AWARDS AND HONORS (YIPPEE!)
FOR ANNA-MARIE ABELL AND HOLY CRAP! THE WORLD IS ENDING!

Abell was Voted Top 40 of *Your Favorite Contemporary Science Fiction Authors* by Book Riot Readers

30th Annual IBPA Benjamin Franklin Awards Silver Medal Winner for Best Science Fiction & Fantasy and The Bill Fisher Award for Best First Book (Fiction)

Shelf Unbound Magazine – 2018 Best Indie Book – Notable Indie

2018 Next Generation Indie Book Awards
Best Chick Lit Novel – Finalist

2017 William Faulkner–Wisdom Competition
Novel Category – Finalist

2017 The Southern California Book Festival
Honorable Mention

"A smoothie of fabulousness that tickles as it goes down."
— Jill Elizabeth, All Things Jill-Elizabeth

PRAISE

"An unexpected story that promises to be one of the most creative fictional discoveries of the year…a fun approach to the entire save-the-Earth-from-alien-invasion scenario which successfully turns traditional approaches upside down."
— D. Donovan, Senior Reviewer, *Midwest Book Review*

"An awesome read! Warm, witty—and thought provoking—a beach read that stays with you throughout the year!"
— Aionios Books

"A rollicking seat of your pants fun ride through the universe!"
— Joan Silvestro, Booktrader of Hamilton

"This book starts with a lot of humour, but quickly gets a very rich storyline with great characters and seriously… this ending? If you like to be blown away, you should read this!"
— Esther, *BiteIntoBooks*

"Anna-Marie Abell has succeeded in weaving her years of study into in the ancient Sumerian culture and their gods with common conspiracy theories, pop culture and random human quirkiness into an out of this world end times romp that will have you laughing out loud at the most inappropriate times and possibly even shedding a tear or two before it's all said and done."
— Jennifer, *JennlyReads*

HOLY CRAP! THE WORLD IS ENDING!*

*OOPS. SPOILER ALERT.

HOW A TRIP
TO THE BOOKSTORE
LED TO SEX WITH AN
ALIEN
AND THE
DESTRUCTION
OF EARTH

ANNA—MARIE ABELL

HOLY CRAP!
THE WORLD IS ENDING!

HOW A TRIP

TO THE BOOKSTORE

LED TO SEX WITH AN

ALIEN

AND THE

DESTRUCTION

OF EARTH

ALIEN
ABDUCTION
PRESS

ALIEN
ABDUCTION
PRESS

San Marcos, CA
AlienAbuctionPress.com

Contact: info@alienabductionpress.com or visit AlienAbductionPress.com

Publisher's Cataloging-in-Publication Data

Names:	Abell, Anna-Marie, author.
Title:	Holy crap! the world is ending! : how a trip to the bookstore led to sex with an alien and the destruction of Earth : a paranormal romance / by Anna-Marie Abell.
Description:	San Marcos, CA : Alien Abduction Press, [2017]	Series: The Anunnaki chronicles ; book one	Summary: In this humorous paranormal romance, a young woman named Autumn and her unbelievably sexy alien boyfriend rush to save all of humanity before the Earth is destroyed.--Publisher.
Identifiers:	ISBN: 978-1-947119-01-7 (paperback)	978-1-947119-02-4 (hardback)	978-1-947119-03-1 (epub)	978-1-947119-05-5 (interactive epub)	978-1-947119-08-6 (audio book)	LCCN: 2017905890
Subjects:	LCSH: Paranormal romance stories.	Extraterrestrial beings--Fiction.	Human-alien encounters--Fiction.	End of the world--Fiction.	Civilization, Ancient--Extraterrestrial influences.	LCGFT: Science fiction.	Paranormal fiction.	Romance fiction.	Humorous fiction.	Apocalyptic fiction.	BISAC: FICTION / Science Fiction / Humorous.	FICTION / Romance / Science Fiction.	FICTION / Romance / Paranormal / General.	FICTION / Humorous / General.	FICTION / Fantasy / Paranormal.
Classification:	LCC: PS3601.B4364 H65 2017	DDC: 813/.6--dc23

Printed in the United States of America
10 9 8 7 6 5 4 3 2 1

This book was edited by David Gatewood. Visit his website at: Lonetrout.com

123RF Stock Photo image credits:
Cow with space helmet (urugvay); scared cow (cteconsulting); interior spaceship (red33); cover spaceship (benchart); cover wine glass (doping)

This book would never have happened if not for the inspiration of two people…

Zecharia Sitchin, the late great overlord of the ancient astronaut theory. Your research led me down a rabbit hole of discovery, and because of it, I will be forever changed, both on an intellectual and spiritual level.

My friend Pam, who excitedly told me about a "super tall hot guy" she saw reading UFO books at Barnes & Noble. And so the story was born.

WHAT IF?

HAMBURGER BOOBY TRAPS, RAMPAGING GIRAFFES, AND TOILET WIZARDS

What if...

Ever since I was a kid I've been fascinated by the unimaginable. I used to gaze at the night sky and contemplate a series of *what ifs*. But I'm not talking about the boring typical *what ifs* such as:

What if I won the lotto?

What if I quit my job and moved to Tanzania?

I'm talking about those outlandish ones:

What if I ran across a herd of three-inch pigmy cows capable of producing solid gold milk, but each ounce I extracted took a month off my life? Would I still do it?

What if we could suddenly have intellectual conversations with all animals? Would we continue to eat them?

What if the whole world went blind and deaf all at the same time? Would we survive as a species?

Another favorite childhood pastime of mine was observing ants clambering atop one another to locate food or gather leaves, like inhabitants of a metropolis bustling to work. Ants are innately oblivious to the threat of a gargantuan foot looming over them. I've often wondered if humans would behave the same way if the tables were turned.

> *What if a jumbo foot came down on us and squashed a city block on a regular basis? After a while, would we just shrug it off and alter course to go around it like ants do?*

Some people go out of their way to squish any and all bugs that come across their path. Not me. I have a strict "no kill" policy with every type of animal.

Well, that's not entirely true. I have an exception for animals I buy in a grocery store. I know: this is incredibly hypocritical. But dammit, I love me some cow. Perhaps I should define my "no kill" policy as "not slaying a creature simply because it annoys you—or simply because you can."

For example, I can't help but wonder:

> *What if I were reincarnated as a fly in my next life? Would I appreciate getting stuck on a glue trap?*

Put yourself in the fly's place. You're ambling along, minding your own business, when out of nowhere the glorious aroma of In-N-Out Burger wafts in your direction. Those freshly cooked fries and juicy burgers fill your senses with food ecstasy. Just when you can't take it anymore, a sign pops up out of thin air that reads:

Salivating, you charge toward the smell all excited. Then—*BAM!*— you step onto a glue pad, unable to break free. Not only are you doomed to a lengthy, torturous death of dehydration and starvation, but your last days are filled with the constant aroma of those heavenly cheeseburgers you can never have.

Not the way I'd want to kick the bucket, that's for sure.

My fixation over these *what ifs* is why I was so into UFOs, ancient aliens, near-death experiences, ghosts, and really, anything paranormal. Truth be told, I'm not sure if deep down I believed in all these things, or if I just *wanted* them to be real, so I'd have something to hope for beyond the monotony of human life. I mean, think about it. What would be more entertaining: cleaning a toilet, or cleaning a toilet haunted by a ghost? (Well, a friendly one. It might get messy if your bowl were possessed by a demon.) Phantom commodes win hands down.

I'll never forget the day this whole obsession got started. When I was six, I asked my mom what life was going to be like when I grew up. She was always one for blunt honesty, and she said, "Well, you'll go to school for a really long time, marry a guy who will lose all his hair, get a job you'll probably hate, have kids, get old, poop your pants, and then die."

I broke down in tears.

My mom ended up regretting having told me all that, because at the age of seven, I convinced myself that those things wouldn't happen to me, and that it was my destiny to one day rescue the planet. I am talking about a Will Smith in *Independence Day* style rescue (except I imagined myself with a breadstick in my mouth instead of a cigar). In one childhood fantasy, I used a butter knife and my badass Barbie Mobile to defend the residents of my neighborhood from a rampaging, genetically mutated, alien-giraffe hybrid that had escaped from a secret government lab. (Kids, if you ever want your mom to get fired as the president of the PTA so she doesn't embarrass you in front of your class, simply splatter your shirt with ketchup and burst into the annual Teacher Appreciation Luncheon with a spork screaming about man-eating giraffes. Trust me, it works like a charm.)

This desire to be the hero had me hooked on stories where people discover they're part of an amazing new reality—a world where the impossible becomes possible. If I waited long enough, I thought, maybe Hagrid and his flying motorcycle would come crashing into my bathroom as I sat on the toilet and proclaim, "You're a wizard, Autumn!"

But it's one thing to dream it, and an entirely different thing to live it. Had I been smart and heeded the advice of the Pussycat Dolls when they warned us to "Be careful what you wish for, 'cause you just might get it," then maybe things would have played out differently.

I wished it.

I got it.

And now I'm about to die.

PART ONE

1

SALTY STICKS OF HEAVEN, A HAIRY DIPSTICK, FLAMING CATS, AND ECSTASY-INDUCING ABS

It was Friday, and my vacation week had officially started. Woohoo! I'd just finished wrapping a shoot for the ad agency I worked for. The product was a rotisserie machine, and after twelve hours of smelling roasted chicken, I craved it so badly I nearly crashed my car when I passed by a KFC. I had to refrain from stopping for food, however, as I was en route to my monthly pig-out fest with my best friend, Emma. We both share the same passion for food. It borders on rehab-level obsession, especially for over-processed, sodium-rich, artery-clogging morsels. If it contains a natural ingredient, we usually pass. (The pinnacle of our eating career thus far was when Taco Bell first offered their tacos encased in a Doritos shell. I will never forget the day we saw the ad on TV. We almost wet our pants.)

Our love for all things edible started twenty years ago, at the age of six, when we discovered my mom's secret "PMS Emergency Junk Food Trunk." (That was not a name we gave it, as we had no idea what PMS was at the time. The trunk literally had a metal plaque etched with that name.) Assuming PMS meant "Pre-Meal Snacks," we dug in and ate it all—then puked. In the subsequent two decades, we developed the ability to pack in more grub than a seven-hundred-pound man at a Las Vegas buffet. Now, I don't want you to get the wrong idea here— we're both quite slim. You see, we have mastered the art of eating large quantities of food without losing our girly figures by fasting forty-eight hours prior to our gorge-fests.

Balance is key.

While driving to Emma's apartment, I was listening to my usual podcast: *Coast to Coast AM* with George Noory. If you haven't heard of the show, it's a late-night radio program on paranormal and conspiracy topics. It covers all the unexplained phenomena: from UFOs, to cryptology, to secret government projects. The topic for this particular podcast was Light Beings, with guest William Henry. To be honest, I usually bypass topics like this one—it's a bit too far-fetched even for me. But it was the only podcast I had left on my iPod, so I gave it a go.

William Henry presented quite the case for Light Beings in his interview—citing ancient texts, pointing out depictions of light bodies in popular classical paintings, and briefly discussing symbolic artwork in the White House. Based on this and other podcasts I'd listened to about Light Beings, the consensus seems to be that they aren't ghosts or apparitions, but are believed to be another type of entity made of pure light, and able to shift from their luminous form into a physical one. Some people are convinced they're demonic, and others feel they are spirits sent directly from God—the "divine light," if you will. William Henry believes that our ultimate purpose as humans is to morph into this "divine light." Maybe there's some validity to that idea. After all, countless people swear they "see the light" when having a near death experience. What if they're evolving into the very light he's speaking of?

As I was pondering this theory, my phone dinged. It was a text from Emma, saying she was running late. Having extra time to play with, I decided to take a quick side trip to Barnes & Noble to search for books on Light Beings. I had to admit, William Henry had piqued my interest.

After I pulled into a parking spot, I stretched outside my car for a minute before heading in. It was a fairly warm night, a typical summer evening in Southern California. A silvery full moon shone above a palm tree. It was one of those nights where the moon appears close enough to reach out and touch. Many people claim to see a face there—the fabled "man in the moon"—but even with the assistance of alcohol, all I see is a bunch of pockmarks.

While I was attempting to identify a face among the contrasting craters, an unnerving chill sent prickles down my spine. It was that feeling you get when you're playing hide-and-seek and you know someone's about to find you. Shivering, despite the warm night, I rubbed my arms to get rid of the goose bumps. I could've sworn there were eyes on me.

But the parking lot was empty, except for a smattering of cars and an abandoned McDonalds' bag (which made me crave fries). Because it had been two days since I last ate—in preparation for my day of gluttony—I was tempted to open the bag and inspect the scraps. My stomach growled its approval at that idea, so I made a hasty retreat to the entrance of the store before it could convince me to join the ants in devouring the leftover salty sticks of heaven.

As the automatic doors slid open, I felt something brush my shoulder, and when I spun to see what it was, a jolt of electricity fired up my leg. I jumped sky high, expelled an involuntary squeak, and then pranced around, afraid to touch the floor until I was a safe distance from the door. Heart thudding in my chest, I studied the ground, expecting to see an exposed wire, but saw only a black rubber mat, a trampled receipt, and a petrified wad of gum.

Looking around to make sure no one had seen my moment of insanity, I composed myself, drew in a calming breath, and continued through the entrance, doing my best to walk like a normal, sober person.

I was not successful. Right as I entered, a dizzy spell had me stumbling into the front book display. I had to grip it with both hands to keep myself upright, knocking several books off in the process. The pistons that kept my wits operating stuttered and hissed—my internal check-engine light flickered on. Embarrassed, I avoided contact with anyone while I picked up the books. One of them had a large tear on the cover, so I hastily shoved it under the rest of the stack, placed them back on the shelf, and casually walked away.

What was wrong with me? I shook my head hoping that whatever had come loose would rattle back into place, but it only made me dizzier, and I staggered into a rack of *ATV Bikini Babes* calendars. At that point, several people had turned to watch the crazy drunk lady in the calendar section. I gave a big thumbs-up to let them know I was okay. I wasn't though. It took a full five minutes of pretending to examine the calendar entitled *America's Best Barns and Feed–Deep South Edition* before I regained my composure.

Given the way my mind was functioning, I decided it wise to ask a friendly sales associate for help in finding a book on Light Beings. If left to my own devices, I was afraid I would end up in the bathroom trying to read the toilet paper roll.

After straightening my shirt (which had apparently twisted up and got snagged under my bra at some point), I made my way to the customer service kiosk, where a shortish lanky dude, I'm guessing in his mid-twenties, scanned a stack of books into the computer with a yawn. His appearance was average until you took a gander at his hair. When I first saw it, I thought the cold front overtaking my mental faculties was making me hallucinate, and I had to pinch my forearm to double-check that what I witnessed was, in fact, real. This anomaly of human nature standing in front of me must have used an entire can of hairspray to create the strangest mountain of brown hair I'd ever seen in my life, complete with twin peaks at the top. It almost defied the laws of physics, towering well over a foot high. I was surprised snow didn't crest the peaks with such an elevation. He had clearly used his hair to make up for his deficiency in the height department. Adding to his overcompensation disorder, he had supplemented his mound-o-hair with that deliberately trimmed haven't-shaved- for-a-few-days-so-I-seem-like-I-don't-care look.

He creased his forehead with an air of irritation as I approached. I waited patiently for him to finish what he was doing, which he sure took his sweet time on. He slapped the enter key a ridiculous number of times before asking me, without even sparing a glance in my direction, "Can I help you?"

What an ass. Despite his major 'tude, my mom did teach me manners, so I put on my best fake "nice" voice and responded with a polite, "Yes, please. Do you have any books on Light Beings?" As soon as the words escaped my lips, I regretted saying them. When you broach paranormal subjects such as Light Beings or aliens, you tend to get the same look you'd get if you'd just dealt a huge fart.

He peered at me with one raised eyebrow. It didn't help matters that I couldn't keep my eyes off his hair. Its sheer presence commanded my attention. And when he caught me staring, he hoisted the other eyebrow to join the first. I hastily pretended to be stretching my neck, rubbing and tilting it up and down, exaggerating extra pain in the direction in which I'd been caught staring.

He didn't fall for it.

"Did you say '*Light Beings*'?" he asked.

I nodded and swallowed hard.

At least he refrained from rolling his eyes as he entered it into the computer. Several pounds of the keyboard later, he gave a cheesed-off sigh and swung the monitor toward me. "Light Beings as in near-death, aliens, or ancient civilizations?"

Deciding I needed to appear educated in order to redeem myself, I replied, "Ancient civilizations. I'm doing a paper for my sociology class." My cheek twitched from the lie. Lying was not a skill in my repertoire—it typically backfired nine times out of ten.

He sized me up, obviously unconvinced by my fib, and clicked on "Ancient Civilizations." In punishment for my lie, what results do you think manifested on the monitor? New Age books, of course. A ton of books on crystals, astrology, astral projection, and the end of the world. He lifted one corner of his mouth in a sardonic smile. I flushed, unable to repress my embarrassment.

Pointing behind me, he said, "You see that super tall dude over there? That's the New Age section."

I zeroed in on the area he'd indicated. On the other side of the store stood an extremely tall guy wearing a gray knit beanie. And when I say tall, I do mean *tall*. The shelves in Barnes & Noble were about six feet high, and this man surpassed that by at least a foot, probably more. I couldn't make out his features because the book he was reading, which had a mystical glowing eye on the cover, concealed most of his face.

"Thanks," I said to my not so friendly sales rep—whom I mentally nicknamed Mr. Hairy Dipstick. Before I left, I dared to take one last peek at the petrified mop on his head—in case it had been only a trick of the light that had made it appear so utterly ridiculous.

Nope, it's just ridiculous.

As I made my way over to the New Age section, my eyes darted from one side of the store to the other, hoping no one was watching me. *Why do I get embarrassed when it comes to aliens and UFOs?* Probably because the media has an unspoken rule that anyone they interview about the phenomenon must:

1. Have been on a minimum of one episode of *Jerry Springer*;

2. Speak with such a thick southern dialect they require subtitles on screen;

3. Have a maximum of three teeth.

Even a casual mention of the word "aliens" among friends or family had them leering at me as if I'd joined a cult and was about to drink the Kool-Aid. Or at least, it did, until I got the idea to pretend I was doing research for a science fiction novel I was writing. Plus, as an added bonus, I could tell people I was an author and sound way cooler than I actually was.

Deliberately ambling, I took the long route to give the tall male beacon in the New Age aisle time to finish and vacate so I could have the section to myself. However, he didn't show any signs of budging, apparently too absorbed in his book. Intuition told me that tucked away behind that paperback was a hot guy, but I couldn't confirm that, because as I walked, he subtly moved the book to prevent me from glimpsing his features. *Weird.* That brought another one of my *what if* fantasies to the forefront: *What if he puts his book down, and upon making eye contact, fireworks ignite and we fall madly in love?*

That was way too normal of a *what if* for me. Mr. Hairy Dipstick had put me off my game. I had a better one. *What if he puts his book down, and upon making eye contact, he shoots flaming cats from his eyes, burning down the store?*

Yeah, that was more like it. Even though I'm an animal lover, cats rank the lowest on my list. I'd rather have a pet tick than a cat.

While enjoying the funny visual of cats shooting out of someone's eyeballs, another chill ran down my spine. What the hell was going on? To make matters worse, with each step that brought me closer to the New Age section, the tingles grew exponentially. By the time I got a couple rows away, my palms were sweating so bad that I had to wipe them on my pants, which left a visible wet mark behind. My god, I was a mess.

And that's when I got lightheaded. *Great.* I escaped to the next row over from Mr. New Age Dude, plunking my butt on a bench with my back to him. Perhaps I was getting sick. That must be the reason for these sudden symptoms.

In an attempt to distract myself from the threatening fainting spell, I picked up the magazine lying next to me—a deluxe issue of *Cat Fancy.*

Karma for dreaming up cats on fire, no doubt. On the cover, one of those hairless feline atrocities glared at me, and the headline next to him read: "The Scoop on Poop." Yes, a pet tick would definitely be a superior companion. Flipping my *what if* scenario, I pictured flaming humans shooting from the cat's eyeballs. That made me giggle.

I tossed the feline periodical aside. It hit the bench and slid off. *Of course.* As I bent to pick it up, this overwhelming sensation that I was about to be attacked had me leaping up, doing a one-eighty, and then swinging my fists like some old-timey boxer, ready for a fight.

No one was there.

This is absurd.

I was in a bookstore—a very *public* bookstore.

Yet I still felt eyes on me.

Holding my breath, I listened for approaching footsteps. At first I only heard Muzak playing through the store's loudspeakers. But then a shrill mechanical hum clicked on in my head, drowning out the music. Soon it was so loud that I had to clap my hands over my ears.

Shit. Shit. Shit. I'm losing my freaking mind.

Between the buzzing in my ears and the pounding of my heart, I thought I might go crazy from all the noise. All I could do was pray that my mental breakdown could wait—at least until I exited Barnes & Noble.

Before I could move, a new sensation struck. Butterflies fluttered to life in my stomach—the kind you get when you're falling in love and you kiss your new boyfriend for the first time. Butterflies at Barnes & Noble? Maybe I was having a brain aneurysm. Then again, I doubted I would be capable of conceiving of lame *what ifs* if an artery had ballooned inside my cranium.

Finally, the loud buzzing faded—only to be replaced by an over-modulated metallic voice. "You must leave now," it screeched in my ear as if someone had shoved a megaphone directly on it.

"Oh my fucking god." I stumbled, lost my balance, and slammed into an end aisle display, which happened to hold an assortment of bobbleheads. Bobble Batman, Bobble Thor, and Bobble Trump all tumbled to the floor, wobbling their oversized noggins at me through their plastic boxes.

"Ignore the mess and exit the building," the tinny voice said, and this time I recognized it as a male voice. "Get in your car and drive away. Don't make eye contact with anyone."

Idiotically, I did the opposite of what the voice said. I spun around and made eye contact with the first person I saw. Mr. New Age stood there—his blue eyes fixed on me. With the book no longer covering his face, his true magnificence was revealed for the first time. My intuition had been right: he was, hands down, the most gorgeous creature I had ever had the pleasure of drooling over in my life. My eyes feasted upon a living, breathing, artistically chiseled statue of a Greek god. His skin was a golden white, and his complexion was perfect, all smooth and velvety; not a single flaw marred his contours. And although I was sure this had something to do with my delirious state, I could have sworn he *glowed*. He looked to be in his late twenties to early thirties. Underneath the knit beanie he wore, his dirty blond hair stuck out in several directions, cut into that long messy style I loved.

Continuing my unabashed admiration of this pinnacle of human evolution before me, my eyes roamed to his torso—clearly God's masterwork. His vintage *Led Zeppelin* T-shirt fit nicely, showcasing his firm chest. Toned shoulders and biceps bulged under the fabric, looking as if Michelangelo himself had sculpted them. I knew his abs would provoke fits of ecstasy if they made an appearance.

I was vaguely aware that my mouth hung open in astonishment. *Oh, yes, me likey very much.* He was far hotter than any fictional character ever described in a book or concocted in my imagination. I shut my slack jaw to hold in the drool, but it just popped open again.

My methodical examination of his physique was interrupted when he cleared his throat. My face went hot as I realized how long I'd been staring at him. I slowly raised my eyes to meet his cool gaze. An unexpected rush of emotions washed over me. I wanted to laugh, cry, overturn the bench next to me, and tackle him all at the same time. But all I managed was a whimper, unable turn away.

I swear his eyes had their own gravitational pull—a pureness that lured me to them. Their blue was reminiscent of the tropical waters in Fiji. I could imagine sailing into those eyes, the cool breezes carrying me away.

Okay, Autumn. Stop ogling him like a deranged creeper woman. Time to cut and run. Your embarrassment level has reached critical mass. Abort! Abort!

Unfortunately, my legs wouldn't comply with the mental command to flee. And to make things even more awkward, he was clearly not as enamored with me as I was with him. He looked like someone frozen during a standoff with a rattlesnake. I had to say something to reassure him I wasn't nuts.

"I'm not nuts," I said stupidly.

He didn't respond.

"Um, yeah. I umm… just think your beanie is super neat."

He still didn't speak.

Suddenly, everything in my peripheral vision dimmed, and Mr. New Age became a tiny point at the end of a dark tunnel. *Oh shit, maybe I am stroking out.* My chest began to vibrate, and the sensation quickly spread to my limbs. I felt like a rocket getting ready to launch. I was gaining all this energy—for what reason, I didn't know.

There was a pop, and the next thing I knew I was floating above my body, watching my physical self standing there gaping at Mr. New Age. Wow, did I look terrible. My darkish auburn hair had partially come out of its ponytail, my already way-too-white skin had turned a few shades lighter, and the mascara on my right eye had smeared down my cheek. Dozens of displaced bobbleheads stared up at me from the floor, shaking their heads in disappointment.

Well, crap. This can't be good.

To my surprise, Mr. New Age snapped his gaze straight at me. And I don't mean at the physical form that I no longer occupied—he stared straight at the floating thing I'd become. Then he flickered, blinking out of existence for a fraction of a second.

Panicked, I drifted toward him, consumed by a desire to reach this captivating creature before he disappeared. The disembodied male voice spoke again, with more urgency this time: "Stop. This isn't the place. Return to your body now."

With the speed of a rubber band snapping, I was catapulted back into my body, and almost toppled into the shelf behind me. I felt as if I'd taken a walloping punch to the gut. Wheezing and ready to faint, I bent over and clutched my stomach.

15

Once I'd regained control of my breathing, I dared another glance at Mr. New Age. There was no mistaking the shock on his face. His eyes were practically bugging from their sockets.

That abruptly ended whatever trance I was in.

"Sorry," I said and turned to leave.

The aisle was empty, thank god. There had been no eyewitnesses to that fiasco. Well, no one except Mr. New Age, whom I could feel staring at the back of my head. I chewed my lip, not wanting to face him again. Implausible as it seemed, I was pretty sure he was the reason I'd left my body.

A radiant flash of light burst from behind me. I whipped around, thinking, strangely, that Mr. New Age had spontaneously combusted. I saw no flames, no puff of smoke, yet Mr. New Age was gone—poofed—vanished.

Flustered, I raced from aisle to aisle, searching for him. People scurried out of my way, not wanting to be anywhere near the deranged lady on a rampage. One gal even clutched at her purse. *He has to be here. No way he's gotten away already.*

Except that he had. Mr. New Age pulled a Houdini and vanished. After all, he was a mile tall; if he had been in the store, I would have seen him. *He must have made it to the parking lot. Maybe I can still catch him before he drives off.*

I barreled toward the exit like I was on fire. Just as I was about to reach the doors, my shin smacked into something hard, sending me flying through the air. I landed on my butt and skidded into the calendar section, knocking the *ATV Bikini Babes* calendars off their display.

What asshat dared to send me sprawling? Mr. Hairy Dipstick was at the top of my list of suspects. To my amazement, no one was around, nor was there a stray book anywhere in sight that I could've caught my foot on—only the squeaky clean marble floor. *Maybe I slipped?* No way. I could've sworn something had slammed into my shin, because my leg still tingled where it had made contact.

The shuffling of feet and the murmuring of voices let me know a crowd had gathered to gawk at me. I flared bright red as it became evident I had most likely tripped myself. Mortified, I kept staring at the floor. If I were lucky, a sinkhole would open and swallow me whole.

A finger tapped my shoulder, and my stomach rolled in response. I jumped, mumbling a few choice curse words. An oversized puff of hair came into view beside me: Mr. Hairy Dipstick. He examined me with the same holier-than-thou look he had given me earlier before offering his hand. I took it reluctantly.

The instant I connected with him, a wave of nausea hit. I pulled away and covered my mouth so I didn't projectile vomit across the entryway. Thankfully, the nausea subsided the moment I let go of him. Seconds later, it was as if it never happened.

He cocked his head. "One of those Light Beings chase you down?"

I gave an uneasy laugh and attempted to play along. "Yeah, and the bastard tripped me."

He took a slight step away from me. Did he think I was being serious? Flushing red again, I did a hasty about face and hobbled out of the store, leaving my pride on the floor next to all the pictures of chicks straddling ATVs.

2

ENDORSING OBESITY, FOOT FETISHES, AND ODDLY SHAPED MOLES

After what had gone down at Barnes & Noble, I needed to keep myself occupied until I met with Emma—and there is no better distraction than food. Emma and I usually shop together, but this time I took the initiative and bought the mother lode. I picked up roast beef sandwiches and Curly Fries from Arby's; a dozen muffin top white chocolate chip pumpkin cookies from a local bakery; pho, fresh spring rolls, and bún from our favorite Vietnamese place; an extra-large veggie pan pizza with double cheese from Pizza Hut; and a bucket of deepfried olive oil chicken with six different dipping sauces. And that was just what I clutched in my right hand. In my left I had a chocolate silk Marie Callender's pie; a bag of Tostitos Rounds with a platter of seven-layer bean dip; and biscuits with apple butter from Lucille's BBQ.

I also had one of the big cans of Red Bull. I figured I'd need extra energy to consume all that food.

After awkwardly stumbling my way to Emma's apartment with all the bags, I had to knock on her door with my foot. The instant she opened the door she eyed me suspiciously.

"Uh-oh," she said, stepping to let me inside. "What did you do?" I entered without a word and placed the pile of bags on the counter.

Emma's an artist, and her apartment showed it. Art supplies were strewn all over. Paint smears, doodles, and splatters covered her formerly white walls. It was how an Aaron Brothers would appear if it had been struck by a tornado. No way she was getting her security deposit back.

We unloaded the food in silence. Emma waited patiently for me to confide in her, allowing me time to sift through events and try to make sense of them. We've known each other long enough that she recognizes when I need a moment to mentally prep.

Emma whisked past me to flip on the kitchen light, and that granted me a proper look at what she wore. She had on a seriously sparkly tank top loaded with tiny metallic sequins, a pair of equally shiny skinny jeans, and thigh-high studded black boots. The reflection of the fluorescents off her upper half temporarily blinded me. She caught me squinting and did a spin, forcing me to avert my gaze from the light that emanated from her tank top.

"What the hell?" I said, blinking the spots out of my eyes. "Did you have to charge that thing?"

"No, battery operated." She lifted the corner of her shirt to reveal a small battery. "I have LED lights hidden under the sequins, so when I spin it makes quite the impact."

Emma is a walking contradiction. She plays the "anti-establishment" artist, yet style-wise she's a carbon copy of a Forever 21 catalog model. Heads turn wherever she goes, not only because of her fashion sense, but because she is a total knockout, with her smooth Asian features, olive skin, and long sleek black hair with a single blond streak down one side.

Turning a knob next to the battery, she increased the tank top's intensity to nuclear.

I blocked the glare with a chicken finger and asked, "And why the electric outfit for our pig-out fest, anyway? Did I miss the memo that said we were wearing light fixtures?"

"I came here straight from a job." She held up her phone, which displayed a photo of one of her paintings: an eighty-year-old man and his forty-something plastic mess of a wife. At least I assumed it was a female next to him. The copious layers of makeup made her more akin to a drag queen, or possibly a circus clown who'd confiscated every set of fake lashes within a ten-mile radius. "I had to paint for a horny old coot and his lip-injected decades-younger wife today. I knew if I dressed like this, the horndog would pay extra. Besides, his leers made the wife so outraged she put a crease in her freshly Botoxed facade."

I snorted out a laugh.

Emma loved to make jewelry and crafts, which wasn't always a big moneymaker, so she supplemented her income with two other more lucrative jobs. Her primary earnings came from doing custom paintings of rich trophy housewives and their greasy ancient husbands on the brink of death. (She hated—I repeat, *hated*—having to paint kept women. If they acted snotty, she would secretly hide a phallic symbol in their portraits. My favorite was the time she painted a hairy mole in the shape of an erect penis on a lady's thigh.) The rest of Emma's earnings came from drawing and selling smutty illustrations. She had uncovered a surprisingly profitable market for fetish foot porn, and was making a pretty penny at it. In fact, my foot was the model for many unmentionable acts. And no, I never actually did anything with it. Emma would just sketch it at the angle she needed and then add it into her drawings, making it perform things that no foot should do.

After we had finished laying out the feast, she said, "Spill it, what happened?"

I bit my lip, not sure how to start.

"Come on, Autumn." She pointed at our ginormous spread with an accusatory finger. "This mammoth stash is either due to guilt or a crisis."

"Complete mental breakdown," I admitted.

I opened the chips, plunged one into the dip, and began telling her all about the Barnes & Noble incident. I must have been overly animated, because Emma had to cover her own food to protect it from the chip missiles launching from my mouth. When I finished, she nibbled on her bean dip-laced Tostitos and knitted her brows in thought. It was only then that I noticed I'd consumed four times the amount she had.

"The way I see it, there are only two options here," she said, tapping the half-eaten chip against her chin as one would a pencil. "Either he thought you had rabies, or he experienced the same phenomenon and panicked."

I thought about that, and then burped. "In comparison, he made that dude in *The Scream* painting seem mildly upset. Therefore, I'm gonna have to say it was rabies." I nabbed a mound of Arby's fries and shoved them in my pie hole. "You think he'll come back? Should I go and try to find him tomorrow?"

"Duh, yes!" she said. "This encounter was obviously a sign. Dare I suggest... soulmates?"

"Or I could have a brain tumor," I offered.

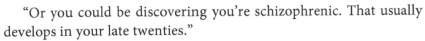

"Or you could be discovering you're schizophrenic. That usually develops in your late twenties."

"Great," I replied, and slurped some noodles from my pho.

"Look, Autumn, I know you. You're gonna obsess over this guy. You won't be able to get him out of your mind. So go for it. What's the worst that can happen?"

I had a flashback of me toppling over an imaginary foot at Barnes & Noble and sliding on my ass. "And what do I say if I see him?" I asked. "I've never asked anyone out in my life, and I'm going to start with a guy who thinks I'm a nutjob?" Frustrated, I slammed down my pizza slice, scattering olives and bell peppers across the table.

"Hey, no need to punish the food," Emma said sternly. When it came to food, we were quite protective.

"Sorry," I said to the pizza, and gingerly replaced the toppings.

I knew she was right. That magnum opus of sexy manhood I'd borne witness to would be trapped inside my memories until the end of time unless I did something about it.

"I can't exactly spend ten hours a day at Barnes & Noble waiting for him to come back," I said.

"What if he's doing the same, searching for you?"

"Fat chance of that."

"Come on, Autumn! If what you've told me is true, then he should have felt it, too. And if he thought you had rabies, he would've asked if you were okay rather than running away like a frightened little schoolboy. No guy is that much of a dick." Emma gave a thoughtful pout. "Well, maybe *some* are that much of a dick." She paused again. "Okay, most. But definitely not a guy who would go to Barnes & Noble and read mystical books."

"I suppose you have a point. Unless I was sprouting horns while it happened, any decent person would've asked if I needed help, right?"

"Totally. I bet he had the same thing happen to him, and that's why he bolted."

"Fine. Say I'm not raving mad and we experienced the same phenomenon. Then what in blazes is wrong with us?" I gripped the table with both hands. "I left my freaking body, Emma. I know I didn't imagine it."

"Hmm... you hear about that all the time. Love at first sight and stuff like that."

"If it *was* love at first sight," I muttered, "it became repulsion at second glance for him."

Emma slid a slice of pie toward me. I refused it.

She drew in a shocked breath. "*What?*"

I brought my legs to my chest and hunched into a ball. "I'm full."

"Impossible! You haven't eaten a single dessert item yet." She made a tsking noise. "This is serious."

I appraised the mound of silky chocolate looming inches from my grasp and salivated. "Well… maybe just one bite."

"Thatta girl."

I picked at the pie slice while Emma slumped in her seat, considering my dilemma. She crossed her arms and said, "Look, why don't you go tomorrow? Browse the clearance section. You don't have to hang all day. Give it one shot. If he's there, then it was meant to be, ya know?"

I chewed on that, and my chocolate-filled crust, for a minute. *What would it hurt?* I could give it one shot. If mystical forces were drawing us together, they would mostly likely do it again.

"Fine. I'll do it!" I pushed my mangled pie slice toward her. "Now you take this slice and give me the rest of the pie. I need to stress eat."

Emma obliged, and I dug in.

3

A COW IN A SWIMSUIT, CHUGGING MERLOT, SUICIDAL MOTHS, AND WET DREAMS

Going to sleep that night proved to be a challenge. Not only had I managed to stretch my belly to twice its normal proportions, but Mr. New Age's blazing blue eyes were burned into the inside of my lids. It reminded me of a *Looney Tunes* cartoon where the lights turn off and you can see the character's illuminated eyes bouncing about exaggeratedly. I tried to think of anything else—politics, gluten-free recipes, a bill I forgot to pay, a bill I couldn't pay, war, famine, Rosie O'Donnell in a swimsuit—anything but those damn eyes!

After hours of tossing and turning I was hot, sweaty, and ready to beat my pillow until only a pulverized carcass of fabric and feathers remained. Finally abandoning all hope of sleep, I stumbled my way to the kitchen to get a bottle of water from the fridge.

Right as I entered, something crunched under my slipper.

"Holy hell!" I said and hopped back.

Under my foot was a picture frame. I picked it up. It was an old photo of me and my parents, taken at a high school band concert. My dad was holding my trumpet while my mom lifted me from behind in a giant bear hug. (She worked out like crazy and loved to show off her man arms.)

My heart began to thud in my chest.

"Who's here?" I shouted and spun around. "I know someone is here!"

That picture should not have been in the kitchen, and certainly not on the floor. Every single image I had of my parents was locked away in my attic. And no, it wasn't due to some falling out. A couple years ago my parents were killed in a car accident, and I lost my freaking mind. They left me the house, and the first thing I did when I moved back in was to remove all the pictures of them, because seeing them made me break down in tears. There were many times that I recognized my mistake and went to go retrieve the photos, but I chickened out each time.

Clutching the frame to my chest, I tiptoed to the attic door, which was located inside a storage closet in the hallway. There was nothing disturbed or out of place in the closet to indicate anyone had entered.

"Okay, Mom," I whispered. "Have you come back to haunt me?" I pushed aside the coats to check the back of the closet. "Dad?"

Maybe I moved the photo while sleepwalking? It wouldn't be the first time that had happened. One time in college I stayed up for three nights studying for finals, and when I finally slept, I sleepwalked to Walgreens. I bought seven bottles of Listerine and a package of nails (the press-on fingernail kind, not the metal ones you put in walls).

Deciding that sleepwalking was the only explanation, I set the picture of my parents on the kitchen table, went to the fridge, and opened a bottle of water.

As the first gulp cooled my throat, I felt a breeze brush the back of my neck. Gasping in fright, I shot water straight up my nose, which triggered a coughing fit.

Behind me, a bright flash of light streaked across the room.

"Shiiiiiit!" I squealed out, then dropped my water bottle, spun, and pressed my back against the refrigerator door.

"Who's there?" I sputtered through the acute burning in my nose.

I waited a moment, but there was no response.

"A car light, that's all. It was only a car light," I reassured myself as I bent to retrieve my water. "And now I'm talking to myself. That's nice."

In an effort to relieve the burning in my nose, I blew it as hard as I could into a wad of paper towels. All it accomplished was making my ears pop.

I eyed the water bottle I had set on the counter. "This day calls for a much, much stronger drink, don't you agree, Aquafina?"

Holding the bottle up like a puppet, I made it nod and say, "Why yes I do!"

After tossing the water back in the fridge, I perused my selection of wines. Since I wasn't having any food and was aiming for a quick buzz, I settled on the cheapest bottle. No reason to waste the good stuff.

Not bothering to take the foil off the bottle first, I jabbed the wine opener in and twirled, taking my frustration out on the cork. Halfway in I got a sudden onset of goose bumps—similar to the ones I'd had at Barnes & Noble—and once again I found myself shivering despite warmth of my surroundings. I turned the opener faster and faster. "Come on, come on!" I pleaded. It finally slid free with a *twoomp*.

My skin became electrically charged, the hairs on my arms standing on end. Wanting desperately to stop the tingling, I drank the wine straight from the bottle. I managed to guzzle down a quarter of the bottle before I choked and spit a mouthful all over the counter. Merlot apparently wasn't a chugging drink.

To my relief, my body warmed from the wine and the tingles dissipated. Excellent! I had found a cure for my problem: alcoholism.

Giving a half-manic, half-terrified laugh, I took one more swig, then shoved the cork back in, and headed back to bed.

I hadn't taken but two steps into the hallway when my stomach thundered with butterflies.

"No no no no no!" I yelled.

A familiar mechanical buzzing commenced—same as it did at the bookstore. Except this time Mr. New Age wasn't around. Guess I could eliminate the "love at first sight" theory. I was just mental.

All at once the butterflies took flight, trying to break free in a mass exodus, and I clutched my stomach to subdue them.

"What the..."

I felt a presence behind me, and I swear I could hear it breathing. I tried to ignore it—to not give in to the hysteria. But when the sweat began seeping through my clothes, I knew I didn't have the willpower. I spun around.

Of course, there was nothing there.

I was about to return to my bedroom—and probably hide in the closet—when a light flashed outside my kitchen window. Without thinking, I ran over, pushed the window up, and peered out.

It was too dark to see anything.

I didn't have a flashlight handy, but there was one of those butane grill lighters on the counter. So I grabbed it, and with the grace of a praying mantis (if you haven't seen them walk, you should really look it up online), I climbed up onto the sink to get a better view and ended up jabbing my knee on the faucet handle. This was one of those "funny bone" type pains that had me grumbling enough curse words to forfeit my whole paycheck into a swear jar. Gritting my teeth, I stuck my entire torso out the window and fired up the lighter.

It provided me a whopping two-inch viewing radius. A moth flapped his way over and attempted to commit suicide in my flame. I put it out before he singed his wings, leaving me in darkness once again.

Feeling a bit silly straddling the sink, I slid back inside, shut the window, and hopped down. The moment I hit the floor, I had to suck in a huge breath. Then another. I couldn't get enough air, as if the atmosphere had thinned around me. The air I did inhale burned my lungs and made my whole chest ache. It didn't make sense. The only way I should've been that winded was if I'd been chased by an evil axe-murdering clown, up a hill, in a snowstorm, wearing five-inch heels.

And that was when the evening went to Crapsville in a hurry. In rapid fire, my vision narrowed, the buzzing grew deafening in my ears, and my legs threatened to give out. It was all I could do to remain vertical as powerful vibrations rocked my core.

"Not again… This can't be happening…"

There was a pop, and then I was hovering near the ceiling staring at my limp body lying on the floor. I looked dead. *Wait*—am *I dead?* When this happened at Barnes & Noble, my body didn't collapse. *Well, shit.*

I felt a tug, and my attention was drawn toward the window over the sink. A pulsating orb of light, with a slight golden sheen to it, hovered just inside the glass. It grew brighter and brighter until the entire room was alight with its glow. Golden fibers began to materialize within it, weaving and coiling together. I felt a tug again; I was being pulled toward it. It was the same gravitational force I had experienced with Mr. New Age.

The pull was impossible to resist. In my ghostly form, I advanced toward the light. Before I could get to it, the light flickered, then zoomed through the closed window to the outside.

Did it just run away from me? I couldn't let it escape. I needed to find out what it was. But how was I supposed to get outside? I no longer had any arms to open a window or a door. Maybe I could go through the glass, just like the light had?

Cautiously, I floated toward the glass surface—and glided right through it. If not for the fact that I was most likely dead, that trick would have been pretty cool.

There were no traces of the light outside, no clues as to which direction it had gone. I moved about ten feet from the house and then stopped. The idea of venturing away from my body had me nervous.

My cell phone rang inside the house. *Who would be calling me at this hour?* I didn't have time to ponder my caller long because, without warning, I was sucked back into my body.

My eyes flew open. I was on the kitchen floor, my cheek pressed firmly against the linoleum, spittle pooling beneath me. My body felt tingly and distant—like your mouth feels when the Novocain is wearing off after a trip to the dentist. A tumbleweed of ashy-blond hair rolled across the floor and hit my nose.

My last thought before I zonked out right there next to the hairball was, *That's odd. My hair is red.*

My phone rang again, jerking me awake. Resolving to let voicemail take the call—mostly due to the fact that I couldn't imagine getting up right then—I shut my eyes.

Ching-a-ling. Ching-a-ling. Ching-a-ling.

The stupid thing wouldn't stop.

Ching-a-ling. Ching-a-ling. Ching-a-ling.

And then I realized, it wasn't my ring tone, but the default one. My usual ring tone was a kid squealing, "I just love Hot Cheetos! I love them so much!" taken from an in-depth exposé NPR did on grade school children and their addiction to the "menace that is sweeping the nation," Flaming Hot Cheetos.

Did I change it? Maybe my phone reset itself? Whatever the case, it refused to stop ringing.

Ching-a-ling. Ching-a-ling. Ching-a-ling.

"Shut up!"

Ching-a-ling. Ching-a-ling. Ching-a-ling.

With a growl of frustration, I rose to my feet and clomped, jelly-legged, to answer it.

"Hel...lo...oo?" I said, slurring the word into three syllables.

My greeting was met with only electrical static.

"Hell-LO!" I said, louder, squeezing the phone, as if that would make it produce a sound.

Still only static. I grunted and hung up.

I felt much better after my nap on the kitchen floor. The butterflies were gone, and I no longer felt like someone was watching me. I was alone again. This should have made me happy—but strangely enough, it didn't. I was genuinely disappointed. The impractical side of me had hoped that Mr. New Age had caused me to leave my body. I guess I didn't meet my soulmate in a mystical, otherworldly, love-at-first-sight episode. I was just nutty as a fruitcake. Fantastic.

Depressed by this, I opened the wine again and drank.

I couldn't shake my desire to hunt down this mystery man though. I needed to explain, to apologize. I needed to drool while gawking at his biceps again. Those eyes... that firm chest... those taut shoulder muscles... oh, have mercy.

That was my cue to go to bed and dream about him. And if I was lucky, it wouldn't be the dry kind of dream, if you catch my drift.

No harm in that, right?

4

ASSLESS CHAPS, ALASKAN YETIS, SEXY ROADKILL, AND EXOTIC MATING DANCES

I woke to the sun cooking the side of my face through a narrow crack between the curtains. *How did I manage to position myself so that a pin-sized opening would hit precisely the right spot to rouse me?* My hand was squished between my left cheek and the pillow. And when I say cheek, I'm not referring to the facial kind. I was contorted in a position only a Cirque du Soleil cast member should be able to achieve. Actually, I couldn't be sure I even had a hand anymore, as it was numb and partially paralyzed. That made me wonder: *What if you slept on a limb for too long? Could you lose it due to lack of circulation? Has anyone ever lost an arm or leg this way?*

I slid to the edge of the bed and let my hand hang over the side until the blood flowed to it again.

On the upside, my plan to have fabulous dreams about Mr. New Age had been a rousing success. For the sake of keeping this story to at least an R rating, I won't divulge the details, but let's just say they were the reason I lay twisted in my bed like a pretzel. They were also the catalyst that finalized my decision to go to Barnes & Noble and officially become a full-blown stalker woman. With a renewed purpose and an extra pep in my step, I stretched and then lumbered to the bathroom to get ready.

After reviewing my present condition, I could see that significant renovations were in order. My usually sleek hair was frizzed into ratty ball on top of my head, giving Mr. Hairy Dipstick a run for his money. My eyes were only slightly bloodshot—nothing a few Visine drops wouldn't fix.

I'm not normally one to put on makeup and do my hair for a routine visit to the bookstore, but I deemed this trip an exception to the rule. That said, I didn't want to arrive in a prom dress and an up-do. Deciding to go the pseudo-subtle route, I spent an hour straightening my hair—then pulled it into a ponytail to give the impression that I didn't try too hard.

As for my stalking attire, I chose skinny jeans and a black tank top. I have the kind of eyes that change color with what I wear: usually they're green, and other times they fade into the gray spectrum. A black outfit would render my eyes a rich avocado color and would be slimming. Double whammy.

As I drove to the bookstore, I cranked up the radio and surfed the channels for a familiar song to distract me—and settled on "Wanted Dead or Alive" by Bon Jovi. I brayed along with everything I had. When the song got to the chorus with the cowboy line, it conjured up an image of Mr. New Age wearing only assless chaps and a cowboy hat. It was sorta hot—in a bachelorette-party strip-club kinda way.

When I reached Barnes & Noble, I pulled into a spot and inspected my makeup in the rear-view mirror. I noticed I had put mascara on my right eye only.

"Dammit, Autumn. You're an idiot."

Of course I didn't have any mascara with me, so I quickly tried to scrape it off my lashes—and pulled half of them out in the process. Satisfied I'd done all I could with what I had to work with, I snatched up my purse and got out of the car.

By the time I arrived at the entrance, I had broken out in a cold sweat. Stalkers are not supposed to be nervous. *Focus, Autumn. You got this.* I sucked in a determined breath and felt several mangled lashes fall onto my cheek.

"Fuck it."

I walked through the door and braced for the chills to overtake me or for the butterflies to burst from their cocoons. The anticipation had me wound so tight, I was afraid my muscles might snap. But not a single butterfly awoke. I felt no chills, no electric shocks, no dizzy spells—absolutely nothing out of the ordinary. (Well, my stomach did growl like a drowning lion because I didn't eat breakfast. And there was the involuntary throat burp that followed. But that really isn't out of the ordinary.)

Not wanting to chance another disastrous encounter with the *Bikini Babe* calendars, I hurried past and then scanned the shelves for Mr. New Age. No luck. I journeyed to the rear of the store, glancing hastily from aisle to aisle, envisioning his godlike figure reclining on a bench, awaiting me, naked and eating grapes.

A familiar voice spoke behind me, making me jump. "Back for more? Get bored of Light Beings and ready to upgrade to poltergeists? Maybe the Alaskan Yetis?"

I turned to find Mr. Hairy Dipstick standing there, his mountain of locks jutting from his scalp. He threw me for a loop by offering me a genuinely warm smile. Reluctantly I reciprocated, stunned that he was able to produce such an expression.

"Loch Ness Monster, actually," I said with a smirk. "In ancient civilizations, of course. And I'll try not to knock anything over on the way out this time."

He frowned and bit one side of his lip, then the other. He kept this up for several moments. Either he was trying to eat his own mouth off, or he wanted to say something more, but was hesitant for some reason. As he mulled over his next move, I took the opportunity to stare at his hair. He reminded me of one of those troll dolls with the crazy hair. I wondered if rubbing his head would bring me luck. He would be popular with the bingo ladies.

"Everything okay?" I asked at last.

"Yeah," he said. "I, uh… I have something for you."

"Me?"

"You know that super tall dude who was here yesterday?"

I suppressed a squeal of delight. "Oh, yes, I think I remember seeing him." I tried to act all casual, but I'm fairly certain it came across as more constipated than nonchalant.

"Well, he tore out of here, practically leaving a smoke trail in his wake—like you attempted to do. You know, before you fell on your ass." He smiled at this, and I responded with my best stink eye.

"Anyway, he left his book bag behind. I looked inside to see if I could find his name or number anywhere, and I found a DVD that was right up your alley." He twisted his foot on the carpet as if smashing an imaginary bug. "I wrote down the title… if you're interested?" He reached in his pocket and handed me a piece of paper.

"You wrote it down for *me*?" Mystified, I took the paper, half expecting it to explode.

"I know. Weird, huh?" He shrugged. "Don't worry, I still think you're nuts."

I glared at him.

"For reasons that are beyond me, I had this feeling I should write it down in case you came in again. I can't explain it."

I read the note:

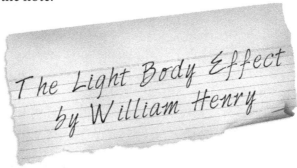

Weird indeed. William Henry was the same guest I listened to on the podcast that made me come to the store in the first place. My mouth flopped open.

"Yep, I'm right," Mr. Hairy Dipstick said. "You're nuts."

"Has the guy come back to get his bag yet?" I asked.

"I believe so. Well, I assume he did, since it is gone from the lost and found."

"Have you seen him again? Was there a name in the bag?"

"No, just the DVD. What's with the twenty questions?"

"Thanks for this," I said, then turned and walked away. I knew that was rude of me to leave like that, and I felt bad—I mean, he was nice enough to write this down for me and all. I decided that, as a token of my appreciation, I would upgrade his nickname to "The Hair" and remove the "Dipstick" part.

As I headed back to my car, I assessed this bizarre series of coincidences. I listen to a podcast, which makes me decide to go to Barnes

& Noble. I'm drawn to Mr. New Age, who leaves behind a bag with a DVD of the very thing I came in for. And then The Hair gets a "feeling" he should write it down for me.

That last part was the hardest to believe. I couldn't imagine that dude expending the energy to scribble a title on a piece of paper for a person he considered repugnant. He didn't even know if I would ever set foot in that place again. Nevertheless, he was compelled to go through a stranger's bag and make a note of a DVD.

None of it made sense.

A car horn broke my concentration. Apparently I'd been standing in the middle of the parking lot for who knows how long. I waved in apology, then hurried out of the way. The driver glowered and skidded off all in a tizzy. Normally that would have earned him the finger, but right now I was too preoccupied to bother.

If I had been thinking straight, I would have realized I was in no condition to drive. The signs were all there. Clue number one was the thirteen tries it took to get my key into the ignition. Clue number two was when I revved the engine to leave and went nowhere—only to discover I had it in neutral, with the parking brake on. And clue number three was the five minutes it took to figure out clue number two.

As soon as I remembered that R meant reverse and shoved the car in gear, the butterflies whipped into a frenzy inside my stomach. The shock of it made me step on the gas, sending the car flying backward. There was bump, a loud thud, and a shriek (the shriek was from me)—and I slammed on the brakes.

"Please let that be a shopping cart," I whimpered through clenched teeth. I closed my eyes and said a prayer to any divine entity who would listen. "Please say I didn't kill anyone."

Terrified beyond belief, I cracked open one eye and peered into my rear-view mirror.

Oh my god.

Mr. New Age was steadying himself behind the car, bracing himself against the trunk.

Holy crap! I hit Mr. New Age!

I hightailed it outside to help.

"Oh my god!" I cried, my voice about three octaves higher than normal. "Are you hurt? Oh my god!" I flailed my arms wildly at my sides, like one of those exotic birds trying to attract a mate.

33

He swiveled toward me, sporting a blazing smile. "I'm fine," he reassured me. "No harm done."

His rough baritone stopped me dead in my tracks—quite literally. My arms hung mid-flutter over my head, one foot suspended in mid-air, as if I were setting up for that winning move from *The Karate Kid*. His voice was gruff and sexy and made my every nerve hum with desire. I never knew a voice could hold such power. The pleasant flurry of butterflies in my stomach was swiftly invaded by a swarm of bees. And based on the stingers they were leaving behind, it was a swarm of blood-crazed killer bees.

Snap out of it, Autumn, you can move now, I thought, abandoning my fancy crane-kick pose. And, as if I wasn't already embarrassed enough, my body decided to start vibrating uncontrollably at that moment. The shuttering was so bad that I had to grab onto the car to keep from falling. I concentrated on breathing. *In and out. In and out.* I knew if I glanced at him, he'd be grimacing at me with revulsion, the same way he had yesterday.

"Hey, you okay?" he purred.

"Yep," I chirped, not letting my eyes leave the petrified bird poop I had become fixated on. I couldn't bring myself to look at him and risk being disappointed by his expression.

There was a long pause, and I became all too aware of him staring at me.

"You sure?" he asked.

"I'm the one that ran into you, and you're asking *me* if I'm okay?" I gave a nervous laugh, snorting in the process. A snot bubble popped from my nose. *Seriously? What's next? A bout of smelly gas?* When I went to wipe the snot sphere away, the palm holding me steady on the trunk slipped from the sweat buildup, squeaking as it slid.

Mr. New Age chuckled—a chuckle that almost had me dropping to my knees from the heat it generated in my core. I couldn't resist any longer; I had to feast my eyes upon him.

The instant I rotated to confront him, the whole world froze except for him—à la cheesy romantic movie style. It wouldn't have surprised me if a musical interlude had blared from the heavens. Mr. New Age towered above me, yet his height wasn't intimidating at all. In contrast, the power of it exhilarated me. The sun shone directly behind his head, creating a halo, and the angelic effect was mesmerizing. His blond hair rustled in the wind, shaping his perfect contours. His luscious lips, cast in the cutest half-smile, would have any girl swooning with just one twitch.

But the crowning achievement of his sexiness was, without a doubt, his eyes. They entrapped me with their brilliance. They blazed almost as vividly as the sky—a shining prism of blue light.

Addicted to his beauty, I drank him in, unable to get enough. The magnitude of emotions this stirred in me made my legs turn to jelly. My knees gave out, and his hands clamped on my waist, saving me from a fall. His grip sent a surge of electricity to my gut, making my breaths shallow and unsteady.

"Whoa, there," he said.

The heat between us had put me in a daze. "Are you a god?" I asked.

He tilted his chin and chuckled again.

No, no, no, no, no! Did I just say what I thought I said? Did I ask if he was a god? I felt my cheeks burn. "I can't believe I asked you that!" Panicked, I decided the best course of action would be to hotfoot it out of there and hide in a restroom or a dumpster, whichever I happened upon first. "If you'll excuse me, I need to go die of embarrassment now." I backed away from him and his hands fell from my waist, making me feel empty inside.

"Hey, wait..." he pleaded.

As he reached out to stop me, his hand accidentally brushed the front of my hips—and that unexpected graze sent the swarm of killer bees down south, if you know what I mean. I lost all ability to walk. I thought I might orgasm right on the spot, and I gave the tiniest moan.

Oh, shit! Did I just moan out loud?

The next thing I knew he was in front of me. A mere six inches separated us. My traitorous legs, not yet recovered, gave way again, and I collapsed into him, our bodies thrust together. I tried to push away, but he held me close. My head barely reached his chest. His solid frame pressed against me, our breathing in sync. Under my hands, his abs were strong and steady as he inhaled and exhaled—his heartbeat drumming against my fingertips. I seriously considered tearing his clothes off right there in the parking lot.

"Wow," I whispered in amazement, all plans of filtering my humiliating thoughts ruined.

My heartbeat slowed to meet his, intensifying the bond between us. It was just him and me; the world outside faded until I heard only the soft breeze. He had me in a trance, and I gladly surrendered to it.

Our hearts beat as one.

We fit together.

Our souls are a perfect match.

A tear trickled down my cheek.

Wait a minute. Am I crying?

That realization dissolved my peaceful haze, and I tried to mumble an excuse for my erratic behavior. But I couldn't get a coherent sentence out.

Without breaking his hold on me, he tenderly wiped away my tear. I vibrated at his touch, steadying myself to leave my body again. But, I discovered I didn't need to go anywhere. He was finally here with me. It was then I knew for certain that he *was* the reason I'd left my body.

"Your soul," he whispered. "It's… it's so…"

"It's what?"

Without warning, his features hardened, and his eyes lost the glow that had captivated me. A storm now brewed inside them. My endorphin-inducing tingles were extinguished, leaving me debilitated. He released me and stepped away.

"I can't do this!" he said. "*We* can't do this."

I staggered to get my footing, disoriented by the abrupt mood change. "Do… what?"

He slid his hands down his face, growling in frustration. "I can't. It isn't allowed."

"Not allowed?"

His darkened eyes bored into me, and dread filled my chest, causing a physical ache. His next words lashed me with every syllable.

"I'm sorry I came for you. I shouldn't have. I won't bother you again. You won't see me again."

"Wait! What?" I sputtered. "Came for me? I was stalking you. I almost made you roadkill!" I was on the verge of hysterics by this point.

With a *whoosh* he was beside me, inches away, heedful not to make any contact. I gasped at the breakneck speed with which he'd reached me. *How did he move that fast?* His closeness didn't give me the butterflies this time. Only sadness filled my gut.

"I've said too much." His eyes softened and gave off the slightest hint of desperation. "Can you please pretend we never met? It'll be better that way."

His request was preposterous. Nonetheless, it broke my insides apart. *This is insane. I've known him for what—all of fifteen minutes in total?* And you could hardly describe our first encounter as a hey-it's-nice-to-meet-you affair. Yet I felt as if he'd just broken up with me. Hell, we'd never gone on a date!

"I don't understand," I said. "What changed?"

If I was hoping for a satisfactory explanation to my question, I wasn't going to get it.

"Nothing. Nothing happened."

My chest hollowed, and my heart sank with a thud into my gut. Then, like I was a ventriloquist's dummy, words came flying out of my mouth, words that weren't mine. "You're right," I said. "Nothing happened. I will go now." I heaved in a huge breath and shook my head, trying to block whatever force was controlling me. "No, wait—that isn't true! How did you do that? You made me say those words, didn't you?"

His posture stiffened, and he narrowed his gaze on me with concern. "How did you… Impossible… How can…?"

"You can get into my *thoughts*?" I was both terrified and angered by this mind trick. It made me feel violated in a weird sort of way.

He stuttered an "I" and a "You," then faltered.

"How did you do that?" I asked.

Instead of answering, he disappeared behind a truck—gone in the blink of an eye.

"Coward!" I shouted after him.

Fuming, I collected myself and stomped off to my car. I got in and slammed the door with a curse, my anger morphing into full-scale anguish. Then my roller coaster of emotions derailed and left me in a heap along the tracks. I slumped in my seat. I didn't understand what I had done to make him so mad. More importantly, I didn't understand why I cared so much. *Why do I feel as if I've lost the love of my life? Why does it hurt so damn bad? I met this guy yesterday! I don't even know his name, for god's sake!*

I should've gone home and slept it off, but the impulse to stay there in case he returned to apologize won out. Surely if I waited long enough, he'd tap on my window sooner or later. *He has to come back, right?*

Tap tap tap.

The sound made me shoot up, and I banged my temple on the visor, triggering a stinging headache. I twisted to the window, ready to burst like a piñata from the elation of his arrival.

Only, it wasn't Mr. New Age, standing there waiting to take me in his arms again. It was The Hair, his jumbo puffball blocking the sunlight. Something in my brain imploded at the site of him. My ears rang from the cave-in. He stood there with his patented smart-ass look. When I didn't react, apart from a dumbfounded blink, he made the old "roll down the window" circular motion.

I pressed the button to automatically open the window. "You know, they don't make those crank windows anymore," I said. He furrowed his brows at me. With a mocking tone I continued, "Those of us here in the modern world have a fancy button that does it for us."

"Well, excuse me," he sneered, and then he made a moronic impersonation of me pressing the button to open the widow. "Is that better?"

I couldn't help but laugh. "Point taken: you do look pretty stupid. The crank gesture wins."

An uncomfortable silence passed between us. Putting his hands in his pocket, The Hair finally said, "You've been sitting there for quite a while. Are you waiting for a Light Being to arrive in the parking lot?"

Little did he know, that was precisely my plan, but I played along. "Yeah. It so happens that this parking spot is home to a portal connecting our dimension to the one in which they reside."

He straightened up, teetering back and forth on his heels. I could tell his mind was whirring, trying come up with a witty retort. After a few spins of his mental cogs, he pulled the keys from his pocket and thumbed through them until he came to a mini flashlight. He pinched it on and shined it in my eyes. "This help?"

I winced when the beam hit my pupils, then giggled. *I can't believe I just giggled.* This day was taking its toll on me.

"What are you doing here anyway?" I asked.

"I dunno. Just had another feeling, I guess. Felt compelled to come outside, and here you were, sitting in your car, staring into space."

He had another "feeling"? I was starting to think The Hair was being used as a puppet. Could Mr. New Age zap thoughts into other people, the same way he did with me?

I examined the lanky figure in front of me. I couldn't conceive of anybody having the ability to penetrate his rock-hard helmet of hairspray.

He knocked on the roof of my car. "Hello… anyone there?"

"I need to go."

I closed the window, revved the engine, and backed out. The Hair shined his flashlight at me with one hand and gave me the crazy *cuckoo* sign with the other. I smiled and put on the brakes, letting down the window while mimicking a crank gesture. He shook his head at me.

"Hey, what's your name?" I asked him.

"Zarf the Light Being from planet Aquanet," he replied, not missing a beat.

I tittered again. *What am I, five years old?*

"Hi, Zarf. I'm Zooloo, High Priestess of planet Melmac."

"Ha!"

I grinned and drove off, leaving Zarf and his flashlight in the dust.

5

GLASS-EYED GURUS, A GENETICALLY ENGINEERED SLAVE RACE, AND FRANKLY, MY DEAR, I DO GIVE A DAMN

This is normally the part of the story where the heroine, trying to uncover the identity of her mystery man, goes online and types in one magic sentence into a made-up version of Google, and it displays everything she wants to know in the top three search results. This triggers the musical interlude, which incorporates a dizzying amount of cursor close-ups, convoluted descriptions, and blurred images. Then, over a drawn-out montage of sleepless nights, she stumbles across the answer in a dusty moth-eaten book hidden in a dingy bookshop run by a creepy gray-haired man with a glass eye who possesses the knowledge of all.

Sorry to put a damper on things, but the truth is, my discovery was way less dramatic than that. I was already ninety-seven percent sure what I was dealing with.

I did need confirmation about one lingering concern though, and I didn't want to have to scour books. Mostly because they were all in boxes inside my garage, and I was entirely too lazy to go dig them all up. Fate was on my side that day. Marshall Klarfeld, one of the premier experts on who (or what) I thought Mr. New Age could be, was on *Coast to Coast AM* that evening. Yeah, yeah, I know: that seems about as much of a coincidence as the Google cliché. But if you've ever listened to the show, you know they had similar guests on a regular basis.

As I dialed in to the radio program, I debated how to best disguise my voice. Even though none of my friends tune in, I was still paranoid they might stumble upon it and recognize me. Ludicrous, I know. After successfully getting past the call screener, I was put into the hold queue, which played the live broadcast while I waited. The host, George Noory, was speaking.

"Now Marshall, you follow the work of the late Zecharia Sitchin. As you know, but perhaps a few of our listeners don't, he was known for translating many of the original Sumerian cuneiform tablets, the oldest records we have of human civilization. Can you give us a summary of what he found?"

"Yes, George. I have studied all of Sitchin's books and was blessed to have had him as my teacher for ten years. Essentially, in translating the tablets, he learned of the Anunnaki—whose name translates to 'those who came from heaven to Earth'—and their creation of mankind using genetic manipulation."

"Marshall, you know I'm a big fan of Sitchin as well, but I gotta tell ya, a lot of people have a tough time believing it. To hear we were genetically engineered by a master race is rather far-fetched."

"Yes it is, George. Yet it's all recorded in these tablets, which were written long before we ever knew such a thing was feasible. Anyone can go online and read them for themselves."

"In a nutshell, Marshall, what do they say?"

"They describe how we were created by mixing clay with the flesh and blood of an Anunnaki, and then implanting that into the Anunnaki female. However, I believe it was really their way of describing a procedure where they replaced the nucleus of the *Homo erectus* female egg with the DNA of the Anunnaki and then planted the egg into an Anunnaki female. Essentially, in vitro fertilization."

"And *Homo erectus* was a primitive version of us?"

"Yes. At the time, *Homo erectus* lacked vocal cords, and their brains were only one third the size of modern human brains."

"Why would the Anunnaki take the time to create us? Simply because they could?"

"The Sumerian tablets state that humans were created to be primitive workers, called Lulu Amelu, to assist in mining efforts. According to Sitchin, the Anunnaki came to Earth in search of gold to protect their dwindling atmosphere."

"When you say 'came to Earth'—you mean they were originally from another planet?"

"Correct. They come from the planet Nibiru, which is part of our solar system."

"Ah, the elusive Planet X. Now, those two scientists from Caltech, Brown and Batygin, believe they have strong evidence for an additional planet in our solar system, larger than Neptune. You think this could be Nibiru? And if that's the case, why are we not seeing it with all our advanced equipment?"

"They're getting closer to finding Nibiru, that's for sure. The thing is, Nibiru is on a highly elliptical orbit that only comes near Earth once every thirty-six hundred years. It has been too distant to observe with terrestrial telescopes unless you know exactly where to look. There's a lot of sky out there, and Nibiru would be much dimmer than Pluto. And as far as advanced equipment goes, I have a feeling NASA and the European Space Agency discovered it long ago, but that information is being suppressed."

"After this Caltech discovery of this so called 'Planet Nine,'" George said, "everyone pointed their telescopes to the night sky to be the first to spot it. It shouldn't be long now before we find out for sure."

"Indeed," Marshall agreed. "Although, you have to realize, even if they do eventually find Nibiru, it isn't their discovery. That very planet was depicted in the Sumerian Cylinder Seals, which are thousands of years older than the Caltech announcement. I'd venture to say the Sumerians were more knowledgeable about the universe than these scientists, or NASA for that matter, even with our so called 'modern technology.'"

"That's true. It's like we're finally catching up to them."

"Precisely."

"So they came to Earth because it was rich in gold?" George asked.

"Yes, there was an abundance of it on this planet," explained Marshall. "But here's the thing. The Anunnaki workers, called the Igigi, soon grew tired of mining the gold themselves. They staged an uprising to get the leaders to bring in more workers. Unable to spare any more from Nibiru, they had to create what they didn't have. So one of the Anunnaki leaders, Enki, genetically upgraded *Homo erectus* into *Homo sapiens* and added them to the workforce."

"What are examples of alterations they made to alter *Homo erectus*?"

"There were many things. For example, vocal cords were introduced to allow communication. Brain capacity was increased. *Homo sapiens'* hands and feet were also altered, resulting in the ability to properly grasp equipment. It took numerous experiments to get everything perfected, but in time, they developed *us*. Adamu was the name of the first successful male."

"Adamu? Now Marshall, do you literally mean Adam, as in Adam and Eve?"

"Yes. The first male was called Adamu, which translates to 'he of the earth' or 'earthling.'"

"You're saying their story of Adam predates what's in the Bible?"

"George, you'd be amazed how many stories from the Old Testament are part of these ancient cuneiforms, written millennia before the Bible, including the epic of the flood."

"When the Anunnaki were manipulating us, from what I recall in Sitchin's books, they made us resemble them, correct?"

"Yes. As the Bible states, we were 'created in His image.' 'His image' being the Anunnaki. George, I am asked many times if the Anunnaki look like us, and I always answer, 'No, we look like them.'"

"I couldn't agree more, Marshall. We need to take a quick break. When we come back, we'll take your phone calls here on *Coast to Coast AM*."

I tried to gather my thoughts during the break. If you hadn't worked it out by now, my gut was telling me that Mr. New Age might be an Anunnaki. All descriptions of them said they were tall, blue-eyed, had white glowing skin, were extremely attractive, and possessed abilities way beyond what we could comprehend. That just about summarized Mr. New Age. Ancient astronaut theorists have suggested they could still be among us, blending in with humans. If that was the case, why couldn't he be one of them?

The line clicked on, and I heard George's greeting. "West of the Rockies, first-time caller. You're on with Marshall."

Panic struck, and I defaulted to a horrible southern accent straight out of *Gone with the Wind*.

"Hi, yes… um… yeah," I stammered. "Mah name is Scarlett." I cringed when I said it. "It's a pleasure to be talkin' to y'all. I had a question about these A-nun-naki fellas."

"Wow, didn't expect that accent from West of the Rockies," George said. "Where are you originally from?"

"Uh, Georgia. Why, yes, Georgia it is." I smacked my forehead at my dumbass response, and waited for him to call me on my BS.

"Well, Scarlett from Georgia, what can Marshall answer for you?"

"If I have read correctly, the Anunnaki are the same as the 'gods' that were written about in these here Greek, Roman, and Hindu mythologies, correct?"

"Yes, Scarlett," Marshall responded. "That's right. Poseidon is said to be Enki of Sumerian pantheon, and Enlil is Zeus, the commander, and so forth."

"My question relates to their personalities. If any of the myths are real, they were downright vile—particularly with such things as incest, war, torture, and all sorts of other devilish acts. Do you believe these stories to be true?"

"Yes, I do. Or at least, I think there is an elementary truth to them all. No doubt they were dramatized in narrative form to pass down as moral tales, and embellished further with each retelling. Nevertheless, they were, originally, based on actual events. It's important to note that *we* are modeled after the Anunnaki—a milder version, if you will. They loved power, were prone to violence and were…" Marshall coughed, "… sexual creatures. No different than us. They just did these things on a grander scale."

George cut in. "Thank you, Scarlett. Next on the line we have…"

I heard a click; my call was over. I sat there for a while, clenching the phone by my ear. If Marshall was right, and these beings behaved anywhere near how they were portrayed in the Greek and Roman "myths," this was not a group I wanted to get involved with.

6
ALIEN TURN SIGNALS, DARWIN'S FACELIFT, SEXY TOES, AND THE GRILLED CHEESE COMMANDMENTS

My preoccupation with Mr. New Age escalated, and soon I was call-ing in sick to work, drinking wine from a 7-Eleven Double Gulp cup, and forgetting to take a shower. I was in desperate need of AA: Aliens Anonymous. To make things worse, the knowledge that the Anun-naki were, in all probability, roaming the streets had made me rather paranoid. Anyone over six feet tall immediately became a person—or I should say alien—of interest. Luckily, I encountered no one who met the prerequisite "godlike" physique that was the staple of their race.

What really had me worried was that Mr. New Age had said we were "not allowed" to be together. Therefore, it would stand to reason that there was a law among them, and hence there must also be "po-lice" at some level to enforce it. What if they could smell my fear and were going to come after me because I was in on their secret?

After a week of sleeping only via alcohol-induced comas, my sys-tem had had enough. This obsession had developed into a rampant infection that had spread into all aspects of my life. Mr. New Age was part of my every thought, every second of every day. If I didn't get my fix again soon, I was convinced I would end up as an alien-seeking crack whore, walking the streets of Los Angeles and turning tricks for any info on where to find the Anunnaki secret lair.

Late one evening, I was at my kitchen sink battling with a dried cork that had dropped inside my bottle of wine. I'd just gotten home from pulling a double shift at work to compensate for all the time I'd missed. The rotisseries were not selling very well, so I had decided to try a "buy one, get one free" promotion for the first one hundred callers. You know, 'cause one rotisserie machine in your kitchen really isn't enough. (FYI: any time an infomercial says to "hurry" because the "exclusive offer" is only for X amount of callers, that is a flat-out lie. Also, the "free" one isn't free. That "shipping and handling fee" you're paying is what the actual product costs, thanks to Chinese child labor, so "free" it is not.) It had taken twenty hours of rewrites and edits to the commercial to get it right.

While jabbing a chopstick into the bottleneck to keep the debris from blocking my much-needed pour, I heard a *pop* behind my eyeballs—as if a synapse in my brain had suddenly crackled and combusted. I looked up to find Mr. New Age standing there outside my window, clear as day.

Or not. I blinked, and he was gone.

That was it.

The last straw.

I couldn't go on like this. I decided, right then, that either I would dedicate the next seventy-two hours to finding Mr. New Age, or I would turn myself in and spend that time in a voluntary psychiatric hold. Mr. New Age won out, of course. I threw the bottle of wine in the trash, fetched my jacket, and hauled ass over to Barnes & Noble to track the sexy bastard down.

It wasn't until I noticed the absence of vehicles in the parking lot that I realized it was three a.m. *At least I won't be interrupted while I lose the last of my sanity.*

I parked, opened my moon roof, reclined the seat, folded my arms across my chest, and hunkered down. Now that I was here, I was determined not to move from this spot until Mr. New Age made an appearance, even if it resulted in me starving to death, leaving only my dusty skeletal remains to be discovered by The Hair.

The stars above lazily traversed the compact space of my moon roof. Since I was in the middle of a city, only the brightest of the bright were visible. Nonetheless, a half dozen or so dotted the cloudless sky. My tense muscles relaxed under their glow.

Suddenly, a flash of light filled my vision. I shot upright in anticipation, only to find that it was a car driving by. I yelled an obscenity at the receding taillights for getting my hopes up, and then nestled back in my seat and closed my eyes.

The next time a flash of light illuminated the night, I wasn't as gullible. I stayed there with my lids shut. But the stupid flash came three more times. Either they had started a road detour through the parking lot, or something was out there. Heart racing, I slowly opened my eyes.

No cars were anywhere in sight. It was dark except for the streetlights. Whatever had been there was now gone.

Disappointed, yet still resolved to see this thing out, I reclined my seat as far as it would go and got comfortable. Not even a minute later, a ball of light peeked over the edge of the moonroof. I jerked back in surprise. Apparently the seat hadn't locked into place, because that movement sent it shooting forward, and my head thunked against the steering wheel.

"Holy mother of Satan," I growled. *That freaking hurt.*

I stayed trapped in that position for way too long, unable to reach the handle to release the seat. Practically dislocating my shoulder to get to it, I finally got the seat back and saw the light had moved to the driver's side window and was hovering there, as if staring at me.

"What the hell?" I said, flinching away from it. Then, after a moment, it floated to the front of my car, where it waited patiently.

By this point, I was sure my heart was generating enough energy to power a small country. I focused on the glowing ball for a clue as to what I was supposed to do. *Should I get out? Should I talk to it? Should I run it over?* A mix of exhilaration and fear made me shake furiously, registering nearly 5.5 on the Richter scale.

The light pulsed, like it was trying to get my attention, then began to inch away from my car. Panicked it might leave without me, I cranked on the engine and cautiously rolled toward it. As I got closer, it moved further away. *Does it want me to follow it?* We did this stop-and-go until we reached the edge of the lot.

Now what? The parking lot was one thing, but navigating the streets in this manner would be tricky, even with so few cars on the road.

The light shrank to a golf-ball-sized globule, zoomed in front of my right headlight, and then blinked on and off.

I gave an amazed little laugh. "Are you signaling?" I asked, though I doubted it could hear me.

I hung a right and trailed it.

We made our way into the canyons of Orange County. My arms began trembling so violently I had to press them straight against the steering wheel to keep from swerving all over the highway. At long last we pulled off onto a narrow dirt road. It led to a dead end about a mile up a steep hill, where I parked.

I couldn't help but notice that there wasn't a home for miles in any direction—and no one even knew I was here. *This would be a perfect place to dump a corpse. No one would be the wiser.*

"Close your eyes," I heard a voice say.

The disembodied words should have terrified me to the point of soiling my pants, but that severed synapse in my brain evidently hadn't stitched itself together yet after snapping in my kitchen. *Speaking of which, I'd have to remember to take that bottle of wine from the trash when I got home.*

"Eyes, please," the silky smooth voice coaxed.

Obeying the command, I shut my eyes and waited for fireworks to illuminate my lids, or something equally dramatic. But all that happened was a dimming of the light. *Why did I have to close my eyes for that?*

"You can open your eyes now."

I took a moment to calm the fluttering in my chest, then ventured a glimpse.

There he was, Mr. New Age in all his splendor, poised in the glare of my headlights. The morning mist swirled in the beams, creating the perfect hot romance novel cover. His tight-fitting vintage Doors tee, weathered and clinging in all the right places, had enough of a worn neck to drive me wild, teasing me with the top of his smooth chest. He had on those leather cuff bracelets, which accentuated his toned forearm and created a delightful tingly sensation in my lady parts. His jeans hung low on his waist, and I desired nothing more than to tug them down.

"You going to get out of the car?" he asked.

I didn't move a muscle, preferring to let the steel and glass of my vehicle form a protective barrier between us. "Umm… can you answer a question for me first?"

He blocked the light from my headlights with one hand. "Yeah, sure."

"Are you an Anunnaki?" I flashed on the brights to let him know I wasn't messing around.

He didn't flinch, but raised his other hand to block the glare as he said, "Yes."

I waited for him to elaborate. But the silence lingered, and it became clear he wasn't going to offer any further explanation. I bit my lip and contemplated my next question. I decided on no-holds-barred bluntness.

"Did you genetically engineer us to mine gold?"

"No."

I sighed in relief and flipped off the brights.

"But one of my relatives did," he added.

My heart skipped a few beats. My brain was slow in processing what he said. When it did, my stomach churned with a mixture of resentment and awe. Reading about us being genetically engineered, or hearing it at lectures, was one thing, but deep down, I had never honestly believed it. It was too fantastical of an idea. Or maybe I hadn't believed it because I didn't *want* to.

"Alrighty then," I said. "I guess that ape-to-human evolution drawing for Darwin's theory is gonna need an overhaul."

"Oh, you still come from apes," Mr. New Age said. "We mixed in a bit of them for added dexterity. There are discarded prototypes wandering the forests of the Pacific Northwest. I believe you call them Bigfoot."

"Great. That solves another burning question."

"We also made mermaids, centaurs, unicorns, dragons…"

"Okay, okay… stop!" I interrupted, "I'm doing my damnedest to get a handle on this right now, and I don't need you making wisecracks."

"I'm not joking. I had a cousin who genetically spliced different creatures in his spare time."

My brows shot up so high they must have hit my hairline. I visualized a creature that had the torso of a moose, human legs, a crocodile tail, and a long, forked snake tongue. Just when I was about to add bat wings and udders, Mr. New Age flashed over to my door and opened it.

I don't know how I did it—must have been due to adrenaline—but I managed to undo my seat belt, scramble across the front seat away from him, and fall unceremoniously out the passenger side in five seconds flat. At times such as these, one presumes their survival instincts would kick in and bring them securely to their feet like a cat, allowing them to sprint to safety. Alas, a face-plant was my fate. Faster than I could spit my mouthful of dirt to the ground, he was sweeping me into his arms.

I shrieked and flailed. He let go of me and backed away quietly, hands raised in surrender. "Calm down. I'm not going to hurt you."

"Is that what you said to the humans before you beat them?" I said, voice cracking from anxiety.

"Hold up. Who said anything about beating?"

"Isn't that what you do to slaves if they don't behave?" I asked, rather judgmentally.

"No. That's what *humans* do to slaves. We treated all ours with respect. And they weren't slaves in the manner you're thinking. They received our help to create and maintain societies if they continued to supply us with gold. If they halted production, we ceased our assistance."

I offered him a skeptical brow.

"Think of it this way; they were paid in knowledge instead of money. No beating involved. I promise."

"And you needed the gold for what?"

"At first we used it to create a shield that enclosed our atmosphere to keep in the heat," he explained. "Ours was disintegrating, and gold was one of the few elements that could regulate our climate while withstanding the intense radiation from the universe. Insulation and a barrier rolled into one."

"At first? You used it for something else?"

"Later, we learned that consuming it made us stronger. It enhances our normal gifts. It is also what allows us to shift into light form."

"Gifts?"

"Each of us has a unique talent, if you will."

I remembered the mind trick he'd played on me in the parking lot before he bailed. "Like putting thoughts into people's heads?"

He gave me a gloriously sexy half-smile. I could get used to that.

Sensing he had more than one of these "talents," I prodded further. "What other 'gifts' are you hiding?"

He just winked.

I returned his wink with a scowl. "I see. What about this shifting-into-light thing? You couldn't do that prior to taking the gold?"

"No. In its monatomic form, gold modifies the way molecules bind to our DNA structure. It has given us the ability to achieve melam."

"What's that?"

"It is what we call our light form."

"I'm no expert on your Sumerian history, but I'm sure I would've heard of a magical substance that manifests superpowers somewhere along the line."

"You have. It's referred to as manna, as in manna from heaven. It's also known as the Philosopher's Stone, the Golden Tear of Horus, the food of the gods…"

I cut him off. "Okay, I get the picture. I didn't think that was real, much less readily available to humans. Does it affect us the same as you?"

"It does. However, to achieve melam, it takes high doses over a long period of time. It is approximately eighty Earth years, give or take, before the effects fully develop, and decades longer until you can transform into light. A human's lifespan isn't long enough. Besides, you can go mad if it's not made properly."

"Hey, is that why gold is so valuable here on Earth? I mean, the world is obsessed with gold. It's like the only universal currency."

"The lure goes back millennia. I believe it had to do with the positive reinforcement it gave humans—almost a Pavlovian response. They provided us with gold and acquired knowledge and technology from us in trade. Plus, since we 'gods' revered it above all other elements, it became the most sought after material in the world. Understandably, humans reasoned that it must be the secret to our power."

"Why aren't you mining it anymore? Don't you still have to take it?"

"We need to take it every day to keep it present in our blood. It acts as the conductor that amplifies and spreads the energy and allows us to shift. But we have plenty on our planet at the moment. We haven't needed to mine for a long time."

I studied his eyes, hoping they would offer a hint as to whether he was telling the truth or not. They glowed a silvery blue in the night.

"I need to sit down," I said.

He hovered awkwardly, trying to help yet not wanting to invade my personal space. I still didn't entirely trust him, so I didn't give off any vibes that I wanted his assistance. Plus, given what had happened at Barnes & Noble, I was afraid his touch would render me a slobbering idiot. Mr. New Age might have the outward appearance of a human, but a human he was not.

Jesus H. Flipping Christ, I'm in the presence of an alien. Breathe. Breathe.

He gestured to a rock that overlooked the city lights. We walked over and sat down; he politely took the far end.

Gazing at the twinkling lights, I tried to organize my thoughts. The faintest hint of dawn's purple light shone on the horizon. I massaged my temples to ward off a headache that was poking behind my eyeballs, and then decided to lay it all out on the table.

"Okay," I said. "So you didn't beat us. What about all those myths? The Greek and Roman writings of these deranged incestuous gods? A horde of control-freak, war-mongering ass wipes. Was that you? Was all that factual information?"

He exhaled. "Nice way to put it. But yes, correct in certain aspects. You have to understand, a majority of those accounts were propaganda to smear one faction or another. No different than what you do at present, spinning news to get the desired effect. That said, the more outlandish stories were simply a way to persuade humans to behave by making them assume they would meet the same dire consequences—moral tales told to children. There is truth to some of them, but we have come a long way since then. We aren't quite the 'ass wipes' we used to be."

"Wait. You were here prior to the Great Flood, right?"

"Right."

"If you were so fond of us stroking your egos and doing your mining while you guzzled beer, then explain to me why you were willing to let us all die during the flood."

"We... made mistakes."

I gave a derisive snort and then placed my hands on my hips. "Oops, did Johnny forget to close the flood gates and kill all of humanity again? I swear, that boy."

Mr. New Age gave his sexy half-smile. *Yummy.* "Our first mistake was that we genetically engineered you a little too well."

"How could that be a mistake?"

"You were designed specifically to work the mines. Therefore we made you resilient to disease to prevent unnecessary downtime, strong and fit so as to not tire or get injured, and extended your lifespan so we could utilize your skills for longer periods of time."

"How long did we live?"

"About two thousand years. And as you can imagine, without deaths, the population quickly grew out of control."

"Two thousand years? How come we don't live that long now?"

"After the flood, when we repopulated the human race, we purposely made you more susceptible to disease and shortened your life to keep the population in check."

"You said that was the first mistake. What was the other?"

"We transferred knowledge to you much too quickly. As a species, you let the instant gratification of vices drive you, forgetting the long-term repercussions. Sex, alcohol, power, and money were your primary obsessions."

"Geez, we couldn't have been that bad. You make us sound like a bunch of demonic fraternity brothers."

"Actually, it was worse. When we created you, we learned that our engineering made you inherently evil. You can be coerced, by fear, into behaving, and that's what we did: hence the stories in your Bible and the creation of heaven and hell. And we were successful, for the most part. The bottom line is that a human will always be drawn toward sin unless there is a will or reason to fight it."

That comment offended me. Granted, I knew that humans could be nasty at times, but not all of us were. *I* wasn't. I huffed in irritation. "So we were no different than you, then. From what I've read, you were no saints. Monkey see, monkey do."

"Touché. You have me there," he admitted. "Evil spreads like a disease. Despite that flaw, we didn't want to give you up. After creating humans, we were mesmerized by your beauty. To be frank, your species was absolutely alluring to us, given your exotic nature."

"Exotic? We look just like you."

"Not true. All of my people have blond hair and blue eyes, without a single variation. You, with your rich hair colors, skin tones, and multifaceted eyes, made quite the impression on us."

The sparkle in his eye made me blush. Never in a million years would I have considered my auburn hair and gray-green eyes exotic.

"The question still stands," I said. "Why kill us all off with the flood? If you thought we were attractive, that's just another reason to keep us."

"It should be no surprise to you that this attraction resulted in… intimacy. And, well, no one expected the genetic anomaly that was born from our unions."

"What the hell did they give birth to? Lizard people?"

"No," he laughed. "Giants. Not only were they upwards of twenty-five feet tall and stronger than any of us, they were also pure evil—all humanity bred out of them. They became the catalyst for the bloodiest battles on record. The flood was intended to destroy them all."

"Hey, that's from the Bible, right? Angels and humans had sex and gave birth to giants on Earth. They were called… uh… oh, man… it's on the tip of my tongue. Nepha-something…"

"Nephilim."

"Yeah, that's it. Why were they so huge?"

"Because time is different for my kind. Humans only carried children for a fraction of the time we did, because of our slower aging process. It was discovered too late that this faster gestation period of the human females essentially sped up the babies' development in the womb."

"How were women able to give birth to babies that humongous? Didn't it kill them?"

"Occasionally, yes. Most mothers ended up delivering prematurely, their infants averaging twelve to fourteen pounds at birth. The major growth spurt for these giants didn't occur until childhood. By the time they reached puberty, males could be in excess of twenty-five feet tall. Unfortunately, this rapid maturation didn't allow time for their humanity to develop, and they operated on sheer animal instinct. A survival-of-the-fittest mentality."

"Dear lord! Why did you keep having sex with humans if these giants were being born? Why not refrain after the first one was conceived?"

Every inch of his exposed skin turned the color of a beet. Fidgeting with the bottom of his shirt, he said with a waver in his voice, "In the beginning, after we ingested the gold, we didn't know how to control melam, our light form, the way we do at present. During high emotional states, it would falter. And sex isn't as… uh… fun when the male and female Anunnaki are shifting in and out of light form." He twisted away from me, embarrassed. "There were various, how do you say it… umm, tricks that males could do to keep whole. Unfortunately, the females were not that lucky."

His foot tapped wildly; if he continued, it might take flight. It seemed to literally cause him pain to have to explain this to me. I should have been nice and stopped him, but my odd fascination prevented me from offering a reprieve. So I waited for him to continue.

"With us, a female always, well, 'finishes' about thirty seconds before a guy. It's what triggers our… you know. And so girls would lose form during their climax, bringing the guy's finish to an abrupt halt. Which was frustrating, to say the least. Humans, however, were solid—so there was no such problem. It was kind of addicting for the males of our species."

He weighed my reaction, then quickly backpedaled at the expression on my face. I think my eyes might've been bulging out of my head.

"The addiction was mutual for human women," he reassured me. "It wasn't until the children were grown that we fully understood what we had created."

"A legion of barbarous jackass blood-letting giants."

"Yes, you could call them that," he conceded. "As soon as it became apparent we had a situation, a law came into effect banning any of us from having sex with, or starting any relationships with humans. Anybody that does is promptly dealt with."

"I'm unclear about one thing. Sexy time created giants, but engineering us didn't? Were we harvested in jars?"

"No. There were no birth pods or tanks of floating babies, I promise you. The Anunnaki females served as surrogate mothers, and we controlled the gestation periods with hormones along with other technology we possessed. Ten months after implantation, normal hybrids were born.

"My god, did you have every female on your planet popping out kids to create all of us?"

"Only fourteen, actually. Then we let humans produce the rest naturally. You have to understand, you matured fast, relative to our long lifespans. The time it took to create a workforce represented just a blip in time for us."

"So what happened with the flood? If the intent was to let us all die, why did Noah and his family get saved? If that account is real."

"One of our leaders, Enki, rebelled against the ruling to let you all perish in the flood. He uncovered a loophole, which he used to protect Noah."

"You've lost me."

"We knew our planet, Nibiru, was going to pass close to Earth, triggering the flood—a near-extinction-level event. A decision was made by the Anunnaki high council to keep the impending upheaval quiet from both humans and the Nephilim—and to let them all meet their final destruction on Earth. We were instructed to tear down all the dams and blow paths in the mountains to allow the waters to engulf the entire planet. And there's the thing, when our leader makes a ruling, it is literally impossible for us to defy it." He drew his brows together in thought. "Well, almost literally."

"Almost?"

"Anu, our leader, has a unique gift. Once he decides on an edict, he is able to transmit the declaration telepathically to us, and we are physically unable to defy it."

"Excuse me?"

"Let me clarify. Say he made a law that we can't eat grilled cheese sandwiches."

That made me smile. I pictured a Zeus-type character sitting on a cloud zapping a commandment on a stone with his mighty thunderbolt.

"All right, no grilled cheese," I said.

"If one was presented to us, we couldn't eat it. Our brains would see it as poison. Simply lifting it to take a bite would result in us heaving."

"That would explain why Anu is the leader," I said. "All he has to do is say no one else can be the leader and he'd be dictator for all eternity."

"Well, not necessarily. There is a flaw in his gift. We must obey only the exact order he forces upon us."

"Lost me again."

"Let's take the example of the grilled cheese. If we wanted a melted cheese sandwich, we could circumvent the ruling by deep frying it, microwaving it, or putting it in the oven to cook. Any other method of making it besides 'grilling,' since the law specifically used the term 'grilled' in it." He got up and stood on the cliff's edge, which gave me a very nice view of his backside. "Maybe that was a bad example."

"No," I said, "I think I get it. Cheese always makes for a perfect analogy. But couldn't he be meticulously detailed in his laws to cover it all?"

"He is, and he's quite proficient at it, too. Regardless, there is always a way to elude his commands. If you're clever."

"Interesting," I said, mostly to myself. The idea of being governed to that extent was frightening. "Sorry. I got us sidetracked. Back to the flood."

"Enki, the architect that engineered you, wasn't exactly okay with sitting back and watching his creation's obliteration. Now, this part of the story is controversial. Enki claimed that The Creator of All, our ultimate God, came to him and decreed that he must preserve the human race. He relayed this news to Anu, but the ruling council didn't believe Enki. They thought it was his weak attempt to get Anu to renounce his mandate."

"You think he was lying?"

"No. Enki doesn't lie. It isn't in his character. This lack of support from the council didn't deter him. He found a way to evade Anu's order. He warned Noah of the flood, and then gave him the blueprints to build the Ark."

"If the flood was that devastating, how could a rickety boat withstand it? And please don't tell me it really did fit two of each animal on it."

"It wasn't a rickety boat; it was a submarine. And pardon me for bursting your bubble of disbelief, but technically it did house two of every animal."

"Now I definitely don't believe you. How the heck is that plausible? The submarine would have to be the size of Texas."

"Not in this case. It housed the DNA of each animal on the planet, including a handful of humans. When the floods receded, Enki planned to restore Earth to its original condition. And that's what he did."

I paused to let all this sink in. Then I said, "There's one thing I don't get. If the gold you came here for was to mend your atmosphere, why didn't you make it easy on yourselves and just relocate to Earth? Why go to all that trouble of mining and transporting gold when you could move to this ready-made planet?"

"Because we age way too rapidly here," he said. "Almost as fast as you do. By spending the majority of time on Nibiru, we are nearly immortal by your standards."

"Why is aging so different on your planet than it is on Earth?"

"It is a simple matter of the speed at which we orbit the sun, and the gravity well of our planet."

Simple matter? What the hell is a gravity well? I didn't get it, but I took his word for it. "If humans were to go to Nibiru, would we age slower, too?"

"Yes."

A thought occurred to me. "Are there any humans there today?"

"The only humans ever allowed on Nibiru were Noah and his wife, and they returned a couple thousand years later to live out their days on Earth. Since then, no human has ever been permitted to set foot on our planet."

"Why?"

"Let's just say it's due to politics."

I wasn't keen on that response, but judging by the determined crease on his forehead, he wasn't going to spill the beans, so I let it go. "Okay. Let's say I go with this. What are you doing here? More importantly, what were you doing at Barnes & Noble?"

"We read, too, you know."

I gave him an unsatisfied glower.

"We have always had people here observing. Making sure you rambunctious humans don't misbehave," he confided with a wink.

I rested my chin on my knees. "How did you get stuck on patrol duty?"

"I'm not on patrol duty. I'm here for… another reason." It was obvious he was hiding something from me. "Okay, enough of the history lesson," he said. "I want to hear about you."

Standing up, I demanded, "What are you keeping from me?"

He blew out a sigh. "I can't talk about that today. I'm sorry."

I rolled my eyes and scoffed, "Of course you can't. Do me a favor though. If you're here to euthanize us disobedient humans, can you give me a heads-up? I have lots of stuff on my bucket list I want to do." Irritated, I kicked a rock and watched it bound off the cliff. To be truthful, my frustration was verging on a childish pout, and I wasn't sure why.

Instantly he was beside me, startling me so badly I nearly karate-chopped him Miss Piggy style.

"Stop doing that," I said, keeping a playful tone, but inwardly annoyed.

He brushed his fingers along my cheek, and static electricity charged the path that he stroked. I closed my eyes and drew in a breath, letting the warmth from his touch travel down spine. My skin buzzed as his fingers slid to my chin, pausing there. With a tender nudge, he tilted it up.

I opened my eyes to find his face only inches from mine. *How is such perfection possible?* His skin was smooth as marble, not a pore to mar its purity. The blues of his eyes were flawless, as if polished from glass; no flecks of brown or black like we have, only a silky aquamarine. And when he moved them just right, they switched to a light gold for a split second. It felt like his soul was calling out to me with each flicker.

"So beautiful," he murmured, casting me into a voluntary submission. He could have asked me to do anything, and I would obey, as long as he promised to look at me this way forever.

His proximity heightened my senses, making me hyperaware of my surroundings. I could hear the birds chirping their morning songs, the rustling of small creatures on the forest floor, and the traffic humming in the distance.

His mouth parted slightly, and his warm breath tickled my skin. I ceased my own breathing, afraid I would gasp and ruin the moment.

He released my chin and shut his eyes, readying for a kiss. I couldn't wait to taste his lips; I imagined them to be cool and sweet. My eyes fluttered closed, preparing for the contact.

An agonizing amount of time passed. The blood thrummed in my ears from holding my breath. I wouldn't be able to sustain it much longer. Finally I dared to sneak a peek—and I found him gone. I heaved in gobs of fresh air and looked around.

"Hey," I said. "Where did you go?"

I wanted to call for him by name and realized I didn't know it.

"Umm. You there? Hello?"

Nothing. *Did he leave me here alone? Seriously?*

"Okay then, I'll just go. It was nice meeting you and all."

I had taken only two steps when he snuck up behind me and whispered, "I'm here." He scared the living daylights out of me, yet again, and I spun, slipped in the gravel, and thudded painfully on my rear end.

He chuckled and offered to help me up.

Miffed and a little embarrassed, I refused his assistance. "I would expect a god to know how to treat a lady."

Ignoring my petulance, he bent down and lifted me into his arms. "Is this better?"

"Acceptable," I replied, trying in vain to maintain my resentful grimace. "I do have another question for you."

He groaned. "One more. Then we are talking about you."

"What's your name?" I asked.

"I do apologize. Where are my manners?" Grinning, he placed me on my feet and extended his hand. "I'm Rigel."

I shook it. "I'm Autumn, but I'm guessing you already knew that."

He didn't say anything, which was all the answer I needed. I wondered about the extent of his knowledge on all things Autumn. *Do they keep files? Or maybe he did a background check?* I was getting a tad paranoid.

"Rigel, huh?" I said. "As in the star in Orion?"

"Yes, that would be the one."

"So you were named after a foot?" I quipped.

He gave a slight start. He was probably surprised by my familiarity of the Orion constellation. The only reason I knew was because of my college astronomy class.

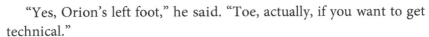

"Yes, Orion's left foot," he said. "Toe, actually, if you want to get technical."

"Hmm… I don't think my mom would have approved of me dating a toe. She always warned me to keep it above the belt."

"Well, I am the brightest star in the constellation," he offered.

"True."

One of his eyebrows rose dramatically. "So, we're dating, huh?"

I went rigid as it registered what I had insinuated. Heat waves of panic flooded my system. I was suddenly very self-conscious, as though I were confronting a grade school crush. "No… I… umm… didn't mean. Wait. What are we doing, anyway? Why did you bring me here?"

"I couldn't stay away." He shrugged. "I tried." He sat down on the rock again and watched the sunrise.

"Same here," I concurred, plopping down next to him. "To be honest, I've been a complete mess, functioning intellectually at the level of an intoxicated turkey with severe brain damage, ever since I met you. And that's putting it mildly."

He laughed. "Yeah, you spilled a perfectly good Double Gulp full of merlot the other night. You should've stuck to the Super Big Gulp container and refilled. It's much easier to hang on to when you're drunk."

My eyes went wide. "That was you at the house!" I said. "You were *spying* on me?"

"More like getting my fix," he confessed.

"Hey, did you take the picture from the attic?"

"I did," he said. "Sorry about that. I was trying to learn more about you. Was your mom a body builder?"

I snorted. "No." By his use of the word "was," he apparently knew she had passed. He really did do his homework on me. "My mom was about total equality between men and women, and it would sometimes annoy my dad. So one day she couldn't get a jar of peanut butter open and asked my dad for help. He raised an eyebrow at her, popped open the jar with ease, and handed it back saying, 'Equal, huh?' I will never forget that day. The calm resolve on my mom's face was frightening. Three months later she was stronger than my dad, or any other man in Irvine for that matter, and never needed to ask for help again."

Rigel was staring at me as if I just told the most fascinating story ever. His attentiveness surprised me.

"So…" I said, drawing it out. "Is that normal? This pull between you and me?"

He shook his head, as if he was coming out of a daze. "No. And that's what concerns me. This isn't normal at all. Our souls seem to be drawn together."

"Is that why I keep leaving my body?"

"I believe so. It's all I can do to keep my own form when I'm with you."

For a while, we both sat quietly, watching the sleeping city awaken.

"Now what?" I asked with a heavy heart.

"I don't know," he said, running his hand through his hair. "If we keep seeing each other, I'm afraid it isn't going to end pleasantly for either of us."

"Is there a rehab I can admit myself to so I can get over you? Because the way I see it, I'm screwed either way."

He regarded me for a long time. Those familiar vibrations stirred in my core from the heat of his gaze, and my soul threatened to launch itself from my body again. The wind tousled his hair, and it fell into his eyes, disheveled and wild. I know I keep saying it, but he was so damn sexy.

He must have been having similar thoughts, because he began to glow along the edges, his shape distorting slightly. Inhaling a calming breath, he shut his eyes. I knew he was doing everything in his power to keep his form. Taking his lead, I did the same thing, breathing evenly until the vibrations subsided.

He exhaled. "I have to go," he said. "I can't take the chance that they'll come looking for me."

I opened my eyes and committed every inch of him to my memory—in case this was my one and only evening with him. "Can I see you again?" I asked with a yearning I wasn't prepared for. My chest tightened as I awaited his response.

He rose, and pulled me up beside him. "I don't think either of us can resist." He cupped my face between his hands, his eyes sparking with emotion. "At least I know *I* can't."

My body thrummed like a jet engine about to take off.

"I need you to seriously consider this," he urged. "Us merely being in the same vicinity could have grave repercussions."

I considered his words. It went without saying that I wanted to rendezvous with him again. He had me worried, though. *What do these so-called 'repercussions' entail?*

"Do you need an answer now?" I asked.

"No. Take today to really think about it." He clasped me tighter. "What they could do to us is unimaginable," he warned before letting go.

"I will, I promise." The fierceness in his eyes brought on a case of the shivers, and I didn't know if they were fueled by lust or fear.

"Meet me here at midnight if you decide you want to see me again," he said.

"Okay."

He studied me, his eyes narrowing, as if he was trying to see inside me somehow. I hoped that mind-reading wasn't one of his "gifts." If it were, he'd be viewing himself naked in my bed at present.

"Close your eyes," he whispered, moving nearer to me.

Without hesitation I did what he asked, praying this finally meant he was about to kiss me. The lightest brush of a finger grazed my cheek, and then a white light brightened my lids and disappeared. So. I wasn't going to make it to first base after all. He had gone, leaving my lips tingling with desire.

I stayed there and watched the sun as it crested the horizon. I already knew I'd be in this same spot again come midnight, repercussions be damned.

7

SEVERED ARMS, BIRTHDAY SUIT FRIDAYS, TINY WEE-WEES, AND A BURNING WHEEL OF LUST

As I drove home, I contemplated the possibility that what had happened to me over the past few days was not actually real—but that instead, I was lying in a coma at a hospital, and this was all one long morphine-induced hallucination.

I was so caught up in my thoughts that when I pulled into my driveway, it felt like only five minutes had passed—which was concerning, since the drive was an hour. Swallowing hard, I tried to recall the details of my trip. *How many people did I almost crash into during my daze?*

I checked the front of my car for any severed arms or critter parts clinging to it. *No carnage. Whew.* Now I'd have to wait and see if one of those photo traffic tickets came in the mail for running a traffic light.

Once I got inside, I went straight to bed, not bothering to take my shoes off. The second I rested my head on the pillow, I was out like a light—getting much-needed sleep at last.

My dreams had different plans in store for me, however.

> *Far underground, cloaked in the cave of a volcano, I hung from a stalactite, my wrists bound, my feet dangling, like a fresh kill ready to be skinned. Towering obsidian rocks contrasted with the flowing red lava that covered a majority of the cavern. The heat came in swells, scorching my naked body.*
>
> *A crack rang out, followed by a searing pain along my upper back. I wailed as my flesh split open. A female cackled maniacally beside me, a bloody whip*

in hand. Through the watery blur of my eyes, I saw another figure dangling over a lava pit across from me. I blinked to clear my vision. Rigel hung there, writhing in agony.

I yelled for him and struggled to get free. Another slash struck, slicing my leg, and I lost consciousness.

When I woke, a bewitching goddess in a white flowing dress levitated in front of me, fondling a serrated knife in her fingers.

"Witness what your actions get you, my pretty," she cackled in a perfect impersonation of the Wicked Witch of the West.

She threw the knife at Rigel. It slashed through the ropes restraining him—and he plummeted into the pit of lava.

I screamed.

I was startled awake by my real screams reverberating off the walls of my bedroom. Several dogs were barking outside, and I hoped a neighbor hadn't called the police in response to my anguished howls. I highly doubted it, though. The days of people reacting to car alarms, gunshots, and shrieks of terror were long gone. Calling the cops entailed getting involved, and that wasn't an option for most people.

I sagged back against the pillows and calmed my racing heart. I couldn't shake the dream. Rigel falling into the pit of lava kept playing over and over on a continuous loop. If I was being honest, I hadn't really, I mean *really*, thought about what could happen if I continued these secret meetings with Rigel.

After repeated slaps on my cheeks to wake myself, I finally rolled out of bed and got ready. Ready to go where, I didn't know. All I knew was I had to leave the house and press the reset button. It was eleven in the morning and warm sunshine topped my to-do list.

Instead of heading to the beach, or some other location equally suited to soaking up the rays, I ended up driving aimlessly around Irvine. If you've never been to Irvine, it consists of mostly modern industrial office buildings, packed in sardine style. If they were any closer together, the city would be a single sixty-six-square-mile office complex. Not exactly what I'd call a rip-roaring vacation destination. But it didn't matter; scenery was not what I needed anyway. I was too lost in my own musings.

I flipped on the radio and tuned to an AM talk station, hoping the usual political BS would help distract me. To my surprise, I didn't find the normal right-wing blabbering. Instead, an unfamiliar host was in the middle of interviewing an expert from NASA.

I increased the volume, intrigued.

"We don't have an accurate calculation for how close it will come to Earth, but we do know for certain we are under no threat of impact."

"Have you officially identified what it is?" the host inquired. "An asteroid or comet?"

There was a long, awkward pause, then the NASA official said, "Actually, it is a planet, with what appears to be seven moons."

The host chortled. "Don't tell me this is the mysterious Planet X that's been prophesied to shepherd in doomsday?"

"No... no..." The NASA official cleared his throat quite loudly. "Although I'm sure you will hear plenty of people claiming we're lying about it passing at a safe distance—conspirators making their own ludicrous calculations. But we assure you, it's not a threat, nor is it the elusive Nibiru or Planet X trending on the Internet. The government would let you know if we were in any danger."

I snorted out loud at that statement. The government wouldn't disclose a damn thing. In all fairness to them, what would be the point? If we were all going to be blown to bits, an emergency alert system would be useless. We'd just go apeshit and murder each other anyway.

The host continued with his questioning. "How close is it to us now? Can we see it in the sky?"

"It's at perihelion and currently blocked by the sun's rays, but its orbit is quite fast; faster than anything we've observed before. You should be able to observe it with the naked eye in about a week as it moves away from the sun."

The broadcast went to commercial, so I cut it off. This new development made me a lot more suspicious about the whole set of circumstances with Rigel. He had said he wasn't here for patrol duty, but for "another reason." And now this mysterious planet just happened to be passing by Earth? It was way too much of a coincidence. It has to be his planet, Nibiru, and the reason for him being here.

I recalled what he had said about the Great Flood—that a passing of their planet had caused it. Alarm bells blared a warning in my gut. *Is he here because it's about to happen again?*

I executed a sharp right into an empty parking lot and completed an impressive donut into a spot—loud tire screech and all. I dug my nails into the steering wheel and considered the possibility.

What if Rigel is here to be an eyewitness as humans drown in another flood? No, that couldn't be. He wouldn't do that. Or would he? Truth be told, I didn't know him at all. We'd had only one date after all, if you could even call it that. Then again, why would he worry about the consequences of us being together if there wasn't going to be an "us" to worry about? Plus, he hadn't said anything after I'd asked for a heads-up if we were about to be euthanized.

Crap. What if I'm entirely wrong about him?

I plunged into atomic meltdown mode, expecting smoke to billow from my ears. Rigel would warn me—I had to believe that. For all I knew, he was here to monitor our reaction to the appearance of their planet—which was making a *harmless* pass by Earth. I had to cling to that theory or I might toss myself into oncoming traffic.

This brooding was getting me nowhere. I decided it was time to do some real research on these ancient "gods" to find out what they were capable of. With a new determination, I pulled out of the parking lot and made my way to the library.

The library was surprisingly busy. Who knew people still actually checked out books rather than just getting them from the Internet? Most of the people were browsing the DVDs, so I had the Greek myths section all to myself. Selecting the largest book first, I pulled it off the shelf and it gave me a view of the next row over, where I spotted a familiar heap of hair.

"Zarf, is that you?" I said.

The Hair, a.k.a. Zarf, toted a cart full of books along with him. A pair of high school girls pranced behind him, giggling to one another, then adopted a seductive stance as they pretended to be interested in the books on the shelf. One of the girls sucked on a pen and the other twirled her gum around her finger.

They have to be joking, right? Did they not see the high-rise hairball protruding from his scalp?

Zarf looked at me through the gap in the shelf. "Ah... Zooloo. What are you doing here?"

"I should be asking you the same thing. Are you that obsessed with books?"

He chuckled. "No. I mean yes, I do love books, but this isn't my choice. Community service. It beats plucking trash off the freeway."

"Say what?" I placed my hands on my hips and gave him my best patronizing scowl. "What did my Zarfie do to earn him some community service?"

"Oh, a little of this, a little of that," he dodged.

"I see..."

"You here for another paper?"

"Huh?"

"Another sociology paper?"

I had totally forgotten that I lied to him, saying the Light Being research was for a sociology paper. This is why I avoid any sort of lie. It always bites me in the ass. At this point, the only sensible way out of it was to shovel more poo on my pile-o-lies.

"Ohh... yeah," I said. "Now I'm doing an essay for my mythology class on torture and punishment by the gods." The lie flowed off my tongue, as if I were a professional.

"Wow. That's a seriously specific topic. Want my help? I could use the break."

I was taken aback by his offer. "Sure, I'd love the help."

His head disappeared from the book hole we were talking through, and he was around the corner by my side in a few strides. With an impressive speed, he scanned the shelf and started handing books to me. It was all I could do not to drop them all. He must have done a lot of community service here to be this adept at finding stuff.

"Excuse me," a female voice said.

I turned to see one of the high school girls standing behind me.

She returned my look with a glare. "Not you." She pointed at Zarf. "Him."

She brushed past me and leaned in close to Zarf. "Can you help me find some books?"

"I am assisting someone else right now," Zarf said. "But if you go to the front desk, they can help you find what you need."

"But I want you."

My eyes darted from the girl, to Zarf, and then to his hair.

Zarf gestured toward me. "Sorry, but she was first."

The high school girl crossed her arms. "Fine." Spinning on her heel, she stalked away, but not without first hissing out a "whore" in my direction.

Seemingly oblivious to what had happened, Zarf took back a majority of the stack in my hands and guided me to an empty study room. Spreading out the books, he said, "Okay, you're looking for different ways the gods tortured people, correct?"

Hearing him say it aloud gave me an involuntary shiver. "Uh-huh," I said, rethinking my plan to investigate in the first place.

He grabbed a couple titles, and I reluctantly took one of my own.

The book I'd selected was filled with images of statues and artwork, displaying the gods naked in various poses. Did they not wear clothes? Then again, with physiques like that, "clothing optional" was the way to go. Birthday Suit Friday would replace Casual Friday in my Roman Empire. I became fascinated by how skimpy their privates were in comparison to their thick frames. I wondered if artistic liberties were taken, or if that was the accurate representation of their wee-wees.

"Here's one," Zarf said, distracting me from stone penis La La Land—and my worry about what that meant for Rigel's nether region. "Askalabos was transfigured into a spotted gecko by the goddess Demeter as punishment for mocking her."

"That isn't so bad," I said. "He could always get a job as the understudy for the GEICO insurance gecko."

Zarf furrowed a brow and carried on with his reading. That was understandable; I didn't deserve acknowledgement for that one. My emotional turmoil had hampered my sense of humor.

After tossing aside three different books based on their gory illustrations alone, I resolved to suck it up and read a freaking sentence already. *That's what I'm here for, right?* I opened a book, closed my eyes, and picked a page at random.

After a reading a paragraph, I said, "Hey, I got something. This psychopath called Lycurgus mistook his own son for a trunk of ivy and cut off his nose, ears, fingers, and toes. And I guess ivy was sacred to the god Dionysus, so he made the land dry and barren until Lycurgus received punishment for his act. In response, the people fed Lycurgus to a herd of man-eating horses to end the drought."

"That's the dumbest thing I've ever heard!" Zarf said. "The dingbat chopped his own son in pieces, not the actual plant, so why in the rusty hamster wheel does Dionysus care?"

I flipped back a page. "Oh, oops, I missed the first part of the story. Lycurgus might've been..." I stopped, suddenly realizing what The Hair had said. "Hold on a sec, did you just say 'rusty hamster wheel'?"

"Yeah." He laughed. "Growing up, my parents were overly strict about cussing, so me and my brother would invent our own phrases."

"Alrighty, then."

"Check this one out," he said excitedly. "Zeus punished Prometheus by having him bound to a rock while a great eagle came by each day to chow down on his liver. And here's the kicker: since Prometheus was a god, his liver regenerated, providing him with endless torture."

The color drained from my face. I massaged the area where my liver was and winced. *Surely, these tales have to be exaggerated.*

On the verge of an anxiety attack, I quickly flipped through another book. That was when I found the coup de grâce of horrific mythos. "Listen to this," I said with a dry mouth. "Tantalus was imprisoned in a pool of water beneath a fruit tree. If he grabbed for the fruit, the branches snatched it away. And when he tried to get a drink, the water receded."

"Nice." Zarf grinned.

I imagined myself chained to a table full of cheese and wine, trying desperately to take possession of it, taste buds watering, just to have it scoot from reach. All that food taunting me day after day; I'd definitely prefer my liver to be mangled to bits by an eagle.

Zarf was now leaning over and studying my book. "Whoa, and you know why he received that punishment?" he said.

I stared blankly at him.

Taking that for listening intently, rather than having a mental breakdown, he read on, "Tantalus was punished because he cut up his son, boiled him, and served him to the gods at a banquet."

I got queasy and had to close my eyes.

"Hey. You feeling okay?"

"Um, yeah," I lied. "Lightheaded, that's all. This food talk made me hungry."

He continued. "Here's another one that involves starvation. Demeter brought famine to Earth because Poseidon raped her in the form of a horse. Ouch!"

"Ohh… nice."

"This is fun." He beamed at me. "Check this one out. This dude Ixion lusted after Zeus's wife. As punishment, Zeus banished him to Tartarus to forever roll around strapped to a wheel of flames to represent his burning lust." He paused and grinned with excitement. "I'm *so* gonna start a band just so I can call it Ixion's Burning Wheel of Lust. Man, you gotta be careful who you crush on with these gods. They inflict harsh punishments."

That did it. I leaped to my feet, almost knocking the table over.

"Whoa. What happened?" Zarf asked.

"Nothing," I said. "I must be getting the flu, so, um, I should go." Conscious that I was being rude, I turned to him, and with an appreciative smile said, "Thanks for all your help. I owe you one."

He looked concerned. "No problemo. Feel better."

I scrambled through the door without another word.

8

TWEEZERS OF DEATH AND LEVITATING KLEENEX

If only the tiniest part of these Greek and Roman "myths" were true, and I had a hunch they were, then I needed to deliver my eyeballs a hearty poke to prevent them from looking at Rigel again. Nothing positive could come from this. It was wiser to rip the bandage off clean before I got too attached. Attaining the resolve to do it was the hurdle.

After the library fiasco, I went straight home. Depressed beyond belief, I pulled into my driveway, dragged myself from the car, and clomped to the front door. For some reason, I hesitated when I clutched the cool metal of the knob, my nerves screaming at me not to enter. I surveyed my neighborhood for anything out of sorts and went on high alert when I noticed the neighbor's dog was barking frantically at me. This may not seem odd to you, but Jib Jab was a thirteen-year-old Corgi mix who usually mustered only one bark per year—saving it for the first firework on the Fourth of July, after which he would immediately fall asleep by his favorite tree, satisfied he'd successfully frightened it off. But now, in the span of thirty seconds, he had barked more than he had in his whole existence. His yelping conveyed a warning, I was sure of it.

Before entering the house, I rummaged through my purse for a suitable weapon. The best I could find was a pair of tweezers. Was it feasible to incapacitate someone using tweezers? My money would be on no, because if it were, you couldn't carry them on an airplane. I was screwed.

Making a mental note to buy a canister of mace the next chance I got, I hid my purse behind the flowerpot and opened the front door with tweezers held high, ready to strike.

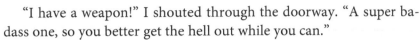

"I have a weapon!" I shouted through the doorway. "A super badass one, so you better get the hell out while you can."

I inched through the entryway and rounded the corner into the living room all stealth like.

"Freeze!" I yelled, pinching my tweezers together threateningly.

I stopped dead in my tracks, my tweezers falling to the floor with a very anticlimactic ping. All my muscles seized in fright when I saw the woman who sat on my couch. She was extremely tall, gorgeous—and had the same glowing blue eyes as Rigel.

"Oh my god!"

"Why yes, I am," she concurred with a smile. "God*dess*, actually."

I scanned the room for anything I could use for self-defense. Collecting statues or knickknacks was not my thing, so this rendered my house void of any easy-to-grab blunt objects. The only plan of attack I could construct was to clock her with the remote control, swaddle her in my area rug, and tweeze her eyebrows out.

"My name is Inanna," she said, then patted the seat next to her. "Please. Sit."

I didn't budge. Her smile broadened, and all at once I was sliding toward the couch against my will. I whimpered and fought to escape, but I couldn't resist; it was like I was bound by an invisible rope. She pulled me along like a piece of furniture she was moving with a dolly until I was standing right at the edge of the couch. *Well, isn't that quite the fancy "gift" she has?*

"Please," she repeated, patting the cushion again. "Have a seat so we can have some girl talk."

Whatever force she had used to bind me was released. Part of me considered making a break for it, but my survival instinct prevented me from attempting it, since I didn't know what other witchcraft this chick had hiding in her fancy bag of tricks. Finally giving in, I swallowed and sat down on the far end of the couch, shaking like a leaf.

"Calm down, Autumn, I'm not going to hurt you," she said in a reassuring tone. "I just want to talk, that's all."

My capacity for speech had hit Kernel Panic status (or for you PC users, the Blue Screen of Death). I fixed my eyes on hers, trembling so violently that it was hard to keep my eyes focused.

An eerie white shimmer danced off her features as she assessed me. Her hair was long and sleek, a waterfall of blond tresses that flowed down her back. She wore no foundation, but didn't need it: her skin was flawless, airbrushed straight off the cover of a fashion magazine. Her eyes were lined in a thick black all the way around, reminiscent of an Egyptian queen. And her lips were a perfect candy apple red, which I suspected was her natural color. That level of perfection should not be allowed in nature. (Rigel excluded; I would give him a pass.)

"It has come to my attention that you are becoming fond of my favorite cousin, Rigel," Inanna said.

I gave a feeble squeak of terror, which she accepted as acknowledgement.

"I assume since you're still considering this foolish plan to see him again, he must not have made you aware of our rules—or rule, rather. Did he fail to mention that?"

"No," I said weakly. "He did."

"Well then, maybe you don't grasp how serious we take it."

Cowering in the corner of the couch, I clutched my legs to my chest, curled into a ball, and assumed the protective posture of an armadillo.

Inanna's lips turned down in an almost imperceptible frown, then she smoothed her brilliant smile back into place. "While we do not perform such heinous acts anymore," she said, "those stories you were reading today are the reason we have these laws in place. A child resulting from an Anunnaki and a human is beyond your worst nightmare. While you and that *Bride of Frankenstein*-haired boy read the exaggerated versions of those myths, that doesn't mean those incidents didn't happen in one form or another. You do comprehend what I'm saying, correct?"

I nodded, blocking out the gruesome images of torture so I didn't lose what little composure I still had (or my lunch). I wasn't sure if I was more terrified by Inanna's presence in my living room, or the revelation that she knew what I had researched at the library. The fact that she had been shadowing me all day horrified me to the brink of tears.

She flicked her wrist, and the Kleenex box levitated to me. I flinched, waiting for it to attack.

"It won't bite. I promise," she said. "Take it."

She made the box nudge my arm over and over until I had no choice but to take it. I grasped it hesitantly between two fingertips, too scared to do anything else. The tissue twitched and I thought it might fly up my nose and suffocate me.

Inanna gave an exasperated sigh. A tissue flew out of the box and hovered next to my free hand. Gingerly, I took it and wiped my watery eyes.

"Autumn, look, I don't want to hurt you. Honestly." Her tone shifted to one of a mother scolding a misbehaving child. "Our punishment is simple. If you mate with my cousin, you die. Under no circumstance will we let another Nephilim be born. Do you understand that?"

Gritting my teeth, I mumbled, "Yes."

These Anunnaki were a bunch of murderous bastards.

Hang on... death. Is that the answer? I had left my body in Rigel's presence—on a couple occasions, in fact. That meant I didn't need a physical form to "live." If my body died, wouldn't my soul be free to do what it wanted? I could be with him, right? How would that work? He had spoken to me as I floated toward him at Barnes & Noble, so I knew we could communicate in that state. Could my soul touch his light form? Better question: could I be physically attracted to an orb?

I gave myself a hearty mental slap. Here I was, contemplating suicide to be with a guy I had just met! This was shaping up to be a real life *Romeo and Juliet.*

Inanna broke into my reverie. "And no, if you die, you cannot be together. When humans pass on, your souls go to another dimension, one the Anunnaki cannot go to. The moment your lungs exhale their last breath, you will be taken from this realm, and from Rigel, forever. So you must quell that hope and any others. Trust me, there's no loophole."

How did she know what I was thinking? Can she read minds?

I decided to test that idea. I thought: *Can you hear me?*

Nothing.

I tried a different approach. *You're an ass.*

"Are you mentally insulting me?" she asked.

My heart thundered in my chest.

"Relax. I can't read your mind, only auras."

I slumped on the couch.

"Honey, I'm sorry," she said with an air of condescension. "I know you two have a connection. You'll get over it. I promise." Her demeanor morphed into that of gossipy girl in a schoolyard as she whispered conspiratorially, "What about that nice boy you were with in the library today? He's cute."

Did I hear that correctly? Was she giving me relationship advice right after she threatened to kill me? The coherent portion of my brain revved up, churning my fear into pure rage. Leaping off the couch, I stalked to the front door, flung it open, and folded my arms.

"I'm clear on where things stand," I said, completely ignoring her lame comment. "If I have sex with your cousin, you'll go all mobster and whack me and I'll never see him again. You can go now."

She sighed and stood up. "I know I've said this already, but I truly am sorry that this is the way it has to be."

"You can go now," I repeated firmly.

She glided, and I mean that literally, through the door, and I slammed it shut behind her with such force that the molding cracked.

9

UNICORN KINGDOM, FOOT-SNIFFING WITCHES, AND EXPLODING SOULS

That evening I wore a path in the concrete surrounding my Honda. It was time for me to leave and meet Rigel, but I couldn't make myself get in. After my tenth frenzied loop, I was concerned that the neighbors might worry I'd lost my mind. In case they were about to report my suspicious behavior to the authorities, I bent down and pretended to check my tire.

Inanna had succeeded in scaring the bejesus out of me. I'd come to my senses and decided to end it with Rigel. But I needed to do it in person; to say goodbye. Problem was, I didn't think I was capable of saying the words. Every one of my cells was wound tight and ready to snap in anticipation of seeing him again.

No longer able to delay the inevitable, I reluctantly opened the car door, crawled inside, and eased the engine on. After adjusting all my mirrors, I wasted more time by fidgeting with my seat. Finally I pulled out and drove slower than a senior citizen on a Sunday drive. I kept darting my eyes from mirror to mirror, checking for any suspicious activity. Thankfully, there weren't a lot of cars on the road. My paranoia caused me to swerve erratically at each passing headlight, convinced it was the Anunnaki materializing to take me down. If circumstances were different, it might have been kind of a turn-on to be chased down by a mob of uber-sexy gods, but after reading all those grisly stories of torture, the Harlequin fantasy was considerably less appealing.

Arriving at the dirt road that led to the canyon, about a mile from where I was supposed to meet Rigel, I had to pull over. My heart beat painfully against my rib cage and my breathing was ragged. I couldn't drive any further. I was too terrified.

I killed the engine and the silence was overwhelming. Never in my life had I felt as alone as I did then. The waterworks started, dissolving me into an uncontrollable snotty mess. Squeezing my eyes shut, I thumped my forehead against the steering wheel with each slobbering sob. Exhausted from all the crying, I slumped against the door and lost myself to a fantasy of Rigel strutting toward me in slow motion, his hair all messy from the wind, muscles flexing, crooked eager smile... and those seductive eyes. That visual made my tears subside and other, more intense, sensations blossom, which in turn awoke those familiar vibrations from their hibernation.

Terrific, all I have to do is fantasize about him and I leave my body. No physical presence necessary. I'm doomed.

Struggling to keep my soul from escaping, I clenched all my muscles as hard as I could. "No, dammit! Not now!"

A flash of light went off in the passenger seat, and I braced for a lethal beheading from an Anunnaki assassin.

"Did you get lost?" Rigel's intoxicating voice purred in my ear.

I shrieked like a little girl, then laughed at the ridiculous noise I'd made. Before looking in his direction, I mentally prepped for the eye candy I knew I was about to devour. And quite the smorgasbord it was. He was sitting next to me in a figure-hugging dark green Jimmy Hendrix T-shirt that showed off his delectable physique exceedingly well—too well, actually. It caused me to lose my resolve.

He frowned at my tear-stained cheeks and stiffened. "I take it you have made your decision?" he said.

"With the help of a relative of yours, yes."

His eyes dimmed; a deadly aura replaced the sexy one. I scooted closer to the door, intimidated by the waves of anger emanating from him.

He exited the car in a rush and paced out front while mumbling in a language I didn't recognize. He was seriously pissed off. His form flickered, and then in a streak of light he crossed to my side of the car. With a yelp, I frantically maneuvered over the days-old Starbucks cup in my console and fell out the passenger side door. This was the second time I'd hurtled across my car because of Rigel. At least this time I didn't eat dirt as I exited, because Rigel was there, scooping me up in his arms. Helpless to repress my desire, I melted into his perfect frame. His caress broke something inside me, and the entire catalog of human emotions inundated me at once, making my tear ducts gush again and prompting the hiccups.

Rigel sat down on a rock with me in his lap. He tried to wipe away my tears, but it was useless: they were coming in torrents.

"Did she threaten you?" he asked.

"I guess that depends how you interpret, 'If you mate with my cousin, you die.'" I shrugged. "Wait, how did you know it was a *her*? You know who it was?"

"Yes. She's in charge of the policing of these sorts of things." He brushed aside a strand of hair that had stuck to my lashes. "Are you okay?"

I didn't know how to answer that. Obviously, I wasn't. He pressed me in tight, making it difficult to breathe, and I cherished every wheeze.

"Honestly, I don't understand how they discovered us this soon, especially given what's going on with—" He stopped himself abruptly.

"What's going on?"

"Nothing. I misspoke. We don't need to talk about that now."

"What are you keeping from me?" I insisted, pulling away to get a better read on him.

"I'll fill you in before the night is over. I promise."

I let it go, not sure if I could deal with any more bad news at the moment. "So there's no magic kingdom we can escape to and be together?" I hiccupped again. "Full of unicorns and fairies?"

He chuckled. "No. I wish there were. I knew approaching you in the first place was a bad idea. I just couldn't help myself."

Caressing his cheek, my fingers lingered on his silky soft skin, and I confessed, "I wouldn't change anything. This connection I have with you is crazy and amazing all at the same time. I don't know how I'm gonna live without you." I nuzzled my head into his chest so he couldn't see my face for the next admission. "This is ludicrous. We've spent what—maybe a few hours in total together? And I'm undeniably in love with you. I feel like I've known you for decades, not days. I must have a screw loose. I mean, I don't even know what you do for a living."

"That's easily fixed," he said. "I'm a research and development consultant for various biological and technological companies on Nibiru."

I popped my head up and stared at him wide-eyed. "Are you messing with me right now?"

"I'm not."

Well, now I was intrigued. I was an emotional wreck, but this might be my only chance to speed date with an alien, so I took it. "What do you do in your free time?"

"Mostly read."

"Any pets?"

He shook his head. "No, I've never had a pet."

"Not even a goldfish?"

"Pets are really a human concept."

"What's your favorite thing to do when you visit Earth?"

"You won't believe me if I tell you."

"Of course I will." I sat up straighter in anticipation of his answer.

"The demolition derby at state fairs."

"No way!" I said. "You're such a liar."

"I told you," he laughed. "I knew you wouldn't believe me."

I tried to envision him hollering in the stands with a trucker hat, ratty T-shirt, and a cup of beer sloshing around. I snorted so hard I coughed. "This is so much fun." I clapped my hands together in excitement. "Okay. Worst habit?"

He quirked his lips in thought, and then answered, "Can't think of one. I am pretty much perfect."

I smacked him. He wasn't lying, though. He was perfection. "Favorite food?"

"My favorite food is a hotdog with ketchup and mayo."

"Eww," I said. "You put mayo on a hotdog?"

"Yes. I love mayo."

"Oh, sorry. But that's a deal breaker for me. I have a strict rule about guys and mayo. Mayo is the devil's condiment."

"Wow," he said. "I've never met anyone who had such a strong opinion about mayo before."

"Good thing you're hot, and we have this unbreakable connection, or I would bolt. That is seriously gross."

He chuckled and pulled me into him, resting his chin on my head.

"Okay," he said. "I'll give up mayo."

"Thank you."

We held each other, lost in thought, and I treasured the proximity. His form shimmered, and I felt his muscles constrict to suppress it.

I ran my hand down his forearm, tracing the contours of his muscles with my finger. He shuddered at my touch.

"I feel so connected to you," I said. "There has to be a reason we are drawn together."

Rigel took a deep breath, as if trying to make a decision.

"What is it?" I asked.

"There is an ancient story—our creation myth," he said. "Prior to genesis, everything that exists in this universe, all matter, all life, was all part of one soul: a splendid blue light. What you would call God with a capital G. There was no beginning or end—he always was—a solitary soul sitting in the void. Our legend tells us that he wanted to create life forms that he could nourish and oversee. So he toiled away, until, finally, he drafted the blueprints for the universe, a master plan, all the way down to the tiniest particle. There was a catch, however. To bring everything into existence, it would require all of his power to ignite the flame—and he didn't know what this would do to him. Unable to resist seeing his flawless design come to fruition, he summoned all his energy into a single point, and the universe was born from the explosion of his soul. In the process his soul was ripped in half, and the two parts were lost from each other."

"I don't get it. If he is everything, why couldn't he locate the other half? Wasn't it still him?"

"A reasonable question," Rigel acknowledged. "The other half of his soul created a universe equal to this one, one that he knew was there, yet couldn't see. A blind spot, if you will."

"That clears it up." I grinned. "Go on."

"There is a Great Prophecy among not only us, but a majority of the other alien nations out there, that one day these two halves will reunite, restoring balance to our currently unstable universe."

"How are they gonna do that if they can't see one another?"

"The prophecy talks of a golden light that will reunite the souls when it entwines itself to a blue light with a single thread. Once fully joined, the universes will become one, and the true Creator made whole again."

"That's a beautiful story."

"To us it isn't a story."

"Does that have anything to do with why our souls are attracted to each other?"

"I don't know. Souls can definitely be drawn together. It's that 'soulmate' bond you all hope for. I'm not sure if all souls have a match… it's possible. It doesn't happen that often between different species. It's pretty much unheard of, come to think of it. Although, that's not what's puzzling. What *is* unusual is that your soul is blue. The color of the Creator."

"I am God," I joked. "That explains why I'm perfection personified."

"Well, you are the only soul I've ever known to be blue."

It took me a minute to process that. "Whoa, whoa, whoa. Press the pause button. I find it hard to believe I'm the only blue soul in the whole universe. You have to be mistaken."

"That's the reason I ran from Barnes & Noble when I first saw you—I discovered your soul was blue. Well, that, and because I was terrified I'd lose my form in the middle of the store."

"What color is a human soul normally?"

"All souls are naturally white. Ours are tinged yellow because of the gold we consume."

A flutter welled in my chest as an idea formed. "Why can't you present this to your people? If it's true, then maybe we could be together? At least buy us extra time?"

Rigel frowned. "Not a chance. They would laugh us off. The Anunnaki are too egotistical to believe a mere human soul could be the catalyst. Plus, say you are this prophecy; who knows for sure if I'm the one you need to connect with? We have no idea how the connection is made."

"If there's even a possibility I could be part of it, don't we have an obligation to explore it? If I am the only blue soul, wouldn't it be worth the risk to look into it? Or would it kill me?"

"I'm not sure. But if you did die, and you're not the catalyst, I would lose you forever. Your soul has no choice; it must cross to the next dimension, and mine can't go there with you. Whatever path we travel, it seems we are doomed to be apart in the end."

So Inanna was telling the truth. Dammit!

Rigel gave a grunt of frustration. "I shouldn't have mentioned it." He repositioned me on his lap and fixed me with a careful expression. "If it's real, and you possess the blue light in the prophecy, *and* I am what will connect us, there will be no preventing it from uniting us when the time comes. You can't alter a prophecy; it will happen no matter what anyone attempts. We don't need to incite trouble by presenting this to my people. If it's meant to be, it's meant to be."

I knew he was right. Plus, I wasn't ready to depart this life. There was a whole world I hadn't explored, and hundreds of pig-out fests to partake of. The concept was absurd anyway: God tearing apart and uniting again in a great prophecy. I was foolish for believing it for even a second. If I *was* this magical catalyst to unite the two universes, I'm pretty sure I would've been clued in to that long before now. It was a nice bedtime story, but altogether inconceivable in the real world.

"This is it then?" I sighed.

"Not quite," he said in a mischievous tone. "I want to have one last night together."

"Oh, yeah?"

"I want to take you to my favorite spot."

That sounded intriguing. "Where's that?"

"Before I tell you, I need to let you know that we have to be careful—because it requires that you leave your body for a while. Are you game?"

"Of course," I said. "I didn't know we could control our souls leaving our body. What do I have to do?"

"Nothing. Just lie down and close your eyes. I'll do the rest."

Lifting me as if I weighed little more than a paper plate, he placed me softly on the rock next to him. "Word of warning. We only have a limited amount of time. If you leave your body for too long, your organs will shut down."

"Uhh…"

"Don't worry, I'll make sure we return in plenty of time."

"Uhh…"

"Don't you trust me?"

"Uhh…" I repeated, meaning it as joke. But he huffed and tramped off without another word. "Wait!" I pleaded, rising and stumbling to catch him. "I was kidding."

Appearing from the shadows with blankets and pillows, he winked and spread them on the ground, then offered his hand. I took it and a zap of electricity crackled between us. And I'm not talking a metaphorical one, a literal current. Shockingly (no pun intended), he didn't seem fazed by it, so I ignored it too.

"Come on," he said.

We lay down on the blanket side by side and gazed into the star-filled heavens. Rigel entwined his fingers in mine, and that simple action cast all my worries aside. I felt relaxed for the first time in days.

Pointing at the sky he said, "You see my star up there?"

"Ahh, yes, the stinky foot."

He jabbed my side.

"Hey!" I jabbed back.

"That's where we're headed. There's a remarkable nebula that sits in front of it, and I know the perfect spot from which to view it. It'll knock your socks off."

I snickered. "Knock your socks off? Are we also time traveling to the fifties?" Unable to help myself, I added, "It's the bees' knees, Daddy-O. Are we going to do a little back seat bingo in the rumble seat?"

He gave me a dirty look.

"Hang on," I said. "Are you talking about the Witch Head Nebula? That explains why she looks all unhappy, having to live next to your smelly foot. Come to think of it, maybe you should refrain from knocking your socks off."

Rigel rolled on his side and tickled me. "Them's fightin' words, missy."

Giggling uncontrollably, I wheezed, "Okay, okay, okay!"

He relented, but not before getting in a couple more pokes to my side. As he lingered there, his eyes glistened, and he leaned in slightly. I thought he might kiss me, and like an idiot, I flinched in surprise. He exhaled and lay back down next to me. *Way to go, Autumn.* Frustrated, I pressed my lips into a thin line. I was determined to get a kiss by the end of the night.

He softly stroked the top of my hand, then twined our fingers together again. "Now, I want you to shut your eyes and concentrate on my star," he said, closing his own eyes.

Unable to resist, I peeked at him to admire his glorious profile. A content smile warmed his complexion, warming my heart in turn. I breathed in, closed my eyes, and pictured Rigel's star as instructed.

Almost instantly, my body trembled, and with a jerk I broke free from it. I was hurtling upward at an unfathomable speed, the wind whipping past me in a deafening roar. My surroundings were a blur of colors and shapes until, as if I had reached the end of a rope I was tethered to, my form jerked to a stop. I found myself floating in absolute nothingness. No light. No sound. No touch. The lack of stimulus frightened me, and I started to panic. Had something gone wrong? Was I trapped?

A familiar pale orb manifested from the void. *Rigel.* I could recognize that man in any form.

Slowly, other things began to emerge, as if the background were being painted on, piece by piece. The first object to appear was a star, which glowed white. I wasn't sure how I knew, but I recognized it as our sun. Rays burst from it in all directions, creating flares of blue and purple. Next, the Milky Way came into existence, lighting up the sky with more stars than I thought possible. Right below it, the moon arose from the darkness. It wasn't all gray and white like in the pictures, though. Very faint blues, greens, and purples dotted its surface.

As amazing as it all was, nothing could top what I saw next. Earth was just beyond the moon. I flew toward it, almost instinctively, needing to be close to my home. Clouds created soft breezy patterns, and the ocean, a deep blue, shone brightly under the sun's kiss. The land was a patchwork of rich browns and greens, the hills and valleys adding texture and dimension. It humbled me to see it all from up here; a single human seemed insignificant in comparison.

You see all these images of Earth from space, but to say they don't do it justice is a vast understatement. I know it's a cheesy thing to say, but it took my breath away. Okay, technically I didn't have any breath to take away, but you get what I'm saying. It was hard to believe that billions of people were down there on the surface going about their day.

Rigel's gold light zipped by me, stealing my attention. His voice rang out. "Amazing, isn't it?"

Without a mouth, I wasn't sure how to respond.

"All you have to do is think what you want to say, and I will hear it," he said.

"Can you hear me?" I thought.

"Yes."

"Wow. This is incredible!"

His golden light appeared different than it had down on Earth. Here, it was much more shimmery and alive somehow. I found myself mesmerized by it.

"You okay?" Rigel asked.

"How come your light form is different here?"

"Because I am not in my light form. You are seeing my soul."

"Really? So your body is on Earth with mine?"

"It is. And the clock is ticking."

His golden light darted away. I chased after him, caught up, and stepped on the gas to pass him.

"Showoff," he said, and whipped past me with ease.

It was exhilarating to be flying through space at a speed that defied the laws of physics—or at least the physics that humans had adopted. The stars warped and stretched as we raced through the infinite expanse, similar to the way they appeared on *Star Trek* when they activated the warp drive.

Without warning, Rigel stopped, and I blew way past him before skidding to a halt.

"What's up?" I asked.

"We're here."

Stars surrounded us in all directions—millions of candles lighting up the night.

"How many stars are there in the universe?" I asked.

"The number is immeasurable," he said. "Now look here."

He swooped to the other side of me, casting my gaze toward a spectacular blue supergiant, the exact color of Rigel's eyes. The moment I saw it, I knew it was Rigel's star. The light emanating from it created a glimmering cross that lit up the sky. I thought I would faint from the sheer brilliance of it, not that a disembodied soul was capable of swooning.

"I see why you were named after this star," I said.

"How do you know the star wasn't named after me?"

That caught me off guard. *How old is he, anyway? He has to be joking, right?*

He jetted toward his star, and I swooshed after him. The rays of light became refracted by a cluster of asteroids, exposing a nebula that harbored a kaleidoscope of colors—green, blue, purple, orange, and red—all glowing in this stellar nursery.

"Not such a smelly foot anymore, huh?" he said proudly.

"I have never seen anything more beautiful in my whole life."

Rigel made a throat clearing sound and gave a deliberate cough.

"Well, besides you, obviously," I added. "I have a question."

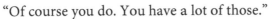

"Of course you do. You have a lot of those."

I mentally scowled at him, but it was in vain since I knew he couldn't see it. "I thought the colors in space weren't supposed to be this vibrant? I read that NASA enhances almost all of their images with false color to bring out specific details. How come it looks as vivid as their photos, if not more so?"

"Ah. You aren't looking through your human eyes anymore. You're looking through your *soul*. Human eyes are restricted by the visible light spectrum. In this form, you have no such restrictions."

"Oooh," I purred. "Do I have x-ray vision?"

Rigel circled me, and the force of it made me twirl several times. Normally I'd be dizzy from the spin, but I wasn't disoriented in the slightest when the rotating ceased. "Yes, but don't get too excited. You can see x-rays as in the true wavelength, not the ability to see unmentionable body parts through clothing."

"This reminds me of that movie *Contact*," I said. "Have you seen it?"

"No. I didn't know it was about unmentionable body parts."

"You're such a dork." I snorted. "There's this scene where Jodie Foster travels deep into space in this machine and gets transported to all these amazing star systems and planets. That's always been a fantasy of mine, ever since seeing it."

"There's nothing stopping us from making that fantasy a reality."

"Really?"

"Follow me."

For the next three mind-blowing hours, we traversed the far reaches of the universe. I saw galaxies in the midst of colliding, stars in a multitude of colors and sizes—including one siphoning the gases from its companion star—and planets teeming with exotic creatures. My favorite was a world where the ocean was a semitransparent violet, and these foamy neon whirlpools covered the entire surface. As we skimmed the waters, a whale-like creature rose from the depths and observed us with a single orange eye located on its tail.

I never want this adventure to end.

And of course, right when I thought it, it happened. Rigel twinkled with finality among the chorus of stars. Even though we were both incorporeal, I had this incredible yearning to kiss him. It was a weird sensation to be all hot and bothered by an undulating ball of light.

"It's time to go," he said, not giving me the chance to protest.

With a lurch, I returned to my body. I felt like I'd been filled with lead; my physical frame was like a prison.

Rigel's hand squeezed mine. It grounded me and made the transition back much easier. I stowed away the memories of our evening traveling the galaxy into a safe place, so that I could call them up later. Taking a contented breath, I turned to him and smiled. "Thank you."

He answered my smile with one of his own and propped himself on his elbow. His eyes scanned my body, appraising my figure. By the scandalous curl of his lip, I wondered if another one of his "gifts" was x-ray vision (the boobie-through-the-shirt kind, not the true wavelength kind).

Leaning in, he gave my forehead a soft kiss.

My body temperature immediately spiked to boiling, coloring my vision blue. An electrical current ran from where he touched my forehead, down my neck, along my arm, and out into the ground. It was as if I'd stuck my finger in a light socket.

The sensation lasted only a few seconds, and then I was back to normal. My vision returned, and I found Rigel about fifteen feet away, gawking at me.

"What was that?" I asked, leaping to a standing position.

"I have no idea. When I kissed your forehead, there was this blue explosion of light and I lost my form."

We stared at each other, both at a loss for words. Rigel suddenly snapped his eyes upward and shuddered. He looked unnerved by something. "I have to go," he said.

"Wait—" I stammered, "what just happened between us—could that be the prophecy? Don't you think we need to—"

Rigel pressed his finger to my lips, and it made blue sparks upon contact. "I can sense them searching for me," he said, "so I can't stay much longer. But I did make you a promise. I said I'd reveal what I was hiding."

He came closer, but hesitated before touching me, as if uncertain whether making contact would incite another reaction. I took the initiative and snagged his hands. Nothing happened, except for the usual chorus of butterflies in my stomach.

"Your world is about to be destroyed," he said without preamble.

"Oh… umm… wow. I… no… okay," I said.

A stupid response, I know. In my defense, a million thoughts were pinging about in my skull, ricocheting from one side to the other in a monumental game of Pong. *What exactly does he mean by 'destroyed'? Is he saying the Anunnaki are going to attack us? An asteroid strike? Another flood? Are we all going to die? Will I die?*

And as idiotic as it seemed, the one question in the forefront of my mind was: *If I am going to die, why can't we be together for the short time I have left?*

He roped me in, probably trying to prevent my forthcoming mental collapse. It had the opposite effect. Instead of savoring the chance to be close to him, I now fought to break free. Reality was sinking in way too fast.

"You must be wrong," I said insistently. "How?"

He held me firmly, his grip doing nothing to stop the tremors that overcame me. They bordered on convulsions, causing my teeth to clatter together. Speaking was nearly impossible.

"Are... we... all... going... to... die?"

"That's what I don't know," he said calmly. "It will be announced that when Nibiru passes close by, one of its moons is going to collide with Earth and annihilate it. It will be then that we will make our decision."

"Decision? What decision?" I was irked with his matter-of-fact tone. "To determine if we're worth saving?"

"Yes," he said, regarding me with desperate eyes. "If more than two thirds of humans choose evil, we will let your species perish with the planet. But if at least one third of you choose good and unite as a race, we are prepared to save those who have made that choice."

"Save us how? Can the destruction be prevented?"

"No. Earth is going to be obliterated. There is no way to stop it."

"Then how are you going to protect us?"

"Those who have chosen the path of good will be transported off Earth and relocated to a new planet."

I pushed away from him. "Let me get this straight. If a majority of humanity goes mental when they hear the news, you won't rescue those of us who *have* chosen good?"

"No," he answered solemnly. "The Galactic Federation has made their ruling. A third of the human race must have advanced to a basic level of peaceful consciousness, or all humans must be left to—"

"To be exterminated?" I yelled, not letting him finish his sentence.

Rigel looked down, and I saw a tear slide down his cheek. "Yes," he said quietly.

I didn't know what to say. I had this irrational urge to attack him for keeping this from me, and even more so for not fighting to save those of us who were worthy—who had pure intentions. My anger toward him subsided when I saw the unmistakable anguish on his face. I knew he had no more authority over the outcome than I did.

He approached me wearily. "They're almost here. I have to go."

"What does it matter if they catch us? I'm going to be part of the massacre anyway."

"You don't know that for sure," he said.

I yelled and flung my hands in the air to release some of the tension before I exploded. This all had to be some kind of joke. Ashton Kutcher was going to walk out any minute announcing the return of *Punk'd*.

I turned and walked to a clearing, where I gazed at the city skyline. For the first time, I saw it as an outsider, and I wondered what choice all these people would make. Who was I kidding? I knew the answer already. Immorality would prevail. If people rioted because of a basketball game, it was a pipe dream to think the end of the world would be any different.

Rigel laid his hands on my shoulders, gentle and tentative. I wanted to pull away and run down the canyon and into the city, screaming into a megaphone to announce the news, a modern day Paul Revere warning the people of the approaching end times. None of that happened because I was rooted to the spot, paralyzed from shock. Crying was the next most sensible response, and that didn't happen either. My despair was so profound it tore at my soul. Not only was I losing Rigel, but Earth was going to be *demolished*. That concept was too horrific to consider. I had always assumed the end of the human race would be our own fault—perhaps a nuclear holocaust, or because we depleted all our natural resources. Not in my wildest dreams had I ever thought Earth itself, the actual planet, would be eradicated.

Rigel spun me toward him, golden tears streaming down his face. It was spectacular to behold the dancing metallic droplets trickling down his creamy soft skin. The ordinary watery drops that filled my eyes must have paled in comparison. We both reached to wipe each other's cheek at the same time, easing the tension with a shared smile.

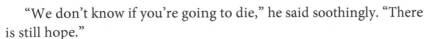

"We don't know if you're going to die," he said soothingly. "There is still hope."

But there wasn't. He knew that too. There was a better chance that Superman would materialize from a comic book and fling the incoming moon in the opposite direction with his pinky finger.

"How long?" I asked.

"I can't tell you that. I'm sorry. I've already broken too many rules."

I couldn't let myself ruin what could be my last moments with Rigel. I had time to figure this all out, but this, these last few minutes—this was all the time we had together. I needed to do what I had come here for: say goodbye.

I pushed my terror and resentment down with a long deliberate breath. Surprisingly, it was easier than I expected to calm myself, given the circumstances.

"Before you go," I said, wiping away my remaining tears, "since it looks like my time is limited here on Earth, I have one thing on my bucket list you can help me with."

"What's that?"

I gave him a sly smile. "A kiss from a Greek god."

He anchored his blue eyes on me. The intensity of them had my heart beating so hard I had to take a deep breath to circulate extra air into my lungs. He clasped my hands in his and lifted them to meet his lips. A mini fireworks display erupted at the contact; I thought I might pass out from the thrill of it.

Letting go, he laced his fingers around the back of my neck, making heat rush to my face. Succumbing to the longing that filled me, I let my lower body collapse against his. He responded by sliding one hand to the small of my back and pressed me firmly into him, his eyes never wavering from mine.

My breathing slowed and my eyes fell shut. I was ready for the kiss. *Hurry up, Rigel.* The pounding of my heart became unbearable. *I will not faint. I will not faint. I will not faint.*

There was a considerable pause, and I worried he might chicken out or disappear on me again. But at long last, his breath teased my moist lips.

And contact.

It was the softest of kisses—tender and promising. Dear lord was it promising. His fingers clenched my shirt with yearning, and I thought that meant he was about take the kiss deeper. But he did the opposite of that and pulled back slightly, his lips just out of reach of mine.

That's it? No freaking way. Not after all this. Was he waiting for me to reciprocate? I didn't care. I was going in. Maybe it was because I was reckless from the threat of the world ending, or maybe it was because I could feel his rock-solid frame tense with anticipation, but I slammed so forcefully into him that he had to steady himself to keep from falling backward.

"Autumn, we shouldn't do this," he said. "If my people find us, we're dead."

"Fuck your people!"

I grabbed the collar of his T-shirt to pull his head down to mine. His brows were drawn together in concern, but his eyes were full of desire.

"Fuck my people," he growled, and he kissed me again, our lips parting to take it deeper. I was greedy for him, my hands groping under his shirt, nails digging in to get more. That blue radiance from earlier flashed on, blazing across my skin. The electricity from it filled me with power and sparked to life a part of me I never knew existed.

Nothing would keep me from Rigel. He was mine.

One of his hands slid up my shirt, and the other tangled in my hair, pulling it hard, which only fueled my hunger for him. I couldn't get enough.

The kiss is not enough.

He reacted to my demands by lifting me until my legs circled his waist. I coiled my arms around his neck, freeing his hands so he could take off my shirt. But instead, he took the opportunity to clamp his hand on my breast and squeeze. I moaned. He slid his hand underneath the cup of my bra, and his soft finger brushed my nipple. It instantly hardened. He flicked it, and I shivered in pleasure.

"If you do that again, I think I might come," I panted.

He growled in response, trailing his hand to the edge of my pants, and tracing his fingers just on the inside. He said with a sexy rasp, "That's the idea."

He grabbed my hips, forcing them lower, the sensation practically setting my inner thighs on fire. He guided me up and down against his jeans, and it sent me shuddering from an orgasm, clothing between us be damned. My legs shook uncontrollably, and he had to squeeze me harder to keep me from slipping.

"Oh, god!" I cried, pawing at his shirt and twisting it violently.

With the force of a rocket, we launched out of our bodies together. Our souls, gold and blue, shot high above the trees, and yet I was equally aware of our interwoven bodies beneath us—his hot breath, his hands unclasping my bra and grazing my hips, his fingers teasing the inside of my jeans.

I was crazed by the red-hot pleasure of his touch. All my instincts propelled me to connect further with him. I had to find a way. His golden light danced and wound around my blue soul, like a vine twines a tree. Intricate gold fibers, radiant as the sun, appeared and formed a fine thread, which began sewing our souls together. Our once separate spirits were becoming one—his desire feeding my desire, my desire feeding his—one building upon the other until I thought we might explode.

Then a crack sounded, followed by a harsh pulling sensation, and for a horrifying couple of breaths I thought my limbs were going to be separated from my joints. The next thing I knew I was back in my body and skidding across the gravel. My jaw cracked against a rock, and black spots dotted my vision. The rusty taste of blood filled my mouth, and I knew the damage was serious.

"No!" I heard Rigel yell, but his voice was a distant echo next to the ringing throb inside my head.

Summoning every ounce of strength I had left, I pushed myself into a sitting position. My jaw was numb and hung at an odd angle.

Through the haze I recognized Inanna. She was positioned between us, giving me a paralyzing glare. "I warned you not to do this," she seethed.

Rigel stepped forward rather sheepishly. "We were saying goodbye, Inanna."

"Yes, I can see that. What were you thinking, Rigel? You know the repercussions."

A storm thundered in his eyes. "Yes, I'm perfectly aware."

Intending to demand she tell me what she planned to do with Rigel, I opened my mouth to speak—but my slack jaw prevented me from forming coherent syllables, much less a sentence. I managed a few grunts before a force knocked me flat as if I were a pesky animal that needed to be put in its place.

"Not a word from you, human," Inanna said.

Rigel snarled. Like an actual animalistic snarl. I rolled on my side and saw he was incapacitated, powerless to do anything. She had an invisible command over him. His eyes implored me to understand that he was fighting to get to me, to take me away to safety. I sagged in defeat, and he closed his eyes, prompting me to do the same. I did.

There was a flash of light.

He was gone.

I was abandoned, broken, and defenseless. I slid along the ground in a futile attempt to escape. Two heaves in and I couldn't fight it anymore; I let myself sink into oblivion.

I wasn't sure how long I remained unconscious, but when I woke, Inanna was hovering by my side, a contraption pointed at my wounds.

"Are you gonna kill me?" I snapped. To my surprise, my words came out normally; my jaw was functioning again. It didn't even hurt.

"No, my dear. I'm afraid that will happen without my help."

She hoisted me upright with her telekinesis and circled me, her device reflecting ominously in the remaining moonlight. My vision was unfocused, but from what I could see, it was a bulbous cross of some kind. *A cross? Is she gonna pray for forgiveness after she murders me?*

Struggling was pointless; I was bound by her invisible restraints. I watched her move the device along my cuts, expecting them to burst open as some sort of punishment. I was confused when a cool sensation replaced the sting of my injuries. When she stepped away, I was completely healed. I gaped at her, waiting for my skin to melt, chest to split apart, or skeleton to implode.

"You should go now," she said.

Her invisible grip on me vanished. My feet touched terra firma, and gravity took hold. Without a word, I strode to my car, keeping my posture strong and erect, not wanting to show any sign of weakness. There was a snort of laughter behind me, letting me know I just looked ridiculous. A flash of light flared and I collapsed to my knees, releasing a breath I hadn't realized I was holding. I sat there in the dirt, fixed my eyes on the purple dawn, and waited for the cleaning crew to mop up the mess from my emotional overload.

10

S'MORES OF DEATH, DOLPHIN SHORTS, AND A COLOR-BLIND TIME-TRAVELING RETRO-TRAILER-PARK FRIEND

After Inanna left, I stayed and watched the city below. I knew that down there, people were getting on with their day, heading off to their places of employment, all oblivious to the fact that their lives were about to end. I was watching thousands of people wandering aimlessly inside a metaphorical glue trap.

Of all the *what ifs* I had pondered since I was five, not once had I thought, *What if Earth is about to be utterly destroyed?* This particular *what if* was made worse by the knowledge that legions of aliens were going to just sit back and watch the show like we were the stars of a snuff film. The bastards would probably pop popcorn and eat Red Vines while they observed the demolition derby between Earth and this asshole moon.

My first thought was to fire up my cell and call everyone I knew. I laughed out loud when I actually pulled out my phone to dial. *What a ghastly mistake that would be.* I could imagine the conversation now. "Howdy, this is Autumn. Dropping you a line to let you know I met these aliens that genetically engineered us, and I fell in love with this irresistible Greek god who said the world was about to end. Thought I'd let you all know so you can prepare for the riots. Okay. By-ee." The first person I dialed would dispatch a paddy wagon full of men with straightjackets.

There was nothing I could do to save them anyway; they might as well have a few more days of blissful ignorance. Emma excluded, of course. I'd tell her. One on one, though. If I called, she'd think I was drunk dialing and blow it off. Then again, she might not take me seriously no matter what I said. How could she, when I was having trouble believing it myself?

A hawk soared lazily through the wisps of clouds above me, and it made me wonder if the Anunnaki were going to preserve the wildlife. It would be such a waste to have all these magnificent species cease to exist. Then I remembered: they already had the DNA they'd taken before the Great Flood, and in all likelihood, they had been taking samples ever since.

A new *what if* popped into my head. *What if there is a rogue Anunnaki scientist who has human DNA stashed in an underground secret lab, and one day he creates a human "Jurassic Park" on Nibiru? "Homo Sapiens Park." No, that's not very catchy. "The Garden of Eden 2" or "The Garden of Eden Redux."* Much better.

By the time I pulled into my driveway, I was completely exhausted. With a heavy sigh, I looked over all the houses on my block—odds were for the last time—and I reminisced about all the epic times I'd had while living here. I recalled the time Emma and I had a wee bit too much to drink and decided we were going to wheel my BBQ from the garage and make s'mores. After opening the gas valve, we discovered we didn't have anything to light it with, so we went to get a match— without shutting off the gas first. Upon our return, we struck the match—and an enormous flame belched forth, setting the neighbor's tree on fire. Due to what could only have been divine intervention, the wind had been blowing in the opposite direction, preventing us from charring ourselves. I smiled, remembering our shrieking and our attempt at battling the inferno by waving our hands wildly.

The *flop flop* of running feet broke my reverie. To my sheer astonishment, I saw Zarf jogging along my street, sporting quite the getup. He had on purple velvet dolphin shorts with a pink stripe down each side, a wife beater tank with an image of a run-down trailer sketched on it, and neon orange shoes with lime green trim and Velcro fasteners. Despite the sweat on his scalp, his hair maintained its perfect formation, gliding along unhampered by the wind.

My first thought was that Rigel had sent him to check on me, the same way he did at Barnes & Noble when he gave The Hair the "feeling" he should venture into the parking lot. *What if Rigel is using him again to communicate with me? If so, why have him put on that gaudy outfit?*

Then it dawned on me. I bet Rigel made him dress that way to make sure I stayed uninterested in The Hair. Not that he even remotely presented any competition to Rigel.

"Hey Zarf!" I called, walking to the curb.

He stumbled to a halt. Downright stunned is the only way to describe his reaction. "Are you stalking me?" he asked.

"Yes. It's the velvet shorts. I can't resist a man in velvet."

He inspected his outfit and cringed as if shocked by what he saw. "I stayed at a friend's house, and it wasn't planned, so I had to borrow this from his brother."

"Uh-huh," I said, crossing my arms. "Is your friend's brother a color-blind time traveler from the seventies who lives in a trailer park?"

His lip quirked. "Worse. A high school emo kid who thinks this is actually cool."

"Ahh. That explains it." An awkward pause fell between us. "Well, I should let you get back to your run."

"Yeah." He hesitated. "Well, see ya," he said, and ran off.

Dammit. I was really hoping it was Rigel that sent him using his mind control mojo. I kicked a rock and turned to head back to the house.

"Hey, Zooloo?" he called.

I did a U-turn, heart thrumming with hope.

"Would you like to maybe get coffee with me sometime?"

I frowned at him, perplexed. I hadn't expected that question. Was it The Hair or Rigel who was really asking me? I searched for any indication that Rigel might be controlling Zarf. If there were any clues, they didn't show past The Hair's douchiness.

I was so desperate for a Rigel fix that I chanced it. "*Yes*," I said, too intensely, so it came across sarcastic. "I mean, yes. That'd be fun."

He folded his arms and copied my earlier expression of disbelief. "Uh-huh."

I tried to cover. "No, really. I mean it. It's been a while since I've dated anyone, that's all."

The Hair's brown eyes gazed at me quizzically. I hadn't noticed it before, probably because of the clown hair, but he was kind of cute. You know, if you're into douchey community-service-serving, dolphin-short-wearing dudes. (Say that ten times fast.) His features were soft, as if he constantly applied moisturizer, he had a trim build, and his eyes were full of milk chocolate speckles that seemed to dance in the sunlight. They matched nicely with his light caramel-colored skin.

I shook my head, shocked by thoughts. *What was wrong with me?*

"Okay," he said. "How about tomorrow evening at Panera? Say seven o'clock?"

"Perfect."

He jogged off without another word. As I watched him bounce away, I got the sinking suspicion that Rigel didn't send him after all— and I had inadvertently said yes to a real date with The Hair.

My insides rolled. *Well, crap!*

11

DING DONG SURVIVAL RAFTS, BEER HATS, AND PORK FESTS

I felt as though I'd been run over by a semi, dragged three miles, and then pushed off a cliff. I wanted to crawl under a rock and hide, and the only thing keeping me from going all ostrich and burying my head in the sand was Emma. I called her and said I needed a girl's night to explain what had happened with Rigel. I didn't mention that the world was about to be smashed to a bazillion pieces, figuring that information would be better relayed whilst consuming heaping slices of pie and vodka shots.

As I walked up to Emma's apartment, I ignored her neighbor who eagerly waved at me as I passed. I knew it was rude, but you know what? I didn't care. The world was ending. She could go fuck herself.

What is happening to me? I can't believe I just thought that! I need to get a grip. I don't behave like this.

Giving in, I waved politely as I rushed past. "Hello, Norma. Good to see you. Gotta run."

When I reached Emma's door, I raised my hand to knock, and then hesitated. I wasn't ready for this. I was scared that if I spoke the truth of the end times out loud, it would make it... concrete somehow. Maybe if I kept it securely tucked away in the attic, it would magically disappear. As they say, what you don't know can't hurt you, right?

I needed booze.

The door clanked open and I leaped into a defensive position, ready to pounce. Emma stared blankly at me.

"What are you doing?" she asked, as I squatted there with my fists raised. Her eyes narrowed and she flicked her gaze from my hands to the ground. She gave me a disappointed frown. What was I missing?

100

Then it dawned on me: I hadn't brought any food, not even a tic tac.

"Oh, shit," she said, her eyes going wide. "Is the world ending?"

A lump formed in my throat. "I think you're gonna need to bust the vodka open for this one."

Emma and I pounded a few back as I relayed the whole story: the genetic engineering, my out-of-body travel to Rigel's star, the orgasmic kiss, Inanna tossing me into a rock, and The Hair in dolphin shorts. I hadn't gotten to the "oh, by the way, we are all going to die" portion of the conversation yet. I made her take another shot with me before revealing that little tidbit.

"If we drink any more," Emma said with a hiss as she slammed down her shot glass, "I will be too drunk to care about your big news."

"That's the idea." I eyed her and released a breath. "What I am about to tell you is the truth, Emma. No hidden cameras. No practical jokes. I need you to know that."

"I know."

I really could count on Emma to believe every word I said, without question. It had always been that way between us, and I loved her for it.

With a resigned sigh, I took one more swig straight from the vodka bottle and then disclosed the whole end-of-the-world thing. After I told her that the human race would only receive a galactic bailout if we all came together in one giant group hug, she gave an almost inaudible "huh" sound and gazed out the window. I gave her time to digest it all.

"Ding Dong raft," she said finally.

"What?" I said.

"We build a raft fashioned from Ding Dongs. It will be our Noah's Ark. And after days of drifting, if we get hungry, we eat the Ding Dongs."

"You know, you may be on to a brilliant idea there. But might I suggest that Twinkies are a superior flotation device? Much spongier."

"Ah, I would argue, however, that spongier soaks up water, and you'd sink. The Ding Dong has the waxy coating that acts as waterproofing."

"Valid argument. I counter with the fact that Twinkies are indestructible and in all likelihood a creation of the gods themselves."

"We must conduct scientific testing," Emma pronounced. "Ding Dong versus Twinkie."

"Cool. We can quit our jobs and dedicate the end days to making a Hostess Ark. The USS Hostess!"

We both laughed. Then I went and ruined the moment by pointing out the one teeny-tiny flaw in our plan.

"Too bad there won't be an ocean left for us to sail on."

Emma gave a sigh. "No chance a habitable chunk of Earth will survive?"

"Nope."

"Then I say we anchor our Hostess boats in the pool and wear one of those beer hats filled with cosmopolitans while we wait for the pyrotechnics to start."

"Sounds like a plan."

We both fell silent. You might think Emma and I would've come apart, cussed, shed tears, or at a minimum punched a wall. The complete opposite was true, however. We just sat there calmly. My mind filled with a vision of Earth exploding, playing out like one of those old atomic bomb testing videos.

"Are you gonna tell anyone?" I asked.

"Hmm. What's the use? They wouldn't believe me anyway, especially not my family. It has cuckoo written all over it."

"Why are we not panicking? We know the world is about to end, and we're talking about constructing unsinkable pastry boats."

"It's 'cause this all seems so far-fetched right now," Emma said. "It does to me anyway. It'll hit us when we least expect it." She paused, then added, "No pun intended."

"All's not lost," I said, taking another swig from the bottle and handing it to her. "If we're lucky, everyone else will react the same as us. The world will remain calm and sane, and we'll be rescued. There will be peace amongst humans at last."

We both busted up laughing at that preposterous conclusion.

"You know what this means?" I said, after the giggles had subsided.

"Fuck yeah. I'm right there with ya, sister."

In unison we exclaimed, "Pork Fest!"

Emma raised her hand in the air and declared, "My goal is to gain twenty-three pounds by the end."

"Well then, we have tons of calories to consume." I tried to calculate the amount I would need to eat to gain that much weight. It was probably way less than you'd think. "All the practice we've had consuming large quantities of food will finally come in handy."

"Yes, we are professionals."

Then I remembered something else I had wanted to ask Emma about. "Before we pillage Costco for our bulk food binge, I have one question."

"Shoot."

"Do I go on the date with The Hair? My gut says it's not Rigel doing the mind-hijacking thing, so I should cancel, right? But what if there's the slightest chance..."

"Bloody hell, Autumn," Emma cut in. "Yes! Go, go, go! The world is ending. What do you have to lose? And you need to get this Rigel moron out of your head. He isn't rescuing you. He's letting you *die*. What the hell is that about? Who lets the woman he loves perish like that without a fight?"

The room went out of focus for a second. I hadn't thought of it that way. I knew he didn't have control over the disaster. Even so—why didn't he at least make an effort to come save *me*? Sneak me away to a secret hiding place for the short time we had left. And when Inanna threw me against that rock, he just stood there. It was evident she had superior power, but he didn't even attempt to fight her. He left me there bleeding. *Am I honestly that dimwitted? Have my emotions transformed me into a blithering idiot?*

I felt faint. A healthy dose of unwanted reality had been injected into my system.

"Are you okay?" Emma asked.

"Ssssure," I slurred, teetering toward the table. Emma flung her arm out to grab me. "He isn't going to save me, is he?"

"You really just now realized that?"

"I guess so. No… wait… yes." A hollow pit formed in my stomach. My throat clenched and I couldn't swallow. I was drowning in an onslaught of grief. Emma held me close while the knowledge that Rigel played me for a fool shattered my soul into a million pieces. Our planet and all the people on it were about to be reduced to ashes, and suddenly, rather than fearing it, I was looking forward to it.

12

ALIEN DEATH RAY, ASSHOLERY, GUSHING GLANDS, AND SPEWING VOMIT KISSES

By the time I arrived at Panera to meet The Hair, I was an absolute wreck. My nervous energy was making my limbs twitch, and my continuous crying had made my eyes swell into red blobs. Add that to my uncombed hair, wrinkled clothes, inside-out socks, and unfinished nails, and I had quite the sexy look going on that evening. He was totally going to think I was a meth addict.

At a bare minimum, I'd intended to comb my hair before going. That plan got the kibosh when I couldn't find the brush. In the temper tantrum that followed, I had thrown a bottle of Tylenol at my reflection in the mirror; it would have been more dramatic had it not bounced off and thwacked me in the face.

Canceling would've been the smartest move. My ability to judge a guy's intention toward me was clearly malfunctioning. If I was being honest, the only reason I'd even come was to spite Rigel. I felt like I needed to show that I'd moved on; that I didn't care. *Yeah, right. Where was an alien zapping death ray when you needed one?*

The tables inside Panera were full of gluten-guzzling families ordering their soup in bread bowls with an additional side of bread for good measure. Even with the plethora of individuals filling the cafe, Zarf could not be missed—thanks to his unique do. He was sitting in the corner tapping intently on his phone.

He hasn't seen me yet. I could just leave. No, I have to do this. Rigel is a fuckwad and I need to prove his assholery didn't faze me.

I headed toward Zarf with determination. As I approached, sweat beaded on my forehead and trickled down my back. I was suddenly flushed like I'd been trapped in a sauna for hours. You'd think I was about to rob a bank.

This is ridiculous. Grow a pair, Autumn.

I drew in a calming breath, wiped away my sweat, and walked up to his table.

"Hi, Zarf," I said, unintentionally finishing the greeting with a burp. Embarrassment intensified my feverish blush, and I knew there was no hiding it at that point.

When he looked up, I squinted in confusion. His hair was only about half its usual height. It appeared strange on him.

He returned my squinty appraisal, and this triggered a geyser of sweat to shoot from every single one of my pores. I had the ingenious idea to subtly rub it off by pretending to swipe away an unruly hair, but all that did was push the perspiration to one side, where it pooled and streamed down my cheek.

"Hey there, Zooloo," he said. "Would you like me to get you a cup of coffee, espresso? You hungry?"

The sweat was getting uncontrollable. It dripped onto my shirt, and when I peered down, I saw a jumbo-sized wet spot on my chest. I could only imagine the marks under my arms and down my back. I had to hope that the dim lighting at Panera effectively hid the downpour. Fat chance of that.

"I'd love a latte, nonfat," I said. Then with a sheepish smile I added, "Umm… I have to use the little girls' room."

Hurrying off without another word, I flattened my arms to my side, trying to hide my massive ovals of sweat. Behind me I heard him say, "Sure, meet you here with the latte."

In the bathroom, I took stock of my drenched shirt. There was no way he hadn't noticed. The moisture verged on cartoonish. What had come over me? I gathered a wad of paper towels, mopped myself up with it, and prayed I could regain command of my gushing glands.

As ludicrous as it sounded, I thought maybe I was having a reaction to The Hair. As I dried my pits with the electric hand-dryer, a thought occurred to me. *Could Rigel be doing this to me with one of his "gifts"? Maybe he's… jealous?*

That thought gave me a mutinous urge to boost the flirt meter to the danger zone and really piss Rigel off. *Oh, it is on now.* I polished up my makeup, tussled my ratty mane, and left the restroom with my sights set on seducing The Hair.

I slid into the booth and positioned my arms snugly to my sides so that my chest stuck out as much as possible. When The Hair returned with the coffee, he evaluated my posture with a frown. "What happened? You hurt your back?"

I slumped in my seat and flushed yet again. "No, I'm right as rain." I reached for my drink. "Thanks for the latte."

"How'd your paper for the god torture thing go?"

"Oh, umm… got an A," I lied.

"Awesome. Hey, if you decide you want a study partner, I'm at the library every Monday from one to five p.m. for the next two hundred fifty hours." He smiled innocently.

"You gonna confess what you did to stockpile those community service hours?"

"Not today. That's second date material."

"Not even a hint?" I leaned in and tossed my hair, copying what I'd seen girls do when they flirted on reality TV shows. In the process, I knocked my coffee cup over. That was not quite the outcome I was after.

The Hair caught my cup in time to prevent major drainage. We both grabbed for napkins.

"You sure you're okay?" he said. "You're acting kinda funny."

Apparently, flirting wasn't my strong suit. The sweat beads seeped from my pores again, and I had no choice but to throw in the towel, so to speak. I drooped into my seat and grumbled, "Yeah. I'm fine."

"You know, I'm getting a bit of a complex," he said. "You get all antsy and flustered when you're around me, and it's not 'cause you are crushing on me… at least I don't think. And no offense, but you look like you just finished a marathon. Did I offend or upset you?"

The manager approached, rescuing me from coming up with some lame excuse. She was a cute, petite girl in her twenties with a pixie cut. Her nametag, placed perfectly level atop her left bosom, read *Gwen*. She didn't acknowledge my presence, and had no qualms about sighing at The Hair in admiration.

"How is everything?" she asked dreamily. "Can I get you anything else?"

"No, we're all set," he said, barely taking the time to glance at her.

She lingered awkwardly. "Um. I, like, totally dig your hair. It's kinda hot."

My mouth hung open. *Does this chick not see me sitting at the same table with him?*

"Thanks," The Hair replied with a courtesy nod. "Now, if you don't mind, me and my date were in the middle of a conversation."

Pixie cut Gwen glared at me and stomped off.

I don't know why that broke me, but it did. Uncontrollable giggles struck me as soon as she left: loud heaves, watery eyes, side ache and all. The thought of a person who wasn't legally blind genuinely finding his hair desirable—it loosened the stress that had had a chokehold on me.

Zarf scoped the cafe to check if people were staring. "What on earth is so funny?" he said in a hushed voice, obviously hoping I would take the hint and quiet down.

"Nothing," I wheezed, wiping my tears. "Look, there has been stuff going on lately that has made me a tad... uh... unhinged." I hesitated, weighing the idea of telling him the whole end-of-the-world thing.

"What happened?" he asked. "Anything I can help with?"

"That's second date material."

"Fair enough. I guess that will be a revealing second date."

"What do you say we start over?" I proposed.

"That's the best idea I've heard all day."

"If we're starting fresh, I think we should formally introduce ourselves." I extended my hand. "My name is Autumn."

"Hi. I'm Devon."

When we shook, a wave of nausea hit me, and I had to swallow it down. I did everything I could to hide it, including bowing my head, but I'm sure he saw it. The feeling instantly subsided the moment he pulled away.

"I have a question for you, Devon," I said.

"Ask away."

"What happened to your hair? Your mountain is sort of a hill today."

"Ahh... well, funny you mention it. See, I usually use a number twelve hairspray."

"Hold up," I interrupted. "Hairspray has numbers?"

"Of course. Twelve is the best. Problem is, I used up my last spray and had to borrow from my mom. She only has a six. So hence it's half as high."

I snorted. "That's amazing."

To my surprise, we ended up talking for two hours after that. We would have talked longer, but the café closed, and a very jealous Gwen kicked us out. Had the circumstances been different—specifically, had I not met the love of my life, who happened to be an alien; and, you know, had the world not been about to end—then I might actually have wanted things to progress with Devon.

As he escorted me to my car, his proximity made the sweat build on my brow again. I became all fevered and thought I might be getting the flu. Devon opened the car door for me, and when I brushed past him to get inside, he hijacked my hand. My stomach gave a lurch, and not in the flutter-of-exhilaration-about-to-be-kissed kind of way. This was more of a holy-shit-I-am-about-to-hurl-all-over-his-Converses kind of way.

"I had fun tonight," he said sweetly.

The nausea ascended into my chest. "Me too," I said, swallowing hard to keep it from creeping any farther.

Devon leaned in and kissed me softly, and I couldn't hold the nausea back any longer. A volcano erupted inside me, and I barely managed to push him away before I heaved all over the parking lot. Vomit spewed everywhere like in a bad '80s fraternity movie.

"What the…?" he said, avoiding the splatter zone. "Autumn, are you all right?"

"Uh-huh." I gulped.

He approached me, and I recoiled. I was now positive that my body was having a reaction to him, and if he touched me it would only make it worse.

"Autumn, your arms," Devon said. "You're covered in a rash."

I scowled at the welts as they snaked their way up my arms.

"You want me to take you to the hospital?" he offered.

"No. No. I just need to get home. I'm sorry."

Without another word I hopped in my car and sped off. In my rear-view mirror I saw Devon standing there with a mortified expression on his face.

As the distance between us increased, the nausea faded and the welts on my arms disappeared. My system had rejected Devon in a big way—and it had to have been Rigel that made that happen.

"Why do you even care?" I shouted angrily at the sky. "You're letting me die!"

That did me in. I started shaking violently and had to pull over to compose myself. Despite my resolve to forget Rigel, the waterworks made an unwanted appearance once more.

I had to snap out of it. I wasn't going to let him ruin my last days on this planet. If I was going down, I was doing it with a bang. I had no idea where my soul would end up after my human form was incinerated, so I had better enjoy what time I had left—Rigel be damned.

My phone rang, and I almost jumped out of my skin. It was Emma. I fumbled to answer.

"Hello?" I sniffed.

"Hey, girl. You wanna come over and spend the night so we can plan our Ding Dong shopping spree?"

I hiccupped a relieved sigh. She always had impeccable timing. We were eerily tuned in to each other's emotional frequency.

"You know it," I said. "I'll be there in an hour."

On the way to Emma's, I hunted down a twenty-four-hour Mexican restaurant and ordered thirty dollars' worth of their most fattening cheese-filled menu items. Hopefully that would keep us full until our Ding Dong lunch break.

13

A THOUSAND PACKETS OF GRAVY, HAIRNETS, RABID SAMPLE HOARDERS, AND THE LAMEST END-OF-THE-WORLD SPEECH EVER

I recounted the whole scene with The Hair while Emma and I gorged on scrumptious lard-and-MSG burritos.

"Sounds like you had a bad hair day," she said.

That made me laugh, easing my sour mood. "That's it, I'm officially not going to torture myself anymore," I said. "No more crying. No more sadness. I say we embrace our last days and go hog wild!"

"Agreed!"

There was a pause.

"What're we going to do?" she asked.

"Besides eat?"

"Yeah."

"Hmm… Well, we obviously aren't going to clock in at our jobs. We have plenty of spare time."

"Speaking of, did you call in and quit?"

"Hell, no," I answered. "For my last bonus they gave me a rotisserie machine. A used one from the set to boot! Delinquency will provide greater fulfillment."

"Cheers to that!"

We tapped our burritos together.

"What to do? What to do?" I said. "We don't have time to travel. Hey, neither of us has smoked pot—we could do that."

A pause.

"Nope, just eat!" we decided in unison.

We didn't leave for Costco until late afternoon the next day because we got caught up conducting experiments with all the delicious stuff we could cook in a waffle maker. The winning experiment involved ironing strips of bacon together and using the resulting product like a tortilla shell to make tacos—a Nobel Prize-worthy discovery right there. Hey, maybe we should offer our bacon shell tacos—which we nicknamed "bacos"—to everyone after the president makes the big announcement. Then people might choose to eat those instead of rioting in the streets.

Deciding that driving separately would give us double the room for our Hostess booty, we jumped in our cars and caravanned to Costco—making a spontaneous side trip to get McDoubles and chocolate shakes for added shopping energy.

Even though I'm a huge fan and would never give up my membership, I don't think Costco is the bargain others tout it to be. Usually you can get cheaper prices at Target, if you compare pound for pound and factor in waste. Unless, of course, you need a silo of soda or one thousand packets of gravy—then Costco can come in handy. I've heard a number of people spout on that the gas prices are worth the membership fees alone. I call BS on that. Gas runs about ten cents per gallon cheaper at Costco—if you're lucky—so on average you're saving a buck per fill-up. I suppose this would be cool, except for the forty-five minutes you spend in line waiting to get it. You forfeit the stupid dollar you saved idling to get the gas in the first place. Once you add the membership fee into the mix, I could argue that you're losing money unless you fill your tank every day of the week.

That said, there is one thing about Costco that's worth the price of membership alone: the free samples. It's virtually a complimentary tapas bar, providing a multitude of scrumptious morsels.

And as if management subconsciously knew the world was ending, they presented us with quite the smorgasbord that day: Hot Pockets, deli sandwiches, sushi, curry chicken, turkey meatloaf, potato salad, chili, Spanish rice, jelly beans, energy bars, chocolate-covered nuts, and fruit juice. Normally, I make it a rule not to be the butthead that goes for seconds, but under the circumstances, I didn't care. On my third trip to the Hot Pocket stand, the lady gave me a dirty look, and I almost didn't snatch another. But the gooey artificial cheese oozing from the slice made it impossible for me to resist snagging an additional helping.

In the refrigerated section, we found a hidden sample station that had jalapeño soft pretzel nuggets with nacho cheese dipping sauce. Score! When we went to grab a box out of the freezer to take home, we discovered a plethora of new products we hadn't yet stimulated our taste buds with. In particular, there were these delectable double-fried pork and shrimp egg rolls. Yes, double-fried, with a bonus layer of tempura coating.

"Those look so flippin' yummy," Emma said.

"Should we get them?"

"I kinda want them now."

Feeling reckless from the knowledge of our imminent demise, I evaluated our options. An empty sampling station with a toaster oven teased me at the end of the aisle. I nudged Emma and pointed at it. She smiled in agreement. Opening the freezer, I snagged a package of rolls, and we took it over to the station.

"Shouldn't we put on some kind of disguise?" Emma asked.

She had a point. We definitely were not dressed for the part. Thinking on my feet, I rummaged inside the station's cabinet and pulled a pack of hairnets from the depths. We snapped a couple on.

"Perfect!" I said, appraising Emma's netted noggin.

Not wasting any more time, we tore open the box of rolls and threw them in the toaster oven. Within seconds, a crowd buzzed on all sides of us, like a swarm of flies after a warm pile of poo, waiting to get their mitts on our precious haul.

I leaned in toward Emma and whispered, "I hadn't planned on sharing."

"Me either. What should we do?"

A ding alerted us that the rolls were ready, and the sound was like a dinner bell for the drooling throng. We withdrew the crispy deliciousness; the smell was intoxicating. The mob gathered closer, a pack of rabid dogs moving in for the kill.

"We do apologize, everyone," I announced. "It appears that these egg rolls might be defective. We need to submit them to quality control."

The crowd moaned in disappointment.

Emma and I each wrapped a roll in a napkin and made a break for it, tossing our hairnets in a passing cart as we went. Behaving like junior high kids who had gotten away with skipping class, we giggled with pride and sprinted into an empty aisle. Hidden behind the wastelands of the toilet paper section, we chowed down at bionic speed, blowing out the heat and fluttering our hands wildly at our tongues because they had been scorched by the nuclear inferno of minced shrimp and cabbage.

Keeping my eyes peeled for any security on their way to nab us, I said, "Can you imagine having to spend our last few days on Earth in jail for looting egg rolls?" Pieces of pork flew out of my mouth as I spoke.

Emma snorted, expelling bits of chewed roll onto a pallet of toilet bowl cleaner brushes. We both broke down laughing, causing us to spit the rest of our food on the concrete, which in turn had us doubling over. As we examined the mess littering the floor, our fits of laughter warped into loud inhalations and ultimately hardcore coughing. People flocked to see what all the commotion was—making sure to maintain a safe distance, probably scared we had an infectious disease.

We attempted to leave the scene of the crime with dignity, exaggerating our composure to hide the laughter mounting inside. We failed miserably and busted up again. I had to hold on to the metal shelving for support.

A full twenty minutes passed before we were back to normal. By then we had loaded our carts with all the Hostess products that were within reach. After enlisting the help of a Costco associate with a forklift, the Twinkies from the top shelf were also transferred into our loving care. Finally satisfied with our stash, we proceeded to the front checkout, our carts packed to the hilt. In fact, they were so full we had to pull them rather than push so that the humungous pile wouldn't block our view. People were gaping at us, which was saying something considering we were at Costco. We ignored them and pretended this was a daily occurrence for us.

As we walked, for the first time since arriving, I became aware of all the people around us, piling twenty-year supplies of paper towels in their baskets or grabbing boxes of Saran Wrap larger than their children. It dawned on me that they wouldn't be able to use a tenth of it before the world ended. The weight of that knowledge lay heavy on my chest.

Glancing at Emma for comfort, I saw the color had drained from her face as well. Our brains were on the same wavelength as usual.

"When do you think they'll make the big announcement?" she asked.

I shook my head. "No clue."

That moment of comprehension we were dreading, that all this was actually happening, was headed toward us at us full speed, and there was no escaping the forthcoming crash. All we could strive for was to curb the hysterics until we made it to our cars.

"All these people are about to die," I said with a shudder, a tightness blistering the back of my throat. "There will be no fucking Earth left, Emma. It will be gone."

"This sucks." Emma stopped in the middle of the aisle. Shoppers swerved around us, irritated. It wasn't until an overweight lady in a mobility scooter squawked at us to move that we rolled over to one side.

"We need to tell people," Emma said, absent-mindedly biting her nail so aggressively I thought she might accidently amputate her fingertip.

"Emma, we're hauling enough Ding Dongs to feed a third-world country. If on top of that we make an announcement over the loud-speaker that the world is ending, we *will* be committed."

"I know. But I feel guilty. I have this burning need to warn everyone."

My conscience was overloaded with guilt too. But what in the hell could we say to get people to believe us? We had no proof of anything.

"We should let it play out naturally," I said. "They can't hold off on the announcement too much longer. Even the government can't hide a big-ass moon on a collision course with Earth."

Emma huffed in exasperation. "You're right. I… I don't know."

Just then my body seized; a savage fire unleashed itself under my skin. I screamed, and my knees buckled, knocking me into my cart. Twinkie boxes went flying everywhere. My first thought was that the end of the world had come early and we were all being scorched by radiation fallout. That assumption was proven incorrect when no one else collapsed with me. The fire struck again—

—and I was suddenly not in Costco with Emma anymore. I was lying on a bed, paralyzed, inside a glass dome filled with a thick mist.

Thump. Hiss.
Thump. Hiss.

A machine thrummed outside the dome. With each thump, red-hot venom coursed through my veins. I tried to cry out, but my mouth wouldn't move.

"Autumn! Autumn!" Emma's voice called for me in alarm. It sounded muted, as if behind a wall.

On one side, crimson blood flowed into my arm, and on the other side, gold-tinged blood was being drawn out.

Thump. Hiss.
Thump. Hiss.

My head lolled to the side, and I was forced to stare at my arm. It was so muscular. *Something is wrong. These aren't my arms, and this isn't my blood.* I was looking through Rigel's eyes. He was the one hooked to these machines.

I heard Emma again, sounding distraught. "Autumn! Autumn! Someone call 911!"

And the next thing I knew I was kissing the concrete at Costco.

"Autumn?" Emma said gently. She was no longer a distant echo but a solid presence; her fingers brushed the hair from my face.

I pushed myself up. A crowd had assembled around me. "What happened?" I asked.

"You started screaming and folded into a fetal position."

My head whirled; I couldn't organize my thoughts. Then the burning flared again, and with a flash, I was back inside Rigel's body. Figures had gathered outside the dome, distorted through the mist, a ghostly jury presiding over the guilty. I recognized one of them as Inanna. At least I thought it was her. She looked anguished, an emotion I didn't think her capable of.

The mist cleared, and the aching eased a fraction. A voice rang inside our glass prison. "It pains us to do this, Rigel. We can't take the chance you will go after Autumn. Your gold will be restored once she's gone, which might be quite soon. They're going to make the announcement any minute. Chances are she will be killed in the ensuing chaos."

The canopy of darkness drew in again, and I returned to the unwelcoming floor of Costco. I heard people above me talking on walkie-talkies. A large hand tapped my shoulder. When I didn't respond, it shook me.

"Miss, are you all right?" an unfamiliar man asked. "Can you hear me?"

With much effort, I opened my eyes to double vision. Despite the disorientation, I was aware that paramedics surrounded me.

"The news…" I mumbled.

"What was that?" the paramedic asked.

"Turn on the news," I repeated with more urgency.

"I think she may have a concussion," he said. "Can you get me the neck brace?"

"The news!" I insisted and started to get up. "We gotta turn on the news."

The paramedic pinned me down with his hands. "There will be plenty of time for television later."

"No. Now!" I said. Adrenaline brought my strength back. I shot up, pushed my way through the crowd, and ran for the televisions at the front of the store.

"Autumn!" Emma yelled, chasing after me. "What's going on?"

"It's time!" I shouted, and quickened my pace.

The paramedics and Emma trailed behind me in an absurd Benny Hill parody. All we needed was a girl in a bikini to make it complete. My heart thwacked in my chest with such ferocity I had to place my hand on it for fear my ribs might crack.

People were congregating at the televisions to watch the live news feed. The president was seated in the oval office with the American flag behind him, his speech was already in progress:

> *"... we estimate about one week until impact. Our planet, in all estimations, will be completely destroyed."*

The lady next to me fell to her knees and wept.

> *"My fellow Americans, there is hope. We can be saved. We have been given an opportunity for redemption. If we, as a human race, join together and prove we are of peace, that we put love above all else, we will be rescued.*
>
> *"Until now, it has been hidden from you that there are aliens among us. Their presence has been concealed for your protection. However, they have been observing and guiding us for thousands of years. These fearless heroes have given us technology and medical advancements; they have protected us from enemies who have wanted to take Earth for their own. These allies are standing by to preserve the human race by relocating us to another planet, virtually identical to this one, ready to be inhabited. It will be a new beginning for humanity.*
>
> *"These saviors have put in place one stipulation for our rescue. We must prove that we are worthy of being saved. We need to unite together and show them the greatness we are capable of as humans."*

His speech reminded me of an overdramatic, overdone, overacted Jerry Bruckheimer film—so, essentially, any Jerry Bruckheimer film. And to add a cherry on the Bruckheimer cake, the broadcast cut away to hundreds of spaceships clustered around the White House.

I actually planted a palm on my forehead and hit it a few times, not believing what I had just witnessed. That asinine camera shot had single-handedly sealed humanity's fate and doomed us all. That scene was going to make people freak out more than they already were. Hadn't they learned anything from *War of the Worlds*?

I turned away from the screen and the cringe-worthy speech. All around me, people were frozen in shock, no doubt processing this bombshell. They had been given two whoppers at once. One, the world was ending. And two, aliens were real, and they were hovering over our cities. Separately, those were brain busters. Together, they were certain to result in mass hysteria. It was only a matter of time before the frenzy got underway.

I found Emma away from the crowd, standing alone among the piles of men's golf shirts.

"Guess we don't need to pay for the Ding Dongs," I said.

"What happened, Autumn? Where did you go back there?"

"I was Rigel."

Emma raised her brow.

"I mean, I had an out-of-body experience again, but this time when I woke I was in Rigel's body, looking through his eyes. We were one and the same. My god, Emma, I felt his pain as if it were my own." I shivered.

"What pain?"

"They extracted his gold."

"Huh?"

I tried to slow my racing thoughts. "I'm sorry, this isn't coming out right. Remember me telling you about how they ingest gold, and it allows them to morph into light?"

"Yeah."

"Apparently they can also extract it from their systems. That's what they were doing to Rigel. They had this machine, and it was transfusing his blood to dilute the gold I think. And my god, Emma... it was hurting him."

"Autumn. It's okay. He's going to be all right."

"That's why he couldn't come for me," I said, tears welling. "They have him imprisoned. They're extracting his gold to make sure he can't escape and find me."

Emma studied me intently. "He *was* going to come for you then." She nodded in approval. "Maybe he does love you."

The thought brought me no happiness or relief. At this point it didn't matter anyway. It was game over. No one was coming for me now.

Emma's arms drooped at her sides. "It's going to get pretty nasty out there. I say we go home and commence with the eating."

A crash let us know that the madness had officially gotten underway. The pent-up beasts had been liberated from their confines and were ready for the rampage. The previously mellow shoppers were now either plundering, on their knees in prayer, or running through the aisles bellowing in rage. One particularly crazed man was mowing down everything in his path with a broom, humans not excluded. The president had succeeded in uniting the people, all right. Too bad it was only uniting them to take part in a worldwide riot.

"So much for us choosing good," I said.

"Let's get out of here."

As we made our way to the exit, a newscast captured my attention. The television on which it played was lying on the floor on its side, screen cracked, but still on. I skidded to a halt.

"What are you doing?" Emma shouted. "Come on!"

The reporter was on location at a shopping center. The buildings were ablaze behind her, and the surrounding cars had had their windows shattered. Glass blanketed the pavement.

"How is this happening so fast?" I muttered. "We're fucked."

The newscast switched to a Fry's Electronics store. And there, retreating from the premises, was Devon—clutching a television in one arm and a Wii U in the other. Not a single hair was out of place on his massive dome, despite the utter chaos.

"Autumn, what the hell are you doing?" Emma demanded. "We gotta go now!"

"That's him!"

"Who?" she shrieked.

"The Hair!" I said, pointing. On camera he kicked a lady in the shin as she made a grab for his television.

Emma finally looked at the screen. "*That's* him?" she asked with a grimace. "What in the hell were you thinking? Be thankful the world is about to end or I would march you directly to the optical section to get you glasses."

There was an explosion of glass at our feet, making us jump. A naked old man was pelting people with jars of pickles like they were snowballs. Without so much as a glance back, we barreled through the crowd toward the exit. (Okay, we might have veered off the path a bit to grab a few snack items along the way.)

To our dismay, the outside was worse. The parking lot was in utter chaos. People and cars were swarming everywhere, with no organization whatsoever.

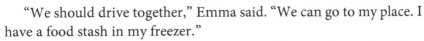

"We should drive together," Emma said. "We can go to my place. I have a food stash in my freezer."

"No, I need to go salvage a couple things from my house first."

She clearly wasn't happy about the idea of us splitting up. I gave her arm a quick squeeze to reassure her and said, "It's important I have them with me when we go. I'm afraid if I don't get them now, with the way things are going, they might be burned in the riot."

Sighing in resignation, she gave me a hug, "You be safe. Get to my place lickety-split, you hear?"

"I promise."

As I watched her walk away, unease welled in my stomach. I knew I would probably never see her again.

14

EVIL CRATER FACES, LOOTING SAMSUNGS, AND SECOND DATES

On the way home I made a mental list of the stuff I wanted to take to Emma's. There were two things I couldn't go without. The first was a raggedy stuffed rabbit I'd had since I was a kid. And second, I had to go the attic to get the photos of my parents. It was silly, but I wanted them by my side when the final moments came.

I felt a pang of guilt when I thought about all the friends and family I hadn't contacted or bothered to visit. Even though I couldn't have told any of them about the world ending without sounding like a crazy person, if I were any sort of friend, I would at least have called to say "hi" one last time. There would be no point trying to call them now. All the phone lines would be jammed up, if not altogether shut down, given the chaos.

A mile into my escape attempt it became apparent that I was going nowhere fast. I thought I was being smart by taking side streets to avoid the freeways. I guess everyone else had the same idea because *all* the roads were completely gridlocked. Ahead of me people were abandoning their vehicles, choosing to walk instead, and I had no choice but to do the same.

By the time I made it to my neighborhood, the sun had dipped below the horizon, leaving a pink glow on the rooftops and windows. The place was a complete ghost town—the perfect setup for a zombie apocalypse movie. There were no people, no sounds, and no lights on at any of the houses. Had everyone left? And if so, where did they go?

My footsteps echoed in the silence, the loose rocks on the pavement sounding like explosions. I treaded more softly, not sure why I was paranoid. I mean, no one was around, right? *That's what the girl thinks in movies right before she gets her head cut off.* A feeling of foreboding swept over me, and I took off at a light run, hoping to make it to the relative safety of my house before it got any darker.

"Hey there, beautiful."

It was a male voice that called to me, but from which direction I couldn't tell. I whirled on the spot, unnerved.

The chilling voice returned. "My friends and I are gonna throw an end-of-the-world party. How 'bout you come here and I'll give you an invitation?"

I whirled again, desperately searching for the mystery man. Gravel shifted. Footsteps thudded closer. The rush of fear that overcame me had the blood pounding in my eardrums, so I couldn't identify where they were coming from.

I ran.

Of course, I chose the wrong direction. From behind a newly graffitied house came a lineup of three goons who looked more than ready to start trouble. The pint-sized one of the trio—I'll call Goon-tini—wielded a knife. Tweedledum, to his left, had a police baton, and leading the pack was a burly blockhead who didn't need a weapon: his biceps were enough. He could easily pop my head like a grape. All three of these dudes had a deranged sneer plastered on their ugly faces. One thing was clear: they were hyenas and I was the wounded gazelle.

I wheeled around to run the opposite direction. Waiting behind me was another man—a man that terrified me more than all the others combined because of a huge crater in his left cheek. It was as if someone tried to dig out the entire side of his face with a spoon. He grabbed my arm, and I cried out.

"Why you in such a rush?" Crater Face hissed. "We're going to throw a party to celebrate the end of the world. We would love for you to come." He smirked. "And I do mean that quite literally."

I screamed until my lungs were too tired to produce another sound. My voice echoed throughout the neighborhood—the very empty neighborhood. Not even a dog barked in response. The psychos merely laughed at me. Tweedledum slapped his knee like some '50s bad boy reject.

Crater Face snatched my other wrist, twisted it painfully behind my back, and shoved me out in front of him to present to the others. Goon-tini came over with his knife and teased the blade against my throat and then down between my breasts.

Anger, not fear, fueled me now. I struggled against Crater Face and managed to break free. As I pivoted to escape, Goon-tini's knife caught me in the shoulder, slicing it open. The pain made me hesitate for a second—and that was a second too long. Crater Face wrapped his arms around me, pinning me tight. Warm blood trickled down my arm.

Tweedledum strolled over and shoved the baton between my legs, almost lifting me off the ground as he slid it back and forth.

"Mother fucker!" I seethed. "What do you want?"

"You," said Crater Face.

"Fuck you!" I spat.

Crater Face and his goons succumbed to laughter again. Pure evil oozed from them, infesting the entire block. It became perfectly clear to me why the Anunnaki were willing to let us all die. A smattering of benevolent folks paled in comparison to the savagery our species could produce.

Underneath their maniacal hooting and hollering, I thought I heard a car approaching. Relief swelled inside of me, energizing my lungs to release a fresh batch of screams. When the car came into view, I gave an ear-piercing screech. My captors didn't even flinch. In fact, they grinned. I was apparently a source of entertainment for them.

As the car drove by us, it slowed to a crawl. I pleaded for help, screaming until my vocal cords seized from the effort. The passengers regarded me with blank expressions. One of them, a young woman cradling her son, mouthed, "I'm sorry," and turned away. The car drove on.

No... no... no... no! This can't be happening!

Without warning, I was slammed down on the road and kicked with such force that I skidded along the pavement, leaving streaks of

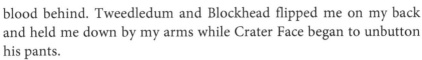

blood behind. Tweedledum and Blockhead flipped me on my back and held me down by my arms while Crater Face began to unbutton his pants.

I fought to free myself; my wrists were on the verge of breaking from the strain. Blockhead pinned my arm down with his knee, then slid his hand down to grope my breast and groaned, "This is gonna be my kind of party."

Tweedledum lifted my shirt, exposing my bra. Goon-tini bent down and, with a flick of his knife, cut it off. "There you go, gentlemen."

Both of them dug in, putting their grubby hands all over my breasts.

Goon-tini slid the tip of the blade down my belly and stopped at my jeans. His smile made my insides turn over, and I had to bite back the bile that rose. "Wonder what we have under here?" he said. "I'm hoping for a thong, but my guess is you're more of a boy short kind of girl."

Crater Face pushed Goon-tini aside. "I get her first."

This is not going to happen. No way am I meeting my maker like this, especially after all I've been through.

When Crater Face bent to straddle me, I bucked my legs and whacked him straight in his balls. He fell to his knees, whimpering. Tweedledum and Blockhead were stunned for just long enough to allow me to slip free. I launched myself to my feet and bolted, not looking back.

I sprinted for three blocks, then took a sharp left and hid in a ramshackle garden shed in someone's back yard. I tried to keep my breathing under control so they wouldn't hear me gasping for air. I heard their voices grow louder, then trail off as they passed me.

I slid to the ground and heaved in a deep gulp of the musty air. With trembling fingers, I tried to somehow fasten my bra back together, but it was useless. Careful not to touch the gash in my arm, I removed my shirt, yanked off my mangled bra, and threw it at the door with a curse.

"Shit!" I thunked my head against the wall. "Shit! Shit! Shit!" I thunked it again and again. What the hell was I going to do? A good first step would be to put my shirt back on. My arm protested this by seeping more blood as I pulled it over my head.

The shed door burst open. I shot up and yanked a shovel off the rack, raising it over my head in a defensive position. "Don't come any closer!" I growled, trying to sound intimidating, but coming off as only slightly less than hysterical.

"It's me, Autumn," a familiar voice said from the doorway.

It took me a minute to register who it was. It sounded like Devon. I craned my neck towards the door to get a better view. And, to my complete astonishment, there he stood, the light silhouetting his one-of-a-kind do. I dropped the shovel and gaped at him as if Jesus himself had entered the shed.

"What the fuck?" I exclaimed.

Was this a hallucination? Did I lose too much blood? I stepped toward him, then hesitated. If he was real, he could be as deranged as the rest of them. "Are you going to hurt me?" I asked.

"What? No. No Autumn, I'm here to help." His eyes found my wound. "Oh crap, your arm!"

He approached, and I picked up the shovel again, clenching it like a baseball bat, ready to pummel him if need be. He lifted his hands in surrender and stepped away.

"I'm fine," I said, giving a threatening twitch of the shovel.

"It's okay, I promise," he said.

"I saw you on TV, stealing electronics. You were practically leading the rabid pack of wolves."

"I know, I mean... I was," he tried to explain. "When I heard the news, my brain misfired. And I'm talking a large-scale shutdown of common sense. I wanted to retaliate, to take vengeance on anyone and everyone. If I was going down, I wanted the best TV on the market when I did."

"Hello! Did you not get the memo? The world is ending. What use is a TV?"

"Look, I know it isn't our second date yet, but—the reason why I did all those community service hours at the library was because of shoplifting."

"What?"

"I'm a kleptomaniac. And when I heard the news, that's all I wanted to do." He cocked his head. "Didn't it happen to you?"

"What? Get the hankering to loot a Samsung?"

"No, the malicious part," he said, rolling his eyes. "Everyone else went nutty as a fruitcake after they learned Earth's fate."

"Hell no," I said. "I can't fathom how people can change at the drop of a hat like that. Didn't they listen when the president said there was help? Granted, a third-grader could have presented the situation more eloquently, but still, there are beings here to rescue us."

"You talking about the galactic band of creatures hovering in the sky, all ready to transport us into their motherships?"

I recalled that horrible *Independence Day*–style scene of the ships ominously suspended above the White House. "Uh, yeah."

"When you hear news like that, you don't think straight. It's a double whammy they hit us with. The world is ending, and there are aliens ready to take us to another planet. Hey, I saw the miniseries *V* from the '80s. Ain't no way I'm going into an alien spacecraft. Besides, why did these 'benevolent entities' wait until now to reveal themselves? If they were smart, they would have informed us ages ago, let it sink in, so we could judge if we trusted them or not. Sorry, but I don't believe they're really here on a rescue mission. It's all a bunch of mumbo-jumbo to keep us calm. So considering all of mankind is gonna bite the big one, keeping my upstanding citizen status wasn't a priority, so my sanity switched off."

"This is hurting my brain," I said, banging my palm on my forehead a couple times. "I need to sit." I plopped down ungracefully. "The real question is, if you became this deranged madman, why are you fine now? And how in the bloody hell did you know how to find me?"

"That's what's bizarre. I was in the middle of Best Buy"—he cleared his throat—"'borrowing' a variety of DVDs and a surround sound system, when I heard a voice in my head. It said, 'Autumn needs your help. It's time to awaken.' I figured it was the last of my sanity sputtering out, so I tried to ignore it, but it wouldn't stop repeating your name. Eventually, it forced its way past my all-consuming need to steal the *X-Files* collector's set, and I got this sudden rush of memories. My family and all the people I care about flashed before me." He glanced at me uncomfortably and added quietly, "*You* flashed before me." He gave an uneasy cough and picked at a piece of paint that was peeling off the wall. "And then I saw a vision of you getting harassed by a gang of evil dudes, and I knew where to go. I can't explain how I knew where to find you. I just did."

"No way!" I shrieked, sending him ducking for cover. "Do you see what this means? Your reversal implies people still have good left in them! They only need a reason to let this fear-driven hate go, to be reminded why life is worth fighting for." I vaulted to my feet. A new idea had begun to formulate. "If this is possible, why wouldn't they just telepathically knock some sense into all of humanity, like Rigel did with you, and give people a chance to overcome this?"

"Huh? Who's Rigel? What are you talking about? I think you need to sit again."

I ignored him. "And Emma and I weren't affected because we already knew. We had made the choice." I clapped my hands together, on the brink of giddiness. "There *is* a way to get people to come to their senses." I staggered over to Devon and grabbed his shoulders. He flinched. "How can I get people to listen?"

A familiar queasiness rose in my gut. Recognizing the warning signs, I promptly let go of Devon's shoulders. I didn't want a repeat of our first date.

"What are you rambling on about?" Devon asked, inching toward the shovel.

"It's not too late!" I yelled in excitement. "We can fix this. All we need to do is make them *listen*! You remember that thing that I said I was saving for our second date?"

Devon nodded.

"Well, how 'bout we consider this our second date?"

15

KNIFE-THROWING THUGS, LAWN MOWER MISHAP, THE WORST SIDE ACHE EVER, FOLLOWED BY THE WORST HEARTBURN EVER

Devon paced as he sifted through the staggering amount of information I had dumped on him. I had spilled almost the whole shebang— although I had omitted the more intimate details with Rigel, to spare us both the awkwardness. I also didn't mention the prophecy, since I hadn't decided if I believed in all that. Plus, publicizing the fact that I might be the one to unite parallel universes might have caused a complete overload.

Devon impressed me with his acceptance of the situation. Who would've guessed that the dipstick employee I met in Barnes & Noble would become my ally while we fought to save the human race? I gave a little laugh when I thought about this ironic twist of fate.

Devon pursed his lips. "There have to be others like you," he said. "People who knew what was going to happen and were able to battle the fear and not give in to insanity."

"Yeah," I said. "I bet the web was swarming with warnings and prophecies. But given the anarchy, riots, and holy terror ripping through the cities, they've gotta be hiding. We don't have the means to track them down. And even if we did, there won't be enough of them. We need to enlighten billions, not just hunt down a few." I kicked the wall in frustration. "What about TV? Maybe I can get on the news to make an announcement?"

Devon scoffed. "You really think these people are gonna listen to *you*? Plus, all the TV stations are probably shut down. You need your alien boyfriend to get in people's heads. If he did it to me, why can't he do it to other people?"

I thought back to the time he had made me say those words that weren't mine. "I'm guessing he can't talk to everyone at once, or it's limited to certain people," I said. "Otherwise, why wouldn't he just order the fucktards who attacked me to stop? Instead he sent you."

"Gee, thanks," he said sarcastically. "You're welcome."

"You know what I mean," I said. "There's a rule or exception we're missing."

"How can we contact him?" Devon asked. "You think he can hear us? If he did his witchcrafty thing on me, he has to be able to hear, right?"

Devon must have said the magic words, because in a flash, I was gone from the shed and in the glass dome with Rigel. It was the Costco incident all over again, except this time I wasn't seeing through Rigel's eyes. My soul was physically there, hovering right next to his unconscious body. In the distance, I could hear Devon calling for me.

"Autumn?" Rigel's voice rang loud and clear around me. "Can you hear me?"

"Rigel, what are they doing to you? Are you hurt?"

"I'm fine. I'm pretending to sleep so they don't know I'm talking to you." He wiggled his pinkie finger to demonstrate. "We don't have much time. They're coming for you. You need to leave the shed. You must go now."

Inanna's eerie glow appeared outside the dome. The condensation on the glass made her bend and distort like a mirage. "I have to admit, you two are determined," she said.

Rigel tried to speak, but Inanna silenced him with a flick of her wrist. His irritation coursed through me, adding to my own.

"Leave him alone!" I snarled.

She fixed her gaze right on me. *How does she know where I am? Can she see me?*

"I wasn't mistaken in the canyon. It's blue," she said, almost to herself. Her expression morphed from confusion, to comprehension, to awe, and finally fear. She rushed at the dome, startling me. "You need to go! They are on their way."

Inanna was showing honest-to-goodness concern for me. But who was she talking about? Then it clicked. She meant "they" as in Crater Face and the gang.

Next thing I knew I was back in the shed, wood splinters from the floor poking my cheeks. I knew Devon was near because my stomach churned.

"Autumn, are you okay?" he said. His voice sounded panicked. "*Autumn?*"

I took in a much-needed gulp of air and pushed myself up. "We need to get out of here!"

But it was already too late. The shed door crashed open to reveal Crater Face and his Goon Gang. Devon grabbed the shovel and hurried to stand in front of me.

"So you thought you could hide?" Crater Face tsked. "But we haven't had our fun yet."

I scanned the room for something I could use as a weapon. The only thing within reach was a can of bug spray and a miniature screwdriver. *Why didn't I get that mace?*

Tweedledum twirled his baton and eyed Devon. "Is this your studmuffin boyfriend? Has he come to save you?"

Devon brandished the shovel and straightened into attack mode.

And then time advanced frame by frame; reality had turned into a slide show. Goon-tini threw his knife at Devon; I leaped at Devon in an attempt to push him out of the way; Devon lowered the shovel to block the blade from slicing into him. But there was nothing we could do to stop the knife from piercing Devon's chest: a direct hit.

I lost my footing and came down on an old-fashioned manual lawnmower, my hand plunging into the carriage. I felt the blades slice my hand, deep; the pain was so great I couldn't even scream. Devon's shovel clattered to the ground. *Hold on Devon. Please hold on.* I strained to turn my head enough to see him. His eyes were fixed on the knife in his chest, bewilderment creasing his features. He fell to his knees.

"Devon!" I rasped. I pulled my hand from the lawn mower, wailing when it broke free. I didn't dare look at it, knowing the damage was severe. That is if there was anything still there to look at.

I reached for Devon with my good hand, but I was too late, he was already falling backward away from me. His head slammed onto the concrete floor.

"No, Devon, no!" I cried. "Stay with me." His eyes dimmed, and I knew what that meant. "Please don't die on me!" His chest was covered in blood—unmoving.

Foolishly, I thought that if I could get the knife out, he would start breathing again. I grabbed the knife by the handle and tried to remove it—but it must have been wedged right into the bone. I had to jerk it back and forth to get if free, opening the wound even more, and that broke something inside me. I unleashed a primal scream. My blood and his blended in a sea of crimson.

In my panic, I had altogether forgotten about our attackers. One of them yanked my hair, whipping me off Devon. I swung the knife, slashing the guy on his temple. He let go and staggered back, cursing. Something cold pierced my side; I dropped the knife and collapsed.

"Rigel!" I begged. "Help me, please. Rigel!" My tears burned as if they were acid.

With a lurch, I was in the glass dome. Inanna was outside, shouting in a language I didn't recognize, and struggling to open the door. Rigel's skin was enveloped by an inky blackness that flaked away like ashes in a fire. Were they *burning* him? He thrashed and screamed.

Inanna opened the dome, and a gust of wind swirled around Rigel. He began to disintegrate, the ashes of his skin blowing away.

"Grab her!" I heard Crater Face bark in the recesses of my mind. I felt something being tugged from my side and then I was in the shed, lying on my back. I tried to get up, but my muscles wouldn't cooperate. I didn't have the strength to fight anymore. It was all I could do to fill my lungs with air.

"Rigel," I murmured.

"In case you forgot, your boyfriend over there is named Devon," Crater Face said. "And he can't hear you 'cause he's dead."

When I twisted my head toward Devon, Blockhead kicked me in the nose with his steel-toed boot. There was a sickening crunch, followed by a distinctive snap, and I could no longer move my limbs.

The bastard had broken my neck.

Squeezing my eyes shut, I tried to go back to Rigel, but I had no control over whatever sent me there. *What are they doing to him? Why is he turning into ash?*

"Rigel, not you too," I begged. "Please don't die."

Crater Face bent down, rotating my head so I had no choice but look at his triumphant grin. Taking his time, knowing I couldn't fight back, he straddled me.

"Rigel's hurt," I spluttered, choking on my own blood.

"Oh, he's not hurt, he's dead. Don't worry, though. You're about to join him."

My vision flicked briefly back to the dome with Rigel. He lay on the floor, barely recognizable, mostly a pile of ash now. Anunnaki—half of them shimmering orbs, the other half in bodily form—now surrounded his remains, arguing with each other. Inanna was kneeling down next to Rigel, her face so pale you could see the blue veins in her forehead.

A slice from Crater Face's blade ripped across my cheek, tearing it wide open, and I abruptly returned to the shed. I saw his wicked grin and his bloody knife poised above me, ready to drive it straight into my chest. All I could hear was the beating of my heart in my ears.

Then he plunged the knife into me.

My heart stuttered and stopped.

I stared into the eyes of my attacker as he pulled the knife free and thrust it down again and again. His laugh was the last thing I heard.

16

SHITBALLS AND VORTICES OF DEATH

I was floating above my body. Crater Face was stabbing me over and over, clearly enjoying himself. Blood sprayed everywhere as if we were in some absurd Quentin Tarantino parody. Devon's body lay beside mine. His eyes were open, but there was no life in them. Tweedledum, Goon-tini, and Blockhead viewed the events as though they were watching a sporting event, complete with cheering and fist-pumping.

An entrancing white orb materialized in the corner of the shed.

"Rigel?" I asked.

It flickered in response.

"Rigel, is that you?" I asked again, excitement welling.

The light grew, forming a disk-shaped vortex about four feet in diameter. It drew me in, tantalizing me with the promise of peace. I could see now that it wasn't Rigel, or any of the Anunnaki for that matter. This had to be the famous white light everyone speaks of.

Well, shitballs. I am officially dead.

I looked down at Crater Face, who was still stabbing my body. *You son of a bitch!* I plowed straight into him, wanting to tackle him, but of course I passed right through him. I did it again anyway.

And then he stood up and began unbuttoning his pants.

No fucking way! There is no fucking way!

He bent down and cut off my shirt in a single swipe. I didn't care if I was dead, I would not let him have his way with my body.

The vortex continued to expand; it now took up half the shed wall. A deep-seated instinct told me to enter it. It was almost impossible to resist its pull, but I knew another dimension lay on the other side, and it was one where Rigel couldn't go. There was no way I would cross if the consequence was losing him forever. And there was no way in *hell* I would leave and let Crater Face rape my corpse.

Not while I had any fight left.

Obviously I had no physical form, but maybe… *can I move objects like a poltergeist?*

Focusing all my anger on Crater Face's knife, I willed the blade to move.

I was almost as stunned as Crater Face was when the knife flew out of his hand and embedded itself in the wall of the shed.

"What the fuck?" He stumbled to his feet.

I've got you now, you sick bastard.

With one more burst of willpower, I sent the knife flying back toward Crater Face. It hit him directly in his groin. The color drained from his face, and he dropped to his knees, gurgling in pain.

God that felt good.

A soothing female voice called from the light vortex. "Autumn, it's time to come home." The voice had a familiarity that calmed me. *Where do I know that voice from?*

Crater Face fell flat on his face, and the other fuckwads turned to run. But I wasn't going to let them off that easy. With a quick surge of vengeance, I slammed the door shut. The panic on their faces filled me with satisfaction.

The portal sent out a ray of light that gripped me forcefully. I struggled against it, but its pull was like quicksand. The harder I fought to escape, the stronger it tugged. It distracted me long enough for the Goon Gang to pry open the door and run wailing into the night. *Dammit.*

My form made contact with the vortex. I was instantly overcome with a feeling of pure love. It coursed through me, filling me with an intense joy. Suddenly the thought of escaping it seemed monumentally foolish.

The familiar voice spoke again. "Autumn, honey. It's time."

I finally recognized it.

"Mom?" I called. "Mom, is that you?"

"Yes," she whispered, her voice tinkling like bells in a gentle breeze. "Come home, Autumn."

I gave myself fully to the light, letting it take me to her. Was I going to be able to see my dad again too? I hadn't realized how much I'd missed them. I missed them with all my soul.

"I'm coming, Mom," I said, sinking further into the light.

Midway through the portal, I jerked to a stop, snagging on something. How could that be? I didn't have a physical frame anymore. Light couldn't snag, could it?

And then I saw it: a fine golden rope had tethered me to the outside. It had entwined in my blue light and locked on—a shackle keeping me in the world I now wanted to leave.

"Mom! I can't get in." I wrestled against the restraint. "Can you hear me? I need help."

There was no response.

"Mom, if you still have man arms, I could really use them right now to pull me in."

The white vortex tugged at me with increased ferocity. My blue light stretched, and the world warped around me.

"Stop!" I yelled. "Something's wrong."

The individual particles of my soul were being pulled farther and farther away from each other. I was literally being torn apart, and I could feel it happening. It was as if I still had limbs and they were being ripped from my body.

"Mom! Help, please! *Mom!*"

It didn't stop. Instead, the white light and the golden tether began a tug-of-war with my soul. The strain was causing all the particles to heat up. One by one they caught fire and turned to ash. I could feel each one as it burned.

And then the vortex began to shrink—with me only halfway through.

"Wait, I'm not in! Can't you see I'm not in yet?"

My vision was split—one side shrouded in a bright white full of love and peace, the other in the darkness and despair of the shed. The fire from my tearing soul grew; it was now a continual blaze so intense that the scream I let out made everything in the shed go flying.

"Mom," I cried. "What did I do? Please tell me what I did to deserve this?"

No answer came.

All I could do was watch in horror as my light, my essence, my very being, was slowly pulled apart. Blackened bits of my soul fell to the ground, creating a snowstorm of ash. I had no adrenaline to protect me, no hope of unconsciousness to ease the misery. There was only pain.

My life's memories came at me in a rush. I saw all the important events that had shaped the person I had become, good and bad. Once a memory finished playing, it melted away, leaving a void in its place— each loss making me forget who I was.

I can't even remember my name.

A scattering of orbs blinked in the darkness. More portals? Would they try to suck me in—to tear me further? I just wanted to die, to slip into a chasm of nothingness, to become numb, to be no more. As the lights approached, I noticed they had a golden tinge. Where had I seen that before? A memory teetered on the edge of my consciousness, then faded away.

The portal was moments from sealing entirely; only a few of my light particles remained. I watched another one burn out and fall to the ground. And with it, my suffering stopped. I felt nothing. It was then that I knew, without a doubt, that when the last particle went out, I would be no more. I wasn't going to heaven, or hell, or any other dimension.

I would simply cease to exist.

A new voice spoke. "Autumn, come with me."

The word "Inanna" fluttered at the periphery of my escaping memories, but I couldn't quite pinpoint who or what that was.

And then there was one particle left. One last piece of my soul. It flickered and—

17

RETURNING FROM THE DEAD, TURKEY LEG UNDERGARMENTS, AND PUBLIC DISPLAYS OF AFFECTION

Thump. Hiss.
Thump. Hiss.

A familiar noise woke me.

Thump. Hiss.
Thump. Hiss.

Where had I heard that sound before?

Thump. Hiss.
Thump. Hiss.

My eyes flew open. I was lying on a table. A machine hovered near my head, pushing a clear fluid into my system. There were others in the room, whispering in an unfamiliar language.

"Ri..."

I tried to call for him, but was only able to croak out the first syllable. *Too weak.*

"She's awake," someone said in English. "Shall I go get him?"

"Yes," said another.

A figure emerged beside me, elongated and misshapen from the bright light and my sleep-strained eyes. It wasn't until it bent closer that I recognized Inanna. *Should I be terrified or happy at her presence?*

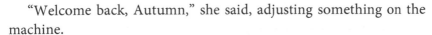

"Welcome back, Autumn," she said, adjusting something on the machine.

Welcome back from where? Had I gone somewhere?

I tried to rise, and toppled back.

"Sleep," Inanna said.

"Okay," I mumbled and then did just that.

A soft, gentle hand stroked my hair. I lay there not ready to open my eyes yet. I knew I was safe, despite not knowing who touched me.

"You awake?" A glorious voice whispered in my ear, and familiar lips grazed my skin.

The sound sent a jolt of exhilaration zipping up my spine, and I flung myself off the table. My legs did not like that at all. I teetered, gave a quick spasm, and collapsed.

Two strong hands caught me and held me close.

"Rigel," I cooed, dreamily blinking up, ready to gaze upon his perfect face.

Except it wasn't perfect. His brows were drawn together, worry lines creased his usually seamless forehead, and dark circles shadowed his eyes.

"I'm here," he said, brushing his finger along my cheek.

His touch made me drunk on bliss. I wanted to dream of only us, his warm body next to mine. Just for a while. My eyes grew heavy and I drifted off to sleep.

When I woke again, I was relieved to find myself in Rigel's arms. He was sleeping next to me, and our legs were entwined. He smelled of lavender soap and baby powder. Not what I would've expected from an alien, but it was oddly soothing, nonetheless.

I fished around in the recesses of my mind for a clue as to how I had gotten here. The last thing I remembered was shopping for Ding Dongs at Costco; after that I drew a complete blank.

Scanning my body, I tried to find the reason as to why I was lying on a sterile hospital bed. Everything seemed in perfect working order. Not a scratch on me. The only thing that raised a red flag was the outfit I wore—a white T-shirt and white shorts. I didn't even own white shorts. Did I buy them at Costco? I stretched open the waistband to see if I was at least wearing my own underwear. Yep, I recognized those: hipsters with an image of a turkey leg over a barbecue.

Rigel's breath heated my neck as he asked, "What's the matter?"

"My undies are on fire," I slurred.

Slurring? Am I drunk? Did Emma and I sneak samples of vodka too? What the hell happened?

A door opened, and a dozen figures drifted in. My eyes hadn't adjusted to the light, so I couldn't make out who they were.

"She's awake," said one of the blurry shapes.

Rigel squeezed me against him. "Yes, but I don't think she's pieced together what happened yet."

"We can't wait any longer," rumbled another voice. "Time is running out."

Something seized my head with a vise-like grip, and suddenly memories were being shoved into my skull, rapid fire and relentless. My head felt like it would split from the pressure. Swinging wildly, I busted free from Rigel's grasp, bounded off the table, and pawed at my head, trying to end the onslaught.

"Ninurta, stop!" Rigel ordered, coming to my side. "It's too soon!"

The scene of Devon with the knife in his chest replayed in my mind as vividly as if it were happening again. Rigel tucked me into his arms, probably thinking his embrace would calm me, but it didn't. How could it when I was being forced to relive my own death?

At last the flood of memories ceased. Rigel let go and gave me space to collect myself. As my vision cleared, I took in my surroundings for the first time, and gasped; my memories were briefly pushed aside by the realization of where I was.

On the opposite end of the room, what must have been millions of stars shone through a giant porthole. A white space pod came into view, slowing as it approached, and then disappeared out of sight.

I was on a spaceship. Like in outer space!

Inside the room, every surface was a muted metallic silver, and so clean that if I dropped an ice cream cone on the ground I would have no qualms picking it back up to eat it. The only items in the room were the bed I'd awoken on and some medical instruments.

And then there were the Anunnaki. Twelve of the tallest beings I'd ever seen, Inanna at the helm, stood formally before me with their hands clasped below their chests in a prayer-like fashion.

Well, one older dude kept his hands behind his back. And by the way the rest were glaring at him, they didn't approve of his stance. They acted as if his position was somehow threatening.

There were too many WTF elements to process at once.

I turned to Rigel. "Devon," I mumbled. "Did you save Devon?"

Rigel pulled me protectively into him.

"Devon's here," he reassured me. "He's alive."

"I want to see him."

"You can," he said, though his eyes were guarded. "Autumn, there's something you need to know before you do."

"No. I can't take any more bad news," I said. The echo of a possibility knotted my stomach. "Oh, shit! Earth, is it gone?" I ran over to the porthole and pressed my face against the glass, searching for the familiar pale blue dot. It was nowhere in sight. "Emma. I need to get to Emma!"

The room spun and pitched, and I had to lean against the wall to keep from falling.

The next thing I knew I was back on the exam table. Inanna was bent over me, holding the same healing device she had used in the canyon, making a sweep over my heart. Rigel stood beside her, his face pale, the dark circles under his eyes even more prominent than before.

"The Earth?" I rasped.

"Is intact, for now," Inanna said. "However, the natural disasters will begin soon."

"Oh, god," I wheezed. "I've got to find out if Emma is okay."

"We will send someone to check," Inanna assured me. "But I need you to calm down. You're going to ruin your new heart. It's still weak from healing."

My eyes went wide and I sat up. "Did you say a new heart?"

"Well, we couldn't exactly keep your old one anymore, now could we?"

"Whose heart did I get?"

"Yours. We can harvest new organs with your existing cells."

"And the bastards who killed me? Are they still alive?"

"Oh, yes."

"What? Why?"

"What I mean to say is, they're alive for now. We shipped them off to the Sahara desert, tied them up, and left them in the sand to slowly burn. As an added bonus, I connected them to an IV that would keep them hydrated until the end, so they can enjoy their blistering skin."

That made me smile. "Thank you for that. I'm not sure why you saved us, but thank you."

Inanna bowed her head.

"What about Devon?" I asked, easing into a standing position. "Were you able to heal him fully too?"

"He is alive and you can visit him. I must warn you though, we could only repair his physical body. He did die, and his soul transitioned to the other dimension. His vessel is now open to him, but it's his choice if he wants to return. If he elects not to, we will have to 'pull the plug,' so to speak, allowing him to fully pass."

"I want to see him," I said. "Take me to him."

"You can, soon. First we must make a request of you."

What could they possibly have to ask me that is more important than Devon?

"When you died," Inanna continued, "your soul was prevented from fully completing your transition into the next dimension."

The memory made me shiver. I remembered my soul being pulled apart, each particle of my light burning away. "Why couldn't I go to the other dimension?" I asked.

"That's what we need to determine. Do you remember the gold thread that tethered itself to you?"

"Was that you?" I asked Rigel. "Were you there to rescue me?"

He deflated at this question, and an unfamiliar emotion flickered on his face before he looked away.

No, of course it wasn't him. The monsters had him imprisoned at the time. I didn't get it. Why was Rigel sad all of a sudden? Maybe because he wasn't involved in my rescue? I couldn't help but feel like I was missing something.

Inanna answered for him. "It wasn't Rigel," she said. "It was a phenomenon we have never encountered before." She glanced at the other Anunnaki who still stood with their hands clasped under their chests.

"You guys are seriously freaking me out here."

There was a silent exchange between the group, and then Inanna said, "We believe when you kissed Rigel in the canyon, a partial soul connection may have been made."

I groaned. "You're not talking about that prophecy thing, are you?"

"It's not a *thing*," Inanna said, clearly offended by my comment.

I thought back to my kiss with Rigel. When it happened, we were, for all intents and purposes, sewn together with a fine gold thread. And now that I had a second to consider it, that thread was identical to the tether that had kept me from passing to the other dimension.

No way. The whole scenario where my soul helps to unite universes is impossible. *Simple as that.*

That wasn't true, though. Nothing could really be considered impossible anymore. After all, I was a genetically engineered hybrid, on a spaceship, who had just been resurrected by a band of supernatural ancient gods. The word "impossible" was no longer allowed in my vocabulary.

With an uncomfortable laugh I said, "That has to be a fable, right?"

Rigel put his hands on my shoulders. "No, Autumn, it's not a fable. It's real."

"How could you possibly know that? What proof do you have?"

"The Creator gave us the prophecy himself," he said.

I snorted. "What, did a prophetic scroll appear out of thin air?"

It was Inanna who answered. "Several hundred thousand years ago—give or take a millennium—we discovered that the origins of our creation and the keys to understanding the cosmos could be found in the microwave background radiation from what you call the 'Big Bang.' We decrypted the information coded within that radiation, and when we did, the Great Prophecy of the Souls was revealed to us, along with many other truths."

I tried to remember the creation myth Rigel had shared with me. At the time I'd assumed it was a poetic rendition of our inception, not a line-for-line retelling. I could only recall fragments of it. He had said God wanted to create life forms that he could nourish and oversee, and in the process he exploded and split in two. Essentially, God got bored and created us for his personal entertainment.

Wow, I know the meaning of life: our sole purpose is to keep God amused.

I didn't know how to react to this epiphany. Shouldn't something happen? At a bare minimum, I would expect divine trumpets to blare in triumph. Instead, I felt royally pissed at being a pawn in God's chess game.

"You okay?" Rigel asked.

"A soul connection, huh?"

"It's a possibility, yes."

I recalled all the times I had seen things through Rigel's eyes, as if we were one. "Are you suggesting I couldn't transition into the other dimension because I was part..." I couldn't come up with the appropriate word to use.

"Me," Rigel said, tracing his finger down my cheek. "I felt it, too. The gold thread manifested from me, Autumn, tearing my soul out of my body with it."

Inanna crossed her arms and sighed. "More importantly, you weren't the only one dying. We lost Rigel too."

"What?" I checked him for injuries. "You died too?"

He swallowed. "My body did, just like yours." I could see the terror in his eyes.

"I thought you were all immortal?" I said. "That you couldn't die."

"Not quite immortal," Inanna clarified. "Our bodies do weaken eventually. And as you have seen, we can cure almost any physical injury or disease, save for a beheading. The thing is, Rigel's body literally transformed into ash when you were dying, and that defies explanation. Never in our history have we beheld such a phenomenon."

My brows knitted together. "No human and Anunnaki have had this connection we have? Ever?"

"No. That's why we must consider the prophecy."

I shook my head. "Nope. Sorry. I don't believe it. I know I glow blue and all, but you are all off your rockers if you think I'm the catalyst to reunite the separated pieces of God." I huffed in total disbelief. "Please."

"Technically, we are all God," Inanna said. "Every particle of us, including our soul, is The Creator of All."

"Yeah, I get that. Nevertheless, there is no way I am *The One*."

"Why do you say that?" Rigel asked. "Why *not* you?"

I had no response for that. It just couldn't be me—that was all I knew.

Inanna plunked her hands on her hips. "Trust me, none of us want a mere human to be *the* one. But the bottom line is, we have to know."

"What are you getting at?" I said. "Are you saying there's some kind of test?"

"Sort of," she said. "We want you to kiss Rigel. We need to witness what happens."

"What?" I just about choked. "Is this a trick?"

"No, it is not."

"In case you forgot, barely a week ago you threatened to torture and kill me if I pursued any relations with Rigel. And now I have your blessing to suck face with him?"

"Well, yes," she said.

I examined Rigel for any sign that this might be a trap. He responded to my scrutiny with that damn sexy half-smile, and I melted.

"To clarify," I said, "you won't zap me into a pile of dust if we do this?" The other Anunnaki in the room remained still and expressionless. Except, of course, for the one dude who wasn't holding his hands in that weird half-prayer position; when I glanced at him, he actually winked at me.

Creepy.

"No," Inanna promised. "I will play nice today."

The anticipation in the room was palpable. I suddenly felt like the headliner act at a fetish club.

"And you *all* have to be here to watch?" I asked.

"Yes."

"Okee-dokee then." I ambled over to Rigel, repressing the impulse to hightail it out of there.

I stood in front of him, shifting on my feet, not quite sure how to start.

"Uh," I said. "So, ya ready to make out?"

His lips quirked in amusement. He ran his finger under my chin and tipped it up, igniting those familiar vibrations. I made a strange whimpering noise, probably more from nerves than anything else. His eyes sparkled, and without further ado, he pressed his lips against mine.

My senses went from zero to brink of orgasm in seconds. I was astonished by the urgency with which our souls ascended this time,

145

his glowing gold and mine blue. As our spirits intertwined, a golden thread materialized and began stitching us together.

I was so overwhelmed with lust that I had completely forgotten that we were being watched. Carnal desire took hold of me, and the part of me that was lip-locked with Rigel tried to rip off his shirt, desperately seeking skin-on-skin contact. I wanted to take him on the spot. I needed to complete the bond.

Same as she had done the last time we kissed, Inanna intervened. She separated us using her annoying telekinetic power—though to her credit, she kept her word and didn't slam me on the ground. Instead, I dangled awkwardly in midair for a second before she set me down lightly.

I brushed myself off indignantly. "Geez, you're welcome!"

"My apologies," Inanna said, her facial expression an odd mix of disgust and amusement. "But I've got lunch waiting, and you were about to make me lose my appetite with your... what do you humans call it..." she waved her hand around, "... 'hanky-panky'?"

I remembered pawing at Rigel's shirt like a wild animal, and my ears grew hot.

"Sorry," I said.

Inanna eyed me thoughtfully and then, as if she had come to some decision, she said, "I need to meet privately with the council. While we do that, why don't you go visit Devon?"

"Okay," I said, still trying to compose myself from the kiss. My god, if that was what a kiss with Rigel was like, I couldn't fathom what sex would entail. I made it my goal to find out the first chance I got.

18

LAME SPACESHIP DESIGN, ALIEN BOYFRIENDS, AND TEENYBOPPER MAGAZINES

Rigel and I walked down a long concrete hallway. It was altogether the opposite of what I would have expected from a highly advanced mothership. At the very least, I envisioned *Star Trek* level technology. Or maybe, you know, glowing buttons, fingerprint keypads, super-shiny metallic walls—the whole sci-fi enchilada. Instead, this ship was monotone: gray walls, gray floor, gray ceiling.

Fancy controls or not, I had to admit that being here was pretty damn cool. *I'm on a freaking spaceship floating around in outer space!* I snickered out loud at the thought.

"What are you laughing at?" Rigel asked, clasping my hand in his. Desire coursed through me, which made me giggle harder.

"I'm on a spaceship."

"And you have an alien boyfriend," he added, giving my hips a playful nudge.

"And *you* have a genetically altered, prophetically-challenged girlfriend."

"We make quite the pair." He winked.

A few weeks ago, I was a single girl whose greatest thrill was sipping wine and eating a mega-sized tray of cheese. Now I was travers-ing the solar system while bumping hips with an alien I fully intended to sleep with the first chance I got.

Of course, there was also a dark side to this fantastic scenario. Too many ends were near: the end of the world, the end of humans, the end of my first and only love, and the end of me. That put a damper on things didn't it? Why wasn't I throwing a fit? I should have been panicking, running in circles, pulling my hair out, something. They must have drugged me with a relaxer when they healed me.

We passed a window in the corridor, and my stride faltered when I recognized Earth shining in the distance, an infinitesimal dot spinning in the vacuum of space. *It's still there.* Even though Inanna said it was, seeing it was a total relief. Stopping to get a better view, I tried to imagine our solar system without it. There would be an empty hole there. Or perhaps a new asteroid belt in its place.

Rigel stepped up behind me. He wrapped his hands around my waist and rested his chin on the top of my head. It felt so normal, so comfortable.

"How long do we have?" I asked.

"Maybe a week."

"Emma," I murmured, gliding my finger along the glass, spelling out her name, as if that would somehow let her know I was thinking of her.

"You only talk of Emma, and never mention your family. From what I gathered while snooping in your attic, your parents passed away. Can I ask what happened?"

I pressed my forehead against the window, enjoying the soothing coolness. "My parents died a while ago. Car accident. I'm an only child and not close with any of my other family."

"Why the rift with your relatives?"

"My mom had abuse issues with her father, which she understandably didn't talk about, and left home the first chance she got. I don't know why my dad never talked about his family, but he had completely lost touch with them. It's strange: I never asked my parents about their relatives, and they didn't volunteer any info. I've only met one grandparent, and don't know the names of anyone else."

"Was that tough? Not having family after your parents passed?"

"No. I had Emma. She's my rock."

I turned to face Rigel. His eyes were reflecting the earth and stars outside. For a frightening instant I saw Earth exploding in the prisms of his eyes.

I jerked, wiping the image from my mind. "We can't save Emma, can we?"

He didn't respond right away, which gave me the answer I already knew. With a heavy sigh he said, "I don't know."

Grief reverberated in my bones, making my whole body ache. I couldn't cry, though. I was done crying. My tear ducts had to be drier than the Sahara desert by now.

Rigel pulled me in to him, his fingers tracing circles on my back. I breathed in his scent and snuggled in tighter, letting all my worries fade away.

After a moment, I put my chin on his chest and looked up at him. "What about your family?"

He immediately tensed.

"Uh-oh."

"My family is…" He paused, considering. "They are…"

"You can tell me anything, you know."

"My mom is equivalent in power to your president."

"No shit." I pushed away to get a better read of his expression, to see if he was joking or not. "I thought Anu would be president."

"Anu and the twelve council members don't deal with everyday matters on Nibiru. That falls on my mother."

"You must be famous then? The hot son of the president and all." A blush spread across his face, and I slapped him on the chest playfully. "Do you have a fan club?"

"Can we change the subject please?"

"You *do* have a fan club!" I couldn't help but tease him. "Are you constantly plastered on the cover of the Nibirubian version of *Tiger Beat*?" I mimicked licking the tip of a pencil and writing on a notepad. "So, Rigel, what is your dream date? Your favorite color? Do you prefer dogs or cats? The Nibirubian fangirls want to know."

"Watch it." He leaned down and nibbled my ear, and my body tingled in response. "The Rigel Nation will not appreciate you heckling me."

My brows shot up. "Your fan club has a name?"

His eyes glistened with mischief. "Wouldn't you like to know?"

He let go of me, and we continued down the corridor, leaving me to wonder if millions of girls were sleeping with posters of Rigel plastered next to their beds.

19

RESURRECTING THE HAIR, CHEESE PIZZA TREES, DIVINE SPONGES, AND TELEPATHIC WET T-SHIRT CONTESTS

We arrived at a metallic door, no different than all the others in this blasé spacecraft. *Don't they get tired of all this stale gray?* Rigel waved his hand at the door—and then with a cheeky side-glance said, "Abracadabra." It opened.

"Dork," I said, smacking him in the arm.

All playfulness drained from me when I saw Devon lying on a sleek silver table.

An attendant was seated at his side. She stood when we entered. "Hello," she said, placing her hands below her chest in that same strange half-prayer position the Anunnaki had back in my room.

"How is he?" I asked.

"He's stable, but still in the other dimension. I will leave so you can be alone with him." She placed her hand on my shoulder. Startled, I eyed her hand warily. The Anunnaki were not an affectionate bunch, so for all I knew this could be the equivalent of a Vulcan nerve pinch. "And Emma is fine," she said, giving my shoulder a gentle squeeze. "She is safe in her apartment at the moment."

My breath caught. "Thank you."

She gave me a sympathetic nod and exited the room.

No tubes or wires were hooked to Devon, like you would find in a human hospital. He rested there peacefully, his chest rising and falling. All evidence of the knife wound was gone. He wore the same style of T-shirt that I did, and a white sheet covered his lower half.

I padded to his side, anxiously chewing my lip.

"You want me to leave too?" Rigel asked.

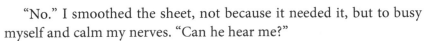

"No." I smoothed the sheet, not because it needed it, but to busy myself and calm my nerves. "Can he hear me?"

Rigel joined me at Devon's bedside. "He can, yes."

I felt as if a spotlight were on me. *What do I want to say? Do I ask him to come back? What if he's happy where he is?*

Leaning against Rigel for support, I admitted, "I didn't think about what I wanted to say."

He smiled and brushed my hair behind my shoulders. "You'll do fine."

I cleared my throat and leaned in close to Devon. "Hey, Zarf, it's Zooloo. Umm… in case you haven't figured it out by now, you died. I mean, uh… crap… you *almost* died. Or you're in limbo. What I mean is… oh, screw it. Look, you can come back if you want. Your body is still here on Earth. Wait. No it isn't. It's on a spaceship. Ahhhhhh!" I turned to Rigel. "This isn't coming out right."

He stifled a grin and spoke to Devon. "What Autumn is trying to say is, if you want, you can return to your body and join us. But it's your choice, Devon. If where you are now makes you happy, then you can stay there."

I wondered where Devon was. Probably in his personal utopia: a lush meadow with trees sprouting extra-large cheese pizzas, flat panel TVs built into giant boulders with free premium channels, and cans of number twelve hairspray growing wild. And here we were, two obnoxious voices butting in and ruining his fun.

"Why would he want to come back here anyway?" I asked. "He's just gonna die again." I clutched the side of the bed and marveled at how peaceful his expression was. Then I did a double take when I noticed that Devon's hair made a heavy indent in the pillow—as deep as his skull did. That number twelve could be used as spray-on armor. "Devon, maybe you shouldn't come back. There's only a week left on Earth, if we're lucky."

Our last dreadful moments together were fresh in my mind—including the conversation Devon and I had in the shed before the Goon Gang came in. *Devon had changed.* Rigel had sent him to me using his telepathy or whatever.

I spun on my heel to face Rigel.

"What is it?" he asked, startled.

"You fixed Devon! You helped him choose good."

He cocked his head and gave me a puzzled look.

"Why can't you do that with all of us? If you can get humans to listen to reason, understand that there is hope, that there is love—like you did with Devon—we can be rescued. Come on, you gotta give us a chance."

"It doesn't work that way," he said. "I can only perform thought transference if I have physically touched a person. The touch creates the bond. I can't help all of mankind."

"That's not true. You spoke to me telepathically in Barnes & Noble. You told me to leave, and we hadn't touched yet."

"Actually, we had."

"I'm pretty sure I would have remembered that."

"I was watching you stare at the moon in the Barnes & Noble parking lot, and then I followed you inside. I touched your shoulder to get your attention right as you entered... but then chickened out and flashed away before you turned."

"I knew someone was watching me." I poked his chest. "Stalker."

He grinned.

"Surely someone here has the power to speak to and persuade the masses to get it together."

"No, none of us are that powerful. But there is a—" Rigel cut himself off.

"What? Is there a way to do it? What is it?"

Before he could respond, the door slid open and the twelve Anunnaki glided in, led by Inanna.

Excited by this new possibility, I ran to her and seized her arm. She stiffened. I doubted any human in history had dared grab her, much less approach her without permission. I let go in time to keep the Inanna grenade from going kaboom.

"You need to give us the opportunity to be saved," I said. "You need to give us a chance to conquer this sickness, 'cause that's what it is. If there's a way to get into people's heads and speak to them, I want to know. Do any of you have that power?"

To my amazement, she tilted her head as if considering my request. Or it was more likely that she was pondering all the different ways she could kill me for touching her.

Rigel grasped my elbow and guided me away. "No, Autumn. Please don't."

"Please don't what?" Had Rigel intentionally hidden crucial information from me? *He wouldn't do that.* I wheeled on Inanna. "What am I missing here?"

"I take it Rigel hasn't told you?" Her eyes widened in disbelief. "I wasn't expecting that."

"Told me what?"

A stillness fell over the room. Inside my belly a trapdoor opened, the pit of betrayal lay waiting below. I teetered on the edge, afraid I would fall in.

I looked directly into Rigel's eyes. "There's a way to save humans… and you didn't say anything?"

"Autumn, it's not like that. It's not…" He trailed off.

Ker-splash! Into the ice cold waters of the River Deception I plunged.

Inanna intervened. "*We* can't do anything. But *you* potentially could." She paused to quickly glance at Rigel before continuing. "It will come at a price to you, Autumn."

"Me? What price? What can I do?"

Rigel answered for her, his voice raspy with emotion. "The Ark. A human can communicate to all other humans using the Ark's power, in conjunction with one of the tools stored inside."

"The Ark?" I said, sure that I'd heard him wrong. "Are you talking about the Ark of the Covenant? That exists?"

"Yes," Inanna said. "However, the Anunnaki are not allowed to use it, due to mandates by the Galactic Federation. A human can operate it, but only for a very short period of time."

I turned on Rigel. "Take me to it, now. I want to use it." I grabbed his arm and tried to pull him toward the exit.

Rigel's posture went slack in defeat.

"What's the matter?" I asked. "Why are you acting like I want to burn puppies alive?"

"Using it will kill you," Inanna said. "Its radiation will cook you within minutes. And we can't heal you from that. Handling it will result in certain death."

"But I can speak to *everyone*?"

"Yes. You'll have about five minutes."

"What about people who don't understand English?"

"It projects thoughts, not words, so it essentially translates itself."

I paced the room. "Have you offered the Ark to anyone else? There's gotta be a line of people willing to sacrifice themselves to keep humans alive, not just me."

"As a matter of fact, we did." Inanna shrugged in a way that led me to believe this was a point of contention for her. "Right after the announcement was made, and humans went ballistic, we met with your leaders. They had managed to get the web and a few television stations back up, and they were actively broadcasting, but it was too late. Not enough people were listening. At least, not enough to get a third of the population to unite. But with the Ark, every single human can be reached, no matter their geographical location. And there is nothing more effective than the perceived "voice of God" to make people stop in their tracks and pay attention.

"So we presented the Ark to all the leaders of your world, thinking they would view it as their last chance to save humanity. But it only resulted in a global temper tantrum over who would be the one to use it. As you can imagine, there are certain countries who want only their people to survive and are willing to flatten the rest of the world if it means their dominance and survival. In the end, we left it to the United Nations to elect an individual of their choosing."

"The UN?" I said. "Dear lord, they're about as useful as a bunion."

"Yes, we learned that very quickly. They are still arguing about it. You all might end up nuking yourselves into oblivion before our moon has a chance to get here."

"Hold on," I said, rubbing my temples in confusion. "How long have our governments known about all this?"

"A year."

"Are you fucking kidding me? A *year*? Why in the hell did they keep this from us for so long? If they had said something a year ago, even a month ago, we would've had time to process all this and get our shit together. It's not rocket science. Be good and survive, or continue being assholes and die. Instead they hid it from us until it was too late."

"None of your governments were willing to disclose the information. The entire economic system would have collapsed. Not to mention what it would do to world religions."

"So what?" I shouted. "What good is an economic system if we're all dead?"

"You're asking me?" Inanna said, raising her hands. "Your leaders made the decision, not us. We made the situation very clear early on, and laid out our recommended plan. We told them that if they didn't reveal the information slowly, in advance, to give the people time to absorb it, the result would be what we have now: utter mayhem. Ultimately, their greed and thirst for power won out. They were confident that you all would come together in the end, and then they could keep the underlying governmental systems intact on the new planet."

"So none of them listened to your advice? No one at all?" I couldn't believe this.

"A few leaders tried to disclose the situation earlier, but that didn't work out so well for them. Two were assassinated by their peers before they could do so. And one actually did make the announcement—but became a laughingstock when the major leaders of the world denied his claim."

"Once you learned how incompetent our governments were, why didn't you step in and warn us all yourselves?"

"The Galactic Federation, which we are bound by, has ruled that we must not personally intervene," Inanna said. "We can assist to some extent, but humans have to come to this decision on their own."

"Well, that ain't gonna happen."

Hope was fading fast, but I was determined to find a loophole. I had to think.

"Okay then, let's go find someone now," I said. "There has to be someone more competent than me, someone capable of writing and delivering a life-affirming speech. Maybe we can talk to the Pope."

Inanna raised her eyebrow at me. "Yes, let's do that." She tapped her finger on her chin. "Maybe we can create a reality show competition: *America's Next Top Martyr.*"

"I'm being serious!" I said.

The air suddenly became charged with energy, my hairs standing on end. "Look human, you have no idea the lengths we have gone through to save your species." I stepped back, and she seemed to try to calm herself before continuing. "After seeing the chaos unfold, the Federation granted us approval to find someone ourselves a couple days ago. We selected several individuals who we thought had potential. You have to understand, finding a candidate isn't as easy as closing your eyes and picking one at random. Not only do they have to be able to deliver a motivational speech, they also have to keep speaking while their skin melts off and their organs bake inside their bodies."

"It hurts like a son of a bitch," an Anunnaki interjected from the corner. It was the first time any of them had spoken, and it took me by surprise. The other Anunnaki were so quiet I had almost forgotten they were there.

This Anunnaki's features were sharp, and his nose came to a point. Not wicked witch pointy, but androgynous supermodel pointy. His ashy blond hair was slicked and cut short, accentuating his manicured eyebrows and long lashes. He was dressed in all black with a brown leather vest. If we were going by cliché stereotypes, he'd be the rebel of the group.

"Yes, Ninurta, that's one way to put it," Inanna agreed, with the hint of a smile.

Ninurta? Hey, that's the SOB that did that memory sandblaster trick on me. I glared at him and his pretentious leather vest.

Inanna uttered an "ahem" to get my attention. "Over the past several days we have put the recruits through a physical and emotional test to see if they would be able to operate the device, and no one has passed. There are still people trying, but I am afraid no one will build a tolerance in time. You are more than welcome to try it if you want."

I opened my mouth to berate them for giving up, and then changed my mind. Truth be told, whoever agreed to that monumental task would, in all probability, fold under the pressure. Can you imagine being charged with preserving all of humanity, only to flub your speech and eradicate them by accident? You get one chance and a few precious minutes to convince the people of planet Earth that they need to love again. And when you consider how many selfish, greedy, warmongering ass wipes there are in the world, the chances are slim to none. Throw Crater Face and his Goon Gang into the equation and you might as well be tasked with turning Rush Limbaugh into a socialist.

"Okay, fine," I said. "How does this device work?"

"Ninurta, you want to respond to that question?" Inanna suggested.

"It would be my pleasure," he agreed with a cocky smirk. He couldn't seem to stop staring at my breasts, and it made me uncomfortable. Rigel noticed and moved closer to me. "After we created you," Ninurta continued, "we needed a way to communicate with all humans en masse, whether they were digging underground in a mine or taking a bath in the river. The easiest way to do that was with a direct transmission to your pineal gland."

"A gland?" I asked. "What good does it do to converse with a gland?"

"The pineal gland is located in the center of your brain. It's what regulates your dreams. It's also known as your 'third eye.' When it's awakened, you can hear and see with it."

"See? Like without eyeballs?"

"Yes," he said, taking several leisurely steps toward me. His height had me craning my neck to see his face. While his tone was all business, his eyes were eager and full of fire, and his pupils vibrated with energy. Either he was having inappropriate thoughts about me or he wanted to eat me for dinner.

I shrank back, and his smile grew bigger. Rigel cleared his throat and assumed a protective posture. Ninurta flicked a glance at him and eased off. Rigel must have delivered a silent warning.

Figuring the boundaries had been established between them, I pressed on.

"I don't get it. If using it means death, then one of you had to sacrifice yourselves every time you made an announcement?"

Ninurta rolled his eyes at me. "No. It only kills humans. When we created humans, we deliberately added this resistance to prevent them from operating it."

Paranoid much?

"So what happens when it's used?" I asked. "Do we hear a voice in our heads or something?"

"Exactly. It's similar to the voice you hear when you're thinking, only it's amplified, and it's obvious that it isn't your own thoughts."

"Didn't people freak when they heard an inner voice ordering them around from out of nowhere?"

"We explained it to the humans prior to using it. They knew what would happen, and we eased them into it. Eventually, it became routine. An intercom system in the brain."

"You said you use the Ark for the power, and also some gadget inside of it. What's this device?"

"A Mullilu."

"What's this Mulliluwawa thing look like?"

"Mullilu," he corrected. "It's in the shape of a pinecone."

Pinecone? Wasn't expecting that. I vaguely remembered watching a conspiracy show that talked about a pinecone-shaped object. "And the Ark, is that a gold chest with winged beings on top?"

"It's a tad more intricate than that," Ninurta said. "But basically that's correct. The Ark holds many of our most prized possessions."

"Like what?"

"So many wonderful things," he said, clapping his hands together. "The Mullilu, of course, a cross, a crown of thorns, the holy grail, a jar of oil, a footstool, a scepter, a sponge, a book of incantations, the tablet of the Ten Commandments, and a flask of manna."

I crossed my arms. "Are you messing with me? A sponge is a prized possession?"

"It is if you need to rub oil all over someone."

Okay, that's creepy. "Excuse me?"

Ninurta laughed. "Most of those items were used to assemble a transportation device. One of the steps to prepare for travel called for the passenger to cover their body in a conductive oil. But none of that concerns you. Only the Mullilu."

"Hey, wait," I said, the conspiracy TV show coming back to me. "I saw this special on the Vatican. They made all this fuss about this knobby doodad that resembled a pinecone. There's a mammoth statue of one in the courtyard of Vatican City, and another on the Pope's staff. They presented all these other instances of the pinecone appearing in art, statues, structures, and secret society rituals. All of those are representations of this device?"

"If only I had a gold star to give you," Inanna said. "Such a smart little human."

I scowled at her remark, and then continued questing Ninurta. "And that's it? I just bust open the Ark, touch this Mulilalalalula and shazam, I can communicate with all humans?"

"Mullilu," he corrected again.

"Can we please call it the Pinecone so I can pronounce it?"

"Fine. The Pinecone it is. It's almost that simple. The Ark must be taken to sacred ground to get the power it needs. Then you must place a pair of conductive bands on your wrists that will prevent your hands from melting off."

"Lovely."

"After that, you will unlock the Ark, and as soon as you touch the Pinecone inside, all humans will hear your every thought."

My mind raced to determine if I could actually pull this off or not. I wasn't feeling confident. The way I saw it, this could go down one of two ways: humans hear my voice in their head and conclude a divine presence is guiding them to salvation, or it backfires and drives everyone to bash their heads into a wall.

I released my exasperation with a growl. "This whole thing is insane. I don't get why you can't save the good ones and be done with it."

"It wasn't only for us to decide," Inanna said. "There are fifty-two other civilizations that have been observing Earth since the Great Flood, and laws have been established for everyone's protection."

"You obviously helped Noah and his family then," I retorted. "I mean, can't you do something similar now?"

Another of the Anunnaki stepped forward. In contrast to the others, he had a formal, almost ancient appearance about him. His silver hair went past his shoulders and was crimped into an intricate chain mail type pattern, alternating between tight square grooves and looser wavy ones, kind of like a basket weave. His beard cascaded down his chest, matching the length of his hair precisely, and was styled in the same pattern—except for the tip, which was ironed flat. If not for the fact he was wearing glasses, his muscular body and sharp facial features would have been identical to the drawings you see of mighty Greek gods like Zeus or Poseidon. Power practically rolled off him in waves, yet his aura was fatherly, caring, wise and comforting. When he spoke, I was glued to his every word.

"That rescue was not a sanctioned one," he said. "Although it was forbidden by Anu, our leader, I entrusted Ziusudra—or Noah, as he is known to you—to preserve your species during the flood." He addressed the next part to the council. "Forbidden, despite my sworn testimony that I had been visited by The Creator of All himself and instructed to save the human race."

Ninurta gave an exaggerated cough, and I distinctly heard him say "liar" under his breath.

Mr. Fatherly Anunnaki continued. "Regardless, I had no intention of sitting back and doing nothing while my beautiful creation perished senselessly in the flood. Therefore I, shall we say, *creatively* found a way around the ruling and secretly instructed Ziusudra on how to build the Ark."

His creation? Then it hit me. How did I not work it out sooner? "You're Enki?"

"Yes." He grinned proudly.

I fell to my knees. Not due to an invisible force, but from the honor of being in his presence. The creator of man stood a mere ten feet from me. Ninurta snorted and rolled his eyes at my attempt to bow.

"No need for all that," Enki said, gesturing for me to stand. "Though I do thank you for your graciousness." I rose as instructed. "There were profound repercussions for what I did—for saving humans."

"Enki, errr, sir…" I spluttered. "Sorry, what should I call you?"

"Enki is fine." He smiled and pushed up the glasses on his nose.

"Enki, despite the repercussions, we are here, and you're here—so it all panned out in the end, right? Can't that happen again?"

"It's not up to just us anymore. You see, when you were created, we, the Anunnaki, were the only ones to ever visit your planet."

"Really?" I said.

Ninurta chuffed, "This solar system isn't exactly a high-rent district."

"If I may proceed without further interruptions?" Enki said. "After the Great Flood, other races arrived to observe the resilient human race I had created. That is when the Galactic Federation got involved. While the human race rebuilt, the Federation monitored your evolution and decided to give you one last chance to evolve from your tendency toward evil. To let you mature without intervention and observe what choices you made. Even though you didn't exactly mature as we hoped, after much deliberation we agreed that when Nibiru approached again—and that time is now at hand—if one third of the human population advanced to an enlightened stage and accepted love, those individuals would be transferred to a new planet."

One of the other Anunnaki stirred at Enki's words. It was the one who didn't have his hands clasped under his chest in the same manner as the others. I had the feeling that signified something important. His hair was pitch black, long and sleek, and unmistakably dyed; his gray roots stuck out like a sore thumb. Dude needed a trip to Supercuts. As if wanting to amplify his phony facade, his beard was colored to match, and was smooth and manicured, forming a perfect upside-

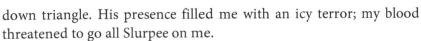

down triangle. His presence filled me with an icy terror; my blood threatened to go all Slurpee on me.

The Iceman continued where Enki left off. "And if you all welcome sin with open arms, as I know you will, every last one of you will be exterminated." He planted a glare on me that made me shiver. "*All* of you." His piercing blue eyes were not alluring like Rigel's. They were lurid and full of hate. "For when you do, it will demonstrate that the depravity of humans has festered into a pustule not fit for existence. You're a genetic mistake that needs to be eradicated."

That's one way of putting it.

Even though Mr. Iceman scared the living daylights of me, I swallowed my fear and asked, "How will you determine if one third of humans are 'good,' anyway? Where's the magic meter that will decide if humans passed the test?"

"You're looking at it," Mr. Iceman said, beaming with pride.

"Oh, yeah, that's totally fair." I raised my hands in forfeit. "Might as well finish us off straightaway if *you* are the judge and jury."

I immediately regretted that statement. I closed my eyes and waited for Mr. Iceman to zap me with his evil witchcraft, or whatever it was, for speaking to him in that tone.

Instead he let loose with a laugh that made me shudder. It was not the "funny ha ha" kind of laugh, more along the lines of: "I am going to enjoy crushing you like a bug and plucking off each limb before I wrap my fingers around your throat and squeeze until your brains ooze from your ears."

Inanna's gaze leapt back and forth between Mr. Iceman and me. What was she doing? Apparently I wasn't seeing the elephant in the room. Based on the gleam in her eyes, it was a big fat one wearing a top hat and sweater vest.

Her lip twitched as she said, "Our oaths bind us to the truth. We will know if he's lying and if he is reading the humans correctly."

Reading the humans correctly? What the heck does that entail? What talent does this dude have?

"I have talents you can't even imagine," Iceman hissed.

Did I say that out loud? All the blood rushed to my head, the pressure thudding with each heartbeat. *How did he know what I was thinking?*

"Because I can hear you," he said.

Oh, shit.

"Oh, shit is right."

You can read my mind?

"Bingo," he confirmed.

Rigel placed his hand on my back in a warning. It wasn't until he touched me that I noticed how much sweat had accumulated under my shirt. My whole body was drenched, and it didn't help matters that I wore a white T-shirt. Between my disaster date with Devon and this, I must have lost ten pounds in water weight alone. With these beings, I wanted to appear confident and in charge, but instead, I was about to kick-start a wet T-shirt contest.

Mr. Iceman guffawed—clearly reading my thoughts—and I covered my chest the best I could with my arms. I desperately tried to picture kittens and daisies, but that proved impossible. His supercharged ESP thing was going to be a problem.

"Well, that sucks." I said.

I returned my attention to Enki. His fatherly presence somehow calmed me. "And let me guess: if you try to bail us out again, including me, a war will arise?"

"That's correct."

Mr. Iceman was relentless with his damn rubbernecking. It was as if he had made it his mission in life to make me lose my concentration. *Two can play at that game.* I fixed my sights on him and thought about a steaming turd, adding a few chunks of carrots and corn for greater impact, then mentally asked, *What's your name?*

"Enlil," he answered, looking thoroughly entertained.

I conjured up an image of a penis, then stomped on it with a foot. He flinched.

"Nice to meet you, Enlil." I smiled.

Inanna must have figured out what was going on, because she intervened before I managed to get myself killed. "So, Autumn," she said. "Do you want to do it? Be the one to use the Pinecone?"

Rigel stepped between us. "Inanna, please. You can't expect her to do this. You know what this means for us."

"I'm just asking if she's interested, Rigel. Nothing is being decided right now. Ultimately, it is up to you both. That is, if she can even handle using it."

All my muscles contracted in fear. It was decision time—for me at least. The question was: Did I even *want* to do it? The skin-melting aspect of it didn't bother me; it couldn't be worse than having my soul ripped apart. In fact, that is exactly why I would be able to succeed when no one else had. I'd experienced and lived through more pain than the Pinecone could possibly deliver. What bothered me was figuring out what to say to people to get them to stop lighting cars on fire and hug it out instead. I mean, of course I needed to do everything in my power to preserve the human race. But what if I ended up sending them to their death by accident? They could be ready to pass the test and catch a ride on the eleventh hour bus to Righteousnessville, and then my nagging rant comes along and ruins it all.

No way they would wake from their evil stupor without intervention though, right? Absolutely not. I had to do it.

"One question first," I said. "You came in here to announce your decision on this prophecy deal. What was it?"

She gestured to the Anunnaki behind her. "We are not in agreement. One of us views this state of affairs differently from the other eleven. We must take the evidence to Anu, our leader, and have him make a ruling."

"I think I can guess who the holdout is," I grumbled.

"Yes," she said. "Enlil is second in command and has the authority to override a majority vote. And he wants you dead."

He gave a sweeping bow.

"Dear lord," I sighed, gazing skyward. "And if you determine that I *am* the catalyst for the prophecy, you're still going to polish me off, right? I'm assuming I have to die for it to be completed?"

Inanna fidgeted with her nails, and that gave me the real answer despite the BS I knew she was about to spew. "We don't know. This is all new to us as well, and a delicate situation politically. I can't stress enough how imperative it is that we keep this quiet until it's understood further. If word leaks that you could be 'The One,' that'll start a conflict that nobody wants."

"I get it," I said, lifting my hands up in understanding.

There was only one way this prophecy could come to fruition. The gold thread was after my soul. In order to take it, I had to die and separate from this body. What destiny I would ultimately have was anyone's guess, but given the hell I experienced trying to enter the next dimension, I knew I wasn't going to ascend into a land of fluffy clouds and harps.

"You don't have to say it," I continued. "I know I'd already be dead if not for my bond with Rigel. My soul would've been shredded back in that shed. Barring any divine intervention from this Creator of All to get humans to see the light, you intend on executing me along with the rest if I'm not The One." I said this last part with a sour expression. "And if you do determine I am The One, you're going to kill me to fulfill the prophecy anyway. Sooo..."

Rigel cut in. "We don't know if your death is the trigger. We don't know how it's fulfilled."

I wished with everything in me that was the case, that this prophecy gave us an option to be together for eternity. It simply wasn't to be. Giving Rigel an unconvinced side glance, I said to Inanna, "If I'm doomed anyway, what do I have to lose? I have a shot to save the human race. I can't say no to that. So I say, why not take a crack at it?"

Rigel turned away from me and walked to Devon's bedside. Was he upset because I had volunteered too easily? Either way my death was inevitable. He had to know that.

Inanna startled me when she grabbed my arm and whispered in my ear, "It's not only you that will die." She motioned to Rigel.

I sucked in a breath. "Oh, god."

My chest became a hollow pit that was quickly filled by guilt and anguish stronger than any I'd felt before—deeper than when my parents were killed. It hadn't registered that my death would equate to Rigel's death, even though I knew the truth of it. Fuck! Of course it would. He died when I did. How could I have been so selfish? There I was, spouting on, making decisions and acting as if I didn't care about dying—about *him* dying. Rigel deserved better than that.

Tentatively, I walked over to him.

He turned to face me, then took my hands and placed them against his beating heart. Mine sped up to match his erratic pace.

"Rigel, I didn't... I don't want..."

"Shhh." His face became stained with golden tears. The sight made my throat tighten and my eyes burn with emotion. Pulling me in, he pressed his forehead against mine. "We might be able to save you, Autumn. We can keep you alive for a while until we understand exactly how this prophecy is fulfilled. We know what it says, but we don't fully understand it yet. Plus, there are four lines of the prophecy we haven't deciphered yet. If we have truly set events in motion, then maybe we will finally be given the key to break the encryption on the last part. Or perhaps one of the other people trying the Pinecone will build a tolerance and can do it." His fingers roamed along my chin and down my neck, which normally would have had me doing somersaults, but right then it just left me numb. There was a finality in his gesture. "If you die, I die too," he said in a whisper.

The room pitched as his words punctured my heart. Unable to speak, I choked on my breath. My vision filled with images of Rigel's charred, limp remains contrasting with the colorless cement below him, and the memory of his screams beat against my eardrums.

I slid to the floor and stared at what was probably the very spot where Rigel had almost died, writhing in pain as he felt every stab delivered to my heart.

Rigel joined me on the floor. He traced his finger along the concrete in a figure-eight pattern. "I will do it for you," he breathed. I couldn't look at him, not after I'd blown him off like his existence was of no consequence. "I'll die… if that's what you want."

That cut me to pieces. I cried like a baby, my tears pattering on the ground. When he slid closer to me, I drew away, wanting to avoid contact of any sort—I didn't deserve it after what I'd done. I crawled to Devon's bed and used the edge to help me stand.

"Of course I don't want you to die," I said between ragged breaths. "*I* don't want to die."

This time when Rigel moved to gather me in his arms, I didn't fight it.

"All of those people," he murmured, "they could be saved." He said this in a way that made me believe he was trying to convince himself, as well as me, that it was the right thing to do. I pressed my face into his shirt in unspoken agreement, and let out snotty sobs of grief.

"I'll do it!" I heard a voice rasp beside me.

We all turned. Devon was sitting upright, all bright-eyed and bushy-tailed.

"Devon!" I exclaimed.

Rigel let me go, and I gave Devon a bone-crushing hug. It didn't even take a second for nausea to strike this time, and I heaved magnificently beside his bed.

"That's what I call a welcome home greeting," Devon said, beaming. "Now, let's pray the rest of the human race doesn't have the same reaction when I strap on my superhero cape and share with them my patented ten-step guide to love and enlightenment." He patted his hair to check its status. "All I need is a can of number twelve hairspray and I'll be ready to rock."

20

TORTUROUS BOWLING BALLS, ELECTRICAL FRO, ERECTILE DYSFUNCTION, AND FUCKFACE FUCKERS

Devon, Rigel, and I crowded in front of a sphere roughly the size of a bowling ball. It was defying gravity, floating three feet above its pedestal, and inside it, a tiny storm brewed. Lightning flashed and clouds churned. The globe itself twisted and rolled, constantly changing directions, but the interior weather remained unaffected. When the storm swirled into a hurricane, Devon grew pale.

Inanna snuck up behind us, making us all jump. "This is what we fondly call the Orb of Agony," she said. "It simulates the excruciating, flesh-melting misery that racks your body when using the Pinecone—but without the horrific death." She plastered on an over-the-top grin when she said that last part, and I swear one of those cheesy commercial sparkle things glinted on her perfectly white teeth. "Word of warning: the nightmarish suffering the orb induces isn't gradual. Once you touch this orb—or the Pinecone when the time comes—the torture is instantaneous. None of the humans that have trained thus far have been able to cope. The record is three words. Well, four if you count *motherfucker* as two words, which I don't."

Had it been appropriate to laugh, I would have, because that was kinda funny.

Devon grinned wide and said, "So my plan of saying 'Wake up motherfuckers' when the time comes wouldn't be the best way to convince one third of the population to love one another? Is that what you're trying to tell me?"

I snorted. I couldn't help it.

The corner of Inanna's mouth rose in a smile. "To each their own. If calling your fellow humans 'motherfuckers' will make them join together and sing 'Kumbaya,' then by all means, 'motherfucker' away." Ignoring our raised eyebrows, she continued, "Devon, ready to take this for a test drive?"

He sure didn't look ready. In truth, he was sort of green. Nonetheless, he shrugged and said, "Um... yeah. I mean, I already died, so how much worse could it be?"

"The best thing about this machine Enki built," Inanna offered, "is that the instant you let go, the pain ceases. There are no lasting effects. It was created that way to allow the trainee to build up a tolerance to it. Unfortunately, no one has developed any sort of resistance yet. We even had to commit one to a mental institution."

"Well, that puts my worries at ease," Devon said, swallowing hard. "Thanks for the pep talk."

"No problem. Now hurry before you lose your nerve." Inanna clapped excitedly as if she were about to witness a baby taking its first steps.

Through clenched teeth, Devon whimpered, "Okay."

Rigel and I both took a few steps back. I wasn't sure about Rigel, but I didn't step away to give Devon room, I wanted to make sure I didn't get zapped by accident.

As Devon readied his hands over the orb, my muscles were as taut as a bowstring; I was scared he might accidentally bump it. Then he sucked in a breath, scrunched his face in anticipation of the pain, and slammed his palms down on the orb like he was playing Whammy.

"MOTHERFUCKER!"

He howled and leaped back, panting, his face contorted in horror. I ran to him, careful to keep a safe distance. Vomit was definitely not going to help at the moment—not that there was a time it ever did.

"Shucks," Inanna said snapping her fingers in mock disappointment. "Too bad that only counts as one word."

Devon gave her an aggravated scowl and said, in a perfect Jackie Gleason impersonation, "Har har de har har har."

I suddenly noticed that Devon's hair was at max volume. "Hey! It frizzed your hair. Instant number twelve!"

He patted it. "Well, what do you know? How does it look?" He hustled over to look at his reflection in the orb.

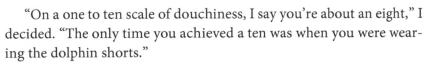

"On a one to ten scale of douchiness, I say you're about an eight," I decided. "The only time you achieved a ten was when you were wearing the dolphin shorts."

We chuckled at the memory. I felt a pang of jealousy emanate from Rigel, so I returned to his side and squeezed his hand in mine.

"You gonna take it for another ride?" I asked Devon.

"You know it!" He bounced from side to side, reminding me of a boxer readying for a fight. His arms flailed a little too much though, making him appear more like Gumby than Muhammad Ali.

He touched the orb again.

"MOTHERFUCKER!"

It took ten more attempts before he was able to graduate from *Motherfucker* to *Cocksucker*. I personally thought that was a promising improvement, but neither Inanna nor Rigel shared my enthusiasm.

"How about we take a break?" Inanna said. She sounded exasperated, and I thought she was ready to call it quits permanently. "You and Devon must be hungry, and I need Rigel to talk to the council about our prophecy *issue*."

She added a mocking tone to the word "issue." That put me off. Granted, she was completely deficient in the humor department, so that could have been her way of keeping things light. *Seriously, though, if I am The One, shouldn't I be part of the debate?*

Mimicking her mocking tone, I said, "Uh, don't you think I should have a say in your prophecy *issue*—as I *am* the issue?"

"You will in time," Inanna said, immediately cutting short my protest. "Please, we need to discuss it among the Twelve right now."

"You mean the Thirteen, don't you? Counting Rigel?" I corrected, crossing my arms in an admittedly childish pout. "Or is Anunnaki math different than ours?"

Her features tightened with irritation.

"Fine, whatever," I said. "Where do we go to get food?"

In answer to my question, the door slid open and another Anunnaki came in. Physically, he was identical to the rest of them—tall, blond hair, blue eyes—but he didn't exude authority or command attention like the others did. And his outfit was weird. He wore some sort of futuristic prison garb: a black, ultra-shiny, full body jumpsuit with matte gray stripes spiraling down it. It had a V-neck with two layers of fabric surrounding the neckband, one red and one black. He set down a tray of sandwiches and veggies. My stomach grumbled at the sight.

"If you need anything," Inanna instructed, "call on one of the Igigi. They will help you.

"Igigi?"

"The men in the jumpsuits."

Without further explanation, she bustled away, and Rigel and the Igigi trailed behind. Rigel gave me an apologetic frown as the door closed behind them.

As soon as they had left, Devon and I dug in like vultures. I assumed the sandwiches would be *out of this world*, no pun intended, since the "gods" made them. But to be honest, they had about as much flair as a five-dollar foot long. The only thing that made these alien subs superior to my beloved Subway Club was the price: free. Therefore, they beat Subway—on a technicality.

"So anyway," Devon said, dipping a carrot in ranch dressing. "What's this 'prophecy' you all are talking about?"

"Oh, that." I waved it off theatrically. "Just an eons-old prediction that doesn't end well for me."

"I figured that much. What's the deal?"

I gave him the play-by-play of all that had happened, including my interpretation of the creation story and the Great Prophecy of the Souls. I described these things from the standpoint of a non-believer, so I'm sure the Anunnaki would have wholeheartedly disagreed with my analysis. I also omitted the part where my soul almost got ripped apart in the shed, mostly because I didn't want to relive that. I did mention the kisses between Rigel and me—which was awkward. For both our sakes, I kept the descriptions sterile—no mentioning orgasms or moaning.

He munched on a pepperoncini, juice dribbling on his shirt. "Not that I have a complex or anything, but is that the reason why you toss cookies when you touch me? 'Cause of the connection you and Rigel have?"

That was an excellent question, and one I didn't have a definitive answer to. I did have a strong suspicion, though. "I think so. I'm fairly certain my soul is rejecting yours. If this prophecy is to be believed, it only wants him, and anyone else it casts off."

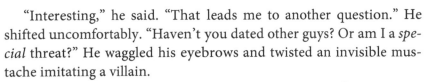

"Interesting," he said. "That leads me to another question." He shifted uncomfortably. "Haven't you dated other guys? Or am I a *special* threat?" He waggled his eyebrows and twisted an invisible mustache imitating a villain.

My cheeks flushed with heat. "Umm... uh... umm..."

"Dang, sorry. I didn't mean to pry. You don't have to say anything."

"No, that's okay," I said, brushing crumbs off my shirt to buy time to decide how I wanted to answer. "After all, you're sacrificing yourself to save humanity. I doubt you'll have time to write a tell-all unauthorized biography."

"There is that," Devon agreed, grabbing another sandwich.

"The thing is, when I was growing up, I wasn't attracted to men." I covered my mouth, realizing I'd made it sound like I was a lesbian. Devon gave me an emoticon-worthy surprise face that morphed into a naughty smirk.

"No—it's not like that," I said quickly. "All through high school I was uninterested, too busy with extracurricular activities. For a while I blamed the lack of free time for keeping me single. Guys would ask me out, but I didn't have time between homework and my after-school stuff. And yes"—I gave Devon the same naughty look he had just given me—"it occurred to me that maybe I was attracted to girls."

His eyes bugged out, reminding me of a bush baby. "You gave it the old college try, I hope?"

"I did." I blushed. "Sorry to burst your bubble, but it was a no-go. In college, I forced myself to date. The first boy I was going to... you know... do it with... He couldn't get it to stand at attention. No amount of play time would make a difference. It just hung there, deflated."

Devon spit his partially chewed sandwich on the polished floor. "That sucks."

"Tried that too. Unsuccessful."

For a moment I was afraid Devon might be choking, then he said, "Autumn! I didn't know you had it in you."

I was about to take advantage of that perfect setup, but Devon shielded his ears. "Stop! I can only handle so much."

"That's what she said."

"No way!" he gasped.

I giggled with pride.

Devon's face contorted in concentration. I could tell he was working hard to make sure his next sentence was clear of sexual innuendo. He settled on, "Please proceed with your narrative," pausing between words to double check for other meanings.

"Okay. Let's see. Guy number two fell off the bed and broke his arm when we were stripping each other's clothes off. Number three was the opposite of what happens with you: *he* heaved on *me*. Number four got explosive diarrhea both times we neared the hot-and-heavy level."

"Whoa, whoa... hold on. At this point, weren't you suspecting anything?"

I chuckled. "Yes, I thought there was something wrong with me. I abandoned dating altogether after number seven."

"Number seven?" he said. "What happened to the other three?" Then he waved me off. "Never mind. I'm not sure I want to know."

"Let's just say the last one spoke an octave higher for a few weeks."

He held up his hands. "Okay, seriously, you can stop now.

"Got smashed by a falling bookcase."

"Anyway... so, you think all of that was because of your soul?"

"Yes. It all makes sense. And it's actually a total relief."

Devon rubbed his forehead as he thought about this. He opened and closed his mouth a few times like he wanted to ask me something, but couldn't seem to say it out loud.

"It's okay, spit it out," I coaxed. "It can't be that bad."

He drew in a breath and puckered up as if he'd eaten a lemon. "Then you... haven't... had..." he stuttered and coughed, "... sssse-ex?"

I wished I could fold into myself and hide at that moment. Instead, I flamed in embarrassment. "No," I said, going for a whispered reply, but my nerves seized my vocal cords, and my voice was loud enough to echo off the walls.

"Wow! I mean... I don't know what I mean," he spluttered.

Then a new thought occurred to me: Was it possible Rigel was a virgin too? *No way.* After centuries of failed attempts at sex, he would have exploded by now, or would be in some galactic prison after snapping some poor schmuck's head off for daring to sneeze in his direction. Plus, girls are always getting gypped in these deals. Periods alone are proof that God is a dude.

"No worries," I said, shrugging it off as if it was no big deal. "I'm thrilled it wasn't something I did wrong. I had self-esteem issues for a while."

"You? You're gorgeous!" he blurted out, and then turned redder than me.

I smiled, feeling shocked but flattered by his comment. "Thanks." Not wanting the conversation to go in a direction it shouldn't, I added, "How about a change of subject?"

He nodded in agreement. Neither of us offered up anything new to talk about, so our discussion went on hiatus while we shoveled in food. The crunching of our raw veggies was oddly comforting.

"What about your family?" I asked once my tummy felt sated. "Did they freak out after the announcement?"

"Honestly, I don't know. I became so obsessed with snatching up anything that contained a circuit board that I never made it home to check."

"I am sure we can find out how they are doing. They checked on Emma for me."

"That'd be cool," he said. "Even though my family bugs the snot out of me ninety percent of the time, I still love 'em. Especially my prick emo brother."

Devon got up and walked to the porthole.

"You okay? I asked.

"How freakin' insane is all this? I mean come on! We are on a spaceship, eating alien sandwiches, and plotting to save the human race like some misfit superhero squad."

"I know, right?" I agreed with a grin. I still couldn't wrap my mind around it.

"Well, I reckon I should keep plugging away at the ol' Orb of Agony." He rubbed his hands together in preparation.

"You don't want to wait till they get back?"

"Nah. Honestly, I prefer having only you here anyway." He cracked his knuckles and pointed at the orb with his thumb like a car salesman pushing for a test drive. "Wanna give this bad boy a spin? It's a hoot!"

The door opened, and Rigel and Inanna entered. Rigel ran over and yanked me into a hug. I felt breathless with the instant connection between us. The kiss he planted on me was supercharged. And, as usual, I forgot we had an audience. I proceeded to grope, eagerly pawing at the muscles on his chest, then sliding lower to his abs, the exquisite ridges causing those familiar tingles. Before our souls could launch from our bodies—and before my roving hands traveled past the point of no return—he broke away.

"That was a stellar greeting," Devon said. "Where's my kiss?" He extended his arms to Rigel.

To my surprise, and probably her own as well, Inanna chuckled.

"How did it go?" I asked, brushing my hair back in place. "I take it you have good news?"

Rigel tugged his shirt down but didn't say anything. It was Inanna who replied.

"We have agreed that, no matter what happens with the humans, we will spare you until we can understand fully this soul bond between you two."

Spare me? I wasn't sure I liked that choice of words.

Rigel put his hands in his pockets. By the glimmer of sorrow in his eyes, I knew he was about deliver bad news.

"I tried, I did," he said. "I couldn't get them to save Emma. I was hoping we could get her here to be with you for as long as we could."

It took me a minute to realize why I was angry. It wasn't the news about Emma—I mean, of course I didn't want her to die, but given the politics involved, I hadn't even considered saving her an option. No, what ticked me off was that they were acting as though they would be doing me a favor by "sparing" me after Earth was destroyed. It was absurd, not to mention cruel, to keep me alive just long enough to see everything and everyone I loved get incinerated.

"And what if this bond is a big fat zero?" I asked, backing away from Rigel. "You open the airlock and toss me into the sun?"

Rigel went pale. It was wrong of me to blame him. I knew it wasn't his fault, but I couldn't help but be pissed that they regarded us as disposable objects. Rats they could exterminate if the lab experiment didn't produce the desired outcome. *Then again, aren't all humans lab rats right now, awaiting the results of the litmus test for righteousness?*

"Autumn, we don't know yet," Inanna said. "We don't want to see you dead. Honestly. But we have made it clear that keeping you is a serious risk for us. Not to be dramatic, but if you're discovered, it will bring about a universal war that could ultimately eradicate a majority of the species alive today."

"Ohhhh…" I said sarcastically. "Well, in that case, let me buy a gallon of SPF one billion for when you send me on a permanent vacation into the molten core!"

I pitched an assortment of veggies at the door, yelling obscenities as each one hit.

Devon broke the tension. "Hey, so… I'm all rested and ready to go, if the pep squad wants to hear me cuss more?"

"I think Autumn may have the cussing covered," Inanna said.

I plopped against the door, exhausted from my hysterical outburst. "I say we go until you say 'fuckface fuckers.'"

"Deal!" Devon agreed.

21

A SIX-PACK SHOCKER, HOMICIDAL HAIRSPRAY, AND BOXER WHIPLASH

Although I cracked jokes to keep the mood light while Devon endured the orb's abuse, it soon became unbearable to watch him struggle. At times I had to excuse myself to hide the tears I couldn't seem to control. The kid had determination. The problem was, he had been torturing himself for hours and hadn't yet managed to scream one real sentence. (Well, that's not entirely true; he did say, "Fuck this!" one time.) Unless humankind was ready to hop aboard the happy train in response to hearing Devon yell every profanity in the book, we were doomed.

After hour six of his labored efforts, Inanna recommended we all take a break. When I went to give Devon yet another pep talk, Inanna grabbed my arm and gestured for me to follow her. Rigel had joined Devon, patting his shoulder in encouragement, so I went with Inanna into the corridor.

Her posture was stiff, her strides quick, and, quite frankly, her demeanor had me worried. She came to a halt as soon as we turned the corner and I almost ran into her.

"Autumn," she said, followed by a pause.

I knew what she was going to say, so I said it first. "You don't think he can master it, do you?"

"I truly honor his effort; I do. But regrettably, we are running low on time."

"I know."

"I didn't want to ask in front of Rigel, because I know he'd never allow it to happen, but... do you want to give it a test run?"

My legs wobbled, and I had to lean against the wall for support. Rigel had been thrilled when he'd learned they weren't going to kill me right away. A few extra days with him—heck, a few extra hours—would be terrific. No, I couldn't allow myself to think that way. This was the entire human race we were talking about.

"I kinda have no choice," I said. "Because of this whole prophecy thing, will I need to get approval from your leader or whatever?"

Inanna leaned against the wall next to me. "No one will oppose your using the communication device. If you are the catalyst, this is one way to find out. And frankly, it saves us the hassle of neutralizing you."

"I don't get it," I said. "Why this dog-and-pony show to prolong my execution? Why not make Enlil's day and serve me up in a body bag right now?"

There was an uncomfortable silence before Inanna spoke the one word that made my insides ache. "Rigel." She pushed herself away from the wall and turned her back to me. "There are many of us who don't want to see him go."

A pang of guilt stung me at the reminder that his death would ultimately be my fault, and it was made worse by Inanna's obvious distress.

She continued, "We both know we can't let a war develop, especially if word spreads that your soul is blue. All the same, it would've been nice to extend this long enough so that Rigel's family could make it here to see him." She faced me again. "Rigel doesn't know this, but the decision was strictly political. His parents pulled some strings on Nibiru to make it happen."

Rigel's family. Of course they would all want to see each other one last time. Rigel deserved that much. Why hadn't I considered his family in all this? Heck, I didn't know if he had brothers or sisters. It was frightening to think that I loved someone I knew so little about. I still couldn't believe his mom was president of an entire planet. I wondered how different things were on Nibiru. *Do they drive cars, or flash everywhere? Do they go to movies? What kind of food do they eat? Do they have heavy metal music?*

Inanna interrupted my reverie. "I'm going to ask Rigel to take Devon to his room for the night. We'll have about ten minutes until he returns, and during that time, I think you should try the orb… to at least see if it's a viable option."

"Rigel will be able to feel it too, you know."

"I know. I thought you might want to do it without asking him first."

"You're right. One kiss and I'm putty in his hands." I pushed off the wall. "He isn't going to be keen on the sudden onset of 'nightmarish suffering,' as you so lovingly called it."

"Devon will comfort him." Inanna winked. "I will meet you at the orb. Why don't you take a moment to prepare yourself." She headed back to the room.

I closed my eyes and thought about Rigel in the parking lot of Barnes & Noble, the sun glinting behind his golden hair as it danced in the wind. That vision was absolute perfection. I decided he would be my anchor when I attempted to use the orb. As the suffering increased, I would escape into the blue of his eyes.

When I returned to the room, Rigel and Devon had already left.

Inanna eyed me cautiously. "You sure you want to do this?"

"Yes." I tried to sound determined, but my insides didn't share the same confidence.

I walked over to the orb and visualized Earth within its depths: the sapphire oceans, the snow-capped mountains, the majestic redwood forests. The fury over all of it being wiped out stamped out my fear, and I zeroed in on the orb's sinister storm, circling it as if stalking prey. Concentrating on the rolling clouds, I let my mounting rage feed my determination.

I inched my hands toward the orb, and my limbs stiffened in anticipation. Before I locked on, I brought forth an image of Rigel: that night I had him trapped in the beam of my headlights, the mist swirling around him like some special effects artist had put it there.

My palm connected with the cold surface, and my entire nervous system erupted with pain—like millions of nails were being driven into my skin, piercing muscle, slicing nerves, and severing tendons.

I screamed.

The vision of Rigel I had worked hard to lock into place burst into an inferno of orange and yellow flames. I let go. The pain stopped instantly.

"Concentrate!" Inanna yelled. "Think of Rigel!"

I nodded and tried again. This time I grasped the orb roughly, foolishly reasoning that causing it pain would make it stop hurting me. Squeezing it with all my strength, I countered the burning by wailing louder than a foghorn. I felt as if I had been tied up with a live wire, doused with acid, and then tossed stark naked into the frigid waters of the Antarctic, where a school of piranhas tore at my flesh until only bones remained. But even with all that, it was nothing compared to how I had felt when my soul was ripped apart. The orb was a cakewalk compared to that.

"Don't just stand there like an idiot!" Inanna ordered. "Speak!"

That was when I noticed that my wailing had stopped. Clarification: I wasn't producing quite the same glass-breaking level of shrieking I'd delivered seconds ago. Involuntary whimpers still escaped.

I conjured up the first kiss between Rigel and me—the soaring out of my body, the heat, the sweat, the passion. I latched on to the image and wrestled to block the pain from taking over.

"I… will… not… let… go!" I forced out.

The pain eased a fraction, and I gritted my teeth.

"I…can… do… this."

Then the vision of Rigel's angelic face and blazing blue eyes came to me, and he offered me that sexy half-smile. The pain lowered to a level eight, one I could actually speak through. "I can really do this," I said much more coherently.

Someone yanked me from the orb, and its assault on me ceased.

"What are you doing?" Rigel panted, embracing me with trembling arms. His skin had turned white and pasty and his eyes were a sickly gray. I couldn't imagine how hard it was for him to get here through all that pain. Shame and remorse punched my gut.

"I'm sorry," I said, looking into his dim eyes. "I had to try. I don't think Devon is going to be able to do it."

On cue, Devon barreled into the room wearing nothing but his boxers. My eyes went wide when I saw how fit he was. Not just "occasional gym" fit, but rock-hard six-pack abs goin' on. I had to force my eyes away so I didn't stare.

"What happened… where's the fire?" he said. "Did the Earth get pummeled? Rigel, you hurt?"

"I'm fine," Rigel said, withdrawing from me.

"Fine?" Devon sputtered. "You dropped to your knees and yowled like a madman. What in the platypus diaper dookie was that about?"

"It was my fault," I said. "I tried the orb."

"You what? What in blazes did you do that for?"

Inanna answered. "Time is almost up. Five days, and then Earth is no more."

"Five days?" Devon and I exclaimed in unison.

I had to lean against Rigel to stay steady. *Earth will be gone in less than a week.*

"Devon, you have shown exceptional strength," Inanna said striding over to him. At first I thought she might touch him, a mere human, but I was wrong. She swept past him. "You've succeeded far beyond what I imagined you capable of." *That's a backhanded compliment if I ever heard one.* "I am one hundred percent certain you could do it with a month of practice. But there isn't enough time."

"I'll keep practicing," Devon insisted. "I'm not ready to tap out yet."

"I can do it," I said, balancing on my own two feet again. "I was able to speak through the pain."

"What?" he said, and then stomped over to me like an angry child.

"I can do it, Devon. I know it."

"No! You'll die, Autumn. You will *both* die!"

"I know." That was all I could vocalize. I should've made an uplifting speech, as heroes usually do at this juncture of the story, to convince the disbelievers that we were taking the noble path. Instead I rallied with all the exuberance of a slug. All possible outcomes led to my demise, but at least this way, if I succeeded, Devon and Emma would live.

"No, Autumn. You can't." Devon stalked toward the orb. "I will do this!"

Rigel held his arm up to block him. Devon made a fist and pounded it into his other hand. He gave me one last plea. "What about your connection thingie-ma-bob? Are you willing to risk interfering with this prophecy? What if your death throws things off?"

"Devon, that's just it, I *do* know. In order for the prophecy to come to fruition, I..." I gulped down a lump in my throat and forced my eyes to meet Rigel's. "*We* need to die."

"We don't know that!" Rigel said.

"Rigel, you know it as well as I do," I said, sounding harsher than I meant to. "We have a death sentence with this thing."

Devon glanced at Inanna for confirmation. The subtle lowering of her head gave him his answer, and he deflated. "But they said they'd save you even if the humans insist on being dumbasses at the end."

"That was to buy time for Rigel to say goodbye to his family," I said.

I was rocked by a spasm of fury—not mine, but Rigel's. He was breathing heavy and shooting daggers at Inanna. I had a sneaking suspicion she was using her telekinesis to keep him at bay, because with the hatred that bubbled inside me, UFC-level fisticuffs would have ensued if Rigel could move about the cabin.

Inanna shook her head and took a deep breath. Apparently she was done with all this for the day. "Autumn, it's up to you," she said. "It's your call."

"No. It's not *only* my call," I clarified.

Rigel stiffened.

"Rigel, I can't do it without your permission. Both of our lives are at stake here. If you say no, I won't do it."

He cleared the space between us in three strides. His fingers brushed my forearms as he whispered, "If you want to do this, you know I'm willing to take the journey with you."

I focused my gaze on Rigel and responded with the only three words that could express how grateful I was to have him in my life: "I love you."

His eyes blazed, making my heart leap and take off at a full-blown sprint. With a growl he grabbed my shirt and pulled me in, kissing me as if this kiss might be our last. *And it very well could be.*

Devon gagged. "Get a room!"

Inanna hurled us in opposite directions. I blushed and straightened my clothes.

"Now that this is settled," said Inanna, "we need to present Devon to the Council of Twelve to determine what to do with him." Inanna stated this as though she were talking about a stray dog that had wandered aboard.

"What?" Devon and I said in unison.

"This speaking-at-the-same-time thing is getting annoying," Inanna said. "Since Devon isn't going to die after using the Ark, we must determine how to proceed with him."

"Excuse me?" I said, poised to attack.

Devon beat me to the punch. He stormed over to Inanna, crossed his arms, and said, "Oh, I'm joining them. I'm going to help Autumn and Rigel, and that's *final*. If the Council of Elders, or whatever you call yourselves, don't approve, you can kiss my shiny white ass."

"Oh, really?" Inanna crossed her arms too. "You think you can take us on? A mere human?"

"Bring it," Devon said, snapping twice. It brought to mind those *Step Up* movies, and I had a weird vision of the two of them doing a dance-off. Their argument was filled with a peculiar sexual tension— quite fascinating to watch.

"Your confidence is cute," Inanna said, pinching his cheek for added effect. He didn't flinch. "What are you gonna do? Hairspray us all to death?"

I wanted to hear Devon's retort, but to my disappointment, Rigel intervened. "Devon is right. He should go. He's part of this now."

"I want him there," I said. "I need him for moral support."

Inanna appraised Devon, her gaze lingering on the two peaks of hair that curled inward like a Tim Burton landscape. "I'll make that recommendation to the council," she said. She advanced threateningly on Devon, towering over him. If she had hackles, they would have been raised. "But be warned: we can't shelter you if this mission fails. If Autumn isn't successful, you will be transported to Earth to meet your fate with the rest of the humans."

"Fine."

"Fine," she said, and she sauntered out the door without another word.

So it was *sexual tension I sensed between them. Two little lovebirds sittin' in a tree!* Inanna put a whole new spin on the term "cougar." But hey, what was a few hundred thousand year age difference anyway? Speaking of age differences. I hadn't asked Rigel his age yet. *Do I want to know?* Unlike in vampire romance novels where a woman's immortal lover is at most one, maybe two centuries strong, mine could be thousands, or heaven forbid, *hundreds* of thousands of years old. That was a substantial amount of time to stockpile names in his little black book.

"We should all try to get some sleep," Rigel said. "We'll head out to get the Ark in the morning, and then make plans from there."

"Sounds good," I said. Although it really didn't sound good. Getting the Ark was the first step toward the end.

Devon twiddled his thumbs, not responding.

"Devon, you okay?" I asked.

His eyes downcast, he said, "Before you lovebirds go off and do things I'd rather not know about, can I ask you a favor, Rigel?"

"Sure. What is it?"

Devon sucked in his bottom lip. "I know this is a lot to ask given the dire circumstances, but... would it be okay if we made an un-scheduled pit stop during our fantastic adventure to save the world?"

"Stop? Where?"

"Umm..." He flushed. "It's my family," he said shyly. "Is there any way you can mind-meld them like you did with me? So I can say toodle-oo to my parents and my baby bro? I mean, just in case."

Rigel looked to me for confirmation and I nodded.

"Of course," he said.

Devon twisted his foot and it squeaked on the floor. "Thanks, man."

Rigel patted his shoulder. "You guys ready?" he asked.

All I could do was stare at Devon. The fact that he struggled to ask such a simple favor of us sent a wave of guilt crashing into me. Because of me he had come back from the great beyond to be human-kind's savior. *Who does that?* He deserved a medal for his bravery, not to be sentenced to death if I failed. I decided that if they hurt a single hair on his head, I would... I would... *What would I do? What could I do?*

"Hey, Autumn," Devon said. "Go."

"Devon, I..."

He gave me a reassuring nod. "You guys go ahead. I can find the way to my room."

"You sure?" Rigel asked.

"Yeah. I'm gonna stargaze for a bit." He gave a weak smile. "I heard reports of UFOs in the area."

Rigel nudged me toward the door.

"Okay, see you in the morning," I said. Devon nodded, and then ambled over to the porthole. When I saw his derriere—not that I was looking there on purpose—I snorted so hard I almost choked. The design on his boxers had me doing a double take that almost gave me whiplash. Plastered across the butt, in thick bold letters, were the words *NUMBER TWELVE.* And below that, two cans of hairspray were printed, one on each leg.

"Hey," Devon said without glancing back, "stop staring at my ass."

22

HUMAN COCKROACHES, '70S PORN MUSIC, AND CUSSING DOOR OPENERS

Rigel and I strolled along the corridor hand in hand. It was surprisingly comfortable, especially when you considered that we hadn't known each other for very long. There was no doubt that I loved him. The thing I didn't know was if this love was genuine, or heightened because of the bond. My heart believed it to be real, and that was the important part, I supposed. Either way, I was happy to have this alone time with him, even if I was dog tired and ready for naptime. I kinda wished he'd whisk me up and carry me to my room, which I prayed to sweet baby Jesus had a soft mattress. Their medical tables were hard metal slabs. I'd give anything for a cushy bed, fluffy pillows, and a down comforter.

"What's on your mind?" Rigel said.

"I'm tired is all. Been kind of a long day."

He raised my hand to his lips. When he kissed it, the surge of electricity from his touch gave me the instant rush of ten Red Bulls. My thoughts buzzed with the tremendous amount of stuff that had happened, including meeting Enlil, the telepathic ass.

"I do have a question about Enlil," I said.

Rigel rolled his eyes.

"Yeah, I know, another question." I did ask a lot of questions, but come on, I was entitled. "Why does he scare the crap out of me? It goes beyond the whole mind-reading ability."

"Come now," Rigel said. "Are you telling me you didn't fall in love with Enlil? Best friend to all mankind."

"Yes, such charisma he has. Can he eavesdrop on your thoughts too?"

"The Anunnaki are immune to that particular gift. You are smart to be skittish, and you should censor what you think when you're near him. He has no regard for the human race at all. In fact, he's the one who campaigned to let you all drown in the Great Flood. I wouldn't be surprised if he pre-ordered a cake to celebrate your impending demise."

"Why does he hate us so much?"

"He can't turn off the voices. Millions of humans continually clamoring in his head has made him a bit cranky."

"Was the flood his first crack at exterminating us?"

"Not by a long shot. He has quite the track record of trying to extinguish you: drought, starvation, sterilizing sheep, plagues, fires… you name it. By the time the deluge hit, he'd brought about so much devastation that humans were resorting to cannibalism to survive."

"That's awful! Why didn't he succeed with any of those? It sounds like he was close."

A slight grin creased the corner of Rigel's mouth. "It backfired in a grand way, thanks to Enki."

"I sensed some serious tension between Enki and Enlil."

"Oh, there is. See, before the flood, Noah sought Enki's advice on what humans could do to get Enlil to end the ongoing punishment. Enki, out of spite for Enlil, told Noah to get all the people to beg day and night for relief—to repeatedly project their thoughts at Enlil, asking him for forgiveness. The masses did as instructed and begged for his help, not knowing that this was the very reason Enlil wanted them all dead. Those were the first prayers to God—albeit the wrong entity, no thanks to Enlil claiming to be their Lord and Savior. Entire cities came together and prayed for forgiveness and salvation."

"That's not good."

"It's worse than you think. When that many people ask for something at the same time, it amplifies in Enlil's brain, driving him mad."

"Wow. Did he give in?"

"Yes. The humans' prayers were answered." Rigel chuckled. "Enlil caved out of sheer desperation to get them to stop."

"I wonder if Enlil can penetrate Devon's helmet of hair to read his thoughts?"

"You guys have gotten pretty close."

Rigel didn't say that with any jealously, but I felt bad. I did have an inexplicable connection to Devon, but it was… brother-like.

I pressed on with the discussion about the jerkwad mind reader. "I bet Enlil was pissed when he heard that Enki helped Noah build the Ark."

"That's putting it mildly. We were on the brink of a civil war due to their, let's call it, difference of opinion. If it wasn't for our leader, Anu, Enlil would've hunted down and exterminated all the humans that survived the flood, one by one."

"Wait. It wasn't just Noah and his family who survived the flood?"

"There were quite a few survivors. We uncovered pockets of people all over that had managed to climb their way to higher ground. Humans are extremely resourceful, which only fueled Enlil's hatred of you. You're tantamount to cockroaches in his eyes."

"Hmm. I think that's too high a status for what we are in his eyes. Discarded chewing gum maybe?"

"Or a rotten piece of fruit?"

"How about a festering septic tank?"

"There you go."

"Oh, hey." Tons of questions crowded my brain now that I had time to ask them. "What's up with Enki wearing glasses? Don't you guys have the ability to correct vision with your advanced technology? I don't scc anyone else using them."

"Ah, far-sighted Enki, yes. No one has been able to fix his eyesight. Our top physicians have tried everything, but it can't be corrected."

"Another thing I found freaky was the way the Anunnaki stood," I said. "What's that hands-clasped-under-the-chest pose you all do?"

"Oh, that. Their formality can be maddening. When they stand that way, it indicates a declaration of neutrality and good will."

"Aha! That explains why Enlil kept his hands to his sides."

"Now that you mention it, I can't remember the last time I've seen him take on the neutrality pose."

"Is that what you actually call it? It has a name?"

"It does. And that's precisely why prayer is usually done with your hands folded together."

"Really?"

"Yes. Humans understood that when one of us came and assumed that stance, we were coming in peace. However, as you can undoubtedly guess, Enlil didn't have a neutral bone in his body. So when he punished them, they all clasped their hands, hoping this gesture would prove that they meant no harm to him. Eventually, it became a staple of prayer—a show of solidarity."

"It's mind-boggling to discover how all this stuff came about."

We walked in silence for a bit, and then out of nowhere, I felt a rush of anticipation swell in my chest. I suspected Rigel was the cause.

"Are you nervous about something?" I asked.

He blushed. "I knew you could feel that."

"What's up?" I halted midstride to read his expression. It was set in what I can only describe as a squirrel about to be flung into the wide-open jaws of a lion. "Are you having second thoughts?"

He avoided eye contact, visibly grappling with his emotions. "No. I'm with you until the end."

"Then what?"

He adjusted his stance and fidgeted hesitantly. "Did you want to stay with me tonight… or shall I take you to your room?"

I froze. My throat went dry and my palms nearly liquefied. That option hadn't crossed my mind, especially since we had previously been tossed to opposite ends of the room when exchanging a simple kiss. (Okay, maybe *simple* isn't the correct word to describe our moments together.) But you could bet your sweet patootie I wanted to play roomies with him. I didn't have to think about that one twice. My thoughts filled with visions of acts that I'd wager were illegal in most states. If a rating system existed for such fantasies, X-rated might be about right. *Cue the '70s porn music.*

It was my turn to channel anxiety into Rigel. I was a virgin, and I highly doubted he was. In fact, now that I thought about it, I had seen him touch Inanna on multiple occasions. Was that an indication he didn't suffer from the same affliction I did?

Rigel coughed impatiently, waiting for my answer.

"Yes, of course I want to stay with you," I said excitedly, digging my mind out of the gutter. "Are we allowed to?"

He sighed in relief. "Considering we are about to die, I'm sure they will give us a pass."

My nerves sprung from the starting gate at this prospect. Somewhere in my gut, a jackhammer flipped on and woke my libido from its hibernation. I had to curb my temptation to do cartwheels as we continued down the hall.

Rigel stopped at a plain metal door. No number or doorknob or anything—just a thick sheet of reinforced steel.

"How can you tell these rooms apart?" I asked.

"It's an alien thing." He shrugged and lifted his hand to open the burnished slab.

"Hold on," I said. "I wanna say the magic word."

He conceded with a bow.

"Open says me," I said.

Rigel burst out laughing.

"What?" I asked.

"It isn't open *says me*. It's open *sesame*."

"What? Really? As in a sesame seed?"

"Well, yes, technically, spelling-wise."

"You mean all this time I've been saying open *says me* like an idiot?" Perplexed, and slightly embarrassed by this lifelong misunderstanding, I felt I had to justify myself. "Truthfully, it makes more sense my way: *says me*. Like I'm ordering the door to open. Open says me. *Sesame*… that's the street where Big Bird and Oscar the Grouch live."

"Okay, okay!" Rigel said, still laughing. "Open *says me* it is."

I waved my hand at the door and said it. It didn't open.

"You ass!" I huffed, jabbing him in the side.

Just then Devon appeared from the around the corner, power-walking, his boxers flapping in the wind. "Open you stupid motherfucker," he called as he rushed by.

The door opened.

Rigel and I succumbed to a fit of giggles as Mr. Supermodel Six-Pack scooted off to his room, his arms pumping and butt shimmying from side to side.

23

POOP-INDUCING WINE, MILLION-MILE-HIGH CLUB, AND A MAKESHIFT TOGA

I had expected Rigel's room to consist of the usual barren concrete quarters the rest of the ship provided. But when the door lifted, I was presented with something straight out of a *Better Homes and Garden* spread—front-page material to boot. It was a huge open space, I'm guessing around a thousand square feet. It had English chestnut hardwood floors with matching wood beams on the ceiling. In the corner was a gorgeous gourmet kitchen filled with stainless steel appliances. The living room had ultra-modern furniture atop a posh area rug.

"How about I open a bottle of wine?" Rigel suggested, guiding me inside.

"Praise Jesus!" I said enthusiastically, salivating at the idea. "That sounds like heaven."

"Please make yourself comfortable," he offered and then made his way to the kitchen to select a wine.

I did just that—kicked off my shoes and dove into the comfy couch. "I have to say, this isn't how I envisioned your humble abode."

"We do *live* on this ship, you know."

"Then why are the other rooms so... so...?" I couldn't think of how I wanted to phrase it.

"So concrete?"

"So freaking hideous," I said, candor winning out over politeness.

He chuckled. "It's practical. Does the job."

"I guess."

He fetched two glasses from the cabinet and poured the wine. The color was unusual—sort of an eggplant shade that shimmered—and very different from the merlots and cabernets I typically drank.

Normally I would go in for the kill, but this time I lingered when the wine's aroma hit my nose. It smelled of orange blossoms, cedar, and springtime. I would totally wear perfume made from this. After breathing in the incredible scent for the fifth time, I took my first sip (or more accurately, my first gulp) and it was phenomenal. The flavors exploded on my palate. I recognized rich dark cherry, chocolate, oak, coffee, plum, pepper, and blackberry. It was pure bliss as it made its way down my throat. By far this was the most exquisite thing to ever tantalize my taste buds—Rigel excluded, naturally.

"Holy hell!" I plucked the bottle away from him to inspect the label. "What varietal of wine is this?"

"The wine of the gods," he said, hoisting his glass in the air. I couldn't help but laugh. "We only have one winemaker on Nibiru. Her blends are perfection. No one else has ever bothered competing."

The label had an image of a radiant woman strategically covered in grape vines to hide anything too revealing. Her figure was slim and elegant. It read:

"What is Geshtinanna Karānuwhatever?" I asked.

"That woman is Geshtinanna," Rigel said, tapping the illustration. "She's our winemaker: the Mesopotamian goddess of winemaking and brewing. Karānu is the Akkadian word for wine."

191

"I thought Dionysus was the wine god?" I said absently as I read the alcohol content. *Wowzer! 33%.*

Rigel snorted. "Don't ever say that in front of Geshtinanna."

"Uh-oh, do I sense a juicy rivalry?"

"While Geshtinanna did produce all the wine on Nibiru, Dionysus stole all the credit for it on Earth, saying he made it himself. Needless to say, it made him popular among the Romans and Greeks. He had quite the business selling her bottles and living the life of a modern-day rock star: girls, gold, food, and lavish accommodations wherever he went. When Geshtinanna learned he was taking the credit for her wine, she was furious."

"I don't blame her. What did she do?"

"She told Dionysus of this delightful new blend she made," he said with a wide grin. "One made exclusively for him. One that put all others to shame with its succulent aromas and sophisticated palate of passionfruit, blackberry, cedar, and smoke. She even incorporated his chubby face on the label as a bonus. Dionysus transported thousands of cases to Earth, planning an extravagant party to celebrate his return. Unbeknownst to him, Geshtinanna had also added an additional ingredient: a generous dose of laxatives."

"What?"

"Yeah. He served it to kings, rulers, nobles... all of the elite."

"Oh, crap!" I laughed at my choice of words. "No pun intended. That must've been a disaster."

"He had to go into hiding for a while."

"That's fantastic!" I did a cheers to the bottle in appreciation.

That modest action made me aware of how fatigued I was; it required way too much energy to lift the glass. Exhaling, I leaned into the couch and nestled into the comfy pillow.

"You look tired," Rigel said.

"I am. This saving-the-world thing is exhausting."

Rigel set down his drink, blasted me with his magnetizing gaze, and slowly wrapped one hand around my waist, pulling me toward him. I quivered from his touch, my skin burning from the fever the sudden closeness prompted.

He took my wine from me and put it on the table. Then, in one steady motion, he whisked me up and placed me nimbly in his lap.

Being able to feel all of his emotions made the desire to unwrap him like a present twice as bad.

He tenderly swept my hair behind my ear and whispered, "I want you so bad right now."

"Do you now?"

I bent to kiss him. The instant we connected, electricity sizzled through our bodies. Groaning, he hastily swapped our positions, so he was on top of me, and pressed one leg between my thighs. One of his hands cupped my breast as he kissed my neck; the other hand teased the skin just underneath my shirt.

"Boy, you don't waste any time, do you?" I breathed.

His sexy half-smile lit up his face and he pressed his knee a little higher. The tingles of an orgasm arose between my legs. *No way am I going to last more than a minute at this rate.* Desperately needing things to progress more quickly, I clawed at my clothes, trying to remove them.

Brushing his lips against my ear, Rigel rumbled, "So impatient." His hot breath against my skin brought on the inevitable vibrations.

"Just a bit," I panted.

With a throaty chuckle, he trailed his tongue along my cheek until he reached my mouth. He lingered there, brushing his bottom lip against mine. One brush… then another.

"What are you waiting for?" I protested.

"Just slowing things down for you."

"Well, stop it." I meant that to be playful, but my need practically had me snarling at him. He was driving me insane.

With another chuckle, he bit my bottom lip, sucking it into his mouth. The building pressure in my core made me moan.

He grinned at me. "If *that* set you off, you'd better get prepared for what I'm going to do next."

My heart pounded. *Oh, god.* "You aren't playing fair."

Placing his arms on either side of me, he brought his knee up, parting my legs until his thigh pressed firmly against me.

I moaned again.

"Who said this was going to be fair?" he said.

He rocked his leg once. Another moan.

"Oh, so we're playing dirty?" Feeling gutsy from the lust, I used my fingernails to stoke the growing bulge in his pants. I felt it twitch. *I can't believe I just did that!*

He let out a long breath and dove in for a kiss. Our lips parted, and he thoroughly claimed my mouth. Any shyness I had melted away once his skilled tongue explored mine. I gave back with the same intensity, my arms wrapping around his neck, fingers lacing in his hair. He tasted like wine and honey. Our breathing became heavy, moving in and out in sync.

The next thing I knew, my shirt was off and flung on top of the lampshade. He carried me to his bed and set me on the down comforter. The duvet was cool against my feverish skin. Towering above me, Rigel stripped off his shirt, revealing his broad chest. His muscles were taut, his skin smooth, abs rippling down to show a faint trail of golden hair leading into his jeans.

"See something you like?" he said.

Blushing, I returned my greedy gaze to his face. *Too much eye candy for a mere mortal to handle.* His hair was messy, partially falling into his face and artistically shaping his features. *That damn hair is such a turn-on.*

I couldn't wait. I was as crazed as an impulse shopper on Black Friday, and Rigel was my ten-dollar toaster oven. Pulling myself to my knees using his jean loops for support, I gave his chest soft kisses. He still smelled of lavender, but now it was mixed with a sweeter smell I couldn't identify. It made me want to lick him all over. Clutching the loops tighter, I began to explore.

As I moved lower and lower with each kiss, his form danced and shone along the edges. I had to rest my forehead against his abs and catch my breath. If I wasn't careful, I might pass out. When I went to unbutton his jeans, this untamed lust that possessed me had my muscles contracting in anticipation, and I lost all ability to use my hands. I couldn't get the blasted button open.

"Dammit!"

With a playful growl, Rigel thrust me back on the bed and finished undressing me... slowly. Way *too* slowly. I didn't know if it was because I was all revved up and ready to go, or if he did it on purpose to drive me nuts, but either way it whipped me into a frenzy. He slid one bra strap down, then the other. Reaching behind me, he stroked my spine, and I arched my back to let him undo the fastener. As he flung the bra across the room, his eyes blazed with anticipation of the feast he was about to devour.

I was so distracted by his firm pectoral muscles that it didn't even register with me that I was completely naked—until I saw he was twirling my panties around on his pinky finger, one corner of his mouth quirked in a smile.

"How did you do that?"

With a smirk he answered, "One of my gifts."

The bastard knew I was about to burst with anticipation, so he taunted me further by slowly undressing himself. First he undid the button on his jeans, then his fingers moved to open the zipper. Inch by inch he unzipped it.

"You are pure evil," I breathed.

He pulled back one side, then the other. No underwear. I gasped. The jeans slid to the ground.

Oh... my... god. He was getting a five-star rating on Yelp first thing in the morning.

Unable to take my eyes from it, I said, "That can't be street legal."

"No, but it makes for a hell of a ride."

I giggled. "You did *not* just say that."

Joining me on the bed, he propped himself on an elbow and ran cool fingers up and down my torso, thrilling every place he grazed. The vibrations began again with renewed vigor. I didn't want to leave my body yet, so I closed my eyes and concentrated on the path of his fingers. They explored my neck, went between my breasts and down my thigh. They teased me, but didn't touch anything too sensitive as to throw me over the edge.

"You okay?" Rigel asked, prying loose my clenched fingers that were digging a hole in the mattress.

"Uh-huh," I whimpered.

With another one of his throaty chuckles, he brushed my nipple once, twice. Then he straddled me, softly kissing both nipples with his moist lips. My breath caught; I hadn't expected the sensations this aroused, the shivers spreading like wildfire.

"More," I pleaded.

He gently took my nipple in his mouth, licking and sucking, his other hand reaching down to explore the rest of me. Those velvety lips sent my vibrations into overdrive, and with an intoxicating jolt we jetted from our bodies. My blue and his gold swirled together, creating a whirlwind of light and color. Where they met, a brilliant golden thread emerged and coiled around us.

And then he slid inside of me. Just a few inches at first, but it was enough to propel my awareness back into my body. My muscles tightened from pleasure as he drove in a little further. I had been warned this would hurt, so I involuntarily tensed.

He paused. I knew instantly what he was thinking, and I flamed in embarrassment. *So much for hiding that I'm a virgin.*

"Are you…?" he asked.

I nodded in answer.

His shining form intensified, arcing off him in a prism. The sight had me growing wetter, and he slipped in a little further. Gently, he placed his hand down between us and began circling the tightness with his finger. My hips rose in reply.

"Rigel, please," I begged.

Each twirl had him sinking deeper, filling me.

The pleasure made my muscles contract with such ferocity that I became immobilized. I launched out of my body again. The golden thread that rippled above us started encasing us in a web, entwining our souls together. Below, Rigel gave an animalistic moan and my consciousness returned to my body. We were gliding against each other from the sweat of our passion. I couldn't think, only feel. His fingers dug into my skin and pulled me closer.

I was on the brink. *So close. So close.* He fed off my pleasure. I could sense his orgasm building inside of me, and it was almost painful. I needed a release, but I was scared to let it come. *It's too much.*

"Autumn, I can't hold on," Rigel groaned in a husky rasp. "It's too much." That did it. I was sent flying over the edge, and he followed, our screams loud enough for the entire mothership to hear.

He kept thrusting, and the orgasm continued on and on.

A flash. The room filled with white light, and I could no longer see. *Did he lose his form? No, I can feel him. He's still inside me.*

Our physical bodies, still joined together, rose from the bed to reconnect with our souls. Floating there in the peaceful glow, Rigel rested his forehead on mine, his soul dancing in his eyes, causing them to shimmer.

"I can see your soul," I whispered.

"Autumn, something's happening."

"Well, duh."

"This isn't…"

The golden tether encircled our feet, snaking its way past our calves to our hips, securing us together with him still inside me. It forced him so deep that we both gave a sharp cry, absorbed by another orgasm. The release continued as the thread finished weaving us together, sealing us in an all-consuming kiss. A blue beam of energy burst from my chest, sending us spinning into…

When I came to, we were lying on opposite ends of the bed, him on his stomach and me on my side, like we had been tossed there haphazardly. The glow from his skin was the only illumination in the room. We stayed there for a minute, catching our breath. Then Rigel sat on the edge of the bed and ran his hands through his hair.

His backside was as nummy as his front.

"Holy shit. I get why sex is an addiction for you," I said. "That last orgasm made me pass out."

"That's not what usually happens."

"Does this mean I'm officially part of the million-mile-high club?"

He got off the bed and put on his boxers. "No, Autumn—I'm telling you, that was not normal." There was panic in his voice.

Without warning, my vision warped into a funnel shape, and I was inside his body, seeing the room through his eyes—looking at my own naked body. *Sure didn't need to see that.* A blink later, I was back in my own body again.

"Why's it dark?" I asked. "Did you turn off the lights?"

Rigel spun toward the entrance and went rigid. I sat up on my knees, trying to figure out what he was doing.

The door opened, and twelve orbs glided in, bathing the room in a soft glow. I quickly pulled the sheets around me in a crude toga and did my best to shrink into the shadows.

Inanna's voice pierced my thoughts. "Rigel, what happened?"

One by one, the Anunnaki shifted into their bodily form. I hurried to shut my eyes, but realized I didn't need to. They just sort of melted and reshaped as they lost their glow. Three remained in their orb form and continued to light the room.

"It happened, didn't it?" Enlil boomed. "Part of the prophecy."

Rigel and Inanna shared a silent communication.

"Why are all the lights off?" I interrupted. Rigel's anxiety and my own confusion clashed inside me. "What's going on?"

"It was you two that triggered the power to shut off," Enlil said. "Wasn't it, Rigel?"

Ninurta spoke up. "The power will be restored shortly."

Through the dim glow of the room, I noticed that only three of the Anunnaki had their hands in the neutrality pose. I hoped this was due to their hasty entrance and not a sign of hostility.

"Is it true, Rigel?" Inanna said. "The prophecy. You need to tell us." Her expression conveyed the opposite of her words. *She doesn't want us to say.*

Rigel's telepathic voice buzzed in my ears, silent to everyone but me: "If they know what happened, Enlil will kill us. If you want to live to help the human race, you must clear your mind now!"

Clear my mind? How was I supposed to do that? By asking me not to think about it, Rigel had ensured it would be the *only* thing I could possibly think about.

Shit. Rigel wasn't kidding when he said that what had transpired was not normal. We had set the prophecy in motion, and neither of us knew the repercussions.

I prepared for a decapitating blow from Enlil, who had to have been hearing my thoughts. But he didn't strike.

"You are all wrong," Rigel lied. "We did not connect."

"You will not lie to me!" Enlil thundered, causing the room to shake.

Rigel flinched. His terror built inside me, forming a lump that blocked my airway. *Well, fuck, if Rigel is this scared, we are in some serious trouble.*

"Okay, so you're all in the loop now," I cut in, wriggling to the edge of the bed to stand while trying to keep the sheet covering all the pertinent areas. "We didn't connect. Now, if you all will excuse me, I'd like to get dressed. This is kind of weird."

An invisible force pushed me back onto the bed. I was immobilized. The fear inside me escalated, and the only sound I could hear was the whooshing of blood rushing to my head. *Is Inanna doing this? But why?*

The answer came immediately. Rigel convulsed, then gave a nauseating howl of pain as Enlil lifted him toward the ceiling. Instantly, my body was consumed with an internal fire. My plasma turned to lava and boiled inside my veins. Thank god Inanna had me paralyzed, or I wouldn't have been able to refrain from thrashing in agony along with Rigel—which would have been a dead giveaway that we *did* connect on some level.

"You will not lie to me!" Enlil roared. "I can no longer hear her thoughts. There is only one thing that could make that happen."

"We... did... not... connect..."

Rigel could barely speak. His body writhed—bending at unnatural angles. I felt a crushing swell of pain as if an invisible stake had been rammed through my skull. Black spots filled my vision.

"You lie," Enlil said, nearly foaming at the mouth. "I say we use the *Suh-Inim-Bala* on her."

"There's no need for that," Inanna said.

Enlil grumbled incoherently and dropped Rigel. The pressure in my head subsided.

"I know one way to get the truth," Enlil said. "Inanna, let her go. If they bonded, I'd wager she can feel everything he can, including pain. And with what I'm about to unleash on him, she won't be able to suppress her screams of torment."

Inanna obeyed. The hold she had on me evaporated, and I lay there limp, helpless against Enlil's plan. All I could do was concentrate on what had kept me sane when I latched on to the orb of agony. *Rigel's eyes, that was how I did it.* I could do it again if I focused.

Rigel was pitched toward the ceiling again. He maintained eye contact with me as he spoke to me in my head, the words ours and ours alone:

"I love you."

That was exactly what I needed to hear, and he knew it.

Rigel suddenly seized, taken by Enlil's torture. The fire struck me with a vengeance. I shuddered briefly, and managed to regain control by concentrating solely on the echo of those words…

I love you. I love you. I love you.

I heard it over and over. It kept me strong.

I love you. I love you. I love you.

His screams. *Oh, god.* I couldn't take hearing him scream. When Rigel's cries threatened to break me, I conjured up images of Devon and Emma. If I gave in, it wasn't only Rigel and I who would be killed; they would die too. That was not an option. *I have to fight the pain.*

The white heat coursed into my bones, and they felt as if they were breaking apart. I filled my lungs with air and emptied my mind, again evoking the memory of Rigel's eyes for strength—the blues of them morphing to form the Earth spinning in a starry sky. My muscles cramped, but I didn't give in.

Inanna's ultra-perfect silhouette came into view above me. "I don't think she can feel it," she said. A subtle twitch of her lips let me know she was aware of my struggle. "They're not lying," she announced confidently to the room.

I began to relax, thinking this test was finally over, when Rigel let loose a bloodcurdling scream that shattered my concentration, and my defenses fell. I was hit by a wall of pain, and I opened my mouth to cry out.

Before the cry could escape my lips, Inanna's paralyzing hold kicked in. She smiled down at me and gave me a wink that the others couldn't see.

Enlil yelled a few words I couldn't understand, and then Rigel collapsed to the floor. Inanna released me from her protection at the same time. I lay there immobilized—not by her grip, but by the residual aching. It took all my willpower not to gasp for breath when my lungs regained full function. As gracefully as I could, I stood up,

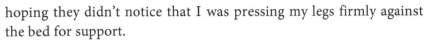

hoping they didn't notice that I was pressing my legs firmly against the bed for support.

"Satisfied?" I asked, giving them all a glare.

The lights flickered on, and I squinted against the unexpected brightness.

Enki approached and evaluated my appearance. I pulled the covers higher, feeling sheepish under his scrutinizing stare.

"It's a shame you have to die," he said.

For a moment I thought he was going to call for my execution, and I recoiled. Rigel must have thought this too, because he flashed over to put himself between me and Enki.

"I don't mean now," Enki said, stepping back and assuming the neutrality pose. "I meant when she uses the Mullilu—sorry, the Pinecone." Rigel backed off, moving to stand beside me. "Ninhursag would have loved to have met you, to study you and discern what makes you different."

The name Ninhursag didn't ring a bell, but he said it as if I should know her. At least I presumed it was a her. With these names, you never knew. *And why the past tense?* I wondered. *Did she die, or is he insinuating that I'll be dead before we could meet?*

"Brother," Enlil cut in. "They're lying! This whole pretense is ludicrous. Rigel almost died when she did. That can only happen with a connection. She is a mere vessel and must be executed to advance the prophecy."

"I agree," said Enki. Rigel stiffened. While those weren't the words I was hoping for, Enki wasn't hostile when he said them. Quite the contrary, he was verging on sympathetic. "Anu has commanded us to not interfere, therefore we must abide by his ruling. Plus, if the last part of the prophecy alludes to what I think it does, we are taking the appropriate path by letting her use the Pinecone. It is being carried out when she sacrifices herself to save humans."

"Why chance it?" Enlil argued. "I say we make them prove it right here! If the connection sealed them together, we must take measures to fulfill the Great Prophecy of the Souls."

"Patience, brother," Enki said.

Prove it? Is he proposing we have sex in front of them all? The thought of doing it in front of an audience made my insides go arctic.

"What are you suggesting?" I said, scrambling to tighten the sheet that insufficiently covered me.

"Nothing," Inanna said. "Let's all take a breath."

Ninurta appeared from the shadows. "Father, I agree with Enki. If it truly is the Great Prophecy, then it has begun. We don't need to, and probably shouldn't, interfere."

Enlil regarded Ninurta like a fly that needed to be swatted. There was no doubt Ninurta would pay later for voicing his opinion. Not that this made me especially sad; Ninurta gave me the heebie-jeebies.

"This is not your concern," Enlil rumbled.

Ninurta bowed his head and retreated, assuming the neutrality pose despite his father's words. *Yep, he's gonna get his ass handed to him.* Half of the group enfolded their arms in a show of peace as well.

"Please," I said, passing Rigel to stand in front of Enlil. I felt like I was on the verge of a nervous collapse. I couldn't stop my hands from shaking. Deciding it might be useful to stroke his massive ego, I kneeled down. "I ask that you give me this chance to save my people," I said. I couldn't help picturing the eyebrow raise Devon would give me if he heard me say *my people.*

Enlil leaned in and spoke softly so that only I could hear. "I know you're lying."

His icy words made me want to run underneath the bed and hide. Clenching my teeth, I focused on those unnaturally dark sapphire eyes of his. He was just inches from my face, but I didn't budge.

Without looking away I said, "I beg you, Enlil, please let me do this."

He stepped back angrily and shouted, "I can't read her thoughts!" The next thing I knew the bed was flying across the room from where he kicked it. It slid about twenty-feet and slammed into the far wall behind us. *Oh shit.* "This evidence alone proves they bonded!"

He pointed at me, and a stream of electrical energy surged from his finger, zapping my chest. I was thrown backward through the air and I landed on the bed with an unceremonious thump. Unfortunately, the sheet didn't travel with me. I lay there, spread eagle, naked as a jaybird. With my skin still crackling from his electricity bolt, I vowed revenge against him.

Rigel ran over and covered me with the sheet. "Are you okay?"

"You mean besides being electrocuted, tossed across the room, and stripped naked? Just peachy. Thanks."

He helped me get my makeshift toga refastened, then guided me back over to Enlil. I didn't have to be bonded to Rigel to recognize that his anger toward Enlil had entered the danger zone.

"Enlil," Rigel said, biting back his fury. "You are my master, and I respect your word and will honor it. But I'm asking you to give us the time to try to save humans with the Mullilu. In only a few days we will be gone and the prophecy fulfilled—if we are, in fact, the catalyst."

In only a few days we will be gone. His words made my legs weak. My heart fluttered in fear, and I had to grab tight to Rigel to stay upright.

Enlil glared at me, electricity still sizzling on his fingertip. I ducked behind Rigel.

"Very well," he agreed. "But be warned, if something happens and you don't burn into a pile of ash using the Ark, I will end it personally." A light flared along his outline, and Rigel shielded my eyes before the full force of his brightness blinded me.

When he uncovered my eyes, everyone had gone except Inanna.

"Thank you, Inanna," Rigel said.

"No need to thank me." She jabbed her thumb my way. "That's one tough human you got there." On her way out she grabbed my shirt, where it lay crumpled on the couch, and tossed it to me. "Now please, for the love of the Creator, get dressed. You're clenching that sheet so tight it's cutting off your circulation." And with a wink, she sashayed through the door.

"Inanna," I called.

Without turning, she flicked her wrist in acknowledgement, "Yeah, yeah. You're welcome."

The door shut behind her, leaving me stunned and speechless.

24

PROPHECY NONSENSE, HULA-DANCING TROLLS, AND THE ALMIGHTY VESSEL OF LOVE

"I need another drink," I said, hobbling over to my wine glass. I guzzled the remnants then unashamedly poured another while Rigel scanned the books in his rather impressive library.

"I know I have it here somewhere," he said. "We need to know what the prophecy says."

Taking another gulp, I shrank into the couch and chuffed, "You think?"

He plucked a stone tablet off a shelf. "Here we are."

"It's on a stone?"

"Lasts longer than paper."

It was frightening to think that Rigel could outlive the biodegradation of a book.

He sat down next to me on the sofa and skipped to the bottom of the tablet. It was written in ancient cuneiform script, but that didn't seem to faze him.

Getting all edgy, I prodded, "You're killing me here. Are you gonna share?"

His muscles visibly tightened as he read aloud:

> In the beginning there was one
> The Creator of All
> All was dark, there was no light
> Alone was The Creator of All
> To be worshiped he desired
> For this another was required

It was decided, a universe he would create
The beings within, he could control their fate
The plan in place, he created a spark
Now all was light, there was no dark
To restore balance, he must start anew
In an explosion, the great soul divided in two

One half Blue, and one half Gold
Their fates were then foretold

The Creator, now divided, the other half he
sought to find
So in time he could again bind
The Dark and the Light
The Gold and the Blue
For when all are as one
It will mean a new era has begun

I sprang to my feet, feeling the need to move in order to release my
building anxiety. "So if the prophecy is fulfilled there won't be light or
dark? How does that work?"

"I don't think that's literal, but a metaphor for good and evil."

"I'm gonna have a heart attack."

"Should I continue?"

"Yeah, yeah." I waved impatiently.

So one day it shall be
Destiny will unite them
A partial connection made
Forced apart by those who refuse to see, their
fated path will resurrect three

With the link in place and their destiny set,
love will gift them with its protection
The true Gold will entwine the Blue with a
single thread
For when the two unite, it will release the
heavenly white light

Rigel paused, and we both went pale. I knew we were reliving the memory of the white light wrapping us together. He swallowed, and with a slight tremble, he finished reading:

> The two halves must once again join
> For in the beginning there was one
> The Creator of All
> They have within their binding power
> To save all during the final hour
>
> Death must claim them
> For the souls to be free
> When ash falls upon the last heartbeat, it will set forth the catalyst for the bond to fully complete
> And in the dark, when they are gone, it will begin again before it can end
> For the end and the beginning are one
>
> A universe will separate one from the other, one will be lost, one found and both unbound
> Only a new love and a true love side by side will ignite the final spark that unites the two universes into one

"It will begin again before it can end?" I repeated. "What the hell does that mean?"

"No clue." Rigel set the tablet on the coffee table.

"That's it?"

"Well, there are still the four lines we haven't decoded yet. Those lines have a different encryption."

"That makes no sense."

"We think the two universes need to be joined before we can crack it."

"Great."

I walked over and collapsed on the bed with a deflated grumble and stared at the ceiling. That part about one of us lost had me worrying about the fate of my soul when I died. Chances were, *I'd* be the lost one.

Rigel's face appeared above me with a goofy expression. I chuckled. "There's no denying that we're the prophecy now," he declared, then plopped down beside me on the bed and stared at the ceiling with me.

"I am God!" I said dramatically, pumping my fist triumphantly in the air. "I shall smite anyone who displeases me."

We erupted in fits of giggles.

"You're going to have to change your favorite expression now," he noted.

"What's that?"

"Oh my god."

"I do say that a lot," I admitted.

He tapped his chin. "I guess it would be 'Oh my Autumn' now, right?"

"Hmm. Then I would be referring to myself in the third person. I would have to say 'Oh my I.'"

"That sounds like you poked your eyeball out."

I remembered us floating in that white light after we bonded. "If we are the prophecy," I said, "how come nothing happened after we… you know… sealed the deal? Over half the verses have already been fulfilled, including the heavenly light thing. If that's the case, why didn't the universe blast open? It was so anticlimactic."

Rigel rolled on his side and gave me a quizzical eyebrow lift.

"Let me rephrase that," I said apologetically, the memory of the incredible orgasm we shared triggered an aftershock in my belly. "What I meant to say is that there's all this connection talk in this prophecy, yet I don't feel any different."

Rigel raised his brow higher.

"You know what I mean!" I said, poking at his chest.

Tracing his finger up and down my arm he said solemnly, "I think that's because we still have to fulfill the last part of it."

"It's official: we must *end* for it to begin. Enlil will be ecstatic."

"He'd be happier if we ended without rescuing humans first. If it wasn't for a majority of the council wanting to prevent your kind's demise, you would've been charred by Enlil's finger rather than merely tossed across the room."

"What's the deal with him?" I grunted. "It isn't our fault he can hear our thoughts."

"I can't blame him."

"Excuse me for a second." I shook my earlobe with my fingers, and then banged the side of my head, pretending to clean something from my ears. "Sorry, must have had a clog in my ear canal. I thought you said you don't blame him."

Rigel gave me a sideways glance. "How would you deal with thousands of radio stations broadcasting in your head simultaneously, powerless to tune any of them out?"

I thought about that. As a general rule, people are stupid—reality shows prove that. And if all those reality stars are so gifted at spewing verbal diarrhea, I can't even imagine what goes on inside their heads. I knew I didn't have it in me to end an entire species, as Enlil clearly did, but I would have most likely drilled a hole in my own head after hearing the inner monologues of some of these privileged spoiled socialites.

Then again, maybe there's nothing going on in their brains at all.

"You have all this medical technology," I said. "Technology that restored my pulverized heart and mangled hand without a scar anywhere. And you're telling me there's no treatment for Enlil?"

"Not without removing part of his temporal lobe."

"Sounds like an outstanding plan to me."

"We had more success trying to breed the defect from you. Ninhursag did succeed in quieting it by a fraction, but that's it."

Ninhursag. That was who Enki had said would love to study me. "Who's Ninhursag?"

"She's the one who created humans with Enki. She's Enki and Enlil's sister and Ninurta's mother."

"Whoa, whoa, whoa!" I choked and bolted upright. "I thought Ninurta was Enlil's son."

"He is."

"Enlil had a child with his *sister*? That's so gross."

"It's not uncommon among us, and not viewed as 'gross' in our society."

"*What?*"

"I'm sure you are aware that human inbreeding produces… well… less-than-perfect offspring. What you don't know is that this isn't a natural phenomenon with humans. We genetically made that happen

to prevent you from evolving to our level. But in reality, the opposite is true. When the Anunnaki maintain pure bloodlines, it serves to retain and expand upon our full potential. Mixed blood has a degenerative effect on our gifts."

"Dear lord, please tell me you didn't sleep with your relatives," I said. "Wait! Do you have kids?"

The briefest flicker of sadness crossed his features, and a feeling of loss hollowed out my chest.

"Rigel?"

He smiled, and the grief instantly subsided. *Maybe I imagined it?* He sat up to join me and stroked my cheek. "No. Calm down. No kids."

I noticed that he hadn't answered the first part of my question. "What about sexy time with relatives?" I pressed.

He didn't say anything. I wasn't sure if his silence was meant to tease me, or was an admission of guilt. I decided to let it be. *Ignorance is definitely bliss on this subject.* And in truth, incest aside, I was a little jealous that he hadn't suffered from the same "no-touchy-the-opposite-sex-ever" affliction I did.

"Have you always been able to touch other women?" I asked without thinking. My face immediately flamed with heat. I mentally slapped myself for saying that out loud.

Rigel's complete confusion made my lip twitch as I fought back a smile. He gave a squeak and said, "Umm... I don't understand the question."

I had to bite my twitching lip to keep from laughing. He probably assumed I was prodding him for the dreaded sexual partner count. Considering how long he had lived, and how famous he was back on Nibiru, that number would be massive. To save him—and me—from further embarrassment, I put an end to that line of questioning.

"Nothing. Forget I said anything."

"Are you sure?" he asked, a yearning for a reprieve written all over him.

I obliged with a change of subject. "Why do I have to shut my eyes when you shift to your light form, and not the other way round?"

Looking relieved, he explained, "When we reorganize from our physical body into melam, our light form, it takes a sizeable amount of energy, and the flash will blind you. When we go the other way, the energy is minimal. We simply *melt* into our forms, you could say."

"Huh. Interesting. Then why did you make me close my eyes when I followed you to the canyon that first time? You were only shifting to your bodily form."

"I figured since it was our first meeting, it'd be best not to morph with you looking. It might have made things awkward between us."

"Smart."

Rigel was still shirtless (and as far as I was concerned he could remain that way permanently—*hubba hubba*), and that made me wonder about something else. "How do you stay fully clothed going from physical form to light?"

"Ah, one of my favorite subjects." Raising his chin proudly, Rigel said, "You are looking at the head scientist for the R&D department that developed our transitional clothing line."

"I almost forgot that I had a nerd for a boyfriend."

"Smart is the new sexy, don't you know?"

"Yes, I see that."

"Our clothes are organic material made from our own cells, so they can transform with us."

"Your clothes are living?" I asked, leaning in to rub his boxer shorts between my fingers. They felt no different than normal cotton. "That should amaze me, but at this point a troll could prance in and dance the hula and I wouldn't bat an eye."

Rigel grinned and laid his head in my lap. I ran my hands through his hair, and his eyes drifted shut. *Dear lord is he gorgeous. Smart is the new sexy.*

"I don't think I'll be able to sleep," I said. "Got too many things buzzing in my head."

His eyes popped open and in a mischievous tone he said, "I may know how to get you to relax."

Trying to maintain a blank expression, I said, "Careful. You are about to seduce the Almighty Vessel. Please me or I shall end you."

"Trust me, that won't be a problem."

And it wasn't.

25

FLOATING FORTRESSES, SLINGING POO, NEFARIOUS NAZI ALIENS, AND A CHIPPENDALES' CONVENTION

When I woke the next morning I felt groggy, yet grateful that I'd slept straight through the night without stirring. Once my eyes adjusted, I double-checked to see if Rigel was still beside me. The glow of the lamp gave off enough light for me to drool over his magnificent shining frame, partially covered by a sheet. He slept peacefully, his chest rising and falling in a steady rhythm. I could have stared at him for hours. *Who needs television when you have a Greek god lying in your bed?*

Part of me wanted to jump on top of him and go to town. I couldn't do it though. He was the picture of contentment. Being careful not to rouse my sleeping immortal, I quietly snuck out of bed. My muscles ached from our "workout" the night before. And the best cure for sore muscles is a good stretch and a hot cup of coffee. *Do aliens drink coffee?*

I padded into the kitchen, and sure enough, right there on the counter was one of those one-cup coffee makers. *Score!* I snapped in a K-cup and brewed a mug of French Toast-flavored coffee.

Since Rigel was still sleeping, I curled up on the couch to enjoy my caffeine rush. On the table was a newspaper titled *Nibiru Today*. How did that get delivered? *That's some freakin' paper route.* I picked it up and scanned the front page. The main photo showed a large city square where hundreds of thousands of protestors held signs. One might think it was a crowd of humans if not for the glowing gold pyramid they marched around. Judging from the surrounding buildings, the pyramid was as tall as a hundred-story skyscraper, and not a single window or door blemished its exterior. This was definitely not on planet Earth.

On the side of the picture, a few callouts showcased close-ups of the signs, which lacked any creativity in wording and design.

A gust of wind tussled my hair and the coffee was snatched from my hands. I looked up to see Rigel standing there drinking it, naked as a jaybird. I gulped.

"Anything interesting?" he asked.

Uh, yeah—and it was beginning to point in my direction.

I averted my eyes from his nether region by escaping back into the pages of the newspaper. "Why are these people protesting?" I asked. "And what are these *Free Ninhursag* signs about? The way Enki talked about her in the past tense, I assumed she was dead."

"She is the reason why humans are alive today. She—"

He caught me staring at his southern hemisphere again.

"Hey, my eyes are up here."

My face heated to medium rare, but I still couldn't take my eyeballs off it. With a smirk, Rigel handed me back my coffee and disappeared. Seconds later, the corners of my newspapers flapped from a new puff of wind, and there was Rigel, fully dressed.

"This better?" he asked.

"Technically, no," I said. "But less distracting. So, how's Ninhursag responsible for humans being alive?"

"If it wasn't for her campaigning and countless protest efforts, you wouldn't have been given the chance to be saved this time. The Galactic Federation's first ruling was to let you all be obliterated: no trial, no possibility of rescue."

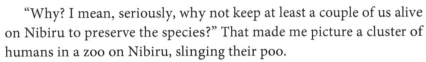

"Why? I mean, seriously, why not keep at least a couple of us alive on Nibiru to preserve the species?" That made me picture a cluster of humans in a zoo on Nibiru, slinging their poo.

"Because of the Galactic Genetic Purification Initiative."

I snorted. "That sounds fake."

"The majority view is that a species created by genetic engineering, or science in general, should not be allowed to exist. A universal mandate was enacted that effectively prohibits anyone from attempting it—unless of course they're prepared for war. According to the law, only those life forms designed by the Creator himself are to be born."

"I understand that, I guess. After all, we argue pretty ferociously over GMOs on Earth. I can only imagine the fight over genetically modified beings. Hey, are they called GMBs?"

"GEBEs, actually. Genetically Engineered Biological Entities."

"If there's this mandate, how'd you get away with it? Creating us, I mean."

"The law wasn't yet in place at the time of your creation."

"Is it a religious-type view, or is there some specific reason why genetic manipulation is banned?"

"Things go wrong when new beings are created by an imperfect one. It usually takes a while to come to fruition, but inevitably evil evolves and consumes any altered species. For example, take the Pleiadians. They're similar to you and me, appearance-wise—slightly taller and lankier. Some time ago a mutant gene manifested among their kind. Mothers were incapable of carrying to term, so their population dwindled to the brink of extinction. The Pleiadians enlisted the help of the Zeta Reticuli—the Greys, as you call them—whose genes don't mutate, to donate their DNA to form a locked supergene that would counteract the abnormality. Scientists created the perfect cross, using only the most desired traits from each species. It was nicknamed the *Superchild Gene*. And to everyone's excitement, healthy babies were born."

"What'd they look like?"

"They were very similar to the Pleiadians, with the exception of the eyes, which were the oversized almond-shape of the Greys, although they still retained the Pleiadian trademark blue and green irises. It was quite the sight."

213

"Strange that I haven't heard any rumors of a species matching that description in the UFO community."

"You wouldn't have. They've been exterminated."

"The Pleiadians were all killed?"

"No, just what they created."

"Geez. I'm not sure I want to hear this."

"I don't have to continue."

I considered it. *Damn my morbid curiosity.* "No, carry on."

"When the children hit puberty, it was like a switch had been flipped: the hybrids turned into evil sociopaths. They lost all compassion and became obsessed with achieving perfection. Once they reached adulthood and had enough power, they covertly carried out genocide on anyone who was not on the same 'level.' Basically any Pleiadian who did not prove to be useful, intelligent, or who was not in sufficient physical condition. The slightest limp was deemed worthy of extermination."

"Dear lord."

"The hybrids eradicated them by any means necessary. Poisoning, undercover assassinations, terrorist attacks, staged accidents, even manipulating weather."

"So they were Nazis with advanced weapons."

"Yes. And now imagine if the Nazis won."

"That's a terrifying thought."

"The elder Pleiadians sought outside assistance," Rigel continued. "An unprecedented number of galactic nations came to their aid, and all of the hybrids were ultimately eliminated."

"You're telling me not a single hybrid was born without this sadistic streak?"

"Not a one, thanks to the locked supergene. Every child was the same without fail."

"Wow. Knowing all this, why does Ninhursag keep up with the fight to save humans?"

"Because during the Great Flood, she witnessed your whole species massacred, including innocent children, and it profoundly changed her. Enki told no one of Noah, so Ninhursag was inconsolable, believing that the human race, which she had helped to create and come to love as her own family, was gone forever. Once Enki revealed what he

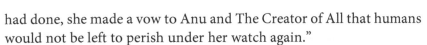

had done, she made a vow to Anu and The Creator of All that humans would not be left to perish under her watch again."

"Ah. Let me guess: she's being imprisoned to prevent her from fulfilling the vow?"

"You got it," Rigel said. "Remember when they removed my gold to keep me from coming for you? Same with her."

I shivered at the memory. "What the hell?" I said. "What's wrong with a run-of-the-mill prison cell? Why such extreme punishment?"

"Removing the gold is the only way to guarantee we can't transform and escape."

"No wonder they're protesting." I pointed to the newspaper. "It's nice to know there are a few of you who don't side with Enlil and spend the day dreaming up ways to off us."

"A few?" Rigel said. "Try most. This situation is creating a political upheaval on our planet. If it were the Anunnaki's decision, I know the vote would be to relocate you. But it isn't up to us. The Galactic Federation has the deciding vote, and their ruling is final. Going against them would mean military action. Trust me when I say a revolt solely on Nibiru is preferable to a war with the rest of the universe. The catastrophic power of the weapons of mass destruction in this galaxy alone could easily take out this entire solar system. Your hydrogen bomb looks like a firecracker in comparison."

I returned my attention to the protestors on the front page. Their modelesque appearance was spectacular. It was like a bunch of *Victoria's Secret* and *Chippendales* supermodels all got together for a super convention. "You all are so good looking, it's comical."

Rigel sighed and confiscated the magazine. "We need to talk about what we're going to do today," he said somberly.

"I know." I groaned. "But it's so nice here. You, me, and a bottle of Merlot. My heaven."

He roped me in and laid us both on the couch. We cuddled there, nose to nose, and his eyes brightened as he took me in. I wasn't prepared for the emotion it stirred in me. Rather than turning me on, it made me sad. Sad that I would be the one to extinguish his light—that brilliant, beautiful light.

"You okay?" he asked.

"Perfect," I lied, kissing him softly on the lips.

"I think we should take Devon to his family before we go get the Ark," Rigel said. "We owe him that closure before things get messy."

I bolted upright and out of his arms, hit with the sudden realization of what today was. *My last.*

"This is it, huh?" I sucked in a ragged breath. "The day we, you know…"

"That's up to you. We need to get the Ark, go to the power source, and then it's ready for you to—"

"Holy shit." My heart actually skipped a few beats. "I haven't even thought about what to say to people."

"I know." Rigel sat up held me close. "We have a little bit of time before anything happens to Earth. You don't have to do it today."

"That's just it: I do. People are killing each other down there. I gotta save as many lives as I can." The tears began collecting in the corners of my eyes. "But I want more time with you. All we got is one night."

"If I could, I would spend eternity with you," Rigel said, resting his forehead against mine. "We just have to make each moment count." He kissed me softly, then lifted me into his lap, brushing a strand of hair off my cheek. "Let's take it a step at a time. We'll get the Ark first, and then we can decide."

"There's still a chance someone else will come through, right? That another person will build a tolerance and can take my place?"

"Yes," he said, lifting my chin. "There's a really good chance of that."

Though he spoke with confidence, I could tell he didn't believe it.

"Where's the Ark of the Covenant anyway?" I asked. "Is it on Nibiru?"

Rigel started laughing.

"What's so funny?" I tried to glare at him, but his laugh was so infectious that I couldn't refrain from cracking a smile.

"No, it's on Earth. You'll get a kick out of where it's located."

"Where?" I asked. Maybe it was in the secret chamber below the Sphinx, or in the White House.

"That, my love, you will have to wait and see."

26

WALK OF SHAME, LEVITATING COWS, FLYING UNDER THE INFLUENCE, AND AN OCTOPUS STOWAWAY

Rigel and I made our way down the corridor to get Devon. There was way more activity on the ship than there had been yesterday. Igigi bustled about going who knows where to do who knows what.

"How many people are on this ship?" I asked.

"Thirty thousand Igigi are here full time, and about twenty or so Anunnaki at any given time."

"Dang! This is a big ship."

We arrived at Devon's door. Rigel raised his hand to knock, but before he made the first rap, it opened and Inanna came rushing out. She practically ran right into us. She looked totally frazzled: her shirt was misbuttoned, her hair disheveled, and she was holding her shoes in her hand.

Inanna was doing the walk of shame!

Nodding to each of us, she said, "Rigel. Autumn."

Lifting my brows at her in accusation, I crossed my arms and said, "Well, hello, Inanna. What a surprise seeing you here."

Rigel looked away, trying to hide his smile.

Inanna gave me a glare that stopped me from saying anything else.

"If you will excuse me," she said, "I have a meeting I'm late for."

Rigel and I stepped aside to let her pass.

When she was out of earshot, I said, "She is such a hypocrite! She breaks my jaw for a kiss with you, but she can"—I shivered in horror at the visual that popped into my head—"get it on with Devon, and that's okay?"

"Actually, it is."

"Wait. What?"

Before Rigel could answer, Devon came to the door, a noticeable bounce in his step. "Oh, hey, guys. You ready to rock?"

I just stared at him, mouth slightly open.

Devon waved his hand in front of my face. "Earth to Autumn. Come in, Autumn."

I gave him a huge grin. "Yeah, sure. Let's go."

We walked down the hallway in an uncomfortable silence. Finally I asked Devon, "So, how'd you sleep?"

Rigel snorted.

"Okay, I guess." Devon rubbed the back of his neck and tilted his head. "My neck is a little stiff."

I wanted to say, *Is that the only thing that's stiff?* but refrained.

"Really?" I said. "Wonder what caused that?"

"There was a lump in my bed."

Rigel and I both started laughing.

"Why's that funny?" Devon asked.

"No reason," I said.

Rigel guided us into an expansive hangar full of hundreds of space-ships—your stereotypical silver disk-shaped crafts, each roughly the size of a convenience store. What had to be thousands of Igigi were bustling about doing a whole lot of clanking on things. It totally looked staged, complete with a perfectly timed spaceship buzzing over our heads.

"Man, this is frickin' awesome!" Devon exclaimed.

"Aren't these ships the ones the Greys are always spotted in?" I asked. "I don't recall any eyewitness reports of hunky gods piloting these saucers."

"They are for the Greys," Rigel said. "We are the largest provider of spacecraft in the Milky Way. These particular commissions here are the newest models, fitted with neural controls that operate via brainwaves. You simply think where you want to go, and it will take you there."

"Cool!" Devon said. "I'm picturing the Greek Isles right now."

"Do we get to take one?" I asked.

Rigel frowned. "No."

I was disappointed. I mean, I was already riding in the mothership. It was silly for me to be picky, but they looked so neat! I wanted to go levitate a cow in a beam of light.

"How are we getting back?" Devon asked.

"We're taking an earlier model, run by touch, not brainwaves."

I gave a jubilant squeak.

Devon's enthusiasm teetered on stroke level. "Sweet corn cakes!" he burst out. "This is the best day of my life."

A ship zoomed in front of us, then came to a noiseless stop and smoothly set itself down. Its surface was flawless—not a door or opening anywhere. *I guess this is our ride.*

Devon bounced about. "How do we get in?" He craned his neck, straining to locate the entrance. "Is the door on the other side?"

"Calm down there, cowboy," Rigel said, patting Devon's head as if he were an overexuberant dog needing to go potty.

"No way! I wanna drive it! Let's go!" Devon ran to the other side of the ship. After doing a full circuit, he said, "What the hell?" Where's the door?"

As if in answer to his question, the craft began to vibrate. A door silently materialized on the front, about fifteen feet above us.

"Open says me," Rigel said—with a smartass smirk and an extravagant flourish.

I was about to smack him when the door shuddered and disappeared, leaving an opening onto the ship. A small platform appeared and an Igigi stepped out, a red cylindrical device in his hand. Both he and the platform descended to the ground.

"Thanks, Alla," Rigel said, shaking the Igigi's hand.

Alla gave us a polite nod and left. Devon didn't hesitate; he steered a ladder over and then darted up the rungs into the craft. I had to stop myself from joining him in an all-out sprint; if I planned on keeping up the facade of a person poised to be the savior of humankind, I figured I needed to keep my composure.

Rigel knew me better than that. "Go on!" he said, shooing me in.

I hauled ass aboard.

My jaw almost hit the floor when I stepped inside. The walls of the ship were transparent; I could completely see through to the outside, as if I were floating in air. I wouldn't even have known I was on a craft if not for a silver chair in front of a navigation panel—the only visible part of the ship.

The sensation of being in midair muddled my equilibrium. "Holy shit!" I said, losing my balance and promptly falling on my butt.

"I know, right?" Devon said, his voice cracking with the thrill of it. "This is the coolest thing ever!" He scurried to the chair, settled in, and made pew-pew sound effects as he rocked back and forth pretending to avoid enemy fire.

Rigel stepped up behind me. "You like it?"

"I've fallen and I can't get up," I whined.

"It was that way for me the first time too," he said. He held out a hand to help me up.

Devon spun in the chair, a grin stretching from ear to ear. "Teach me how to drive this? Please?"

Rigel exhaled. "I will. I promise. Just let me get us into an open area first."

"I can totally steer us outta this place. I was the star student at my elementary school's space camp."

"I don't think that quite qualifies you to drive," Rigel said. "Now, up you go."

Devon rose, his expression sullen, as if his mom had confiscated his favorite toy. "Fine."

Rigel sat down and placed his hands on the arms of the chair. Straps emerged and snaked over each of them. He slid his hands forward, and the ship moved in the same direction. I dropped flat and hugged the floor with a whimper.

"It takes getting used to," Rigel said. "This craft has a stabilized interior so you'll barely feel any movement. You need to acclimate to the visuals, that's all."

He wasn't lying. It didn't *feel* like we had moved at all—my eyes, however, were communicating very different things to equilibrium. We entered a tunnel with a strip of lights leading off into the distance.

"Get ready," Rigel said.

"Oh, sweet mother of everything holy," I mumbled, and then squeezed my eyes shut.

"Weeeeeeeeeee!" Devon squealed.

"Why don't you inch your way over here and hold on to me for support," Rigel offered. "That may help."

Not yet daring to open my eyes, I had to crawl blindly across the floor. When my fingers brushed the metal of the chair, I stood and clutched Rigel's lusciously firm and sexy shoulders. I let one eye slide open. We were drifting in space. I could handle this. The darkness totally helped.

"Can I fly now? Can I?" Devon begged, clapping his hands and shuffling from foot to foot.

"All right already!" Rigel said.

Rigel had barely gotten one butt cheek off the seat before Devon had scooted in. He moved with such speed I was surprised he didn't produce scorch marks. Devon placed his hands on the arms of the chair the same way Rigel had, and the straps wrapped around them. The moment they were in place, he shifted his hands abruptly to the left—which caused the ship to spin. The swirl of stars made me fall down again. I covered my eyes and moaned from queasiness.

"Slow down there, young Jedi," Rigel said.

"Sorry."

"Subtle, reserved motions."

"Roger that."

"Autumn, you okay?"

"I just threw up in my mouth."

"Better than on me," Devon said.

I kept my eyes glued shut. "Rigel, please let me know when he has it under control. I'll stay here in the fetal position until then, if you don't mind."

It felt like an hour passed before Rigel finally said, "I think he has it."

Cautiously, I opened my eyes and slowly got up. The view shocked me. Earth was before us, a vibrant blue, clouds covering its surface like a patchy blanket of snow. It reminded me of the night Rigel and I had explored the galaxy together.

Rigel must have read my thoughts. His arms enveloped me from behind, his touch now wonderfully familiar and comforting. "That was quite the night, huh?" he said.

I pressed closer to Rigel and reached back to grab his hips.

"Oh, yeah."

Devon broke in. "Hey, Rigel. How do I go faster?"

"Just nudge your hands forward."

Of course, in classic Devon style, he launched his hands forward—and we went barreling toward Earth. I screamed, and Rigel zipped over and pushed Devon's hands back.

"You've had enough fun for today, young man," he mock scolded.

"But—" Devon began.

Rigel cut him off and shooed him from the seat. Then he turned to me. "You want a turn?"

"I don't know."

"You gotta fly it," Devon insisted. "It's so fun!"

"Um, okay."

Hesitantly, I sat down. I placed my hands on the armrests, and the straps secured me in. Not wanting to send us plunging toward Earth like Devon did, I made only the most microscopic maneuvers.

The ship didn't move.

"You'll need to put a smidge more muscle into it," Rigel advised.

He came up behind me and placed his hands atop mine, gently guiding me along. His touch had me instantly dizzy with lust.

Giving me a sly smile, he said, "Whoa there." I knew he wasn't talking about the speed of the ship. Flushing, I focused on my flying again.

"We don't have to be stealthy, since humans know about us," he said. "We're free to roam about the earth if there's something you want to see."

"Oh, hey, can we go to the pyramids of Giza?" I said, mimicking Devon's exuberant bouncing.

"Sure." Rigel chuckled.

With his hands directing mine, we dove into Earth as if it were a giant swimming pool. The outside of the ship shone red for about five seconds, and then we were drifting through a cloud bank and arriving at the pyramids.

"They look so small from this high up," Devon said.

Kissing the top of my head, Rigel asked me, "You ready to take the helm by yourself?"

All it would take was one sneeze and I'd ram us into one of the pyramids, but I said, "Okay."

Rigel released my hands, and I began to steer on my own. It was way easier than I expected—the ship moved at my will.

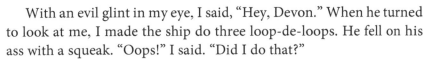

With an evil glint in my eye, I said, "Hey, Devon." When he turned to look at me, I made the ship do three loop-de-loops. He fell on his ass with a squeak. "Oops!" I said. "Did I do that?"

"Showoff!" he exclaimed.

Satisfied, I lingered in front of the grand pyramids, taking them all in. I noticed that dozens of people were gathered beside the smallest one. I was about to mention it when Devon spoke.

"Hey, why is the top missing off that one?" he asked, pointing to the tallest one.

"Drunk driver," Rigel answered.

Devon and I snorted and waited for Rigel to join us. But his expression was serious.

"You're kidding, right?" I asked.

"Nope. A drunk Altairian sideswiped it," he said. "Quite the fiasco. After that, the Galactic Federation launched a wide-scale anti-drunk flying campaign. In fact, you have the logo for the campaign on your dollar bill."

I highly doubted there was a spaceship or a can of beer hidden in the spider webs of artwork on the dollar bill. There was only one item that could possibly fit the bill—no pun intended. "The capstone with the eye on it?"

"You guessed it," he said. "That was the logo for our campaign. Below it they wrote, 'We Are Watching You' as the tagline. And if I remember right, the subheading was, 'Keep an eye out for drunk-flyers.'"

"Really? I always thought that the eye in the triangle belonged to that secret society, the Illuminati."

Rigel grinned. "It does. They excavated a campaign tablet that some alien probably tossed off a ship along with his empty beer bottle. The last line—'Keep an eye out for drunk-flyers'—was missing from it, so they translated the 'We Are Watching You' and thought it was a bona fide warning that the gods were keeping track of their every move. They stole it and adopted it for their own symbolic messaging."

I laughed so hard the ship pitched to the side. Catching myself, I steadied the craft.

I immediately sobered when I saw what was happening at the smallest pyramid. It was shaking, and billows of displaced sand were rising from it. As I watched, a chain reaction of explosions detonated around the base of the pyramid, and its stones began to crumble and fall. The bottom layers gave way, and the upper layers collapsed down onto them, until the entire thing was hidden under a massive cloud of dust.

Rigel motioned for me to relinquish the controls, and I did. He maneuvered the ship to the other side of the rubble, where we saw a line of trucks dumping explosives beside another pyramid.

Devon asked, "Why would they even bother?"

"A show of dominance," Rigel muttered in disgust.

"I don't want to see this," I said.

Rigel flew us away from the disturbing scene.

We were all silent as we sailed past mountains, deserts, forests, valleys, and lakes. I committed to memory their splendor before this world was lost forever.

When we reached the ocean, Rigel dove us down beneath the surface. We explored the world below, one that I had only seen on TV. Schools of fish turned in unison, creating a silver sheen as they adjusted course. We reduced our speed to follow a pod of dolphins, and in the process, an octopus suctioned itself to the ship. We took it on a spin for several miles before it let go and disappeared into our bubbling jet stream.

By the time Rigel lifted us from the ocean, a profound sadness filled me. "Are there other worlds like this?" I asked.

"There are," Rigel responded. "Not all are this impressive, yet others contain wonders that defy imagination."

Devon joined me, and both of us stared down at the vast waters below, tipped with whitecaps. The wonder of our travels had worn off, and was replaced by a foreboding. The countdown to the end had officially begun. The sands of the hourglass were about to bury me alive.

"You know," Devon said with a heavy sigh, "I've never traveled outside of California."

"No way."

"Yep. Born and raised. Not a family trip to the Grand Canyon or anything."

I didn't know what to say to that. He wouldn't get to travel to any of those places now. Come to think of it, I hadn't done much traveling either—a few cities in the U.S., and once to Canada for a high school band competition.

I wanted more time to experience it all—to climb Mount Everest, swim with a platypus in Tasmania, and drive a go-cart along the Great Wall of China. Those things would never happen.

Time was going…

going…

gone.

27

BLOWUP MONOPOD ELVIS, EXPLOSIVE SPACE MODULATORS, AND AN ACID-FILLED CACTUS

We soared south along the coastline of California, the barren rocky cliffs gradually being replaced by the mansion-lined sandy beaches of Malibu. Veering inland, we sped over Los Angeles, where pillars of smoke were billowing from the riot fires that extended all the way to Orange County.

"Can you guide me to your place?" Rigel asked Devon.

Despite the unfamiliar perspective from the air, Devon was able to direct Rigel to his house. We soon drifted high above a typical tract home community; a patchwork of stucco and manicured lawns. From this height, the neighborhood appeared quiet enough—but when we descended, it looked like a war zone. Abandoned cars were scattered on the road, with a disturbing number of them overturned. Alarms were flashing. Smoke was rising from the smoldering remains of houses that had recently burned down. And a busted fire hydrant was shooting a geyser of water into the air.

(Normally this waste of water would drive me mad. It's one of my pet peeves. I have a borderline anxiety attack when someone keeps the water running while they're brushing their teeth. But considering it was all going to evaporate in a cataclysmic explosion in a couple days, I figured it didn't matter in the larger scheme of things.)

Devon twisted his shirt in his hands, and his face turned a light shade of green. Seeing his neighborhood in that state had to be devastating.

"We should devise a plan," Rigel suggested.

Devon gave an anxious nod of agreement.

"Do you have any idea what their mindset might be?" Rigel asked. "Are you sure they're still here?"

Devon wiped his sweaty palms on his jeans. "Well, when I went on my shopping spree, I kind of 'borrowed' their car. So unless they hoofed it out of town or jacked the neighbor's SUV, they'll be here." He shook slightly as he ran his hands down his face. "My house is the last one on this street. The one with the pink flamingos and garden gnomes covering the front yard."

He wasn't joking about the decorations. The lawn was covered in more tacky ornaments than anyone should be allowed by law. The highlight of this Reddit-worthy display was a humongous blowup Elvis with a punctured leg. He lay flopped on his side, his mangled plastic bell bottoms fluttering in the wind.

"Wow. Now *that* is a yard," I said. "I bet your neighbors love you."

"Be glad you weren't here to witness the destruction during the Portola Hills Lawn War of 2000."

"It's scary when the least tacky item in a yard is a pink flamingo."

"Yeah, I know. My parents are strange. Very introverted."

"And your brother?" Rigel asked. "You sure he stayed behind with them?"

"He wouldn't leave my folks, even if he did go mental."

"Okay then," Rigel said, parking the ship over the back yard. "I suggest you two to stick together while I go find your family and do my thing. It shouldn't take too long. Devon, when I know it's safe, Autumn and I will leave you alone to talk with them. Take your time and join us on the ship when you're ready. Does that plan work for you guys?"

We agreed.

Rigel murmured something in a foreign language, and the outside of the ship darkened. You could still see through it, but it was like a tinted window, and I could now see the curves and lines of the craft. My equilibrium instantly righted itself now that there was a semi-solid surface below me.

"Hey," I said. "Why didn't you do that earlier?"

"Thought you might like an unobstructed view."

I folded my arms together and glared at him. "Uh-huh."

Rigel waved his hand, and a console emerged from the ceiling. He pressed a series of buttons, and the door of the craft opened, revealing a platform outside.

"What, no welcome mat?" Devon asked.

Rigel gave a wry smile and pressed another button. A welcome mat materialized on the platform.

Devon's eyes went wide. "What, no diaphanously clad female runway models?"

Rigel waved his hand over the screen, and for a minute I thought he might actually be conjuring runway models. Instead, two red cylindrical objects dropped from a light beam below the console and hung there suspended. They looked like petite sticks of dynamite. Rigel grabbed the objects and held them out to me and Devon. "Here. Each of you take one of these."

We accepted the mysterious devices, handling them gently in case they were genuine explosives.

Devon smiled and said with a boyish enthusiasm, "Oooh… is this the Illudium Q-36 Explosive Space Modulator?"

"Where's the kaboom?" I added, doing my best imitation of Marvin the Martian. "There's supposed to be an Earth-shattering kaboom." I frowned after I said it and then admitted, "I suppose that isn't funny, considering."

Rigel shook his head at us. "This is what you'll use to get back on the ship. It's your key."

Placing the modulator to his heart, Devon said, "A key? So soon in our relationship? I'm flattered."

Ignoring him, Rigel continued. "It memorizes your unique fingerprint. When you're ready to come back aboard, you press the long button at the end and it will usher you up."

I inspected the smooth red surface of my key. Devon gave me a mischievous grin, and I knew exactly what he was thinking. At the same time we jabbed the cylinders in the air and yelled, "Duck Dodgers in the twenty-fourth and a half century!"

Rigel finally laughed. "Okay, that's enough, Looney Tunes. Let's go."

We followed him out the doorway onto the little platform.

Devon peered over the edge. The yard was at least a hundred feet down. "Don't tell me we have to jump?"

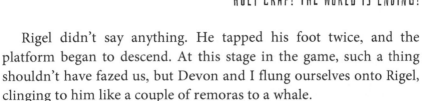

Rigel didn't say anything. He tapped his foot twice, and the platform began to descend. At this stage in the game, such a thing shouldn't have fazed us, but Devon and I flung ourselves onto Rigel, clinging to him like a couple of remoras to a whale.

When we landed, Devon confessed to Rigel with a nudge, "You know, I think I'd be willing to be gay for you. Your voodoo seriously kicks ass."

If Rigel responded to that, I didn't hear it. I was too focused on the uneasy vibe around us. There was no sound of sirens, or people, or birds—not even a cricket. *Where is everyone? Are they all hiding inside, or have they all left? Where would they go?*

"… and that's how I ended up kissing him," Devon finished.

Did I hear that correctly? What were they discussing while I was zoned out? I made a mental note to ask about that later.

We tiptoed to the rear door of Devon's house. Rigel signaled for us to stay behind him, then he cracked open the door and peered in. With a rush of wind, the door flew open and Rigel was inside, gesturing for us to enter.

Devon and I gave a start.

"Coast is clear," Rigel said with a sparkle in his eye.

"No joke, dude," Devon said. "You have my number if you change sides."

"Wait here in the kitchen," Rigel said. "I'll only take a minute." He was gone before we could nod in agreement, leaving us in another gust of wind.

To occupy myself while we waited, I checked out the photos displayed on the fridge. A Polaroid held by a fish-shaped can opener magnet caught my eye. It was of Devon and his family, obviously taken some time ago, as Devon couldn't have been more than sixteen. They were all posing by a barbecue that was blazing with smoke—whatever they were cooking was on fire. Devon's dad had a beer in each hand, and his mom made rabbit ears behind Devon's brother with a pair of tongs. His brother was a stereotypical emo kid of maybe thirteen, his face all scrunched up, clearly annoyed by having to be in the picture.

"This your family?" I asked.

No response.

"Devon?"

I turned to find him staring at the entryway. From around the corner, a guy stepped into view. His hair was a rat's nest, and his face and hands were caked with dirt.

"Derrick," Devon said. "Is that you?"

Devon knew this person? This Derrick guy moved further into the kitchen and that's when I noticed he had and axe behind his back.

"Oh, shit!" I called to Devon. "He has an axe."

Derrick spun in my direction, I think only now realizing someone else was there. It was then that I recognized him: this was Devon's brother.

"Derrick, what are you doing?" Devon asked, his voice shaking.

"Who's *this*?" Derrick spat, glaring at me in disgust.

I spread my arms to show that I wasn't armed. Devon slowly backed toward a rack of knives on the counter.

"Hi," I said, trying to keep my calm. "I'm Autumn, Devon's friend."

Without another word, Derrick lunged at me, his axe swinging straight at my head.

On instinct I put up my hands to block his swing, and was amazed when I managed to deflect it downward. Unfortunately, I didn't quite knock it completely out of the way, and the blade grazed my stomach, creating a bloody slash. With my newfound ninja skills, I grabbed Derrick's arm in one hand and twisted him around so I held it behind his back. I wrapped my other arm around his body and tried to keep his axe hand pressed to his side.

Devon came over with a butcher knife and stood an arm's length away from us.

"Derrick, stop!" I barked as he thrashed, trying to break free. "You don't have to do this. Look at your brother. He's here. He came back."

Derrick stiffened, and abruptly stopped struggling. He stared at Devon and blinked several times.

"Put the axe down!" I ordered, tightening my hold on him.

He did as I said, and Devon kicked it away. I let Derrick go.

Derrick slumped into a chair and slammed his fists against his temple repeatedly. "What's going on?" he said. "I don't understand."

Devon ran to me clenching a dish towel in his hand. "Shit, Autumn, you're bleeding."

I looked down and my shirt was covered in blood. It didn't hurt. *That must mean I'm okay, right?*

"I'm fine, I promise," I said, waving away the towel. "And did you just cuss in your own home? Isn't that against the rules?"

"Moldy honeydew melons spiked on an acid-filled cactus," he said feebly. "That better?"

"Umm… sure."

"Fuck!" Devon yelled. "Rigel is going to flip."

I kneeled next to his brother who was still sitting in the chair. "Hey, are you okay?"

"What are you asking *him* for?" Devon said behind me. "He sliced you with a freaking axe!"

Derrick sank further into the chair and said, "What did you do to me?"

"What did *she* do to *you*?" Devon snapped.

"Devon, quiet," I demanded. "Derrick, how do you feel?"

"Like I just woke up from a nightmare," he replied. Then his gaze fell on my bloody shirt. "What the fuck." He stood so quickly, he knocked the chair over. "What the fuck!"

"Hey, everything is fine," I said reassuringly. I righted the chair and guided him back into it. "It's not your fault."

I started to kneel beside him again, when I was abruptly pulled away, and the next thing I knew Rigel had me on the other side of the room.

"Autumn, what happened?" he asked, scowling at the blood on my shirt.

Before I could respond, Rigel seized Derrick by the neck and lifted him up, leaving his feet dangling off the ground. "What did you do?" he growled.

"Put him down!" I ordered.

Derrick was fighting for breath, his face quickly turning a bright shade of red.

"Did *you* do this to her?" Rigel demanded, raising him higher.

Derrick sputtered, clawing at the hands squeezing his neck.

"I said *stop*!" I boomed this so loud it echoed off the walls.

Rigel finally let Derrick go. He fell to the floor, gasping for air. Devon ran to his brother, and at that moment, both parents burst through the door from the living room. They hesitated for a moment, and when Rigel nodded, they rushed over to gather Devon and Derrick in their arms.

Rigel came over to me. "Are you hurt?" he asked, examining me thoroughly.

I wanted to succumb to the concern in those panicked eyes, to let him take charge and carry me away. I didn't though. This was about Devon and his family, and I needed to be strong for their sake.

"I'm fine," I said. "Let's give Devon time with his family."

On our way out, Derrick approached me. Rigel leapt between us.

"It's under control," I said, gently pushing Rigel aside. "I promise."

"No it isn't!" Rigel said. "I haven't reached into his mind. To get him to see reason."

"Trust me," I assured him. "He won't hurt me."

Reluctantly, Rigel relaxed his stance.

"I'm sorry," Derrick said.

"It's okay," I replied. "It's not your fault."

Derrick offered me his hand and said, "Thank you."

I shook it and gave him what I hoped was a warm smile. "You're welcome."

"Hey," Devon said. "How come you can touch him without tossing chunks?"

He had a good point. *Perhaps Devon really is a 'special threat'? Nah.*

"Maybe all this time I've just been allergic to your hairspray?"

Devon frowned and patted his head as Rigel and I walked out the door.

28

HORRIBLE ACCENTS, EVEN WORSE ACCENTS, SUPERPOWER-WIELDING SOULMATES FOR SALE AT TARGET, AND MORE TERRIBLE ACCENTS

Once we were back aboard the ship, Rigel tended to my wound with a familiar metal instrument—the same one Inanna had healed me with. Now that I could see it closely, it appeared to be one of those ankhs the ancient Egyptians were always holding in the hieroglyphs. Rigel tapped it on the console, and it vibrated like a tuning fork, emitting light and cooling my stinging gash.

"All right, Lucy, you got some splainin' to do," he said, doing a horrible Ricky Ricardo impersonation.

"Wow! That was the worst attempt at an accent I've ever heard!"

"What? My accentasses are magneeefeeeeco." As if to prove his talent, he shared another accent. "Yer bum's oot the windae."

I doubled over laughing. "What the heck kind of accent is that supposed to be?"

"Come on epp and see me urchins," he said proudly, acting like he had just delivered a showstopper. I thought he might be imitating a pirate, but I couldn't tell for sure. It came across one tenth cockney and nine tenths downright unintelligible.

I struggled to catch my breath. "Uh, no."

"Frankly my dear, I dooon't give a da-ham." Okay, I'm pretty sure that was supposed to be a southern accent, but it totally sounded like a British man suffering a stroke. It reminded me of my call into *Coast to Coast AM* when I botched the *Gone with the Wind* accent.

I made a buzzer sound effect at Rigel.

"Fine. Let's hear you do one," he said.

"I never said I could do one!"

"Well, your injury is clearly affecting your judgment. My accents are fantastic. No one else has said otherwise, and I do them all the time. As a matter of fact, I am well known for it."

My eyes widened, and I had to refrain from frowning in disbelief. "Oh, I bet you are."

Rigel stalked off to the console. Worried I might have offended him to the point of not healing me completely, I inspected my stomach. It was thoroughly mended, all traces of the cut vanished.

"Thank you," I said.

He gave me a forced smile as he poked at the screen with more pressure than was necessary.

I decided changing the subject might be the best approach. I relayed to him all that had happened in Devon's kitchen. His interest was piqued when I explained how I was able to subdue Derrick easily, and how I thought I might have gotten in his head too—the whole thought transference thing that Rigel has—since Derrick came to his senses right after I touched him and tried to explain what was going on.

"So you think you have my powers?" Rigel said.

"Yeah."

I pondered what other talents I might have siphoned from him. There had to be a way to make them useful. Unable to resist, I flexed my muscles, hoping for a Popeye bicep or for my forearm to inflate with a slide whistle sound effect. No such luck.

"Hey, will these abilities help me when I use the Pinecone?" I asked.

"I don't know," he said. "I'm curious about something, though. Come try this." I joined him over by the console.

He brushed his hand across the screen, and a female computer voice chimed, "Sign out successful. Goodbye Rigel."

Rigel guided me to stand in front of the panel. "Place your hand on the monitor," he said.

"Why?"

"Trust me."

I shrugged and did what he asked. And as soon as I raised my hand to the screen, Rigel's photo and stats appeared on the display. The computer voiced hummed, "Welcome, Rigel. How may I help you?"

"Would you look at that?" he said.

"It thinks I'm you?"

"It recognizes people by their energy fingerprint."

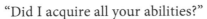

"Did I acquire all your abilities?"

"I doubt you can shift into light, because you haven't consumed gold."

"What about your speed?"

"It's plausible. We had the ability to flash prior to taking it, but it was significantly slower than what we can do now."

"How do I do it?" I asked enthusiastically. "What do you do? Should I just run?"

"No. It doesn't work like that."

"Then what should I do?"

"I don't actually know. It's sort of instinct for us. Maybe… try picturing where you want to end up?" Rigel crossed his arms. "I don't know if your clothes will go with you though."

"Are you trying to get me naked?"

The corners of his mouth twisted. "Yes, that would be nice. The thing is, I don't know how much of me you procured. This is uncharted territory here."

"You could flash in regular clothing prior to consuming gold, right?"

"Yes. The amount of energy we use to flash takes us into the first stages of our light form. We can't do it without partially turning into light, so anything solid falls through us."

"Worst case, I end up naked? Would that be so bad?"

"Hell no. Go for it!"

I marched to the corner of the ship and faced the door. It wasn't that far, but it would have to do. I visualized myself being at the doorway.

And in an instant, I was there, precisely where I had intended, my hair rustling from the wind—and my clothes intact and on my person. *Holy crap, that was cool!*

"Rigel, did you see that?" I squealed as if I had won the lotto. *Heck, this kicks the lotto's ass!*

His face lit up. "That could come in handy."

"Let's go outside where there's more room!"

I readied myself to flash out the door, but stopped short when I saw Devon on the platform floating toward the ship holding his space modulator. My exhilaration drained instantly, replaced by concern.

The platform locked on to the entryway and Devon wiped his feet on the welcome mat before stepping through the doorway. "I know I keep saying it, but that's so freaking cool!" He kissed his modulator with a loud smack.

"How did it go?" I asked.

"Awesome," he said, thrusting his chest out in mock pride. "I informed them that their gallant son was off to save the human race, and that made them proud."

"I'm sure they were proud of you anyway," I said.

"True, but this makes up for me not going to college. Hey, what were you kids doing before I arrived? You looked like you were about to dash off. Everything okay?"

I couldn't wait to share my new super speed with Devon. "Watch!" I said. I flashed to the opposite side of the ship. "Ta-da!"

"What the hell? I want to do that!"

"Sorry. I think I gained some of Rigel's abilities when we... you know... bonded."

He gaped. "Now I'm officially jealous. Where do *I* get an alien prophetic soulmate to gift me with superpowers?"

"Hmm... maybe Target carries them," I teased. "We can check."

Rigel interrupted. "There is a far more pressing issue we need to discuss with Devon." Devon and I fell silent. "Autumn here believes I can't do accents. What's your opinion?" He cleared his throat, then said, "I think yer the cat's pajamas, babeee."

Devon's face remained blank. I had no doubt he was wondering what the hell was going on. "Irish?" he said hesitantly.

"No," Rigel answered. He crossed his arm and sniffed.

"Cockney?"

"No."

"Chinese?"

I about hit the floor. Devon gave an innocent shrug.

Rigel narrowed his eyes at us both, then stomped over to the navigation chair. With an evil smirk at me, he made the ship see-through again, and shot us into the sky. I fell on my butt.

"You are so gonna pay for that," I said.

29

SPACESHIP DRIVE-THROUGH, DECAPITATED GORILLAS, ALLIGATOR SNORTING, AND DING DONG DOMINATION

As we skyrocketed into the clouds, the city blending in with the countryside, I thought of Emma somewhere down there and was hit with a swell of remorse. With all that had been going on, it hadn't occurred to me to try to contact her. What a horrible friend I was. *How could I forget Emma?* She probably thought I'd been killed, since I'd never made it to her apartment.

"Wait!" I said.

"What's the matter?" Rigel asked, worry lining his features.

"Emma," I said. "I need to see Emma. Can we go there? It won't take long, I promise."

"Of course," he said. He removed his hands from the controls. "Why don't you take the reins?"

I sat down at the helm, more confident than last time, and guided the ship to her apartment complex, which was located next to a shopping center. As I passed over all the stores and restaurants, I realized that I didn't have any food to bring. *Unacceptable!* Foodstuff was a strict requirement when visiting Emma. I wouldn't dare go to her house without at least a pound of grease, especially with the story I was about to reveal.

I redirected the ship and brought it to a stop over the drive-through of Arby's.

"Emma lives at Arby's?" Devon asked.

"No," I said, rolling my eyes at him. "I gotta get food to take to Emma's. It's kind of our thing."

"Uh, I don't think, given the circumstances, anyone is going to be manning a fast food joint."

"No problem. I had an illustrious career at Arby's in high school. I can fry, slice, and assemble like no other." I said that a little too proudly. "You guys want anything?"

"Ooh! Ooh!" Devon perked up. "I'll take a Meat Mountain Sandwich with Horsey Sauce and a silo of Curly Fries."

"Wow, you aren't messing around," I said, impressed. "Rigel, how 'bout you?"

"Not sure. Never had Arby's."

"What?" Devon and I gasped in unison.

"I'll whip us up all the Arby's staples then," I said. "You're in for a treat."

"Get extra Arby's Sauce, too," Devon said. "I love that with my fries."

"Totally! No true Arby's meal is complete without the signature sauce."

Rigel moved to open the door for me, but I raised a hand. "Let me," I said with a sly smile and then boomed, "Open says me!"

The door obeyed. I grinned at them both, gave a quick salute, and then visualized the inside of Arby's—and faster than I could take a breath, I was there.

Putting safety first, I washed up before springing into action. I fired up the deep fryer, nabbed the Curly Fries from the freezer, and sliced plenty of roast beef. In under thirty minutes I had made a cal-orie-packed feast, including several different types of loaded meat 'n cheese sandwiches, Curly Fries, Jalapeño Bites, Mozzarella Sticks, on-ion rings, and enough sauces to fill a kiddie pool. On the way out, my sweet tooth whined in protest. Not wanting to ignore the dying wish of my sugar-addicted molars, I confiscated a heap of cherry turnovers and a half dozen molten lava cakes before returning to the ship.

When I flashed in, Rigel stared at the bags in my hands. "You can carry things when you flash?"

"Umm… I guess so. You can't?"

Rigel frowned.

"Oh, that's right. The gold and all." I beamed at him. "Wow, my gifts kick your gifts' ass!"

Devon swiped the bags from me and divvied up the spoils between them. While he did this, he gave Rigel a serious lecture about when to properly use Arby's Sauce, when to use Horsey Sauce, and when to stick with ketchup. I headed back to the navigation chair and flew us to Emma's place. The smell of the food had my stomach growling, and the hunger shakes made my flying somewhat haphazard. Along the way I narrowly avoided decapitating a King Kong-sized gorilla statue perched on the roof of a car dealership. And I might have nicked a traffic light when I maneuvered into Emma's apartment complex. And possibly I took off a few roof tiles from the clubhouse. And maybe a balcony… or two. Hey, in my defense, the ship was invisible, and I couldn't tell how far the outside of it reached.

In contrast to Devon's desolate neighborhood, Emma's was quite the hotspot for mischief and mayhem. A group of boys were busting a gut trying to roll a MINI Cooper (sadly they had only managed to lift one tire about a foot off the concrete), a decrepit gray-haired man was lighting a dumpster on fire with a blowtorch, and atop a delivery truck, a collection of naked college-aged kids snorted blow off what appeared to be a taxidermy alligator.

As the ship approached, the crowd wrangled whatever they could find to lob at us. One heaved a lawn chair pretty far, but unfortunately it nailed his buddy on the forehead when it landed. Wanting to distance us from these crazies, I flew over the complex and parked inside a courtyard, taking out another balcony along the way. *I hope Rigel has this craft insured.*

When I rose from the chair, I found Devon and Rigel devouring their food. Rigel's mouth was filled to the brim, the curly ends of his fries sticking out like frightened little worms. He dribbled some out as he spoke.

"Devon ate that whole Meat Mountain monstrosity. Did you see what was on that thing?"

"Uh, yeah. I made it for him."

"That's something you came up with, right?"

"No, as frightening as it is, that's a real thing."

(For those of you not fortunate enough to know about the contents of a Meat Mountain Sandwich, let me give you a breakdown, because it simply is amazing: chicken tenders, roast turkey, ham, swiss cheese, corned beef, brisket, Angus steak, cheddar cheese, roast beef, and bacon. And that's all on one sandwich. Even Emma and I, who are professional eaters, draw the line at this one.)

Rigel and Devon chomped away, happier than two kids who had raided a secret cookie stash. When I gathered up the rest of the food to take with me, I was shocked by how much they had already consumed. At least they saved the Jalapeño Bites for us. I went to put the container in a bag when a hand snatched it away.

I turned to see Rigel clutching it protectively in his arms, Arby's Sauce all over his chin.

"Not the Jalapeño Bites, please?" he said.

"I take it you like Arby's then?"

He nodded.

"Okay, you guys can keep the Jalapeño Bites."

He and Devon both dug in like savages.

I flashed from the ship onto Emma's patio and peeked through a crack in the blinds. Emma was inside, painting on the wall. Despite the chaos outside, she was dressed in her Forever 21 finest. She had on '80s acid-washed jeans with tons of holes in them (in fact, there were more openings than actual material covering her legs), a long flowing tan sweater with several layers to it, and suede ankle boots. I knocked on the glass door.

Emma dropped her paintbrush and scooted from view. The next thing I knew, a shotgun barrel was pointed right at me.

"Holy mother of hell," I gasped, and quickly stepped out of range.

The shotgun was replaced by her eyeball as she peered at me through the blinds, then the door swung open and she nearly bowled me over.

"You're alive!" she said, squeezing me so hard I couldn't move my arms.

"I am. Are you okay?"

When she pulled back, she had tears in her eyes. "Yes. At least I am now that you're here. I'm also, oddly enough, suddenly craving Arby's. When you didn't show I thought something had happened to you. Where have you been?" She noticed the blood all over my shirt and went pale. "Shit, Autumn, is that your blood?"

"How 'bout I tell you as we demolish a pound of Curly Fries?" I held out the food bag, and she clapped her hands in delight.

She invited me inside and I got to see what she had been painting. I stopped dead in my tracks to stare at it. She had converted the one entire wall of her living room into a grand canvas: a spectacular landscape of an exotic island, complete with an aquamarine ocean, white sandy beaches, and tropical vegetation. The light and shadows she used made it seem real. The highlight for me was a tea party taking place on a cliff in the background. Toucan Sam, Cap'n Crunch, a Keebler elf, Count Chocula, and the smoke monster from *Lost* were sharing cakes and sipping from dainty cups.

"Emma! This is amazing!"

"Thanks," she said. "Look over there."

She pointed to the corner of the mural where she'd painted us lounging on a raft made of Ding Dongs. And next to it… was a sunken Twinkie boat.

"See?" she said. "The Ding Dong raft lasted longer. Your Twinkie ship sank, and I had to come rescue you."

"Hmm…" I tapped my finger against my cheek. "Not to rain on your parade, but you definitely took artistic liberties there."

She glanced again at my shirt. "Before we do anything else, I have to get you a new outfit. That blood is grossing me out."

She stepped out, then returned with a blue scoop neck T-shirt and a pair of stretchy black pants.

"Thanks," I said. I held them up. "You have normal clothes? This seems way too plain for you."

"Are you kidding? Those are yours. You left them here a few years ago."

"Oh, whew. I was worried for a second."

After I changed my clothes and cleaned up, we plunked our behinds between the palm trees and chowed down while I gave Emma a summary of the madness that had transpired since we split up at Costco.

"Autumn," she said with a sigh, resting her head back on the wall, "I don't know what to say. I wish I had some meaningful words of advice, but I don't." She turned to me. "There's one thing I do know."

"What's that?" I asked, licking the residual curly fry residue off my fingers.

"I really should have given you badass high-heeled boots and a sexy red corset instead of that T-shirt. You need to look hot while saving the planet."

"I'd totally fall on my ass."

Emma nudged me with her shoulder. "Seriously though, I know you're gonna save us."

"I have no idea what to tell to these people," I said, burying my head between my knees.

"It'll come to you. I have faith."

"That makes one of us," I grunted. "So, anyway, what happened to you after Costco? How did you make it home?"

Emma grinned. "Like you, I didn't make it far before I had to abandon my car. I found this cycle shop and stole one of those really cool electric bikes. The charge only held for about five miles though, and when that sucker ran out, let me tell you, it was impossible to pedal. Probably because I haven't ridden a bike since I was like twelve."

"I think the last time we rode was in junior high," I said. "Do you remember that?"

Emma squinted, then her face lit up with the memory and she slapped the table. "Dean Madigan."

I busted up laughing. "You told Dean that if he could pop a wheelie for thirty seconds, you would make out with him."

"That bastard!" Emma huffed and crossed her arms. "He tasted like onion rings and breath mints."

"Ewww." I laughed. "I can't believe he did it."

"He totally played me."

"And then you had a tantrum and tossed your bike in the dumpster."

"Because every time I got on, it would only remind me of his slimy wet mouth and those sucking noises he made."

"I had completely forgotten about that."

"Me too." She gave me a playful shove. "Gee. Thanks for the reminder."

I laughed again.

"Anyway, after the bike ran out of juice, I walked back."

"You didn't run into any wackos like I did?"

"Well, there was this one dude dragging a taxidermy alligator down the street."

"Oh, I saw him. He's outside your apartment right now snorting cocaine."

"Seriously?"

"Naked, too."

"I don't need to see that."

We fell silent for a while after that. We both knew it was time for me to go.

Emma was the first to speak. "This is the last time I'll see you, huh?"

"Probably."

We stood and stared at the painting for a while. Emma's eyes were glassy with emotion. "Who knew my best friend would be the one to save the human race?"

"Well, I haven't done it yet."

"You will."

I felt tears forming in my eyes. No more pigout fests, no more penis-shaped moles, and no more time with Emma. This was it. I latched on to the notion that she, at least, might be saved—if by some miracle I persuaded the masses to listen to reason.

"I wish you could come," I said.

"You'll do fine."

We flung ourselves into a drawn-out, tear-filled, way-too-tight hug. I didn't want to let her go. But with great sadness, I released her and headed to the patio.

"Autumn," she said.

I glanced back.

"I love you," she whispered.

I smiled and said, "Are we reenacting the Lifetime movie of the week?"

She laughed. "No. This is much bigger than that."

"So true."

"May the fork be with you."

"And also with you." I gave her a sweeping bow.

After I closed the door behind me, I heaved in a breath and had to lean on the railing for support. My chest was a hollow pit, the breaths painful as they left my lungs. *The term 'having your heart ripped out' makes sense now.*

Emma's eye appeared at the crack in the blinds. I whispered the words "I love you, too," then flashed to the ship.

30

ARTIFICIAL PASTRY KILLERS, HOT RUSSIAN GIRLS, DRUNKEN WOES, AND PRESIDENT LINCOLN'S BUTT WEDGIE

Rigel and Devon were polishing off their turnovers when I returned. They beamed and waved hi, their teeth covered in cherry filling as if they were two vampires feasting on a fresh kill and not an artificial pastry. Fate has a strange way of bringing people together: an other-worldly Greek god, a vomit-inducing kleptomaniac, and the unwit-ting vessel for the Lord Almighty—all joining forces to save humanity from the clutches of evil.

Now that's a great logline for a movie.

Rigel rose to greet me, holding a chocolate lava cake. "This will cheer you up."

I accepted it and bit in. It was all warm and gooey inside. "You warmed it up?"

"He sure did," Devon answered for him, patting his belly in satis-faction. "Rigel made it taste fresh from the oven."

Within seconds I had devoured the whole thing—the melty choco-late satisfying a craving I didn't know I'd harbored. It wasn't until I was jonesing for another that I noticed Rigel was no longer beside me.

Whirling to find my sugar pusher, I saw him watching me from the other side of the ship. He was leaning against the almost invisible wall, one leg propped up. His arms were folded casually on his chest, exposing taut biceps. He could have been an airbrushed model torn straight from the pages of a catalog; T-shirt clinging to all the right places, pants hanging teasingly low, and that brooding pout. Granted, Rigel could have worn a chicken suit and would still have been hotter than hell.

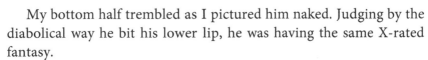

My bottom half trembled as I pictured him naked. Judging by the diabolical way he bit his lower lip, he was having the same X-rated fantasy.

Devon gave a whistle and said, "The way you two are staring at each other, you remind me of characters on a telenovela. What are those faces you're making?"

Rigel pushed off the wall all seductive like, and I gulped. My desire was abruptly extinguished when he proclaimed in the saddest excuse for a Mexican accent I'd ever heard, "Your pass-eon eeegnites my ffflame."

Devon and I spoke at the same time. "Nope."

Rigel glared. "If you two talk in unison one more time, I'm going to speak in accents for the rest of the trip."

"No!" we both shouted together, then covered our mouths in horror. Of course this sent us into hysterics.

It was with regret that I spoiled the fun by asking Rigel, "So what's the plan?"

"Next destination is the Ark."

"Are you going to tell us where it is?"

"I bet it's in a cave deep within a tropical jungle," Devon said. "Do we get to go all Indiana Jones?"

"No," Rigel said with a grin.

"What are you smiling at?" I asked.

"I tell you what: if you can guess where it is, I will never do another accent as long as I live."

Devon and I rose to the challenge. I took the first stab at it. "Vatican?"

"No. Very cold."

"Stonehenge?" Devon tried.

"Colder."

"The dark side of the moon?" I asked.

"Nope."

"Donald Trump's Apartment!" offered Devon.

Rigel raised an eyebrow.

"Anywhere in Africa?" I said, remembering a rumor it might be in Ethiopia.

"Hmm... no. But we will have to go there."

"Why?"

"South Africa is where we have to go to activate it."

"What's there?"

"The Abzu."

"Is that a thing or a place?"

"A place. It used to be our center of operations for mining gold and home to Enki's genetics lab. More importantly, it's where we will get the power to operate the Ark."

"Power?" Devon asked. "Can't we just plug into the Hoover Dam? It's way closer."

"If only it were that simple. The Abzu is home to a colossal energy grid we built when we first arrived."

"Why is that ringing a bell for me?" I said, trying to fish the memory from the depths of my mind.

"Have you heard of Michael Tellinger?" Rigel said. "He collaborated with Johan Heine, who uncovered our elaborate networking system and activation device."

"Tellinger! Yes, I know who he is." I recalled an old podcast. "He was on *Coast to Coast AM*. I think he claimed to find Enki's home and a calendar—a Stonehenge-looking thing, but older. He called it Enki's Calendar? Or was it Adam's Calendar? Anyway, I did a search on him, and I found images of all these huge circular structures, hundreds of thousands of them, spread throughout South Africa."

"Those stone circles are all part of the energy grid. 'Enki's Calendar,' as he called it, is the activation mechanism for the grid."

"All that infrastructure to power the Ark? That's a lot of work for a communication device, isn't it?"

"The energy grid was created for much more than that. It provided electricity to all our cities, ran the gold mining equipment, and fueled our transport ships to Nibiru."

"Hold on," I cut in. "That single location powered *all* your cities? Didn't you have cities throughout the world?"

"We did. Energy was transported wirelessly from city to city using special towers. Power lines without the lines, if you will. The relics of those towers can be found in almost every country in the world. Functioning ones, in fact. Humans just haven't recognized them for what they really are. All you see is rubble, when in actuality they are massive transmitters placed on a series of ley lines, each convergence serving as an amplifier. The Great Pyramids, for example, were used to receive power and provide communication between the rulers of our cities."

"Did you have cell phones back then?" Devon asked.

"We had something similar, a tablet type device, but Enlil monitored all transmissions through his central base of operations."

I shook my head. "What, all the humans filling his brain with endless chatter wasn't enough? He needed to hear what you all were saying aloud, too?"

"Well, you guys know the lore behind the Tower of Babel, right?"

"I think so," I said. "That was the tower that God destroyed to 'confound' the people, or some mumbo-jumbo."

"Sort of," Rigel said. "You see, Marduk, Enki's son, loathed Enlil, and he used every resource at his disposal to bring his rule to an end."

"That's understandable," I chuffed.

"In a ploy to establish a resistance and overthrow Enlil, Marduk built a secret communication tower in Egypt in order to bypass the central system and send unmonitored messages to the other cities in the hopes of inciting an uprising among humans."

"What provoked him to attempt that?" I asked. "Overthrowing Enlil seems like a suicide mission to me."

"Inanna…" Rigel hesitated. "Um, maybe I should skip that part."

"No, you can't skip it now!" Devon said. "What about Inanna?"

"No way. She'll kill me."

"Spill it!" I insisted.

Rigel twisted uncomfortably. "You can't repeat this to anyone."

Devon and I made a zipping gesture across our lips.

"I first need to explain one of the underlying social structures of our civilization in order for you to understand. You may have noticed that the Anunnaki are kind of control freaks?"

"No," I said sarcastically. "Really?"

"In our society, it's important that qualified individuals govern all political and social affairs. Every infinitesimal detail must be accounted for and overseen properly. And when we came to Earth and created humans, we discovered that you needed to be monitored or you would quickly become unruly, and that meant we had to share the babysitting duties to keep things in order."

I glowered. "I'm not going to enjoy where this is going, am I?"

"Probably not," he said. "Enlil recorded each of these responsibilities on separate tablets, which are called *mes*."

"Called what?" I asked.

"It's an old Sumerian word spelled M.E. but pronounced 'may,' similar to the month. These tablets were a way to organize who got to command what function. For example, one *me* might give someone jurisdiction over money, another over art, another over the exalted scepter, and so on."

"Exalted scepter?" Devon interrupted. "That sounds medieval. Does it do anything cool?"

"It was used to steer boats."

"Blah." Devon pouted.

"It's the same as Poseidon's trident in Greek mythology. Dropping it can generate a ripple of energy capable of incinerating all living creatures within a ten-mile radius." Rigel twitched as though reliving an actual incident. "Anyway, whichever individual received a particular *me* would have dominion over that area, and would be responsible for all associated duties. For instance, if I had the barley *me*, I'd govern the crop cycles and either make them flourish or wither, based on how the humans behaved."

"That totally makes sense now," I said. "That's why in mythology you have the god of rain, the goddess of wine, god of this, goddess of that. . ."

"Exactly."

"And that's why people prayed to the gods and gave sacrifices," I reasoned. "They had to, or you jerks would take their crops away."

"Yes, that's true too," Rigel conceded. "These *mes* were also used as bargaining tools among us. Let me give you an example, which, before you ask, is in no way a real story."

I squinted in disbelief, but nodded for him to continue.

"Say a particular human family did something to upset me. Maybe they didn't pay their taxes, or they lied about something significant. I might want to punish them by taking away their land. In that case, I would go to the owner of the Kisura *me*, which controls and marks borders and boundaries, and strike a deal with that Anunnaki to shrink the family's lands in exchange for either money or use of one of my own *mes*. The more *mes* you had, the more you commanded, and hence the more powerful you were."

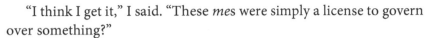

"I think I get it," I said. "These *me*s were simply a license to govern over something?"

"Yes. A license is a perfect analogy."

"What deterred an ambitious Anunnaki from doing what they wanted anyway?" I asked. "If I wanted to destroy crops, let's say, I could easily light them on fire. I wouldn't need a stone tablet for that. For that matter, what would deter me from stealing the scepter and zapping anyone who tried to take it back?"

"That was not an option," Rigel said. "If someone used or interfered with a *me* that didn't belong to them, the owner of the *me* could take any recourse he or she saw fit. No holds barred. The Anunnaki would band together for the opportunity to flaunt their *me*s and give a clear message that theft was not tolerated."

"Was there a *me* that controlled all the other *me*s?"

Rigel nodded. "It's called the Tablet of Destinies, and was owned by none other than Enlil."

"That sounds fancy," Devon said.

"It was. It could instantly take possession of any *me*. The person who had the Tablet of Destinies essentially had at their disposal the means to enslave everyone if they so desired. It was nicknamed the Enlil-power."

"And you relied on a slab of stone to track all this important information?"

"Not just stone. Each *me* was a fine piece of computerized lapis lazuli with the owner's energy fingerprint programmed into it."

"Lapis la-what?" Devon said.

"It's a brilliant ultramarine stone that the Anunnaki are fond of. If a *me* was given or sold to another, the fingerprint had to be reprogrammed with the approval of either Enki or Enlil."

"How did you initially divvy up the *me*s?" I asked. "Knowing you guys, I'm guessing they weren't dispersed fairly."

"At first, they all belonged to Enlil and Enki. No one else was allowed to use, borrow, or be in the same room as them without supervision. And that, finally, is where Inanna comes in." Rigel fidgeted a bit. "Bored with her time here on Earth, she... sought a new challenge, let's say. She was—and still is—quite the spitfire." Devon leaned in, eyes sparkling like a high school gossip queen about to hear the dirt. "As I mentioned, the more *me*s you possessed, the more leverage you had. Inanna, shark that she is, wanted the lion's share of the *me*s for herself."

"Oh, I bet she did." Devon grinned. "This is gonna be good."

"Inviting herself to Enki's place for dinner, she wore a revealing outfit and gushed seduction from every pore. And I do mean that literally. One of her 'gifts' is seduction. She spent the night getting Enki drunk, and then charmed him into giving her more than a hundred *me*s, including seven of the exalted ones."

"Nice!" Devon said.

"What made a *me* exalted?" I asked.

"A *me* was exalted if it gave one ownership of an object that wielded remarkable power—or if it was bestowed to one of us directly by our leader Anu."

"I bet Enki wasn't too happy the next morning." I said. "A hangover and all those *me*s gone."

"No, he wasn't. He hunted her down—after he remembered what happened, that is. But she went straight to her grandfather Enlil, who concluded that Enki did willingly give them to her, drunk or not. Therefore, she was able to keep them."

"Oh, man." Devon laughed. "She is something else."

"After that incident, Enlil made Enki divide the rest of the *me*s among the Anunnaki to be fair. When Inanna heard about this, she threw a fit and insisted she get a cut too."

"But she'd already gotten hers," I said. "That was the whole point."

"I know, but Inanna has a way of getting what she wants. She complained to Enlil, and the next thing we knew, she had doubled her collection—getting several *me*s that had been promised to none other than Marduk. In fact, he lost over half of his collection to her. This pushed him over the edge, and he decided to overthrow Enlil no matter the cost."

"Why didn't he go after Inanna?" I said. "She's the one that bargained for all those *me*s."

"Oh, he did, later. But remember, it was Enlil who granted them to her. He had ultimate power over who got what *me*s, not Inanna. If Marduk wanted this favoritism to stop, he needed to take down the source of the problem, which was Enlil. Besides, Inanna wasn't the only one getting special treatment as one of Enlil's family line. So with

the help of some of the Igigi and Marduk's human supporters, the construction of the Tower of Babel began."

"Not to get sidetracked, but who exactly are the Igigi?" I asked.

Rigel became noticeably uncomfortable.

"Uh-oh. What is it? And don't you dare say, 'We don't think like you do.'"

Rigel seemed to be considering his words. "The Igigi are the working class and military in our society."

That in itself wasn't so bad, but I could tell there was more. "By 'working class,' are you actually referring to slaves?"

"No, they're free. The males have to serve in our military when called upon, no different than your drafts. The only thing is, the Igigi can't advance their way to the status of an Anunnaki. You have to be born into it. Similar to a royal family."

"Well, la-di-da," Devon sing-songed. "Shall we call you Prince Rigel? Perhaps Emperor Rigel? Oh, how about Baron Rigel von..." Devon paused. "Hey, what is your last name anyway?"

"Oh, shit," I blurted. "I don't even know. How can I not know that?"

"Calm down, you two," Rigel said. "The Anunnaki don't have last names."

"I wish *I* didn't," Devon said, and then covered his mouth quickly.

"Why, what's your last name?" I asked.

He paled and shook his head.

"It can't be that bad?"

"Sore subject for me," he grumbled. "Not a great childhood."

"Come on, what is it?"

He sighed. "Fine. It's Potty. My last name is Potty."

My eyes went wide. "That *is* unfortunate." I cleared my throat to cover up my laugh. "Devon Potty, huh? What's your middle name?"

He flamed red. "No. I don't speak of my middle name."

"Oh, come on!" I said. "Please. Don't make me play the dying savior card."

He looked away, and in a mumble I could barely hear, he said, "Whent."

Whent? I thought I must have heard him incorrectly. "What was that?"

"Devon Whent Potty, okay?" he huffed. "You happy now?"

Rigel and I couldn't contain our laughter.

"Why on earth would your parents give you that middle name?" I asked.

"Every guy in my mom's family has that middle name. It's tradition. And when she married my dad, well, a lifetime of unrelenting ridicule for the two Potty boys ensued."

"No wonder your brother is an emo," I said.

"All right, you've had your laugh," Devon grumbled. "Can we get back to the freaking tower now? Enlil pissed Marduk off, he built a tower to send smoke signals for an uprising, blah blah blah."

Biting on my nail to hide my smile, I turned to Rigel. "Yeah, if that many people were on board to take Enlil down, why didn't it work? I mean, I assume it didn't, since he's still running things."

"It didn't work," Rigel said, "because Marduk had a spy in his rebellion. Enlil got wind of his treachery and flattened the tower."

"Question," Devon said. "I always thought Babel was about discombobulating speech. Isn't that the reason all these different languages exist in the world?"

I stared at him. "How did you know that?"

"Because I use BabelFish to translate phrases online occasionally. You know, when I need to chat with a hot Russian girl."

"Ahh," I said. "Valid question. How does the Tower of Babel relate to languages?"

"To stop another uprising by humans, Enlil had Enki install an encryption failsafe. Each region of the world was forced to learn a separate and unique language from all the others, and they only received messages in their designated dialect. They were no longer able to converse without going through this monitored command station where transmissions were translated into the appropriate language. He also had Anu mandate that the Anunnaki and Igigi were only allowed to learn the single language of their region. If they wanted to communicate to other regions, they had to go through this translation system. In time, the original language was lost among humans."

I wanted to ask if such a mandate was still in place, but Devon spoke up first.

"Hey, wait a minute," he said, his face full of curiosity. "Do *you* have any *mes*?"

Rigel darted his eyes nervously. "*Mes* aren't relevant anymore," he said. "They're only for nostalgic purposes now."

"Okay, but did you have one?" Devon pushed.

I cocked my head. "Yeah, do you have one?"

Swallowing hard, Rigel said, "Yes."

"Annnnnd?" Devon asked. "It does what?"

A bead of sweat trickled down Rigel's forehead. Whatever this *me* gave him control over, he sure didn't want to say. His face turned so pale I was afraid he might faint.

"Rigel?" I asked, "You okay?"

"Dude. It must be something major." Devon poked him in the shoulder. "You *so* have to spill the beans. What is it?"

Rigel opened his mouth to speak, then shut it. I was beyond curious, but he seemed to be in complete anguish at having to admit what *me* he owned, and I couldn't endure seeing him that upset.

"It's not important," I said. "Rigel, you really don't have to say."

He heaved a sigh.

"Booooooo!" Devon griped. "Are you at least going to tell us where the Ark is then? Is it wedged under Lincoln's butt at the Memorial? He looks a bit strained sitting in that chair."

"Warmer," Rigel said. "Arkansas."

"Arkansas?" Devon and I said—accidentally speaking in unison.

"I warned you." Rigel said, and in a unidentifiable hodgepodge of accents, he continued, "Y'all are askin' for it neeow. Yup. This here Ark is hidden in Bentonville, Arrrr-kansas."

"What's in Bentonville?" I asked.

"Do you guys shop at Wal-Mart?"

"Wal-Mart?" Devon and I said together.

"Stop doing that!"

"What does Wal-Mart have to do with the Ark of the Covenant?" I asked.

"Everything."

31

GRANNY KUNG FU MASTER, THE PORTAL TO HELL, AND A LEWD ACT IN A PUBLIC TOILET

"Here we are," Rigel said, bringing the spaceship to hover next to a dilapidated Wal-Mart. It clearly hadn't been remodeled in thirty years: the walls were cracked and chipped in places, and the paint was peeling off in big chunks. Did management fail to notice all the painting supplies at the ready in their home improvement section? They hadn't bothered to update the Wal-Mart sign with a logo from this century either: each letter was written on a separate white block of wood, reminding me of a solved *Wheel of Fortune* puzzle.

"The '70s called and they want their Wal-Mart back," Devon announced.

Rigel laughed. "We purposely keep this one outdated so the traffic stays down."

"You think it's hidden in the garden center?" I asked Devon.

"By 'garden center,' do you mean that couch parked outside the entrance?"

I snorted when I saw the ratty brown couch sitting between the pony ride machine and a line of lawnmowers.

"No," I said. "There's a real garden center over there." I pointed to the far corner where a bougainvillea, an open bag of dirt, a half built demo shed, and a chainsaw lay.

"Hmm. My first guess was in Sporting Goods," Devon said. "But on further reflection, it would be pretty dumb to put it next to all those guns and ammo. This is Arkansas, after all. Therefore I'm gonna go for the least obvious location and wager it's in the fabric and crafting section. Most likely next to the multi-colored spools of yarn."

Rigel rolled his eyes.

"Seriously," I said to Rigel, "Why in the hell are you guys stashing the Ark of the Covenant at Wal-Mart?"

"Actually, Wal-Mart was created specifically to be a cover for the Ark," he confided. "Before that, it was kept in a warehouse we have at Mount Ararat. That location became troublesome when the Galactic Federation started hosting parties here on Earth. They would put in requests for viewings of the Ark on a regular basis, but the safeguards we have at Mount Ararat to protect the items stored there are quite elaborate, making it difficult to host hundreds of guests at one time— and moving it in and out all the time can be dangerous. So we had to figure out where we could showcase it while still keeping it hidden from humans. The current placement came about when Inanna de- vised the clever plan to hide it beneath a discount department store. To be honest, she was two bottles of wine in when that vision came. After consideration, however, the Anunnaki thought the simplicity genius. We enlisted an Alpha Centaurian who lived as a human on Earth at the time to oversee the project. He had recently opened up Walton's 5&10 in Bentonville, creating the perfect opportunity to expand the franchise to a larger facility where we could hide the Ark and hold the Federation parties. And so Wal-Mart was born in Rodgers, Arkansas. We later relocated to Bentonville when more room was needed."

I gawked at him. "Sam Walton is an alien?"

"He was, yes."

"Trip out on that," said Devon.

"Wal-Mart offered an ideal ruse; it was the last place anyone sus- pected the Ark would be. As a bonus, it also proved to be profitable. In fact, it was so successful, the U.S. government now uses Wal-Marts across the country to secretly store weapons and supplies. That's why there's one in virtually every city."

"You're totally messing with us right now," Devon said.

I crossed my arms and squinted at Rigel suspiciously. "You're tell- ing me that while I'm wheeling my feminine products down the aisles of my local Wal-Mart, in reality I'm traipsing on top of an arsenal of lethal weapons?"

"Odds are, yes," he said.

"Well, slap me upside the head and color me zebra," Devon exclaimed.

"I'm not even going to ask what that means," Rigel said.

"It means hot damn, we're going to Wally World!" I translated, in the best redneck accent I could muster.

We descended from the ship into the Wal-Mart parking lot. I had been so distracted by watching Rigel's muscles flex as he steered the ship that I didn't notice how much things had changed outside. The horizon was blanketed by a smoky orange haze, as if the hills were on fire. This haze dampened the sun's rays, and you could see Nibiru and its moons off to the side. To get a better view of Rigel's planet, I blocked the sun with my hands. It was unreal to finally see it. Even though it was still small in the sky, you could tell the planet had fiery wings that extended from each side.

"So that's your home?" I asked.

Indulging me with a gentle neck massage, Rigel said, "Yes, that's Nibiru."

The sight made me think of a phoenix in flight about to be reborn. Beautiful—if not for the devastation it foretold.

"Which one of your moons is the bastard that's plowing us down?"

"The brightest one—there, at five o'clock. It's called Tiamat-min, ironically."

"Why is that ironic?"

"Explaining it would involve a boring history lesson on the formation of our solar system."

"I could use boring about now."

"Well, a long time ago, before either of our species existed, Earth's location in the solar system was not between Venus and Mars, as it is now. You were farther out, between the orbits of Mars and Jupiter. At that time, Earth was called Tiamat, and your moon was called Kingu.

During a pass of Nibiru around the sun, one of its moons collided with Tiamat and split it into two. Now we had Tiamat I, Tiamat II, and Kingu. On Nibiru's next encounter with your planet, thirty-six hundred years later, another of its moons struck Tiamat II, pushing both it and Kingu into orbit between Venus and Mars. Tiamat II eventually became known as Earth, and Kingu is your moon.

"Tiamat I was destroyed when Nibiru clipped it on the way back out. The fragments of Tiamat I became your asteroid belt—except for one large fragment, which was captured by Nibiru's gravitational field and fell into orbit. Nibiru had added a new moon to its collection."

"And that moon is called Tiamat-min," I finished. "Hence the irony, since that's the one that's going to destroy us."

Devon yawned dramatically behind us. "You two done with the history lesson?" he asked. "I wanna go shopping for the Ark." He hopped on a stray cart, scooting ahead of us, and squealed, "Oooh, I call dibs on one of those electric cart things."

With one last glance at the menacing sky, we walked through the deserted parking lot toward the Wal-Mart entrance. I should clarify: Rigel and I walked, while Devon inched along next to us in a motorized cart he had found, honking its horn.

As we approached, a young man dressed in a Wal-Mart vest strolled out of the store and began gathering up stray carts. He was acting like it was a normal day on the job.

"Did he not get the memo about the world ending?" Devon asked.

The enthusiastic cart collector spotted us and waved cheerfully. "Hey, Rigel!"

"Hi, Mike!" Rigel waved back.

"Is he one of you?" I asked.

"No. Secret Service."

Before Devon or I could say anything, Rigel's hands flew up. "Please don't speak," he said in an exasperated tone. "I know you were about to talk in unison again I can't take it."

Devon and I shrugged innocently, and we all headed inside.

In true Wal-Mart fashion, a senior citizen greeted us at the door. She was a cute old lady with grayish purple hair and curls fresh from their rollers. She shoved a basket at us whether we wanted it or not.

"Hi, Rigel dear." She beamed, showing off the whitest set of false teeth I'd ever seen. "It's delightful to see you again."

Rigel gave her a hug. "It's wonderful to see you, too." He gestured to us. "Marge, may I introduce you to Autumn and Devon."

I extended my hand to shake hers, and she used it to yank me into a hug instead. It was way stronger than I had expected her capable of. This old lady could have easily cracked my rib if she wanted to.

"My dear girl," Marge said. "I heard what you're doing for us. 'Thank you' doesn't even begin to cover it. Such a special girl you are."

"No problem," I wheezed.

She loosened her freakishly strong granny arms and fixed her eyes on Devon. "What in god's name did you do to your hair?" she said, wrinkling her nose as if she had smelled something rotten. She licked her fingers and then patted his hair down, only to have it pop up again.

"Hi," Devon said shyly.

She surveyed him for a long time. "You look like a moron," she concluded.

Rigel and I snorted. Devon grimaced, and his ears turned pink.

Marge shifted her attention to Rigel. "They're ready for you in the basement, dearie."

"Thanks, Marge."

Marge gave a nod and went about lining the carts up.

"Nice meeting you," I said before turning to leave.

We made our way into the store and I did a double take when I saw cashiers at their registers, like they expected shoppers to come busting through the door any minute. And then we passed a middle-aged man stocking the shelves and another who was reassembling a display that had been trampled.

"Why are all these people still working?" I asked.

"It's their directive."

"Directive?" Devon said. "No way! Are these all Secret Service agents?"

"Sixty percent of this Wal-Mart's staff is made up of government operatives," Rigel said.

"Cool!" Devon said. "Are they trained in martial arts and able to scale shelves in a single bound?"

"I'll let you in on a little secret," Rigel whispered conspiratorially. "At one time, Marge used to be a highly skilled Kung Fu master."

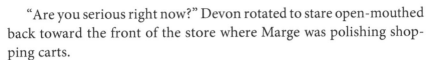

"Are you serious right now?" Devon rotated to stare open-mouthed back toward the front of the store where Marge was polishing shopping carts.

"No," Rigel said, laughing. "You watch too many movies."

With Devon scowling behind us, we headed to the furniture section, where Rigel plunked down and stretched luxuriously on a green recliner.

"Alien boy needs a rest already?" Devon scoffed.

With a twinkle in his eye, Rigel replied, "Just tryin' out the merchandise."

I immediately knew he had a trick up his sleeve and waited for the inevitable theatrics to arise. And boy, did they. He grabbed the handle to recline, and a panel swung up in front of the chair. It was identical to the navigation system on the ship.

"Just when I thought this day couldn't get any better!" Devon exclaimed. "End of the world notwithstanding," he clarified. "Is this Wal-Mart a stealth rocket? Are we gonna launch into space?"

"It's official, you need to curb your movie viewing," Rigel said.

The floor rumbled beneath our feet, and like a real-life Transformer, the aisle in front of us collapsed and reconfigured itself into a grand elevator entrance.

Devon and I stood there gawking. After a moment, Devon raised his hand to his face and made a static sound, pretending to talk into a walkie talkie. "Cleanup in aisle six," he said. "Repeat. Cleanup in aisle six."

Rigel swept his hand toward the elevator, Vanna White style, and said, "Welcome to the Portal to Hell."

"Portal to Hell?" I took a step back.

"Don't worry," he said. "That's just the code name the CIA gave it."

Devon looked thrilled. "Operation Portal to Hell!"

I straightened and gave Rigel a formal salute. "Permission to enter the Portal to Hell, sir?"

Devon saluted alongside me. "Sir, yes sir. Permission to enter Hell, sir!"

Rigel gave us a sideways glance as he pressed the elevator call button. "Stand down, soldiers."

We dropped our salutes.

"Okay, I have a real question," I said.

"Of course you do." Rigel sighed.

I narrowed my eyes at him. "So any time you all want to access the Ark, the entire furniture aisle of this Wal-Mart has to be disassembled? I could be mistaken about this, but I'd think customers might become suspicious if half the store transformed into an elevator shaft."

"This is the after-hours VIP entrance for special parties," Rigel explained. "We have a plain old boring service entrance, too, but I figured Devon would appreciate this more."

"Shit howdy!" Devon whooped.

We got on, and the doors dinged closed behind us. The elevator seemed no different than every other elevator I'd been on—no fancy blinking instruments or anything. Muzak even played softly in the background. Although there was something about the particular song...

Devon almost choked when he worked out what it was. "Is that the Muzak version of 'Highway to Hell'?"

"Yes," Rigel said. "A joke the builders implemented after they heard what the code name was going to be. On the ride up it plays 'Stairway to Heaven.'"

We descended for a full minute before the elevator lurched to a stop and the doors dinged open.

"How far down are we?" I asked.

"Three hundred feet," Rigel said.

"What?" I gasped, flicking my gaze upward. "That's like thirty stories down!"

Suddenly feeling panicked, I stumbled back to the corner of the elevator and squeezed the handrails for support. Claustrophobia wasn't a fear I usually suffered from, but traveling thirty stories underground didn't exactly sit well with me.

"What's wrong?" Rigel asked.

"Umm... I didn't know we would be this far down. Shock, that's all." The handrail I had a death grip on gave way; the wood crumbled in my hands. "Oops!"

Devon studied the damage. "For an advanced species and all, that's awfully shoddy construction."

Rigel furrowed his brow at the splintered rail, then shook his head. "Come on," he said, and then led us out of the elevator.

What I saw on the other side totally shocked me. We were in a beautifully decorated lobby. Polished stone columns rose up to reveal a domed ceiling with red stained glass panels and a massive glittering gold chandelier. The floors were covered in a matching gold and red carpet, and the walls were blanketed with red velvet curtains. I felt like I was about to go and see a grand opera.

"What the hell?" I said.

"Impressive, isn't it? Rigel said. "The Federation parties were lavish affairs."

"I guess so."

There was a loud crack, followed by a hiss. Rigel and I spun around, hands raised in a defensive stance. It was only Devon. He was standing behind a small concession stand holding a soda can he had just opened. It fizzed and popped as he slurped it down.

We stared at him with blank expressions. "What?" he said. "I was thirsty. There's Diet Dr Pepper here, you want one?"

Even though that did kind of sound good, I declined. "Why's the Ark still down here anyway?" I asked Rigel. "Shouldn't you have it somewhere that isn't going to be destroyed in a few days?"

"We were keeping it down here in the hopes that someone would come through and be able to use it. If not, we would have moved it in time."

Rigel led us through a door marked "Employees Only." He stopped abruptly once on the other side.

"What's wrong?" I asked.

"There are usually guards here."

"Maybe they're on break?" I suggested.

"Possibly." He frowned. "Something doesn't feel right."

As if to prove his point, at that moment we heard the unmistakable rumble of an explosion far above, and the floor shook beneath us. Devon and I pressed ourselves against the wall, but Rigel remained where he was, seemingly unconcerned. Three more explosions thundered overhead, one right after the other, and each time the hallway rattled and bowed, sending tiles cascading from the ceiling.

Devon shrieked, "Holy high roller on a Frisbee, what was that?"

"It's underway," Rigel replied, disturbingly calm.

"What's underway?" I asked, realizing immediately how dumb that question was. *Durr, the end of the world.*

"The final destruction," he answered somberly. "The first phase is a global meteor shower."

"Those explosions are meteorites hitting Earth?" I gulped, unnerved by that prospect.

"Yes."

Another *durr* moment hit me. Idiotically, I had thought everything would be hunky dory until the moment their moon incinerated us all. But I should have realized: an object that enormous approaching us would wreak all sorts of chaos on Earth long before it made actual contact.

"Are they dropping everywhere," I asked, "or is this a fluke that's only happening here?"

"We expect one quarter of the planet's landmass to be ravaged by meteorites," Rigel said. "This is a just light sprinkle. In twelve to twenty-four hours, the real storm arrives."

Another explosion rumbled above us, and more tiles fell from the ceiling.

"This is a sprinkle?" Devon blubbered, picking a piece of tile from his hair. I tilted my head to the side, confused. The tile piece was on the back of his head. How did he know it was there?

Rigel waved us forward. "Come on."

After we took several more turns through the complex of underground hallways without encountering another soul, Rigel said, "Okay, something is definitely wrong. We should have met a minimum of three guards by now."

"How far is the Ark from here?" I asked.

"It's right at the end of this hall." He gestured at an unguarded door about fifty feet ahead of us. "Wait here, I'll check it out."

He flashed to the door and made a thorough examination of it, including putting his ear against it. Then he flashed back.

"I don't know what's happened here," he said. "But I don't think it's a good idea to go in there without a weapon." He ushered us through a side door and then into a small cramped side hallway. "You guys hang here—I'll be right back."

And without another word he zoomed away.

Devon and I stayed quiet as church mice. I wouldn't have been surprised if you could have heard the cogs in our brains squeaking while we processed what was happening.

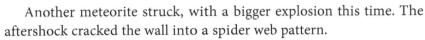

Another meteorite struck, with a bigger explosion this time. The aftershock cracked the wall into a spider web pattern.

"That can't be good," Devon said.

"No, that's not encouraging."

"I don't know about you, but this is getting uncomfortably real for me."

"It's just *now* real to you?" I said. "Returning from the dead, the Orb of Agony, flying a spaceship... none of that felt real?"

"No, I said that wrong," he said. "I mean the end. That Earth is going bye-bye for good. I don't know. I was in denial, I guess. Until now, there haven't been any signs. It's been picture perfect, apart from the humans going mad and all."

Another series of explosions rocked us from above, and the lights flickered on and off. The wall beside us cracked down the middle, bits of plaster spilling into the corridor.

"You're right," I said. "I apologize. *Now* it's real."

"Rigel has been gone a while," Devon said. "You think he's okay?"

"I'd know if he was in trouble."

"Oh, yeah. The bondo twins."

There was another blast, and it sounded like it was right over our heads. We both looked up as a chunk of the ceiling broke loose. We dove away, just barely escaping in time.

"I don't know about you," Devon said, "but I'm ready to blow this popsicle stand before it caves in."

"I couldn't agree more."

We clambered to our feet and were about to flee when Rigel appeared carrying a duffel bag.

"Devon, do you know how to shoot a gun?" he asked.

"Depends. Do video games count?"

"Close enough," Rigel said, and held out a small handgun for him to take. Devon pinched it daintily in his fingers, holding it from his body like it was a stinky piece of laundry. "I've removed the safety," Rigel explained. "All you have to do is cock this back and fire."

Rigel riffled through the bag and pulled out a long knife. "This is for you," he said, and then handed it to me.

"Hey! How do you know I've never used a gun?" I asked.

"Have you?"

"No."

"Take the knife. We need to do this quickly. It's not looking good up there. They're evacuating everyone in the store right now. I don't know how widespread the meteorites are yet, but if they're this bad in other areas, we must—"

"—light a fire beneath our pert behinds and scurry the hell outta here pronto," Devon finished, with his own artistic flair.

Rigel's demeanor turned intense, his authority all-encompassing. "Stay behind me."

He led us back into the hallway and toward the door where the Ark was. Devon held his gun like a rookie cop on a TV drama. I thrust my knife out as if brandishing a sword. At first I felt vulnerable with a plain ol' piece of cutlery, but then I remembered that I had super speed *and* could carry things when I flashed. That had to be an advantage.

"Rigel, you got any intel on the situation?" Devon asked. "We lookin' at a six-four-seven delta?"

Rigel cocked his head. "A lewd act in a public toilet?"

"No, grand theft."

"Grand theft is four-eight-seven."

"What? Are you yankin' my chain?"

"I can tell you with all certainty that I am not, nor will I ever—in any context—yank your chain."

"My cop friend is gonna get it if we survive this."

Rigel kicked the door open. Devon covered the entrance with his gun extended and shouted, "Freeze!"

We all peered into the room. It was spacious, probably five hundred square feet, and completely empty—save for one person:

Enlil.

He sat in a folding chair eating a sandwich with one hand and holding *Nibiru Today* in the other.

Rigel held out his hand in front of us. "Lower your weapons," he said in an uneasy tone.

"What?" Devon asked, not dropping his gun. "Are you sure?"

"Drop your weapons, now!" Rigel said with absolute authority.

We complied. Through the bond, I sensed Rigel's fear, and it made me start to panic.

Enlil tossed his sandwich over his shoulder, licked his fingers clean, then stood, folding his paper. "You know, the deli sandwiches here are a bit dry. I might have to talk to management about that."

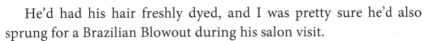

He'd had his hair freshly dyed, and I was pretty sure he'd also sprung for a Brazilian Blowout during his salon visit.

"Oh, it's one of you," Devon said, startling me with his casual attitude. He ambled into the room and looked around.

Enlil rubbed his beard and reviewed Devon. "Hmm. What interesting thoughts."

It occurred to me that Devon didn't know this was Enlil. Worse, he didn't know that Enlil could read minds—unless he happened to overhear us talking about that when he was in limbo, but I highly doubted that. *Oh, shit.*

"Devon," I said, my voice strained. "You might want to come over here."

"Why? No one's here except us, and..." Devon raised his brows at Enlil and snapped his fingers like he was trying to remember something. "Forgive me, I don't know your name."

"Enlil," he said with a smile.

Devon's face went pale. "Oh. I've heard a lot about you."

"I see that, yes."

Devon looked confused. "Okay, well, where's the Ark? Are we in the right room?"

"You are in the right room. And it isn't here."

"All right..." Devon said with a frown. "Are you going to tell us where it's at?"

Enlil's expression reminded me of a scientist observing a rat in a maze, and I suddenly feared for Devon's safety. Without thinking, I flashed between Enlil and Devon—and immediately regretted it. I had just given Enlil confirmation that Rigel and I had bonded. *Double shit!*

Enlil raised one side of his mouth in a knowing smirk. "Well, well, well..." he said. "Isn't this an interesting turn of events? I knew you two weren't being honest in Rigel's room." Wagging his finger at me, he finished with a baleful, "Tsk, tsk, tsk."

This time it was Rigel's turn to flash, putting himself between Enlil and me.

Devon raised his hand high in the air to get our attention, "Anyone want to fill me in on what I'm missing here? Are we playing Red Light, Green Light?"

I grabbed Devon's arm and dragged him away from Enlil—and needless to say, the contact with Devon made me heave. Enlil laughed, and the sound was bone-chilling—like Chucky come to life.

"He can hear your thoughts," I warned Devon through a clenched jaw.

Devon stiffened beside me.

"Yes," Enlil said, staring at Devon. "Uh-huh … No, not anymore." I understood what was happening: Enlil was answering the questions running through Devon's mind. "I wish I could … No, I can't shut it off … I would be, as you so eloquently put it, shitting my pants if I were you, too… No, I am not going to, uh, 'send you down the river.'"

The hungry way Enlil stroked his beard belied this last statement. And I could have sworn he added a "yet" under his breath.

"Where's the Ark, Enlil?" Rigel asked.

"About that," Enlil said with mock concern, presenting us with pouty lips for effect. "I'm afraid I have a teensy bit of bad news for you. You see, I was quite nervous the Ark would be stolen during these troubled times. For the sake of your precious little human, I wanted to make sure there were safeguards to protect it. You understand, I'm sure."

"Where is it?" Rigel repeated angrily. Then, with a deep inhale, he regained his composure. "Please, Enlil, we're running out of time."

"Acting only in your best interests, I assure you, I personally transported the Ark of the Covenant to the vault in Mount Ararat. I placed it on the platform where Ziusudra's Ark was showcased before the clearing, so it would be easy-peasy for you to find."

"Easy-peasy?" I echoed. "Seriously?"

Enlil's eyes widened innocently. "I did the right thing, didn't I? If it had been stolen, I would never have forgiven myself."

I half-expected him to dress in a tutu and pirouette around the room. His show of concern was such a joke. I didn't get it. Did he honestly think we were falling for it? And who was Ziusudra? The name sounded familiar, but I couldn't put my finger on it.

Devon must have been wondering the same thing, because Enlil said, "Devon, I do understand your confusion." He gave an exaggerated sigh. "I always forget how you humans have a knack for changing names. Ziusudra's Ark is better known to you as Noah's Ark. You know, the boat with all the animals crammed on it?" Enlil let out a deep belly laugh. "That one never gets old. How your kind came to the conclusion that he stuffed thousands of animals on there, I will never know." He wiped a pretend tear from his eye. "Just so we're clear, his name was never Noah. He was born Ziusudra. You all couldn't pronounce it, so you changed it to Noah." He gave an indignant huff. "Morons."

Devon swallowed. "Thanks for the clarification."

"Yes," Rigel said. "And thank you for your concern, Enlil." He was playing the same "nice" card as Enlil did, except Rigel's smile displayed way too many teeth, making it more of a snarl. "We are in your debt. And I assume the key to open the Ark is with it?"

"Oh, dear." Enlil gasped. "Thanks for the reminder. I would have forgotten all about the key. That would have cost you some precious time." Enlil produced a skeleton key from his pocket and handed it to Rigel. "Here you go."

Rigel nodded but said nothing, as if waiting for the other shoe to drop.

"Don't you worry, now," Enlil said. He tapped his temple in that universal "I've thought ahead" gesture. "Because I wanted to ensure the Ark was safe and sound for your arrival, I activated all the safeguards when I left."

"Thank you, Enlil." Rigel's smile coiled into a venomous sneer. "We should be off to retrieve that directly, since we are short on time and all."

"So true. Time is not on your side. Yes, indeed." Then Enlil snapped his fingers, giving a Razzie-worthy performance of pretending he had just remembered an important piece of information. "That reminds me! Rigel, the Council asked me to pass a message on to you. Despite our meticulous calculations, the first phase has begun, and it might be progressing a wee bit faster than predicted." His eyes glinted in delight.

"Thank you for delivering that message," Rigel said, almost robotically. "I owe you one." I felt his rage welling inside me, and I wanted to take my knife and stab it through Enlil's heart. My gaze flicked to the knife on the floor. Rigel saw me and quickly took a pacifying breath, and that helped to suppress my desire to commit homicide.

"Let's get going," Rigel said.

Rigel guided us from the room. We didn't even make it to the door before Enlil called to us. "Oh, Rigel. There is one more thing I forgot to mention."

Rigel went rigid. "Yes?"

"When I activated the safeties, I may have accidentally damaged a panel or two in my haste. I do hope it doesn't present too much of a problem for you."

Game. Set. Match.

"Not a problem at all," Rigel said, his teeth grinding as we strode out the door.

We hotfooted it back to the elevator.

"What the hell was that about?" I asked in a low voice. "Why didn't he just destroy the Ark instead of moving it?"

"I'll fill you in on the ship," Rigel replied.

We burst through the door into the lobby. It was almost unrecognizable. The floor was littered with bits of glass from the chandelier, and the curtains all lay in heaps against the walls.

We skirted the glass to get to the elevator, and Rigel pressed the button to go up. The door dinged open. We all got in and rose from the Portal to Hell as the Muzak version of "Stairway to Heaven" played in the background, a flute solo creating a nice crowning apex to the musical monstrosity.

"That is some serious flute playing," Devon said.

The elevator began to vibrate, and dust fell from the ceiling.

"What the—"

Devon was cut off when the elevator came to an abrupt stop. He stumbled, and would have been impaled by the broken handrail if Rigel hadn't caught him.

"Thanks, dude," Devon said. "What happened?"

"The meteorites," Rigel said. "They must have damaged the store."

My claustrophobia started to kick in again. "Please tell me we're not trapped in here."

"We're about to find out," Rigel said. "Autumn, you pull that side of the door, and I'll take this side."

"Me?"

"Trust me," he said.

I did as instructed, and the metal bent open at my command.

"Whoa!" Devon gasped.

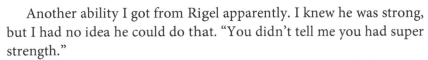

Another ability I got from Rigel apparently. I knew he was strong, but I had no idea he could do that. "You didn't tell me you had super strength."

"I couldn't have you doing anything stupid now, could I?"

He was probably right. Had I known, I might have hastened my demise by punching Enlil right in the nose.

"What else can I do?" I asked.

Rigel offered me only a mischievous wink.

Light streamed in through an opening about a foot high. Not enough for us to squeeze through, unfortunately. I checked what floor we were on, and it said ground level, so that light had to be from the top floor.

"Maybe we can dig our way out," I said.

"Get down!" a female voice bellowed from outside the elevator.

We all eyed each other.

"Did you hear that?" I asked.

"Yes you did," the woman said. "Now get down and cover your head."

We barely had time to comply before an explosion sent an avalanche of rocks and dirt raining down.

"You can get up now," the woman said.

Dusting myself off, I rose to see that the entire top of the elevator was gone—as was the roof of the Wal-Mart. A smoke-filled sky lay above me, the sun muted to a dull flicker. An enormous fireball zoomed by. Seconds later a distant rumble could be heard, followed by a shockwave of energy that rippled across the horizon.

A silhouetted figure peered at us through the dust. Inanna. "A little birdie told me Enlil came to help keep the Ark 'safe,'" she said.

"It's safe, that's for sure," Rigel said, shaking his head.

"Let me get you out of there."

She disappeared. I was expecting she'd return with a rope or a ladder, but the next thing I knew, all of us became airborne, and were lifted out of the elevator and set gently on what was left of the floor of Wal-Mart.

"Okay, you win," Devon said, drooling at Inanna. "You by far have the coolest superpower." He held his hand up apologetically to Rigel. "No offense, Rigel, your telepathic thingie is neat too, but levitation... wowzer."

"No offense taken."

Devon's banter ground to a halt as the scene in front of us sucked all the humor from the room. The store was completely unrecognizable. Most of the walls had crumbled, and the products were buried under heaps of charred rooftop. A gigantic crater now occupied the area where the parking lot used to be.

"Where is everyone?" I asked. "Marge?"

"All safe," Inanna said. "They were evacuated in time."

Rigel began to fill Inanna in on Enlil's shenanigans.

In a state of shock, I picked up a still smoldering lampshade off the floor and mumbled to myself, "I can't believe this all happened so fast."

"This is insane," Devon said, coming up behind me. "You okay?"

"Yeah," I said, blinking a few times. I tossed the lampshade back into the rubble. *I sure hope I have the strength for this.*

"There's no time to waste," Inanna snapped. "Let's take my ship." She gave a wolf whistle, and the craft popped out of thin air, hovering next to us. It made the vintage model we were using look like an old Ford Pinto. Easily three times the size of ours, her ship had a triangle shape to it, and waves of energy rippled off it.

Devon gaped at it. "Wow! Does it go faster than ours?"

"Naturally," Inanna said proudly. "Designed it myself."

"Inanna is an amazing pilot, too," Rigel added.

Before Devon could swoon like a teenybopper at a boy band concert, we were lifted inside.

"You really designed this?" Devon asked Inanna.

"Helped build it with my own two hands." She gave Devon a nudge. "If you make it through this, I may let you take it for a spin."

"Oh, I wouldn't do that," Rigel warned. "If the destruction of the planet doesn't kill him, driving this thing most certainly will."

"Hey!" Devon said. "I kicked ass navigating the other ship. I can't help it if you're an old grandpa driver."

Inanna laughed. Not a chuckle, but a full-blown laugh. It was rather unsettling: a cross between a walrus and a fire alarm. She probably didn't get much practice at it. From the little I knew about her, she took life way too seriously. Whatever happened last night between her and Devon had sure put her in good spirits.

Ew, ew, ew. Must not think about the possibilities.

32

SOLID DIAMOND GRILLZ, HAIRY HIDING PLACES, POISONOUS PENIS DARTS, AND A GASEOUS FIRE-BELCHING BUNNY

The inside of Inanna's ship was transparent like our own (the tinted window version, that is), but the layout was completely different. A main control panel spanned a good twenty feet at the front of the craft, and several smaller substations were scattered about the rest of the space. On the rear wall were display cases full of female combat gear, armor, and weapons galore. This was clearly a battleship (or an homage to the television show *Arrow*).

Inanna sat down at the helm and promptly switched into pilot mode, attending the controls in what I could only describe as a futuristic game of Simon Says. Lights would flash in sequence, and she'd flutter her hands, repeating the pattern.

"Normally I could get us there in under ten," she said, "but since we have to contend with meteors, it'll take longer."

"I trust your judgment," Rigel said. "We couldn't be in more skilled hands."

We zipped through the sky, darting to and fro around the falling rocks. I watched Inanna, amazed by her mastery of the ship, and thought back to when I first met her. Not to sound ungrateful, but she was a bitch. And now here she was, risking herself, once again, to keep us safe.

"Why are you helping us?" I asked. I instantly regretted it. I should've kept my mouth shut, but curiosity got the best of me. "I mean... I'm sorry. I appreciate everything you did. That came out all wrong. It's just... you saved me in Rigel's room, too. That's such a one-eighty from when we first met, considering you broke my jaw and all."

Inanna was silent for a moment, then replied, "Ninhursag and I share the same ideas on humans. For argument's sake, let's say I'm helping her keep the vow."

Rigel eyed her curiously. "You're the leader of the Earth Initiative, aren't you?"

"Perhaps."

"What's that?" Devon asked.

"It's an underground crusade whose mission is to uphold Ninhursag's vow during her imprisonment," Rigel explained. "A substantial number of our kind are doing everything they can to keep humans alive, regardless of whether a third of your population comes through or not."

"Are those the same people I saw protesting on that magazine?" I asked.

"Yes."

Devon stared at Inanna in awe. "An aeronautical engineer, a rebel leader, *and* you can make things levitate. God, you're sexy."

"That isn't even the half of it, honey," she said, giving him a wink.

Oh yeah, they totally had sex.

I bit my lip and considered my words. "Really though, Inanna, I do want to thank you. I'm tremendously grateful for everything you've done."

"Aw," Devon cooed. "You two lovebirds made up. Now I think you should kiss."

I groaned. "Okay, now that we're safely away from Enlil, can you please fill us in on what the hell happened down there? Why did Enlil move the Ark? If he wanted to stop us from using it, why not destroy it? Or assassinate me to bring this all to an end?"

"Because a decision has been made not to interfere with your attempt to save humans," Inanna said. "Anu set this decree, and as a result, it's physically impossible for anyone to defy it, including Enlil."

"Uh. Isn't that what he's doing?" I asked.

"That's the tricky part," she said. "He was acting to keep the Ark 'safe.' He didn't prevent you from getting to it, therefore he isn't technically breaking any laws."

"Come on!" Devon protested. "It's obvious why he did it!"

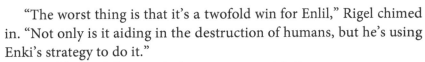

"The worst thing is that it's a twofold win for Enlil," Rigel chimed in. "Not only is it aiding in the destruction of humans, but he's using Enki's strategy to do it."

"Enki?" I said. "I thought he was on our side."

"He is," Inanna said. "When the Great Flood occurred, Anu gave us orders not to announce it was coming, but Enki found a way around it, same as Enlil is doing now."

"I don't get how Enki got away with helping Noah," I said. "The bottom line is he broke the decree. He told Noah how to construct the Ark."

"Ahh... no he didn't," she said. "He went to Noah's house and stood outside his room and spoke to the *wall* about the upcoming flood, how to build an Ark, and what to put on it. Noah, with the help of his people, constructed it using the plans he heard from the 'wall.' And since Enki communicated the warning to an inanimate object, he wasn't violating the order."

"Genius!" Devon said.

"Yes, it was. And Enlil is pulling the same trick right now. By slowing us down, he is assuring that more humans will die, which in turn gives you less of a chance of succeeding."

The meteors grew thicker ahead of us. Inanna kept zipping around them. Even if she was this pilot extraordinaire, I couldn't help but feel antsy at the possibility we could slam into one.

Rigel must have channeled my worry, because he pressed me against him and kissed my cheek tenderly. *God that feels good.* "Trust me when I say she's the best pilot in all the universe," he said confidently.

Devon regarded Inanna proudly. "You kick ass!" he shouted after she dodged a barrage of six meteors that were coming at us in a pack.

"I have to alter our course," she said, a bead of sweat forming on her forehead. "The meteors are thicker than projected for this first phase."

"Do what you think is best," Rigel said. "I have faith you will get us there."

"You guys keep calling this the 'first phase,'" I said. "Is there an order to these disasters?"

"Yes," Rigel replied, releasing me but staying close. "One of our moons, which has a highly elliptical orbit from our planet, has slammed into the asteroid belt, sending many of them toward Earth. That is what we are seeing now."

"Oh, shit."

"Let's just say we should try to finish our, uh... mission, prior to phase two. That's when the approach of our planet begins to cause tidal stress. Oceans will rise and the earthquakes will begin. In phase three, Earth's plates will shift and fissure from the immense pull of gravity between Earth and Tiamat-min, producing volcanoes, earthquakes, and tsunamis. This, sadly, triggers the caldera at Yellowstone to let go, which is phase four."

"The U.S. will be leveled!" I cried.

Rigel closed his eyes. I could feel his sadness in my gut. The situation weighed heavy on his shoulders. "It will destroy much more than the United States"

"How many phases are there?" I asked.

"Five is the last phase. Tiamat-min will collide with Earth, resulting in the total destruction of both."

"I don't suppose there's any chance you're off on your calculations," I asked.

Rigel squeezed my shoulder and then Devon's, silently answering the question. I sat down at one of the control stations and spun in the chair, staring at the meteors pelting the planet. It didn't seem real. Asteroids pierced the atmosphere, ignited into red balls of fire, and disappeared before crashing into Earth, creating grisly mushroom cloud explosions visible from even this height. The shock waves spilled across tremendous distances, dissolving clouds and warping the air. Entire pockets of the planet became enveloped in a roiling inferno of black smoke and fire. I couldn't take my eyes off it.

Devon joined me. "How ya holdin' up?" he asked.

"Peachy keen," I lied.

"It isn't bad on the other side, you know."

At first I thought he was talking about the other side of the destruction. Then it registered that he meant death and the next dimension. It felt like it was years ago that we died in that shed. I realized Devon didn't know that I was unable to cross over; when I filled him in on everything back on the mothership, I had omitted that part.

"It's peaceful," he said, trying to comfort me.

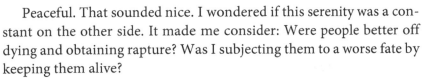

Peaceful. That sounded nice. I wondered if this serenity was a constant on the other side. It made me consider: Were people better off dying and obtaining rapture? Was I subjecting them to a worse fate by keeping them alive?

"Why am I doing this?" I asked. "Why bother? If it's this wonderland on the other side, I would be an ass if I didn't let everyone go there."

Devon thought for a moment. "I think the universe needs us," he said. "It made us for a reason."

"That's not true," I said. I threw a glance at Rigel and Inanna, who were in deep discussion. "*They* made us. The universe had nothing to do with it."

"They helped us along, sure. But humans were here before they added their hocus pocus. The un-evolved version of us, anyway."

"Nevertheless: If humans are all going to a peaceful place, why keep them from that?" I asked. "Why prolong the inevitable? I should liberate them into this magical dimension of pure happiness without further ado."

"If all humans die, there will be no new souls to join us on the other side."

"So what? The people they love will all be there, either going with them upon death or already waiting on the other side."

"What about those who haven't met their soulmate yet?"

"Can't they meet that person over there?"

"No. The other dimension isn't material... well, it is kind of, but not really."

"What's it like, then—an infinite gas cloud?" I asked. "Do you keep your human form? Are there Targets there?"

Devon smiled. "No. I... I can't explain it with words."

My frustration surfacing, I clamped my hands behind my neck. "What is the *sense* to all this? If we don't truly die, only our physical bodies, why do we have to undergo a horrific death? All this pain and suffering, for what? Why can't a portal simply open when it's our time, and we step in, and bypass the agony of murder, injury, and disease?"

Devon put his feet up on the control panel and sighed. "So essentially, you're asking me for the meaning of life?"

"We both know we're only here because God was bored and wanted some toys to play with."

"There is that," he agreed. "But I have a feeling that, sometime after that, his creation evolved into a higher purpose. Maybe when he discovered love, it all changed?"

That comment blew me away. Devon had quite the noodle under all that hair. It was nice to see that side of him.

"Wow, that was incredibly wise," I said.

"I amaze myself all the time."

"Oh, wise master." I clasped my hands together under my chin and bowed my head. "Please tell me, what's the meaning of life?"

I could almost hear his hard drive searching for the folder containing the explanation. Apparently the search came up empty, because he just shrugged.

"Hold the phone," I said. "King Zarf, the wisdom master of the universe, doesn't have that answer for me?"

"Afraid not. I sold the knowledge of all things to the devil in exchange for my sexy locks."

I snorted. "Quite the bargain you got."

Below us, the ocean came into view, the water churning and whirling chaotically.

Devon took his feet off the panel and rested his forearms on his legs, watching the water. "I might have an explanation to give you, but I'm afraid it may require a cheesy underscore to go with it."

I opened my mouth to crack a Bruckheimer joke, then decided against it.

Devon straightened, an intense and profound expression on his face. "All I know is, the universe is better with you in it. I can't imagine one where you were never born. Can you imagine a world without Emma or your family? Heck, if I hadn't been born, for god's sake!"

At that moment I wanted to be able to touch him. Not sexually or anything, just take his hand in mine. Trying to keep the mood light, I said, "Ah, yes, you are correct. I hear the music building to a dramatic climax now."

"It should be. This is Academy Award stuff here," he said. "Who are we to know what achievements humans are capable of, what beauty we may create? Sure, by letting everyone pass on, you give them peace. But consider this: by doing that, who are you preventing from being born? No new human souls would be created—they'd be lost for eternity. If we choose good, maybe we're destined to become enlightened or some crap, and do remarkable things."

"Well, who am I to not let humans achieve 'some crap'?"

"With crap on our side, humans will live long and prevail," Devon said, jabbing his arms upward.

"To crap!" Inanna chanted from her station.

"To crap!" we all shouted together.

"Thanks for that," I whispered to Devon.

He gave me a wink. "Anytime."

"We're almost there," Inanna said.

Devon and I stood up. We were positioned aside a colossal mountain. The winds gusted violently, causing flurries of snow to rise hundreds of feet in the air, limiting visibility. It wasn't until we were almost on top of it that the rocky summit was distinguishable.

Inanna lowered the ship carefully down the slope.

"This place is way too arctic for my taste," Devon said. "Why couldn't Enlil have stashed the Ark at the lost city of Atlantis or someplace more exotic? I heard there are kickass beaches on Atlantis."

"You were already on Atlantis," Rigel said.

"I think I'd remember that."

"Our mothership *is* the mysterious lost city of Atlantis," Rigel said. "We used to have it docked in what is presently the Persian Gulf. It didn't sink or become engulfed by the sea, as your tales suggest. We simply launched it into space."

Devon made a fake gesture of writing on a notepad. "Great. I can check that off my bucket list."

"You have a bucket list?" I asked.

"Of course. Who doesn't?"

"What else do you have on it?"

"Let's see. An evening with Kate Upton, create and eat the world's largest quesadilla, replace my front teeth with solid diamond implants so I can bite through steel, and audition for *America's Got Talent*."

"You want to be on *America's Got Talent*?" I asked, stunned. "What's your talent?"

"Modern dance."

"Shut up! You're such a liar."

"Wanna bet?"

"Yeah."

Devon assumed a fetal position and started twitching. Then with a jerk he slammed his fists on the ground and undulated like a worm.

"What the hell?" I said. "Are you convulsing? Do I need to get the ankh?"

He paused with one leg lifted over his head. "You doubt my skills?"

"Hey, you guys," Rigel interrupted. "You'll want to see this."

Devon untwisted. "Tell ya what, when you save us, I'm going to do a real dance recital in your honor."

"Deal," I said, and we air shook on it.

The ship hovered beside what appeared to be a natural ledge.

"What are we looking for?" I asked.

"Be patient," Rigel said.

The side of the mountain began to shake. Great chunks of snow broke loose and slid down the ridge. For a minute I thought phase two had come early and the mountain was about to explode.

"What's going on with the mountain?" Devon asked. "It's not gonna belch lava on us, is it?"

Rigel swished his hand in that familiar mocking way and said, "Open saysa meea." He wasn't going to let the accents go.

"To your credit," I said, "I knew you were striving for an Italian accent that time, so that's an improvement."

"It wasn't Italian," he grumbled.

"Indian?" Devon guessed.

"No."

"Come on, guys," Inanna broke in. "Are you deaf? That was clearly Spanish. Chilean, to be precise."

"Thank you!" Rigel exclaimed, sounding relieved. "They think my accents are horrible. Can you believe it?"

"No way!" She gasped. "These humans don't know the first thing about your incredible talent."

Rigel gave us a satisfied look. Inanna turned so that only Devon and I could see her face, and then she mouthed the word *awful* while giving an over-the-top eye roll.

Dreadful accent or not, the mountain apparently understood his command. An enormous chunk of rock, ten times the size of our ship, hinged skyward, revealing an entryway.

"Whoa!" Devon jumped. "That rocks! No pun intended."

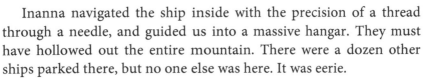

Inanna navigated the ship inside with the precision of a thread through a needle, and guided us into a massive hangar. They must have hollowed out the entire mountain. There were a dozen other ships parked there, but no one else was here. It was eerie.

"Are there usually Igigi here?" I asked.

"Yes," Rigel growled. "I'm sure their absence is courtesy of Enlil. Having assistance would make it too easy on us."

"Come on, now," Devon said. "That has to be defying a law, to leave this place unguarded?"

"Not if he had a legitimate excuse."

"Seriously?" I said. "What reason could he possibly pull out of his ass to evacuate a whole base?"

"That is what terrifies me."

Inanna muttered a curse and left the helm. "I simply must remember to give granddaddy a thank-you basket when this is all done." She snapped her fingers at us. "Well. You all ready to march blindly into an Enlil minefield?"

The hangar was nice and cozy; the Anunnaki must have accrued a hefty power bill each month keeping this place heated. It was also perfectly illuminated, even though there were no light fixtures—or at least, none that I could see. The smell in the cavern was crisp and clean, not at all musty or re-filtered, like you'd expect for a sealed room inside a mountain. Not that I had any real reference. The air actually gave my lungs a boost of energy.

Inanna led us to an elevator carved into the rock wall. Intricate gold symbols outlined the trim. And it was there that we were presented with the very first Enlil bomb. The buttons on the control panel were giving off electrical sparks. Below them on the ground was a coffee cup that oozed a syrupy, amber-colored mess. Whenever the substance dripped on the floor, the stone sizzled and hissed. *Definitely not coffee, then.*

On the elevator door itself was a Post-it note. It was stained and burned with what I assumed was the same toxic sludge in the cup. Rigel grabbed the note and read it.

Rigel crumpled the message into a ball and threw it on the floor.

"Is there any other way down?" I asked.

"Yes, but you're not going to like it."

"What's new?"

The ground shook beneath us, and we all planted our feet wider to brace ourselves in case it worsened. It didn't amount to anything but a quick hiccup, as earthquakes go.

Inanna frowned and tapped her finger on her chin. "That's curious. Not time for the next phase yet."

"Could it be a meteorite strike?" Rigel asked.

"I'm not buying it," she said. "Especially with the ghost town we have going on here."

"Is this a volcano?" Devon asked. "Is it gonna go boom?"

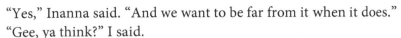

"Yes," Inanna said. "And we want to be far from it when it does."

"Gee, ya think?" I said.

Rigel opened a door located next to the elevator. A plaque above it read:

I thought about that. The only way an all-stone structure would be on fire is if the volcano belched lava. *Wouldn't a stairwell be futile at that point?* I wondered if they posted it as a joke.

The emergency door led to the top of a spiral staircase. I peered down. It stretched on and on, with no bottom in sight.

"We have to walk down all that?" Devon grunted. "There's no way we're gonna make it in time. At least not me. I don't have fancy-schmancy powers like you all."

Suddenly we were all lifted into the air. "I got you covered," Inanna said with a wink at Devon. We began to descend right down the middle of the shaft, bypassing the stairs altogether.

Another earthquake hit, making the staircase wobble and sway like a giant pulsating slinky.

"I may need to speed up a bit," Inanna said. "You newbies should cling on to each other."

I started to reach out to Devon, but when the nausea grew, I scooted away from him and grabbed Rigel instead. That left Devon dangling awkwardly by himself.

"It's okay, sweet cheeks," Inanna said. "You can hold on to me." She pulled him next to her.

We jetted down practically in a free fall. I pressed myself against Rigel with a squeak. Devon, of course, was as thrilled as if we were on a ride at Six Flags.

"How far down does this thing go?" Devon shouted through the wind.

"Three miles," Inanna answered.

"What?" I shrieked.

Devon's eyes bulged. He was either scared or about to burst a blood vessel from all the excitement.

"Is this mountain even real?" I asked.

Inanna gave me the stink eye for doubting it. "Yes. That's why we want to vacate this place sooner rather than later. If this volcano lets go, the lava doesn't have much rock to break through, since we gutted most of it."

Devon patted his hair and said, with dire concern, "Oh no, I can't let these lovely locks get singed."

The light faded as we descended, and by the time we touched down at the bottom, it was pitch black. Our landing was gentle, but we all ended up falling on our butts anyway when another earthquake hit.

"*Lumos*," Devon said after the tremor subsided.

"*Lumos*?" I snorted. "Okay, Harry."

To my astonishment, the light came on. I gawked at Devon, who sat there stupefied.

"No freaking way!" he hooted. "It worked!"

"*Accio* Ark," Inanna said.

Devon and I pivoted in her direction. She was leaning on the wall with her hand on a light switch. "Awe, too bad. That would've been convenient."

Devon glared at her.

"Let's get going," Rigel said.

We followed him to a multi-story wooden door. Soaring at least fifty feet, it was made of thick cedar, and about halfway up was a giant gold doorknocker in the shape of Enlil's smug face, the knocker part dangling from his mouth. To the left of the door was a panel made of cobalt, marbled stone, and crystal. There was a hole on the front of it, where it looked like something was broken off.

"Is that where a lever used to be?" I asked.

"Yep." Rigel sighed. "The handle that opens the door."

"Don't figure 'open says me' will work on this one, huh?"

Rigel bent down to retrieve the broken handle, which was lying on the floor. It had another Post-it note on it.

"What does it say?"

Rigel held it out for us to see.

"That's a dumb security system," Devon said. "You pull a lever and the door opens? Any Tom, Dick, or Harry could do that."

"It will only function for those on the current Council of Twelve," Rigel explained. "One of them has to touch the lever to deactivate the safety."

I looked to Inanna. "So if we can get into that panel, you think you could disarm it and open the door?"

"Yes. I just need to be able to touch what is left of the lever."

"Can't you bust open the box with your super strength?" Devon suggested.

"No," Inanna said. "It has a failsafe. The security system will go on lockdown if someone breaks the enclosure."

Studying the console like a mechanic would diagnose a leak in an engine, Devon said, "There's a maintenance lock here on the side. Will that get you in?"

"Yes."

"Do you have a key to it?"

"I do," Inanna said.

We all sighed in relief.

"Except it's on the mothership. When I came to get you hooligans, I wasn't thinking I would need to open the Chamber of Secrets here."

"You know," Devon said, "the fact that you've read the Harry Potter books makes you damned sexy."

With a smirk she countered, "If you can do an *Alohomora* spell on this lock, I will be forever yours."

With a triumphant gleam Devon said, "Then go get a ring and get ready to propose, baby, 'cause I may be able to help with that!" He reached into his mountain of hair—which stayed perfectly in place by the way—and extracted a petite leather case.

"What the hell?" we all said at the same time.

"Wow, that *is* annoying," Devon said.

"You store stuff in your *hair*?" I asked.

"You never know when an opportunity might present itself," he said, opening the case to reveal a set of tools.

"Opportunity for what?" Rigel asked. "You pick locks often?"

"He's a klepto," I whispered.

Devon tinkered with the lock. Within a few seconds, he had the panel open.

"Now, *that* is damn sexy," Inanna said. "What else you got stashed in that hair of yours?"

"Wouldn't you like to know?" He winked.

"You show me yours, I'll show you mine later," she said, brushing past him and grazing his hip. She pressed down the stubby remnant of the lever.

The door slid up into the ceiling, revealing a fountain that spanned the entire width of the room. An eerie refulgent green water shot into the air and splashed against the ceiling. It was a way freakier version of the Bellagio fountain in Vegas.

"What's that green stuff?" I asked, tiptoeing into the creepy room.

"Acid water," Rigel said. "Safety number two."

Once we were all in the room, the door shut with a loud bang behind us. Devon and I both jumped.

"Holy bamboo butt plugs!" Devon said.

"Dear lord," I said. My heart was pounding in my chest. "A little warning next time?"

"Oh, did I forget to mention that?" Inanna said. "All the safeties reactivate automatically."

"Thanks," I said with an eye roll. "How many of these traps are there?"

"Twelve. One designed by each member of the original Council."

I lost it. "You guys are fucking killing me with the dramatics. What's wrong with a door? A *single* door with a lock. It can be a fancy one—maybe one with a handle that turns into a lion and bites your hand off. Just the one door would do if the result were a dismembered limb. Even you have to admit that this is overkill."

Inanna shrugged. "What can I say? We have a flair for theatrics."

"I'm being serious."

"So am I."

Rigel placed his hand on my shoulder. "It's true. As you saw at Wal-Mart, the Anunnaki like to put on a show. That is kind of what we are known for. The Council couldn't agree on what to do to protect this place, so they decided they would each make a safety. And that started a competition, as each member tried to top everyone else with their design. That's why we ended up with this crazy obstacle course. Visitors from across the universe come just to see the safeties in action."

"And you're telling me there is no service entrance to this place?"

"Not for this," Rigel said. "The items stored here were too valuable. Only the Twelve were allowed to escort people in, and when they did, these rooms all were part of the experience. It was essentially a museum for the very elite."

Another earthquake rolled beneath our feet, making the green water swell.

"Time to jet!" Devon said. "This safecracker needs to break outta here before the walls cave in and muss my do. What's next?"

"Safety number two," Inanna said as she escorted him to a control panel beside the fountain. It, too, had a broken lever. Devon immediately set to work on the lock. I had to admit, it was impressive watching him pick a lock with such skill.

When he opened the panel, Inanna touched the lever and the fountain stopped spurting, the water going still. A steel bridge lowered from out of nowhere, creating a path across the acid water. We walked carefully along it. Once we were over it, the bridge retracted and the fountain turned back on.

"If this fountain is safety number two," I asked, "then that big wooden door was the first?"

"Yes, Enlil's contribution," Rigel said.

"How lame," Devon said. "No sense of creativity."

Inanna scoffed. "He couldn't be bothered to design anything for this. A Nephilim named Gilgamesh gave the door to him as an offering several thousand years ago, and Enlil thought this was the perfect opportunity to dump it." Turning to Devon she whispered, "Wait until we get to mine."

"Let me guess," he said excitedly. "A real-life game of Centipede? No! Better yet, Frogger?"

"No."

"Fire-breathing dragon?"

"No."

"Zombies?"

"No."

Devon continued to make guesses as we made our way through this alien version of the Temple of Doom. Thankfully, Enlil had only broken the first two levers, so we sailed through the rest pretty fast. After the acid fountain we encountered a lethal laser light show, a Hummer converted into a Roomba complete with razor sharp bristles and super suction, a *Wipeout* style obstacle course where the water was filled with box jellyfish, a room where the walls were heated Teflon plates that came together to flatten you into a panini, a dungeon strewn with claw traps, mighty medieval blades that swung from the ceiling, sexy humanoid robots that shot poisonous darts from their privates, an anti-gravity chamber filled with floating live wires, and a riddle room where you had to solve a conundrum or get mauled by a sphinx.

Finally, after what felt like hours of walking, we got to Inanna's pride and joy. It was obvious it was hers because the giant wall where you entered had a mural of her plastered all over it. And it wasn't just her face either; it was ten renditions of her buck naked, and in each one she was in a different erotic pose. Devon's cheeks flushed red as he tried to avert his eyes.

"Everyone be quiet now," she whispered.

She pressed the lever, which was strategically located on one of her painted breasts, and a hidden door slid open to reveal an airy and cheerful room. Above us was a fake aquamarine sky with puffy cotton ball clouds, and below us was a pristine field of perfectly manicured grass. In one corner, an insufferably cute bunny with floppy ears grazed happily. It inspected us, twitched its teeny nose, and then continued munching away. After a second of chewing, it expelled a tiny toot, and fire came shooting from its backside. It didn't seem fazed by this.

"Did it just fart fire?" Devon asked.

"Yep."

It produced another little *poot*, and another jet of flame shot from its furry derriere.

"Huh." Devon rubbed his chin.

As we stepped forward, a tree noiselessly sprouted from the middle of the field. A wooden sign dangled off a limb, which read:

PET BUNNY
TO PASS

"Ooooooh…" Devon wheezed with excitement. "Does the rabbit unleash a flaming gaseous burp if you approach?"

Inanna gave a wicked smile before replying, "No."

"Does it kill you with cuteness?" I asked, raising my eyebrows.

"No."

Rigel laughed.

"You're driving me bonkers!" Devon said. "What does it do?"

"It poops land mines."

I thought Devon's head was going to pop. He belted out a torrent of laughter that echoed throughout the room. At the sound, the bunny sprang four feet in the air and scurried off—setting off one of his own land mines and combusting into a puff of smoke. Bunny fur went flying in all directions, lightly drifting to the ground like falling snowflakes.

Gaping at the charred patch of grass where the bunny used to be, I realized I hadn't heard an explosion. "Why didn't I hear a bang?" I asked.

"Silent but deadly," Inanna said.

Rigel mimicked a rim shot behind us.

Devon barked with laughter again, and had to sit on the floor because of the spasms it brought on. When Rigel joined in with a chuckle, I gave them all a shameful *tsk*. *Devon just killed a bunny and they are laughing about it?*

"Don't worry, honey," Inanna said. "It's a robot."

I felt utterly stupid. *Of course.* Like they would keep a live bunny that poops weapons of mass destruction alone down here.

As I covered my face to hide the embarrassment, a violent earthquake hit, sending us all to the ground. The tree swayed wildly, bending and groaning—and then with a loud crack, it came crashing down. Upon impact, it detonated scores of bunny land mines, and flaming tree parts flew everywhere. I shielded my face with my hands, but that didn't do much. Burning splinters pierced my arm and side. I swiped them away before the flames burned my skin.

Thankfully, the quake didn't last long. I climbed to my feet to assess the damage. Inanna and Rigel had flashed into light to avoid the splinters. Devon, on the other hand, had smoldering wooden shards protruding from his helmet of hair.

"How did your hair not catch fire?" I asked.

"Fire-retardant hairspray."

I rolled my eyes. "You are the strangest person I have ever met."

Rigel and Inanna melted back into their forms. "That shouldn't have happened," Inanna said. "We should have a full day until this thing blows."

"This reeks of Enlil," Rigel grumbled.

"We need to grab the Ark and get out of here," Inanna said. She quickly transported us over the landmines.

A glass entryway awaited us on the other side of the room. There was a giant plaque in the center covered in complex symbols with connecting lines and circles.

"Is this the legendary lost original language?" I asked.

"Yes," Rigel said. "But now you found it. Congratulations."

"What do I win?"

Devon waved his hands. "Please, for the love of everything holy, don't reply with anything sexual, unless it involves Hooters girls, powdered donuts, and a slip-n-slide."

When we neared the entrance, the doors automatically slid open, department store style. Beyond them was a vast exhibit hall. Rows and rows of empty glass display cases stretched so far that I couldn't see the other end of the room. Whatever was on show here was gone though. Only moving materials remained: a couple of hand trucks, a ladder, some crates.

"All of those traps to protect this empty showroom?" Devon asked. His voice echoed in the vacant cavern.

"Usually it's full," Inanna said. "But in preparation for the destruction of Earth, we transferred all the items to our planet, for us to either keep or auction off. An Earth estate sale, if you will."

"What was in here?"

"About three thousand of the most valuable artifacts and works of art from Earth's history."

"I don't mean to belittle your capabilities," I said, "but you're telling me you relocated three thousand items through that obstacle course of booby traps? That would take years."

"Don't be silly," Inanna said. "We drilled a hole on the other side of this chamber, hauled the artifacts out, and sealed it when we were done."

"Why bother sealing it?"

"We were still using this as a command center."

To one side of us was an enormous roped-off platform, maybe half the size of a football field. Next to it was a sign with words in several different languages, one of which was English. It read: "Ziusudra's Ark (Great Flood)." A shiny golden chest floated nearby on the platform. "Is that the Ark of the Covenant?" I asked, pointing.

"The very one," Inanna said.

I walked toward it, mesmerized by its glow. Devon followed close behind.

"Make sure you guys don't touch the Ark itself," Rigel said.

It reminded me of the one Indiana Jones found in *Raiders of the Lost Ark*, but more ornate. Etched into the side facing us was a male Anunnaki standing inside a winged disk. He had a long wavy beard and wore a funky square hat. The wings that spread out on both sides of the disk were bird-like, fanning all the way out to the corners of the Ark, and each row of feathers was leafed in a different shade of gold, going from a golden brown at the top of the wing to a pure white gold at the bottom. The Anunnaki grasped a large ring in his hand, and he was holding it up, as if handing it to someone. At the center of the ring was an old-fashioned keyhole. Below him were twelve human males, their arms stretched out toward the Anunnaki in adoration.

On top of the Ark were two statues: one winged female on each end. They were kneeling, facing each other, their heads bowed, their wings extended forward so their tips were touching one another's. Each corner of the Ark had a metal ring attached, and threaded through the rings were two wooden poles, presumably for carrying.

I almost succumbed to tears at the beauty of it; it was a work of art unmatched by any other.

"Hey, guys," Devon said. He pointed to one of the wooden handles.

That's when I noticed that stuck to it was an all too familiar Post-it note. "Oh, dear lord," I said. "Not another note from Enlil. What's his deal with those things?"

"He owns stock in 3M," Inanna replied, coming up behind me.

Rigel pulled off the note and an accordion of other attached notes came with it.

"Uh-oh," Devon said.

Rigel read the notes aloud:

Hi guys! *I should really stop working out so much. I don't know my own strength sometimes.* Happy you made it to get the Ark. Hopefully the (broken levers) didn't hinder your progress too much, since the volcano is due to go kaboom earlier than anticipated.

Rigel gritted his teeth and continued:

I sure hope with everything that's going on I don't forget to mention the early eruption when you come get the Ark in The Portal To Hell.

I simply must remember to tell you! If not, at least you know now.

I wish you all the best!

Hugs and kisses,

♥ENLIL

"That has to be a lie!" Inanna roared at the Post-it note as if it was Enlil himself. "I would have been informed if the volcano was due to, as Enlil so eloquently put it, 'go kaboom' early! They would've called a meeting with the Council of Twelve to tell us!"

"There's more," Rigel said.

P.S. Inanna, I know you will be upset you didn't know about this. The instant I heard the news from our chief scientist, my immediate concern was evacuating all the staff in time.

I am planning on notifying the council upon my return to the ship. Looking forward to seeing you at the Federation dinner tonight! They are serving filet mignon, your favorite! Granddad ENLIL

Inanna mumbled a string of curse words under her breath, then said, "I knew he had an vengeful streak." She kicked an abandoned ladder that was nearby, and it skidded off the platform. "But I honestly didn't think him capable of this. To his own granddaughter?"

Rigel crumpled the notes and threw them on the ground. When they hit, the room quaked violently. And this time it didn't relent.

"I think that's our cue to go," Devon said.

"Listen," Inanna said. "I'll transport Devon and the Ark with my telekinesis, and you and Rigel flash." We nodded, and I zoomed to the

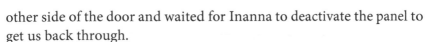

other side of the door and waited for Inanna to deactivate the panel to get us back through.

There was a shout, and the next thing I knew Devon and the Ark were sliding across the room. I flashed over to grab the Ark to keep it from hitting Devon, but before I even got there, it stopped, righted itself, and hovered above the ground.

"What the hell?" Devon said, rubbing his head.

Inanna stood in the doorway with a horrified expression on her face. A substance was streaming from around the doorframe, covering her in some kind of dust.

"That son of a bitch!" Inanna hissed.

"What's wrong?" I asked, panicking. "What is that?"

"Inhibitor spray," she spat. Staring directly into a security cam perched atop the doors, she raised one long finger and said, "Consider yourself marked, Enlil."

As soon as she said his name, a Post-it note fluttered to the ground. None of us bothered to pick it up.

"What does that 'inhibitor spray' do?" I asked.

"It weakens our power for a short period of time."

The mountain shook again.

"Fuck!" Rigel said.

"I can't transport Devon fast enough to beat this now." Inanna eyed Devon up and down. "Your own feeble legs will provide quicker propulsion."

"Hey!" Devon said. "I'll have you know I was on my high school track team. I bet I can run faster than you now that you don't have fancy superpowers."

"I doubt that, human."

Bits of the ceiling began to rain down on top of us.

"We're not going to make it if we wait for my power to return," Inanna said. "These earthquakes mean this thing is going to blow any second. We need to move now."

Move. That gave me an idea.

"I'll be right back." I zipped back into the warehouse and collected a hand truck and some rope from a display.

I returned and parked the hand truck in front of Devon and Inanna.

"What's that for?" Inanna asked.

"Both of you get on," I said.

She raised a brow at me. I raised my brow back.

"You have got to be kidding," Inanna said.

"Can you flash or turn into light in your present condition?"

"No."

"Then this is your ride. *I* will flash us out of here."

Devon grinned and jumped on the hand truck. "It's okay, sweet cheeks," he said to Inanna, opening his arms wide. "You can hold on to me."

She gritted her teeth and got on with Devon. I tied the rope around their waists. I so wished it was appropriate to laugh, because the two of them tied to a hand truck was the funniest thing I'd ever seen.

"You ready?" I asked.

"Shit howdy!" Devon said. "Let's do this."

"I'll be right behind you guys," Rigel said.

I tipped the hand truck forward in front of the control panel so Inanna could deactivate the trap and allow us to cross the room. The anger rolling off Inanna was a tangible thing. Enlil was going to pay for this one.

With one hand I held on to the hand truck, and with the other I held the handle of the Ark. I envisioned the entrance to the next safety in my mind's eye, and off we went.

"Holy shit!" Devon shouted. Because of the wind, his lips were flapping, so it sounded more like "Oleeee ibbbbt."

In a few short minutes we were through all the safeties and back at the stairs that led to the exit. Devon's eyes were huge, and his mouth was frozen open in a silent scream. His hair, however, hadn't been fazed by the wind at all.

I stared up at the thousands of stairs. How the hell was I gonna flash them and the Ark up all of those?

I didn't have time to ponder the problem long. A mega quake hit, so powerful that I fell to the ground and couldn't stand back up. Rigel rushed to my side. He said something, but I couldn't hear him over the rumbling of the quake and a metallic groaning sound. I looked up to see that the metal rail of the stairs was bending, the steps themselves falling away, breaking free of the wall.

"Well, fuck," was the last thing I had time to say before the stairs came crashing down, and I descended into darkness.

33

RAW MEAT, A ROCKIN' CHEST, AND FLIPPING ON THE PAIN SWITCH

It was quiet… too quiet. No more rumblings from the earth, no booms of stairs crashing. *Does that mean we're safe?*

I was lying face down on a cold, hard surface. My eyes were closed, and I couldn't seem to open them. They were too heavy; or maybe someone had glued them shut. I couldn't be sure. There was a dull, throbbing pain throughout my body, but I couldn't locate a specific injury—everything hurt. And I was pretty sure a hippopotamus was squatting on my back. My lungs hissed with each breath. At least the pounding of blood in my limbs meant they remained attached—or so I hoped.

When at last I managed to peel my eyes open, I immediately shut them with a groan. It felt like the light from the room was going to drill a hole into my sockets. I tried again, squinting this time until my eyes could adjust.

There was a blur of color below me. I blinked a few times and realized I was back on Inanna's ship, staring through the semitransparent floor as we shot into the sky, barely escaping the plume of an erupting volcano.

"Holy shit!"

I scrambled to my feet, was hit with a dizzy spell, and promptly fell flat on my face. *What is wrong with me?*

Rigel appeared next to me holding the ankh. He was pale, his features sunken, and flakes of ash fell from his skin.

"Rigel, what—"

Then I saw Devon.

He lay next to me, unconscious. Vomit rose to my throat, not because I was touching him, but because of his injuries. He was a slab of bloody raw meat.

"Devon," I whimpered.

Rigel tried to heal me with the ankh, but I batted him away.

"No," I said. "Devon... help... Devon... please." Every word was such an effort that I had to pause between them.

Rigel shook his head and attempted to heal me again.

"No," I insisted. "Devon."

Rigel collapsed, the ankh clattering to the floor.

"Rigel?" I said, and crawled to his side. I was confused. He didn't show any signs of injury. I lifted his shirt to see if I was missing something. There wasn't a single wound, yet his skin was flaking away like he was dying. "Inanna. I need... help."

I grabbed the ankh from Rigel's hand and tried to run it over him like I'd seen him do to me, but nothing happened.

"Inanna!"

The next thing I knew, the ankh was taken from me. I looked up to find Inanna standing there, a golden tear staining her cheek. *Okay. I must be hallucinating. A tear? From Inanna?*

"It's not Rigel that needs healing, honey," she said.

And that was when I finally looked at myself. Almost all the skin on my arms was gone, and in places I could see all the way to the bone.

Inanna kneeled down in front of me. Her expression freaked me out worse than my injuries. She was scared.

"Before I can heal you," she said to me in way too calm a voice, "I need to pull this out of your chest. There's nothing I can do for the pain."

I didn't understand what she was talking about. She must have seen my confusion because she pointed between my breasts.

I looked down to find a spur of rock, as thick as a baseball bat, protruding from my chest. *Why am I not screaming in pain? Why don't I feel anything?*

"You ready?" Inanna said, lifting my chin to meet her eyes.

I nodded.

She grabbed the end of the rock shard and pulled.

As if she had flipped on an invisible pain switch, my body seized, and blood began pouring out of my mouth. Black spots filled my vision until there was nothing left. Was I about to die, *again*? Hopefully I was like a cat and had nine lives. Either way, at that moment, I didn't care. I welcomed the darkness.

34

A SCALY SIDEKICK, ALIEN APPS, AND STRESS-RELEASING SQUEEGEES

The surface under me wasn't the smooth metal of the ship; it had a spiky texture. I brushed my fingertips along it. *Dried grass? No, how could that be?* A gentle heat penetrated my limbs, breathing life into them. The familiar smell of lavender soap and baby powder filled my lungs.

I opened my eyes to see Rigel staring down at me in all his glory, the sun framing him in an angelic glow. It reminded me of that time not so long ago in the Barnes & Noble parking lot.

"Are we in heaven?" I asked.

Giving me an easy smile, he stood, unblocking the sun and forcing me to squint my eyes against the brightness. He offered me a hand, and with his help I negotiated with my wobbly legs until they could support my weight.

We were atop a grass-covered cliff that provided a spectacular view of surrounding mountains. The vegetation was dry in places, and that somehow added to the beauty of the area. The cliff we were on was steep, and down below was a valley filled with grass plains, patches of tightly packed trees, and dirt roads. Inanna's ship hovered about forty feet away. The exterior was mirrored and reflected the surroundings, almost acting as camouflage.

In the reflection, a red glowing object caught my attention. I turned to the sky to see Nibiru. The planet and its moons were clearly distinguishable now; Nibiru itself was already the size of our own moon. Its expansive atmospheric wings extended from both sides.

Stretching my sore muscles, I said, "Where are we?"

"South Africa. The Abzu."

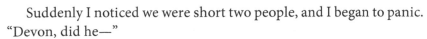

Suddenly I noticed we were short two people, and I began to panic. "Devon, did he—"

"Hey, look," hollered a familiar voice behind me. "I found a chameleon!"

I whirled around—and saw Devon headed our way. I put my hand to my chest and sucked in a breath. "Oh, thank god."

There was a multi-colored lizard on his shoulder. He stroked its chin with his pinky finger as he walked.

"As you can see, his hair survived too," Rigel said.

Indeed it had. If anything, it looked even fuller.

"Where's Inanna?" I asked.

Rigel picked a strand of grass from my hair. "She's gathering the things we need to activate the power grid."

"And the Ark?"

"On the ship."

"This is it then." I spoke with a finality I wasn't prepared for. My heart sped up, and I felt kind of lightheaded.

"This is it," Rigel repeated, caressing my cheek. "You ready?"

"She'll do great!" Devon said encouragingly. The lizard had nestled in his shirt pocket like a content kitten. "Meet Howard," he said, proudly motioning to his new pal.

I plunked onto the grass. "Wow. This really is it."

"You need help with what to say?" Rigel asked.

I thought about it, and decided that a spur-of-the-moment approach was my best bet. A scripted speech would probably sound fake, and if this was going to work, it needed to be heartfelt. I was ready to leave it all on the table, and I hoped humans would appreciate that.

"No thanks," I muttered.

My thoughts went to my imminent demise. *What am I leaving behind?* A will was useless, obviously. There would be nothing left to give anyone. I knew I wouldn't cross to the next dimension, given the circumstances, so what remained to solidify my existence?

"Too bad Earth is coming to an end," Devon said, petting his lizard in contemplation. "This little adventure would've made the *New York Times* bestseller list."

A light bulb flicked on above my head. "That's it!" I exclaimed, hopping to my feet.

"What's it?" Rigel asked.

"I need to tell people our story. If they survive, they should know what all of you did."

"What *you* did, Autumn," he corrected.

"What we *all* did," I said.

"Can I write the screenplay for it?" Devon asked.

As I reflected on all that had happened—the good, the bad, and the ugly—I realized there was no time to jot it all down. "Never mind," I said, my shoulders sagging. "It won't work. It would take months to tell it all, and we don't even have hours."

Devon frowned at his new scaly sidekick. "Guess we'll have to find another way to fame and fortune, huh, Howard?" He cradled Howard in his arms like a baby. I couldn't help but giggle at the sight.

Rigel snapped his fingers, gave me a kiss on the cheek, and flashed onto the ship. He returned almost immediately, carrying an MP3 player. Dangling from the headphone jack was a pair of EEG wire type things.

"What's that?" I asked.

"The *Suh-Inim-Bala*."

"Isn't that the torture device Enlil wanted to use on me?" I said. "The way he spoke of it, I thought it ripped your fingernails off one by one—or worse."

"Nothing quite that dramatic. It's a mental recording application, not a torture device. It records and transcribes what you're thinking into words. It was originally developed for authors and important leaders to allow their thoughts to literally flow onto the page. Later on it was revamped and used to get information from hostiles. Due to its versatile nature, developers created plug-ins, add-ons, and apps, including one that can convert your thoughts into a novel."

"Ha!" Devon laughed. "Aliens have apps."

Rigel gave me the device and placed the wire pads behind my ears.

"How does it work?" I asked.

"If you mentally recall all that happened," he said, "it will record it in words. It's a very intuitive app. It has a character recollection feature. Once you establish the person, anything you recount them saying will automatically be put in with a 'Devon said' or 'Inanna asked.' It will also recognize the emotion in which they say it. It's a well-developed tool. You can mentally erase things too."

"That kicks ass!" Devon said.

I swallowed hard. "What about all the stuff between now and…"

Rigel winced slightly at that. "You can keep it attached and it will record you in real time going forward."

"Okay."

"You have a while before Inanna finishes her errands," Rigel said. "Why don't you give it a try?"

Suddenly put on the spot, I felt this extreme anxiety about doing it. "Um, how am I supposed to articulate the details of this convoluted story? My mind is going a thousand different directions."

"I know," Rigel said. "On the ship there is a device called the *ĝeš-ni-dub*, or what we nicknamed the 'tranquility tool.' It operates similar to hypnosis and allows complete relaxation. You can use that. I'll wake you when Inanna returns."

I pushed my nerves aside. "All right. Let's do it!"

Rigel and I went aboard the ship, leaving Devon to play with his new best friend. Rigel pressed some buttons on the console, and a plush couch materialized.

No longer fazed by magically appearing items, I plopped down on it, snuggled in, and stared upward. Buzzards circled above. I hoped that wasn't an omen.

"Where would you like to start?" Rigel asked. "Do you want me to ask you questions to get you into the flow?"

"First I want a kiss," I said. "Then, I think I should introduce myself before I recount these last days. So maybe lead by asking me to address the survivors?"

"Sorry, what was that?" He grinned. "I didn't hear anything after you said you wanted a kiss."

"Then by all means…"

He leaned in and kissed me. It was playful at first, but quickly grew impassioned. As much as I wanted to rip his clothes off and take him right here, I had to stop. *Recounting our tale is more important than raw, passionate sex, right? Dammit!* Somehow I got control and pried myself away from him.

It occurred to me then that the times back in Rigel's room were going be the sum total of my short sex life. If so, well… that was the way to do it. It'd be hard to beat an out-of-body orgasm while bound by the soul of God.

Rigel's eyes sparkled, and I knew he could read my dirty thoughts. I blushed.

With a cocky smirk on his face, he conjured up a glowing white wand and swept it across my shoulders and head. My muscles relaxed as though someone had used a squeegee to wipe them clear of all tension. When he spoke, his voice gradually faded to a murmur in the background.

"Autumn, the survivors are ready to hear your tale. Can you introduce yourself and recount your adventures on the planet formerly known as Earth?"

PART TWO

I wake from a sound sleep, content and relaxed, and keep my eyes shut to preserve the feeling for a few minutes longer. The sensation of someone's breath on my face wakes me further. A cool minty smell fills my nose, burning it in a refreshing way. A soft kiss brushes my lips—and then the mouth grazes my cheek and continues down my neck. My heart pounds against my chest, and I can't help but give a slight moan. The kisses trail their way back up the other side of my face. When I open my eyes, Rigel's blazing blues greet mine, shining so brightly my heart skips a beat.

Entwining my fingers in his hair, I pull his lips to mine, and the connection of our kiss illuminates the room in blue sparks. I rise in an effort to lessen the space between us. He responds by pressing me down on the couch, pinning me with one hand while sliding my shirt and bra off with the other. He kisses my bare skin, working his way from my belly button to my chest. We're uninhibited, our passion driven by a profound anger at the universe—for bringing us together only to tear us apart. Pulsating in a white radiance, he straddles me, his jeans doing little to hide his excitement. *Oh, god. This is it. The last time we'll have this experience together. And we both know it.*

He cups one of my breasts, his nails digging in, spurring my lower region to quake, and I'm forced to clutch his biceps to steady myself. He presses his pelvis into me, the edge of his zipper sliding against... *Oh, god...* The threat of an orgasm builds with each thrust.

"You finish?" Rigel asks, wild and electrified.

"Finish?" I say with a rumble of ecstasy. "We haven't even taken off our pants yet."

Rigel gives a throaty chuckle, stirring a rush of pleasure. "No. Finish with your thoughts. You wrap up the story?"

I'm such a dope. "Oh, that." I blush, drunk with sexual desire. "Yeah."

Placing his chiseled arms on each side of my shoulders, he leans into me, hair tickling my face. He whispers in my ear, "I'll make sure you finish the other thing too." Executing another masterful thrust, he gives me a kiss filled with a craving so intense that I *do* finish, right then. Rigel stiffens when my spasm hits him too, and he rapidly removes the rest of my clothes, barely able to forestall his own orgasm.

Once he slips inside me, I use my newfound super strength to force us together. *I want him inside me, all the way inside. No space between us.* I wait for the vibrations to begin and for our souls to launch out of our bodies. But they don't. The only vibrations I experience are the uncontrollable spasms rocking my core.

My initial orgasm lingers, making every nerve tingle, my skin hypersensitive, putting me on the brink of insanity from overstimulation. It builds and builds until it hits again, practically shattering me. I cry out Rigel's name. He lifts me from the couch and we slam into the side of the spaceship, his abs rippling against mine as he leans into me.

It's beyond bizarre to see through the walls to the outside while we're in the throes of passion. I soon forget that when Rigel takes one hand and places it on the small of my back, pressing me into him, deep—*so fucking deep*—the other hand braced firmly on the wall. Our orgasm hits, and we are both breathless. His pleasure fuels me, and in turn my pleasure increases his. It's too much, and my muscles contract, my back arches... and we scream.

I'm frozen, my mind bursting with white lights, little stars dancing in my vision. *Holy shit.* Our sweaty bodies fold into each other and we stay there, unable to move while aftershocks hit us in waves.

"If I had to pick a way to end things," I confess, "I think this would be it."

He laughs and kisses me on my forehead, his eyes searing mine with an intense affection. "I love you, Autumn."

"I love you, too."

I take a mental snapshot of this moment in time and lock it away, because this is what will keep me strong when I use the Pinecone. No amount of physical torture could distract me from the love we're sharing right now. I know I can take on anything as long as I have those electric blues to guide me.

A single golden tear runs down Rigel's cheek. I wipe it off and kiss the place where it teased his skin. It tastes sweet, not salty like human tears.

"Can I ask you something?" I say.

"What is it?"

"Where did you go... when you died?"

He doesn't answer right away, taking a few moments to study me. "My soul was pulled from my body by the golden tether, and then everything went white."

"Did it hurt?"

"I felt all the pain you experienced from those assholes in the shed, but there was no pain after I died, *we* died, no sensation, only this white glow." He furrows his brow. "Why? I know you couldn't enter the other dimension, but what happened after you died?"

"Nothing," I lie. "Couldn't get in is all."

"I can read your emotions, remember?"

There's no way I am going to tell him about my experience, not now. It's a huge relief, though, to know he won't suffer the same fate as me. He will be at peace. My chest begins to tighten, and my nerves prickle at my stomach, making it ache. "Are you scared?" I ask.

"No," he responds with surprising confidence.

My backbone clearly isn't as strong as his. "I'm scared shitless," I admit. I bury my head in his chest, fisting his shirt tight in my hands as I fight back tears. "I'm going to miss you so much."

He lifts my chin and rests his forehead on mine. "Listen to me." We're eye to eye and both of us are letting the tears fall freely now. "Our love, our souls, our light will be one after this. We will be together, Autumn. Fully. You must know that by now. You are not going to lose me."

"But you'll go into another dimension."

He places my hand over his heart. "Feel that?" His heartbeat thuds hard against my palm, matching exactly the beat of mine. "We are one."

My breath hitches, and we stay there, forehead to forehead, for a long moment.

Finally I say, "Hope you don't mind being with me for eternity then."

"Even that won't be enough."

I give him a playful nudge with my nose. "Okay, now that was a little cheesy."

Rigel grins and brushes the hair behind my ears. "You ready?"

"Yes."

We break apart and get dressed in silence. I try to enjoy my remaining alone time with him, but my thoughts turn to the monumental speech I need to make in a matter of hours. I'm faced with the biggest *what if* of my life. *What if I fail?*

By the time I put my shoes on, I'm shaking so badly that Rigel has to help tie my shoe. That's when I see that he's wearing a different shirt from before. This one is a Van Halen vintage tee.

"I'm guessing those aren't replica vintage T-shirts you wear?"

"No, they are. I had to re-create them with our organic material. But I did make them based on shirts I purchased at actual concerts."

"Who was your favorite?"

"My favorite band is Led Zeppelin, but my favorite concert was The Doors in Miami in '69. That was wild. But that might've had something to do with the acid I dropped."

"No way!" I say, shocked. "What did you hallucinate?"

"A unicycle."

I snort. "A unicycle?"

"When Jim Morrison ripped his shirt off, I hallucinated that he leaped on a unicycle and rolled around the stage buck naked. I was snapped out of it when everyone in the crowd started taking their clothes off too. The rest was a blur of sweat and chaos."

"Any unicycle flashbacks?"

"Not that I can remember."

"Too bad. It'd be fun to see you trip out."

We walk off the ship into the warm sunlight. It's eerie that this location boasts blue skies and cool breezes, while the rest of the planet is being torn apart by meteorites and fire. Knowing I might never get the chance to savor it again, I fill my lungs with the fresh and familiar Earth air and bend down to feel the grass between my fingers, digging in to let the cool dirt lodge under my nails. Straightening, I brush my hands on my pants and watch a cloud pass by. It changes shape as it glides along without a care in the world. Rigel regards me curiously, but doesn't say anything.

"So where's this magical power device?" I ask.

"Right there." He points. "That's Enki's Calendar."

I look where he indicates and notice for the first time a series of stones near the edge of the cliff arranged in a circular pattern: a South African Stonehenge. They're considerably eroded with age, but it's undeniable that they were at one time carved into specialized shapes. In the center of the circle are two tall gray rock slabs, their flat sides facing one another, reminding me of a very ancient and worn version of the ape monolith in *2001: A Space Odyssey*. About fifty feet on either side of the monoliths are two trees that mark the edge of the circle, square boulders placed at their bases.

"Are those trees part of the device?"

"No, just the stones at their bases," Rigel says. "Those are the north and south markers. The trees were planted later during an anniversary celebration."

"How old is this place?"

"Seventy-five thousand years old. However, it's considerably more worn than it should be because of use."

We walk closer, and I study one of the stones. The curve of it has me curious. "What did this used to be?"

"Have you heard of Horus?"

"Isn't he the Egyptian god with the bird head?"

"Correct. Horus was actually part of one of the oldest alien civilizations, the Abgal. They have the head of a falcon and bodies similar to ours. The Abgal are our closest allies and assisted with building this power device. This stone, along with several others, was carved into the shape of a perching falcon in commemoration of them. It's the same as the statue of the Horus bird you will find throughout Egypt."

I trace my finger over the curve of the stone and try to imagine a creature such as the Abgal roaming around.

"Yo Rigel, I have a question," I hear Devon say behind us.

Needing to clear my head and prepare for what I am about to do, I leave Rigel to answer Devon's question, and retreat to a flat rock on the edge of the hill. Sitting there, I soak in my surroundings: from the dung beetle rolling its treasure across the terrain, to the mighty new sapling fighting to push itself from the soil. Both are working hard to survive, not knowing their struggle is pointless.

My attention wanders to the opposing hill, about a half mile away, that has a single lonely tree perched on top. It's a rich green, which is strange, since all the other trees in the area are fairly sparse. And beyond the tree, I see a figure. I'm pretty sure it's human, but it's too far away to know for sure. I hear the grass crunch, and feel Rigel approaching.

"There's someone over there," I say, pointing.

"That's Inanna."

"What's she doing there? Don't tell me Enlil buried the parts we need to activate the device all over Africa?"

"No, nothing like that. Beside that tree is Dumuzi's grave."

"Is that like her dog?"

"Dumuzi was her soulmate."

"She had a soulmate?" I say, amazed. She didn't strike me as the "soulmate" type.

"Believe it or not, their love is legendary—the inspiration for poems, songs, and works of art."

"What happened?"

"Many thought their marriage would lead to peace between Enlil's and Enki's families, because she's a descendant of Enlil, and Dumuzi was a descendant of Enki. Remarkably, both Enlil and Enki gave their blessing for the marriage, and even threw a party in their

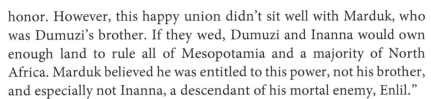

honor. However, this happy union didn't sit well with Marduk, who was Dumuzi's brother. If they wed, Dumuzi and Inanna would own enough land to rule all of Mesopotamia and a majority of North Africa. Marduk believed he was entitled to this power, not his brother, and especially not Inanna, a descendant of his mortal enemy, Enlil."

"Was this before or after Marduk got pissed that Inanna got all those extra *mes* from Enlil?"

"This was after that, but prior to the Tower of Babel incident. I personally think Marduk had a secret love for Inanna that she didn't reciprocate, but that's just conjecture. Anyway, Marduk made it his quest to sabotage their union."

"Okay, Marduk is a moron if he tried to mess with Inanna."

"Well, you know how I said Inanna was power hungry?"

"Yeah."

"After she and Dumuzi were wed and had a couple of children—"

"Inanna is a *mother*?"

A flicker of pain crosses Rigel's face, but he immediately covers it. I know I didn't imagine it because I feel this sorrow all of a sudden.

"What's the matter?" I ask.

"Nothing."

"But I—"

"Inanna was a doting mother, in fact," he says, stopping that line of questioning. I decide not to press further. "Life became tedious for her, so Inanna decided she needed new land to rule. Her sister Ereshkigal had more land than her at the time, and as you can guess…"

"That was simply unacceptable," I finish.

"Yes. Inanna told Dumuzi of her plan to conquer her sister, and he wanted nothing to do with it. In fact, he forbade her to act, which only made her want it even more. Long story short, she went behind his back and tried to defeat her sister—and Inanna was killed."

"Usually when people say 'long story short' they end up telling a super long story. I think you're the first person I've ever met that meant it. Wanna elaborate?"

"Before she went to conquer her sister, Inanna told her plans to her best friend, and instructed her to go to Enki if she didn't return. And when Inanna didn't come back, they discovered that she'd been imprisoned and executed. Enki used his contacts to smuggle in the elixir to resurrect her."

"Where was Dumuzi during all this? Didn't he freak after hearing his wife was killed?"

"He had no idea any of this was happening. As far as he knew she was visiting her family, which technically wasn't a lie, I guess."

"Obviously Enki was successful with the resurrection."

"He was, but Ereshkigal kept Inanna prisoner. The only way Ereshkigal would give Inanna her freedom was if she provided Ereshkigal with someone to take her place. And it had to be someone close to Inanna, not a stranger or enemy. Inanna didn't think it through; she just wanted out of there. So she agreed.

"First, Ereshkigal tried to take both of Inanna's sons. Inanna refused. Next Ereshkigal selected Inanna's best friend. Inanna refused again. By this time she realized what a terrible bargain she made. Unsure what to do, she went to Dumuzi for advice—and she found him hosting a party, drunk on wine. She was so angry that he wasn't mourning her death, she gave Dumuzi to her sister as her replacement."

"Wait! I thought he didn't know anything about what was going on. He didn't even know she went to her sister's, much less that she had died."

"That's right."

"Holy shit."

"He tried to tell her that, but she was overcome with rage and didn't listen to his pleas. Ereshkigal's men seized him. When she finally discovered the truth, it was too late."

"I change my mind," I say, feeling queasy at the thought that I'm trusting Inanna with my life. "I'm ready for the shorter version now. Where does Marduk come in?"

"Dumuzi managed to escape, and Marduk jumped at the chance to go after him. So he put together a team of mercenaries to track Dumuzi down."

"Did Marduk kill him?"

"The official report is that Dumuzi tried to hide behind a waterfall, slipped into the rapids, and drowned. But no one believes that. The prominent opinion is that he was captured and thrown over by Marduk. He wanted Dumuzi finished."

"How come they didn't resurrect Dumuzi like they did Inanna?"

"It was too late. After three days, the soul is fully transitioned into the other dimension. Dumuzi was washed down the river and they

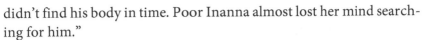

didn't find his body in time. Poor Inanna almost lost her mind searching for him."

"It was her fault!" I say, disgusted. "She sent him in her place. Who does that to someone they love? I mean, she didn't even give him a chance to explain!"

"You have to understand Inanna."

I stare at him. "You're *defending* what she did?"

"No, no. It's just. How do I say this? Inanna is…"

"It's not important." I wave him off; I don't want to start an argument. "What happened to Marduk? Did he pay for what he did at least?"

"Ultimately, he did. A war arose, with Inanna leading the charge to annihilate all who were on Marduk's side. Enlil stepped in and ruled that Marduk be sealed inside the King's Chamber at the Great Pyramid and left to die a slow death."

"That's quite the punishment."

"Yes, except for the fact he was rescued."

"What? You have to be kidding."

"Anu heard about what Enlil did and freed Marduk, deciding his sentence should be exile to Egypt."

My blood pressure rises just thinking about him getting off like that. "Is he still alive?"

"My guess is no. Eventually, all traces of him vanished. Later, a tomb was found that allegedly contained his remains. Trouble is, there are no written records explaining how he died, and no one came forward as a witness to his death. We have only rumors and speculation to go on."

"Do you think Inanna…?"

Rigel nodded. "I think she hunted him down and sealed him in a tomb to suffer the slow demise he was originally sentenced to. She vehemently denies it, though."

If anyone hurt Rigel, I would stalk them down until I brought the bastard to justice by breaking every bone in his body one by one. The thought of it has my insides roiling.

"Wow, I can feel that," Rigel says, patting his abdomen. "You've got a protective spark in you."

I'm unprepared for that. *How can I be protective, yet willing to have Rigel join me on death row to save humanity? I'm such a hypocrite.*

Rigel helps me to my feet. "We're going to be killed anyway," he says, hooking his finger in the loop of my jeans to pull me into him. "Enlil will make sure of that. You need to do this. You're the only hope left for humans, and you have to fight for them."

This should ease my guilt, but it doesn't. The thought of being mankind's last and only hope doesn't exactly liberate me. "Yeah, piece of cake."

All this talk about Inanna and her family suddenly reminds me of something. "Oh, no!" I say. "You didn't get to speak to your family."

"Actually, I did," he says. "When you were using the Suh, I set up a communication with them. I got to say goodbye to everyone back home."

"Oh, good." I sigh in relief. "I bet they love me."

He gives me a wink. "Let's just say it's lucky you don't have to meet my mom."

Rigel pulls me in so my back is to his chest and wraps his warm arms around me. We watch Inanna as she sails through the air toward us with a train of items following her. She's holding a pitchfork-type thing that is at least four feet taller than she is. And considering she's almost seven feet tall, that's quite impressive. As she gets nearer, it registers with me what it must be.

"Is that the exalted scepter?"

"It sure is."

"That's one of the *mes* she stole from Enki, huh? His trident?"

"The very one."

"Wow."

Inanna lands softly on the grass beside us. Devon hurries over to join us, Howard clinging on to his shoulder for dear life.

"Nice lizard," Inanna teases, making Devon glow with pride.

I check out the other items Inanna brought. Levitating next to her are three stone rings, a stack of metal bowls, three cone-shaped stones, four pairs of sunglasses, two down jackets, and a bulbous rock about Devon's height (hair included).

"What's with the mondo bowling pin?" Devon asks, squinting at the rock. Now that I look closer, it could have been a sculpture of a human at one time.

"This is Sam," she says.

"Nice to meet you, Sam," Devon says. Then he raises a brow at Inanna. "Is he gonna come alive and do the jig?"

"No." She scowls. "Sam here used to be in the west corner of the circle until some bird enthusiasts decided to relocate him to the entrance of this nature preserve. The moronic boobs removed him from sacred ground and made him a shitting post for swallows."

"Poor Sam," Devon says. "How come he gets a name?"

"Sam is short for Sound Amplifying Mechanism."

"It's not just a rock?"

Inanna glares at him and sends Sam flying toward Devon.

Devon jumps out of the way as Sam zooms past. "Hey!"

"Oops." She sets Sam down along the rim of the circle, and then turns to Rigel. "Sorry it took so long," she says. "Enlil was here." Reaching into her pocket, she pulls out a wad of Post-it notes. "He was careful to record all he did to 'keep us safe,' and he provided plenty of messages to explain how apologetic he is about the last-minute changes."

Rigel takes the notes and throws them over his shoulder. "This has ruined Post-it notes for me," he says.

"Unfortunately, due to a newfound 'safety measure' that Enlil, to borrow a human phrase, has pulled out of his ass, we are going to have to go old school in order to get our power. Hence"—she gestures to the various instruments floating beside her—"all this."

"Wow, this brings back memories," Rigel says. "Are there enough of us to pull it off that way?"

"It would be better if there were more of us, but if I hit the stones hard enough with the scepter, it should trigger."

"This oughta be interesting," Devon says, rubbing his hands together.

Inanna clears her throat and sounds suspiciously casual as she asks Rigel, "Were you able to touch base with our sources to verify what phase we are in?"

Rigel shifts uncomfortably and loosens his hold on me—the telltale sign that he's hiding something. Almost in a mumble he says, "Phase three is in full force, and we only have about an hour, maybe two until the caldera breaks open."

Devon drops to his knees. "Oh, god."

"What the hell did you say?" I roar, pushing Rigel away. I pace, my brain going into shock. *Must keep moving or I will collapse. Must keep moving.* "You have to be mistaken." I gesture to the sky. "It's fucking blue sky and chirping birds here."

"We are in a safe zone," Rigel says. "There is a reason why we placed the circle here."

I can't seem to catch my breath. "This can't be happening."

Rigel reaches for me, but falters when I give him a glare that would put Medusa to shame. He keeps his distance as he explains, "The pressure on you is overwhelming, Autumn. I didn't want to make things worse. It was pointless to mention it until we retrieved everything we needed for the activation. All it would do is upset you."

Balling my fists to suppress my anger, I bite back the scream that is building inside me. There's no time for emotions. "We must do this now."

"Let's fire this bad boy up!" Devon says.

Inanna distributes a metal pot, a stone ring, a pair of sunglasses, and a cone to each of us. She hands Devon and me the down jackets.

"How come Rigel doesn't get a jacket?" Devon asks.

"He doesn't get cold like you."

"Does the device change the weather?" I ask.

"No. But we're going to need to get out of the way of the energy beam, so I'm going to levitate us off the ground. I thought I may as well take you up high enough to see the show."

Devon's face lights up. "Cool!"

I examine the instruments she gave us. The ring is about the size of a donut and is carved from a shiny brown stone, or possibly dark glass. The cone is decorated with elaborate writing I don't recognize. While it resembles an artifact you might unearth at an archeological site, it doesn't seem to be an antique; it's way too pristine to have been lying in a field for thousands of years. The pot I received is the largest of the bunch. It's one of those Tibetan singing bowls.

"I'll need you all to run your ring along the rim of your bowl," Inanna instructs. "The sound activates the grid. This will create the precise vibrational frequency to trigger it."

Inanna takes my ring, lays it flat against the edge of the bowl, and slides it against the rim to demonstrate. It sings from the contact. "It's imperative you sustain a uniform speed," she says. "Once all of you

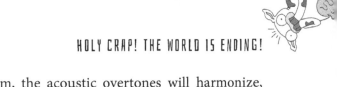
establish a similar rhythm, the acoustic overtones will harmonize, causing the rings to vibrate. When the vibrations get to where you feel you might lose control, let the ring go. It will levitate and spin above the bowl vertically." She holds the ring so the hole is facing us. "When this happens, I need you to place the cone's flat side against the ring." She presses the bottom of the cone on the lip of the ring. "This will send out a concentrated energy beam. You want to direct it to the taller of the center stones. Word of warning, don't touch the ring with your hand; it will burn you. Simply aim it in the right direction using your cone, which will remain cool."

"My aim isn't the best," I say.

"Then I'll duck until you guide the beam over. Once it hits the stone it will lock on."

"Okay," I say shakily, not at all confident in my death ray piloting skills.

"Once I give you the signal, you can place the bowls on the ground. The ring and cone will stay in place. Now, I need you all to spread out and position yourselves outside the circle."

There's no time for any more Q&A. We all spread out as she requested. I organize my stuff while the others get into place. I hook the glasses on my shirt, secure the cone in my pocket the best I can, and tie the coat to my waist. Once we're all ready, Inanna waves her hand, and we begin.

I glide the ring around the bowl, creating a low hum. The acoustics in the circle make it so that I can hear the others' bowls as if they were right next to me, each giving off a different tone. At first it's chaotic, like an orchestra tuning before a concert. But once we get a flow going, a perfect harmony arises, and it's an entrancing arrangement of notes. Energy tingles in my fingertips, moves along my arms, prickles my spine, and travels to my toes.

As the harmonic tone gets louder, my eardrums whir and tickle from the vibrations. I clench my jaw in an attempt to stifle it. The need to scratch is overwhelming (like one of those sudden itches on your foot that practically has you seizing as you try to rip off your shoe to scratch it). I am actually considering sticking the tip of the cone in my ear when there is a thunderous clap, and the whole earth rolls underfoot. I almost lose my grip.

"Don't stop," Rigel shouts. Planting myself firmly in place, I keep my otherworldly song going.

Inanna glides around the perimeter and chants in a poetic, mesmerizing musical language. It's definitely not English. *Their native tongue, perhaps?* I never asked what their language is called. *Nibirubian?* Whatever she's speaking, it's hypnotizing. As she passes by the stones that are on their sides, they rise to what must be their original positions.

Once she completes an entire circle, Inanna quiets. She straightens her arms toward the sky, as if possessed, and tilts her head all the way back. It's at such an unnatural angle that I expect her to go full-on *Exorcist* style and spin her head around, but she doesn't. Instead, her form shimmers, turns iridescent, and emits tiny particles—dancing fireflies of energy surround her. *Holy crap.*

And then I feel my ring start to fight me. It trembles and forces itself away from the edge of my bowl, like a magnet being pressed against its opposite pole. I let go as Inanna instructed, and it zips into place above the bowl, spinning rapidly. Instantly it glows red and heat pours off of it. In the center of the ring a white pinpoint of light flickers on.

Retrieving the cone from my pocket, I use the flat end to stop the ring's spinning. A stream of energy immediately shoots from the cone's tip... which I haven't aimed yet.

"Shit!"

I look to see if I hit anything, and spot Inanna crouched on the ground, staring daggers at me. My death ray is a mere foot from drilling a hole in her head.

"I told you." I shrug and hold back a smile.

Carefully, I aim the cone at the taller center stone, and it locks on. Rigel and Devon already have theirs secured and are laughing at me.

After a few seconds, the rock begins to glow red like a coal in a fire.

Inanna's voice resonates through the circle as if she's using an invisible loudspeaker. "I am about to activate the Zalag," she says. "It's going to create a frequency that will render us all deaf for several minutes." Devon and I give each other a worried frown. "You can put the bowls down now."

I place the bowl on the ground. The ring, the cone, and beam of energy remain in place.

Inanna walks around the two main monoliths, which I assume is the "Zalag" she mentioned, and runs her fingers along the crown of the smaller stone searching for something. She must locate whatever she was looking for, because she places both hands on the scepter, raises it high in the air, and with all her strength slams it down hard on one rock, then on the other.

The noise that resonates is instantaneous, and the intensity of it nearly knocks me off my feet. Braying trumpets, thousands of them, echo off the surrounding mountains, as if announcing a divine presence. There is a blast of wind from the stones that whips my hair. Then all the air is drawn back in, the noise going with it, leaving us in complete and utter silence.

Sweet baby Jesus, this is weird. No noise at all. I can't even hear my own breathing. The absence of sound is sending all my other senses into hyper awareness, and I start to *feel* the sound rather than hear it.

A musical thumping beats inside my chest. I reach up to feel it with my hand, and it leaves a trail of particles in its wake. Curious, I move my arm from side to side, and the air undulates with luminescent specks. I look over to see that Devon is doing the same thing, waving his hands with childlike fascination.

The particles begin to vibrate and lift toward the sky. There is a shaking under my feet, and I see that anything not rooted down is lifting off the ground, including me. This isn't Inanna's power; this is different. Almost as if there is no more gravity. I kind of float there like an astronaut on the International Space Station. Devon, of course, is taking full advantage and doing loop-the-loops.

Inanna rolls her eyes at Devon, then with a wave of her hand the four of us shoot up into the sky. The wind whips my skin, making goose bumps appear on every exposed inch. Quickly untying the coat from my waist, I put it on, grateful that Inanna had thought of it.

When we finally stop and hover, we're at a dizzying height. I'm talking skydiver altitude. The patchwork landscape below us is spread out for miles in all directions.

My hearing returns with a painful thwack.

"Holy goat babies," Devon says. "That flippin' hurt."

"Hold on, we're going for a ride," Inanna says.

Not giving us time to actually "hold on,"—*and to what?*—she jets us away at a speed that has my skin stretching from the force of the wind. I try to scream, but we are going so fast that no sound comes out. Seconds later, Inanna brings us to a screeching halt.

"What the fuck was that?" I yell.

Inanna smiles broadly at me. "Payback for almost frying me with your energy ray."

"You almost killed Howard!" Devon splutters. He has his lizard pal pressed up against his chest.

"I have hold of him. Nothing would've happened to him."

Devon glowers at her and coos soothingly to Howard.

Inanna lowers us until the details of the landscape start coming back into view. Thousands of stone circles litter the countryside; they are everywhere. As we get closer, I see they are clustered together in groups, reminding me of a massive beehive—lines of stones connecting the circles like some ancient highway system.

A blast of heat hits us from below, and all the circles flare with a blinding light, forcing me to cover my eyes. *I guess this is why she gave us sunglasses.* I slide them on so I can watch the show unfolding below.

Each stone circle is filled with a churning whirlpool of light. One by one, spheres of energy wink into existence in the eyes of these vortexes. The spheres pulse once, then suck all the surrounding light into them like a vacuum cleaner. These new bulbs illuminate the landscape in a *Guinness Book of World Records*-winning Christmas display. The rings themselves begin to heat and glow a bright orange, appearing to draw power from the spheres, and give off a low pitched hum that I can feel in my gut. The energy from the circles flows into the stone roads, creating tendrils of interconnecting light.

Inanna sails us—gently this time—back toward Enki's Calendar. The illuminated roads flow in the same direction we are, like veins pumping energy into the heart of the Calendar. She brings us to a stop outside the circle.

All the power is now being fed into the two center monoliths. It forms a ball that crackles with electricity (Tesla lightning ball style). The hum increases until, with a crack, a geyser of energy rockets into space. The buzzing fades, and the only thing I hear is Devon's rapid breathing.

"Holy shit," Devon squeaks.

"Holy shit is right."

Inanna does her wolf whistle, and her ship zips over to us like an obedient dog. The door opens and Inanna lifts us inside.

The instant we touchdown, Inanna busies herself at the ship's controls, and Rigel jabs at one of the substation screens, on which are some kind of schematics. I watch with a mixture of fear and awe as they maneuver in an intricate and seemingly choreographed routine. Rigel slides his finger down the display, and the ship's walls appear. The room is steeped in darkness, save for the glare of the screens—until a light flickers on. Just like in the mountain cave, I can't pinpoint the source of the illumination. I'm going to have to ask Rigel about that later.

Scratch that. I won't have the chance. My stomach lurches at the thought. I'm a hop, skip, and a jump away from dying—to use a phrase my mom loved to hammer into my head when I did something stupid (which was a lot). *My mom. My dad. Would I see them again if I couldn't transition into their dimension?* I might be going somewhere that separates me for eternity from everyone I love, including my parents, Rigel, Emma, even Devon.

The world spins, and the next thing I know I'm slamming into the floor. In a rush Rigel is there, his gentle hands picking me up.

He places me in a chair, rubbing life back into my limbs.

"I know you can do this," he whispers in my ear. "I love you. Remember that." He hurriedly goes back to work on his screen.

Devon sits in the seat beside me. I can tell he's trying to hide the fact that he's nervous. "Anything I can do?" he asks.

I exhale shakily. "I don't think so." My breaths are shallow and labored, my chest pains transitioning into cardiac arrest territory. *Wouldn't that suck if I died of a heart attack right now, after all this?*

On Rigel's screen, a visual appears—a view from outside of the ship. The energy geyser continues to gush into the atmosphere a couple of hundred feet away. Rigel waves his hand across the monitor, and a golden rod with a thick silver ring at the end begins to extend toward the energy beam.

"Antenna is in position," Rigel says. "Is the ship ready to receive the power?"

"Confirmed," Inanna says. "You can make the connection."

Rigel presses an emblem on his monitor, and the silver ring lights up with a purple glow. Bands of electricity break off from the geyser and move toward the ring. The craft starts to vibrate.

"Contact in five, four, three, two…"

When he says "one," the energy connects, and the ship groans and quakes.

"Contact," Rigel announces.

"Well, duh," Devon says.

My temples pulse, and I realize I'm not breathing. I heave in a lungful of air, which results in hiccups.

Devon frowns. "You don't look so good, Autumn."

"I'm fine. I have to be fine." I close my eyes and attempt to regain my composure.

A swirl of wind tosses my hair, and then Rigel has me in his arms. His blue eyes blaze with emotion.

"Rigel I—"

He doesn't let me finish the sentence. In the next breath he is fully claiming my mouth, fisting my hair to force the kiss deeper. I slide my hands up his shirt, grabbing onto his shoulders to pull him in. This kiss is filled with an intense desperation. *One last kiss.*

Pulling away too soon, he hovers inches from my face. "You ready?" he whispers.

His kiss and his strength have given me the fuel I need to keep going. A full tank, in fact. I click into ready mode. And not because I lost all fear, but because I can feel that Rigel is ready. His resolve resonates through me. Together we are unconquerable. Together we are one.

"I love you so much," I say.

"I love you, too," he says with his patented gloriously sexy half-smile. He gives me one last kiss on my forehead, and then breaks away to join Inanna. "We're ready," he says. "All systems go?"

"Almost," Inanna says, eyes flicking to the door impatiently. "I'm waiting on something."

"What's that?" I ask.

"It's a surprise I organized for you. It should be here shortly."

I can't help but give her a blank expression. "Hold up. You got me something?"

"I did. While we wait, let's juice up the Ark, shall we? Would you like to do the honors, Autumn?"

I catch sight of Devon swaying anxiously behind us, and I make a decision. "I'd like Devon to do the honors, unless it's painful. Does it hurt to do it?"

"Not at all," she says.

Inanna practically skips to the Ark, and with a dramatic flair, she opens an elfin-sized door located underneath. Devon and I bend down for a better view. Out of it she pulls a plug—and it's not some fancy alien design, it's a regular ol' three-prong plug. She walks to Devon, the cord extending from the Ark.

My mouth falls open in bewilderment.

"A plug?" Devon asks.

I can't believe it. "Are you telling me we went through all this effort to power up the Ark—*only to plug it into the wall?*"

Inanna shrugs. "Kind of anticlimactic, huh?"

"That's freaking awesome!" Devon shouts. "Where do I plug it in?"

She points to a socket on the side of the ship. "Right there."

Brimming with enthusiasm, he takes the plug from her and sticks it into the socket on the wall. The Ark splutters like an old-timey crank engine. I tilt my head at Devon, and he gives me a palms-up shrug.

"Is there an engine in there?" I ask Inanna.

"What were you expecting, hamsters on wheels?"

"Not an engine, that's for sure. Why didn't you make it run on gas?"

She raises an eyebrow. "At these prices?"

I roll my eyes. This is an odd time for her to suddenly gain a sense of humor.

"Actually, we needed a pinch more power than your antiquated gas could provide. Hence the light show outside."

Inanna's eyes widen, and she claps her hands together. I'm surprised by the uncharacteristic giddiness. *Maybe this misadventure is getting to all of us.*

"Your surprise is here!" She beams.

The door to the ship opens, and two figures drift in. One is a tall, extremely stunning woman with short blond hair. She has a motherly presence about her, strangely reminding me of Tinkerbelle. Her beauty contrasts with her torn and dirty clothing—it looks as if she barely survived a bar fight with her dignity. Around her neck is a necklace of… petrified flies? *Okay, that is a weird fashion choice.*

The other figure steps forward. I recognize her immediately, and I squeal in delight. It's Emma. She waves a box of Ding Dongs in one hand and Twinkies in the other.

"Is this where the party is?" she says.

"Emma!" I flash over to her and give her a hug, sending the pastries high into the air. "What are you doing here?"

"Ninhursag came and rescued me seconds before a meteorite destroyed my whole apartment complex."

My jaw drops, and I turn to the strange woman. "You're Ninhursag?"

"The one and only."

"I thought they had you imprisoned?"

"They did. Luckily for me, there was a global uprising on my planet, and the Council was, let's say, persuaded to let me go."

"Let you go?" I ask. "You look like you've been on the front lines. No offense."

"None taken." She reaches into her pocket, pulls out a wad of Post-it notes, and sighs. "Enlil wanted to ensure my safety."

"For the love of god!" I shout.

Rigel cuts in. "Wait, rewind. Uprising?"

"They broadcast coverage of the calamity unfolding on Earth. Those who weren't on our side were persuaded to change their minds after observing humans being executed in such a grisly fashion."

This reignites my sense of urgency. Every minute we waste equates to thousands, if not millions, of innocent people dying. "Shit!" I yell.

Everyone freezes at my outburst.

I collect myself and face Ninhursag. "Forgive me. I'm extremely honored to meet you, and I want to thank you for the incredible things you've done for my species, especially for creating us. But there won't be anyone left to rescue if we wait any longer."

"You're welcome," she replies, regarding me with a motherly pride. "And you are right, my dear. Time is of the essence."

Emma waves an unwrapped Ding Dong at me. "First you need one of these."

"Nice try," I say with a smirk. "But I think I'll take a Twinkie."

She tosses me one. I open it and take a bite. "This would so kick Ding Dong's ass in a flood."

Expecting her to give me grief for my blasphemous remark, I am surprised when she instead flings herself at me, giving me one last hug. Everyone in the room moves in too, encircling me, and I realize my inevitable "Dorothy" moment has arrived. This is my last chance to say goodbye to my friends before tapping my ruby slippers together to leave Oz.

Only there's no going home for me.

After breathing in a whiff of Emma's scrumptious blackberry body lotion, I'm suddenly craving pie. I pull away and say, "Every year on this day, you must have a pig-out fest in my honor. If you don't consume at least three thousand calories, you will be disgracing my memory."

"You got it. We'll call it the Autumn 3K." She lifts her Ding Dong, and I toast her with my Twinkie. We finish our tasty treats in two bites. True eating professionals.

Next I go over to Inanna. "Thank you for arranging this," I say. "Actually, I have a ton of stuff to thank you for, but this… this is exactly what I needed."

She wraps me in a hug. *Is she drunk?* Unsure what to do, I give her back a quick pat.

"I have faith in you," she says. "I know you're going to save humanity."

"Thanks."

I leave her, shell shocked by her show of emotion, and move toward Devon. My heart sinks into my gut when I see him. His jaw is clenched and tears are pooling in his eyes. I know that what I'm about to do will make me puke, but I don't care. I seize him in my arms and cling to him with everything I have. Miraculously, I don't heave, and I thank the Creator for this temporary relief.

Devon hesitates at first, but then responds with an even tighter embrace of his own. I force myself to pull free in case I really do throw up.

"When you sell the film rights to this story, do me a favor and don't let Bruckheimer anywhere near it," I insist. "I want it to be watchable."

"Are you nuts? I wouldn't let him touch it with a ten-foot pole. I'm thinking Spielberg and Howard."

I bite my lip to keep from crying. *I'll miss you most of all, Mr. Scarecrow.*

Closing my eyes and breathing in deep, I face Rigel one last time, a lump forming in my throat. *I can't leave him. I can't.*

"I have a gift for you too," he says.

I can't imagine what it is. "For little ol' me?" I say, batting my eyelashes.

He gestures behind me, and I turn to see a walnut-stained wooden chest sitting there on the counter of the control station. *Where did that come from?*

We walk over to it, and Rigel waves his hands over it, "Open says me." I'm about to give him a joking shove when the lid lifts to reveal a gift that makes my breath catch. Inside is my raggedy rabbit, and the photo of my parents I had gone home to get before the Goon Gang nabbed me.

I cover my mouth in shock. "When did you do this?" I say, unable to talk louder than a whisper.

I reach out for them, but I'm shaking so hard Rigel has to pick them up for me and place them in my hands. I pull them to my chest and sob, my life playing out in flickering snippets inside my mind. Images of my mom comforting me after I scraped my chin running from a kamikaze hummingbird, failing my driving test because I nicked a short bus, Emma presenting me with our first twenty-seven-inch pizza, tossing my cap into the air after graduating college—only to have it snag on my bracelet and poke me in the eye—Devon's tower of hair...

... and Rigel.

Rigel's tender caress brings me back. "You ready?"

"Let's do it," I say, way more confidently than I feel. I place my treasures back in the box and rub the tears from my face.

Inanna appears with the key and two solid gold bracelets that have a circular flower design on the front and back.

I remember what Ninurta said about them. "Are those the bands that keep my hands from melting off?"

"Lovely, aren't they?"

I put them on. "They could look like a dog's butthole for all I care. As long as they work."

"They will direct the flow of the current between you and the Pinecone, preventing it from accumulating in your hands."

A jumbo TV lowers from the ceiling. On screen is Enlil's hideous grinning mug, in high definition and five feet wide. *Not a pretty visual.*

I'm beyond fear at this point. A pure hate stronger than anything I've felt before surges through my veins. "Goddammit! What the hell do you want?" I roar. "Can't I have these last moments to myself? I know you're sick of humans, but you're such a fuckwad! You know what? Why don't you take the Post-it notes you made us and shove them up your ass!"

You could have heard a pin drop. Rigel, Inanna, and Ninhursag all stare at me stunned, eyes bulging. Enlil raises his overly dyed eyebrows and the camera zooms out to reveal the rest of the Council of Twelve behind him, all wearing the same bug-eyed expression.

"Well, shit," I say.

I can see several Council members trying to stifle a laugh.

"Thatta girl!" Emma says behind me.

"That's quite the greeting, Autumn," Enlil says, sitting back and folding his arms across his chest. "I'll let that one go, since you *are* about to die and all." He waves his hand as if this is no concern to him. "I say we let bygones be bygones."

I'm about to go off on him again, but before I do, Rigel wraps a hand around my waist and gives me a little warning pinch. I plaster on a fake smile. "Yes, bygones be bygones," I say through clenched teeth.

Enlil snaps his eyes to Devon. "Yes, I can hear your thoughts, fluff top, all the way from here."

Then Enlil cocks his head and slowly turns to Emma. "And who do we have here?" he asks. "She's a feisty one."

Emma beams with pride and says without fear, "My name is Emma." *Crap. She doesn't know he can read thoughts.*

Enlil inhales and fans his hands on his face as if *verklempt*. "She thinks I'm kinda sexy for an older dude."

Emma's mouth opens, and then closes again. A blush spreads across her cheeks.

"Thatta girl," Enlil says, clapping with mock pride.

"Don't let him get to you, Emma," I say. "He's a dick."

"You know, you human girls always tend to fancy the bad boy," Enlil says.

I snort. "You definitely don't qualify as a boy, and 'bad' isn't the word I'd use to describe you."

"I bet," he says, clearly amused. "It is unfortunate I can't read your thoughts. It would be thoroughly entertaining."

"No need. I'm happy to broadcast what a fucking asshole you are."

Rigel clutches my shoulder firmly in warning.

Ignoring him, I continue, "What do you want anyway? Here to witness my death, are you?"

"You always assume I have the worst intentions."

"Because you do."

Enlil's facade of kindness disappears, replaced by unadulterated loathing. A spike of fear stabs me in the gut. I may have taken it too far. But what could he possibly do to me at this stage of the game?

"I thought I would offer you visual inspiration for your speech," he says with a cold smirk.

The screen changes to reveal a leveled city next to a body of water. Not a building is left standing, and smoke and flames rise from the rubble. I scan it for a landmark to identify the location. That's when a massive green hand, its fingers clasping a torch, bobs by in the water.

Devon, Emma, and I breathe in at the same time.

"Oh my fucking god," Emma says.

"Is that...?" Devon asks.

I stumble forward, closer to the screen and it switches to another city—an all too familiar one. It's Orange County, where I live... or lived, I should say. A hailstorm of meteors are striking, leveling buildings like they're straw huts. The camera zooms in to show a meteorite disintegrate a family that was running for cover under an overpass.

"Stop this!" I order.

Enlil is showing me all this to throw me off. The ass wants me to lose my concentration and fail. And I'm afraid it might be working. A raw and consuming fire fills my gut; my throat constricts and I find it impossible to swallow. Digging my nails into my palms hard enough that they bleed, I make an effort not to give in to the immense sorrow that's threatening to take me down. *I will not let him get to me.*

Enlil reappears on the screen. "Oh dear, is that upsetting you?"

"You're *trying* to upset me," I spit at him. "Sorry to disappoint. It won't work."

"That look on your face says otherwise."

"Enough!" a male Anunnaki shouts from behind Enlil. I don't know who it is because Enlil's big head is blocking everything.

Rigel presses against my side, lending me support in case I need it. But I find that I'm perfectly fine. Enlil's plan has failed. He has

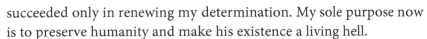

succeeded only in renewing my determination. My sole purpose now is to preserve humanity and make his existence a living hell.

"Enlil, terminate the feed this instant!" Ninhursag commands. "Council, this is clearly interfering with what you agreed to let Autumn do."

The camera zooms out from Enlil to unveil the rest of the Council. Their expressions show a mix of confusion and outrage.

"Yes, I agree," says Enki, rising. "You did not make us aware you were going to do this. This is unacceptable!"

"No need to get your panties in a wad," Enlil says, raising his hands in surrender. "I'm done. Well, except for one last thing."

"Enlil, so help me," Ninhursag warns.

It's too late. On screen appears another place I recognize: Yellowstone Park. The entire place is bulging as if a mutant balloon was inflating below the surface. Before I can comprehend what I'm seeing, the whole ground ruptures—and explodes. The transmission goes snowy, then switches to an aerial view. The caldera spews fire, rock, and mud miles into the sky.

Without another thought, I grab the key from Inanna, flash directly to the Ark, and put it in the keyhole. Before I open it, I glance one last time at Rigel. He gives me a nod, letting me know he's ready. This simple gesture has me trembling. I have to squeeze the key with all my might to regain focus.

"I love you," his voice hums next to me, causing me to shake even harder. A heartbeat later his lips are pressed against mine. We embrace, passion and tears mingling together, fueling my adrenaline. He lets me go, pushing me away. And I'm glad he does, because I wouldn't have. I would have stayed in his arms forever.

I turn to the Ark without looking at anyone else. I need his face to be my last memory. I twist the key, and the chest opens.

Inside, the Pinecone sits in a woven basket next to all the other items Ninurta listed. I can't help but smile when I see the beat-up sponge sitting next to a fancy jar of oil, appropriately labeled "OIL" in giant block letters.

As if sensing I was ready for it, the Pinecone rises from the basket and hovers above the Ark. There is no reflection on its surface, making it look more like a mini black hole than a solid object. The energy it gives off draws me in, calling me to it. With the memory of Rigel, Devon, and Emma strong in my mind, I clasp it firmly in both hands.

The torment is immediate. I scream and fall to my knees, but I don't drop the Pinecone. My vision is a blur. A searing heat seizes my spine. My skin is literally bubbling and melting off. I want to let go, to make it all end.

I hear a voice in the recesses of my fading sanity. "I love you," it says. It's Rigel. "I'm here with you."

There is a flutter in my chest as my heart responds to his voice.

I close my eyes and picture only him, towering above me with that sexy cocky half-smile. It takes envisioning his soft lips on mine, his naked body pressed against my thighs, for the screaming to stop.

"You need to get up, Autumn," Rigel says.

My body is shaking so badly, I'm not sure I can. With a cry of pain, I force myself to my feet, still holding the Pinecone.

Rigel's voice comes to me again. "Let your heart guide you."

And I do.

I begin to speak:

Hello. Umm. Please don't freak out. I mean, don't freak out any more than you already are. You're not hearing voices. Well, you are, but you're not going crazy. Shit, I should've memorized a speech. Oops, I forgot you can hear everything I think. Ahhh! This isn't going well.

Let me start over. My name is Autumn, a fellow human, and I'm here to help you. I need all of you to listen to me because I don't have much time. You have a choice in what happens to you. You don't have to die. None of you has to die.

The universe is boundless, more beautiful than we ever imagined. I have seen it for myself. It's teeming with life… with beings more advanced both technologically and spiritually than we are. And I'm not talking about little green men, but beings just like us. They're ready to rescue you, but you must first prove that you want, and deserve, to be saved.

Look, I know you're scared. You want to lash out. I get that. But you don't have to end it this way. You don't have to end it at all. You can survive, be with your loved ones, and live a new life full of abundant opportunities. Think about it: you can have a clean slate. A fresh start. But before that can happen, I need you to remember love. You have forgotten it because of the grief, anger, and chaos. But listen, it's there... waiting to be claimed again.

Bring to mind the one thing you love the most. It can be a person, an animal—hell, even a hobby. Whatever you treasure above all else. I want you to visualize that now. I want you to recall how it makes you feel—the warmth, the excitement, the happiness, the thrill.

I need you to remember that.

Rigel materializes in my mind, as if he has joined me in my thoughts, tangible and real. I have flashes of our time together. The first time I saw him at Barnes & Noble holding that book. His sexy silhouette in my headlights. I see us racing through the starry heavens. Then I see Emma scarfing a whole fried chicken, grease covering her face. I see Devon power-walking through the corridor in his number twelve boxers.

Now I want you to recall a time you laughed so hard you couldn't stop, no matter how much you tried. Remember your first kiss. Eating your favorite food. Hanging with your friends. The heat of a fire when it's cold. The cool breeze on a hot day. The gentle touch of the person you love. Remember happiness. Remember love.

A warmth builds in my chest, leaving a flood of affection inside me. All the physical torture melts away, and I'm left with only a soft tickling against my skin.

You can push away that veil of terror that has blackened your soul. It's not too late. All you have to do is give yourself over to love. It'll all be okay, I promise. You'll live. You'll thrive. We humans are capable of incredible things. Our emotions can either be our biggest strength or our biggest weakness. Right now they may be the latter, but if so, that's only because we have stopped believing in ourselves. Take that flutter in your chest when you think about the person you love, and let it grow. Let it consume you. Let the bitterness and resentment leave your body. Force it out and give in to the warmth that's building in your heart.

I wonder, as I'm composing these words on the fly, if Bruckheimer had an influence on me after all. Devon would be cringing if he heard what I was saying. Oh wait, he can. *Hi, Devon!* So can Bruckheimer for that matter.

My soul begins singing from the love that's growing all across the planet.

Yes, that's it. Can you feel that? I can feel the love. It's amazing. Come on. Keep it going. Unite as one, and you will be saved. You will be saved.

You will be saved.

You will be saved.

I savor the feeling for a moment, open my eyes, and then let go of the Pinecone. It floats gracefully back into the chest.

I try to see past the fog that has built up in my head. All my pain is gone. In fact, there is no sensation at all. I glimpse my hands and see why. They're just a melted mass of flesh. I don't think I have any nerve endings left. My vision narrows, and the next thing I know, the back of my head is cracking against the floor. I'm unable to take a single gulp of air.

The video screen is in my line of sight. It shows the feed from Orange County again. A row of people are standing hand in hand, staring upward. More are joining them.

The sky plunges into darkness.

I'm gripped with the fear that I am too late, that the sinister darkness must be the rocks from the caldera about to rain down on them. My chest hollows out. *I failed.* But instead of rocks, beams of light fall to Earth—and the people are lifted into the sky.

Not the eruption. Spaceships. They've come to rescue us.

Inanna, Devon, and Emma step into view above me. Spots are popping into my already narrow vision. I try to speak, but only blood spills from my mouth.

"It worked," Devon says with a smile, his eyes welling with unshed tears.

I try to return his smile, but can't.

"You did it," Rigel's voice murmurs in my head. "I'm so proud."

I push myself onto my side and see Rigel on the floor mere feet from me. His skin is scorched beyond recognition. Ashy flakes swirl around him, carrying him away from this existence layer by layer. Beneath the shroud of blackness that covers him, the fading sky blue shimmer of his eyes draws me in.

"I love you," he whispers.

With all my remaining strength I flip over and crawl toward him, inch by inch. But I can't make it. I collapse, my entire body starting to spasm.

Then I feel myself leave the floor. At first I think I'm leaving my body, then I realize that Inanna is helping me get to Rigel. I hear sobbing, but I refuse to look at anyone but Rigel. He is the last thing I want to see.

I land softly by his side. We stare at each other, and I take his hand in mine.

"I love you, too," I mouth, my vision now barely a pinprick.

One last super sexy half-smile appears on his face, and my pain is replaced by the warmth of pure love.

I give one last cough of blood before death at last comes for me.

The End

Or is it?

AUTHOR'S NOTE

This book is based on existing ancient Sumerian cuneiform texts and artifacts. On my website, you will find links to all the texts, cylinder seals, and artifacts I reference in the book and used to create the story. You will also find a full glossary and blog posts that discuss the "truth" behind the different aspects of the storyline. If you have questions about any of the companies, places, facts, researchers, or anything else, you will most likely find the answer on my website.

Visit: WrittenByAnna.com

Throughout the book, I reference many different theories from the ancient astronaut community. Some I believe, and some I don't. So just because I mention it in the story, doesn't mean I think it is true. The goal of this book was to present many different theories in a fun way, and to open up a discussion about them. I have amassed twenty years of research into the topic, and I will be presenting it all on my website. I invite you all to join me, read the evidence, and come to your own conclusion. Hopefully we can discover the truth together!

That said, I do want to point out that most of the backstories of the Anunnaki and the character names I used for them are based on documented accounts from the translations found in *The Electronic Text Corpus of Sumerian Literature* at the University of Oxford, and a few other universities. I also pulled from *Atrahasis* (which talks about the creation of humans and the flood), *The Epic of Gilgamesh* (also recounts the flood story), *Anzu* (Tablet of Destinies), and of course, the Old Testament.

The interactive version of the e-book has links so you can see first-hand some of the items and places I mention, including links to all the ancient alien stuff.

WHO'S WHO

I mentioned some great researchers and shows in my book, so I wanted to give them credit and tell you where you can learn about them.

Zecharia Sitchin

Oh, where do I begin? Two people are considered the granddaddies of the ancient astronaut theory: Erich von Däniken and Zecharia Sitchin. While they each present different theories—and even have a bit of a rivalry—they both deserve credit for all the work they have done on the subject. For the purposes of my research, Zecharia Sitchin was my inspiration. Because of him, I have taken up the study of the Sumerian culture, and discovered some truths about humanity that have completely changed my perspective on our place in the universe. While I don't agree with all of Sitchin's conclusions, his work on the subject is extensive, powerful, and well worth the read!

Website: Sitchin.com

Coast to Coast AM

This is by far the best radio program on the planet (and possibly in the universe). It covers paranormal topics, fringe science, ancient aliens, UFOs, conspiracy theories, metaphysics, cryptozoology, remote viewing, climate change, predictions, and religion—just to name a few.

If you are at all interested in the subject, then I highly suggest you become a Coast Insider. You'll be able to stream or download a large archive of online programs, commercial free. I know it sounds like an advertisement, but I get nothing from it. I just really enjoy the shows.

Coast to Coast AM website: Coasttocoastam.com
Coast to Coast AM Insider: Coasttocoastam.com/coastinsider

I especially want to thank George Noory and Rachel Nelson from Premiere Networks for granting me permission to use George's likeness and mention the program in my book.

George Noory

George Noory is the top-notch radio host at the helm of *Coast to Coast AM*. George is the most open-minded and generous host I have ever listened to.

Bio: Coasttocoastam.com/pages/george-noory
His events: Coasttocoastam.com/pages/events
George also hosts a fantastic show on Gaia TV called *Beyond Belief*: Gaia.com/series/beyond-belief

If you are looking for that special someone in your life, you can check out George's two dating websites.
Paranormal Date: Coasttocoastam.com/pages/paranormal-date
Conspiracy Date: Coasttocoastam.com/article/conspiracy-date

Marshall Klarfeld

Marshall is a Caltech graduate engineer, and has dedicated his life to discovering the truth behind the origin of man. Zecharia Sitchin's writing can be a bit "clinical," and Marshall (who studied under Sitchin) does a great job of breaking it down for the general public. As an introduction to the ancient astronaut theory, I highly recommend his book: *Adam: The Missing Link*. If you become a Coast Insider, then you should check out Marshall's episodes. He is a regular on the show.

Thank you so much Marshall for allowing me to use your likeness in the book.

Website: Adamthemissinglink.com
Coast to Coast AM podcasts: Coasttocoastam.com/guest/
klarfeld-marshall/6545

Michael Tellinger and Johan Heine

Michael, along with Johan Heine, discovered the "South African Stonehenge," which they named Adam's Calendar (also known as Enki's Calendar). Not only did they discover this circle, but they also found that there were hundreds of thousands of stone circles throughout Africa. Extensive electronic measurements of these circles indicate that they are, in fact, generating energy.

Michael also uncovered what he believes to be the ruins of the home of Sumerian god Enki, and the grave of the Sumerian god Dumuzi.

Website: Michaeltellinger.com
Watch his show on Gaia TV called *Hidden Origins*: Gaia.com/lp/
hidden-origins
Coast to Coast AM podcasts: Coasttocoastam.com/guest/
tellinger-michael/6680

William Henry

William Henry is by far my favorite speaker. He is one of the few researchers I know who continually works and adapts his findings to present new material at each lecture. William blends historical, scientific, religious, and archeological symbology to present a case for the ascension of our soul. Even if you don't believe in such a thing, once you hear one his lectures, you will realize what a profound influence this concept of ascension has had on the human race throughout all the cultures of the world. It will blow your mind.

"The Light Body Effect," which I talk about in my book, was one of the first of his lectures I attended.

Website: Williamhenry.net
He also hosts a show on Gaia TV called *Arcanum*: Gaia.com/series/arcanum
Coast to Coast AM podcasts: Coasttocoastam.com/guest/henry-william/5629

Giorgio Tsoukalos

While Giorgio is not mentioned in my book, I must give him credit for one of the jokes in it. The joke about the number twelve hairspray was based on an actual conversation Giorgio had with someone at a party he and I attended. His hair was only about half as high as usual that day, and when someone asked him about its diminished volume, Giorgio's response was that he had to use a number six hairspray that day, rather than his usual number twelve—and therefore, he could only achieve fifty percent of its regular volume. That was too amazing not to use in my book, especially given the character of Devon. Giorgio has borrowed a couple of my jokes, so fair is fair.

Website: Legendarytimes.com

UFO Documentary to Watch

UFO sightings receive such poor mainstream media coverage that most of the time these events are completely misrepresented. The subject is still seen as a joke by a majority of the population. But well-documented and credibly witnessed sightings have occurred. I highly suggest, as a good introduction to these credible cases, the documentary *I Know What I Saw*, produced in 2009. You can find the entire thing online. I also have a link to it on my website: WrittenByAnna.com

ABOUT THE AUTHOR

Anna-Marie Abell grew up in a trailer park. Well, several actually. Her trailer was on wheels so she got to experience the Pacific Northwest's vast array of mobile home parks as her parents moved her from one to the other. Somewhere along the way, she got totally into UFOs. Probably because she was hoping extraterrestrials would come and abduct her. But they never did. Luckily for her she was smart, because her only hope of escaping trailer life was college and a full scholarship. Moving to sunny California on her almost full ride to Chapman University, she was well on her way to her new life. Two bachelor degrees later (Film and Television Production and Media Performance), and several honors and awards for her accomplishments, she managed to start working in an almost completely unrelated industry from her majors: infomercials.

It was in college that she got bit by the "ancient alien" bug after listening to Zecharia Sitchin on *Coast to Coast AM*. In her pursuit to uncover the truth, she has spent the last twenty years researching the ancient Sumerian culture—in particular their "gods" called the Anunnaki—and their connection to the creation of the human race. What she found changed her life, her beliefs, and her understanding of the universe (and beyond). Her humorous science fiction trilogy, The Anunnaki Chronicles, is a culmination of all her research, her borderline obsession for all things paranormal, and approximately 2,300 bottles of wine.

Ready for contact?

Website: WrittenByAnna.com
Twitter: @writtenbyanna
Facebook: @booksbyanna
Instagram: @booksbyanna

Want to be a galactic hero and leave a review?

Interdimensional review portal: WrittenByAnna.com/review

CPSIA information can be obtained
at www.ICGtesting.com
Printed in the USA
LVHW052311070519
617046LV00001B/75/P